The Chosen Queen

The Chosen Queen

∙ ∙ ∙

A NOVEL OF THE
PENDRAGON PROPHECY

Sam Davey

DIVERSION
BOOKS

Diversion Books
A division of Diversion Publishing Corp.
www.diversionbooks.com

Copyright © 2025 by Sam Davey

All rights reserved, including the right to reproduce this book or portions thereof in any form whatsoever. No part of this publication may be reproduced or transmitted in any form or by any means, electronic or mechanical, including photocopying, recording, or any other information storage and retrieval, without the written permission of the publisher.

Diversion Books and colophon are registered trademarks of
Diversion Publishing Corp.

For more information, email info@diversionbooks.com

First Diversion Books Edition: June 2025
Hardcover ISBN: 979-8-89515-039-9
e-ISBN: 979-8-89515-033-7

Design by Neuwirth & Associates, Inc.
Cover design by Jonathan Sainsbury

Printed in the United States of America

1 3 5 7 9 10 8 6 4 2

Diversion books are available at special discounts for bulk purchases in the US by corporations, institutions, and other organizations. For more information, please contact admin@diversionbooks.com

The publisher does not have any control over and does not assume any responsibility for author or third-party websites or their content.

For Kyra Rose

The Chosen Queen

PROLOGUE

I sit here, looking back along the hard, dark tracks of used-up time. My present is spent remembering the past. I have no future, confined as I am outside of time, behind the castle walls of Carbonek, sustained by memories and the pictures in the scrying bowl.

My name is Igraine, eldest daughter of Amlawdd, King of the Welsh borderlands and vassal of Constantine, the last Emperor of Britannia. Back then, after the Romans left and the civil wars began, I had my people to protect, my land to fight for.

I have observed that many mothers believe their children are remarkable. They foster in their bosoms happy hopes and plans of greatness, only to watch these visions fade as the fates dole out their judgements. That tiny child whose precocious chattering and perfect curls inspired his mother's dreams of fame and fortune will end his days a blacksmith or a ploughman like his father. Greatness, power, and majesty are not bestowed upon the many. But perhaps the many, in their humdrum and seemingly unremarkable existences, can find a happiness that is denied to those whose fate it is to rule.

Was I so very different when I held my babes but briefly to my breast? Did I, in those rare and borrowed moments dream-see my daughters as women grown in wisdom and in beauty, imagine my son assume his man's estate with courage and compassion? I really can't recall, and in any case, my erstwhile and ill-remembered thoughts are surely neither here nor there, for History has recorded on her bloody pages the doings of my children.

My children, two girls, one boy, whose destiny was to shake the world, each carrying inside them the seeds of mutually assured destruction. Morgause, Morgan and, Arthur. A queen, an enchantress—and a king.

I was mother to all three of them right enough and my girls were true-born children of my lord. But Arthur—Arthur was another matter altogether—and it is from his beginnings that my story will unfold.

Chapter One

It was still dark when I woke, stretching my toes and turning toward my sleeping husband, who had drunk a little too well last night and as yet showed no sign of stirring. I nestled close beside him, resting my cheek against his shoulder and breathing in his sweetly familiar scent, directed my fingers questing downward, slowly, past his hips and into those dark and secret places where our pleasure hid its head. Gently, my fingers moved, stroking and teasing as I kissed his back and urged him to wake up and love me.

Afterward, I fell asleep, and by the time we woke a second time the sun was high in the sky and we had missed our breakfast.

"I'm starving," grumbled Gorlois, who was getting dressed in a hurry and as a result had mis-fastened his tunic. It now hung crookedly over dark green trousers tucked rather haphazardly into his new deerskin boots.

"They will laugh you out of the hall if you go down looking like that," I responded and without bothering to pull on my robe, got out of bed and went toward him. Undoing his belt, I adjusted his tunic so that it fell into neat folds. Bending down, I picked up his cloak, which was lying in a crumpled mess on the floor where he'd thrown it the night before. I shook it out in an attempt to rid it of the worst of the creases and then reaching up, hung it elegantly around his shoulders, fastening it in place with the brooch I'd given him as a wedding gift some eight years before.

"That's better," I said, nestling up against him, feeling the rough wool of his tunic press against my naked skin as his arm encircled me. "My husband is the equal of any man at Uther's court and should dress accordingly."

"And my wife shouldn't get dressed at all—at least not when she's alone with me." Gorlois' hands ran lovingly down my back and pulled me hard against him. Then, giving my buttocks a quick caress, he released his grasp, holding me at arm's length. As he looked into my eyes he said, "But I would rather you presented yourself modestly before the court this morning. I did not like the way the King's gaze rested on you last night."

So he had noticed the way that Uther had been staring at me. I'd hoped that Gorlois had been too engaged in talking politics to see the way his liege-lord's eyes had followed me at supper. My husband had but one fault, a temper as high and harsh as the winter storms that lash the cliffs of Tintagel, our castle by the sea, and although he was not quick to anger, once his wrath had been unleashed it was a mighty task to calm him.

I moved toward the bed and seized my undershift, pulling it over my head whilst thinking of words that would allay his fears and forestall an outburst of his anger.

"Oh, I don't think he noticed me that much," I lied. "And anyway, I really wasn't paying him any attention. I was far more interested in talking to the Lady Vivian."

Placing a belt around my waist, I turned to the glass to tidy my hair and arrange it neatly beneath a veil. Gorlois grunted appreciatively at this ostentatious display of wifely modesty and, reaching within our closet, brought out my kirtle and helped me into it, lacing the neckline as high as it would go.

"I'm not so sure I trust the Lady Vivian," said Gorlois, giving my laces a final pull to settle them in place. I sighed, realising that my words may well have turned his thoughts from Uther, but only by introducing another equally inflammatory subject.

My husband had become increasingly interested in the new faith the monks and traders had brought to Britain. He even wore their symbol, a simple wooden cross, on a thong around his neck, although today I had made sure that it was tucked in securely beneath his tunic.

In the past few years, these in-comers had started to build churches, encouraging our traditional holy sites to fall into disuse and disrepair. There were even stories of whole communities turning from the old ways toward the promise of a life eternal. I knew from many an anguished late-night conversation that Gorlois was seriously considering rejecting the Mysteries in favour of the new religion and the Risen God. As the Lady Vivian was also the Lady of the Lake and High Priestess of the Goddess, it was no wonder that he felt uncomfortable in her presence.

Nevertheless, I felt both fondness and respect for the stately priestess who had taught me much and whose grace and intelligence I greatly admired. Before I married, I'd spent five years within her household being schooled in craft and wisdom and, unlike Gorlois, I saw no reason to question the Mysteries. Indeed, I hoped to place my younger daughter Morgan in Lady Vivian's care when she was old enough to leave me. It was this that we had been discussing last night, when King Uther had decided to pay me so much obvious and unwanted attention.

"I understand, my love, but I have known her for so long. It would have been rude to ignore her when she chose to sit beside me." I put my hand upon his arm. "But let's not worry about such things. We have something more important to consider."

He looked at me questioningly. "Breakfast," I said. "You have quite worn me out and if I wait much longer for my meat and mead, I think I'll faint away."

He laughed, his humour restored at the thought of a good meal, and we left the room to break our fast at a time when the rest of the court was probably beginning to prepare for mid-day dinner.

◆ ◆ ◆

AFTER WE HAD EATEN, GORLOIS went to join his men. Although there was now an uneasy peace between those loyal to the Pendragon and the invading Saxons, my husband was keen to ensure his troops were kept in order and never failed to undertake their daily drill. He was the Duke of Cornwall and of royal blood himself, but Gorlois spent at least two hours a day at practice with his men. It kept him strong and healthy, and they loved him for it.

I decided to go in search of Vivian. Since my marriage, I had spent much of the last seven years in Cornwall, and I hungered to find out more about what was happening in the Kingdom.

As I wandered through the corridors, I let my mind roam, thinking about the past. After the murder of King Constantine, Uther and his older brother Aurelius were helped to escape to Brittany by Vivian and the Lord Merlin, a wise and rather mysterious Druid who many credited with supernatural powers.

The two young princes grew to manhood at the court of the King of Brittany, where Merlin continued to train and advise them. Well-schooled in warcraft and driven by the slow burning fire of righteous revenge, the brothers returned to England and declared war upon the usurpers. Sadly, not long after their return, young King Aurelius was killed in suspicious circumstances. I could remember hearing rumours that he had been poisoned as he lay in his tent after defeating the Saxons at the battle of Conisburgh.

It was said that on the day Aurelius died, a great and fiery dragon blazed across the skies, foretelling the might and wrath of Uther and heralding his righteous war to force the invaders from our shores and unite the land. That was three years ago, and since then Uther, who now styled himself "Pendragon" in honour of the portent, had fought and won many a bloody battle. And my husband, Gorlois, was one of his most trusted Generals.

Now that the rebels were subdued, we were called to celebrate the peace at Caer-Lundein, where Uther had made his court. For the first time in years, the roads were safe for all to travel and the

Court was full of lords and dukes, princes and princesses, knights and their fair ladies, called together to rejoice in Uther's victory and to show the world that the realm was now at peace.

As I made my way swiftly through the castle, I nodded briefly to those ladies who I recognised from my previous visits to the court, but I paused to talk with no one. It was a beautiful day, and many were taking advantage of the sunshine; choosing to wander through the gardens or sit peacefully beneath the trees. When I finally arrived in the Ladies' solar, the shady room was quiet and almost empty apart from two cats asleep beside the hearth and, as I'd hoped, the Lady Vivian, sitting by the window, her hands resting lightly on her lap.

She was looking out onto the courtyard, watching Gorlois and the other warlords putting their men through their paces. She didn't notice my approach and I took the opportunity to gaze on her, revelling in the chance to look at the woman who had been such an important part of my childhood. I had known her for twenty years or more, but whilst those years had seen me grow to womanhood, time had appeared to bring no changes to the Lady. She was small, finely made with delicate features, pale skin and hair that was just a shade lighter than a raven's feather. Her eyes, as I well-remembered, were of a clear and startling blue and she had a demeanour that was both graceful and—perhaps surprisingly given her slightness—commanding. She was a woman whom no one could ignore.

As I moved closer she must have sensed my presence, for she turned and held out her hand. I reached out to take it and found that my knees and shoulders bent involuntarily into a deep curtsey. I might now have become a Duchess and of higher rank than a mere Lady, but my years of training and study in the Lady's household on the lake isle of Avalon had created responses in me that I could not break. Without even being aware that I was doing so, I bent my knee and lowered my head to take her blessing.

"Come child, sit beside me." As she spoke, she moved slightly to one side and indicated a space on the window seat. I obeyed, following her gaze down into the courtyard. To the right, just in the shadow of the Keep, I could see the Cornish men at practice. Two soldiers were engaged in mock battle, using wooden broadswords, heavy shields fastened to their arms and helms upon their heads. One of them was my husband, stripped to the waist, his hair pulled back in a long plait which reached halfway down his back. I watched as he thrust and parried and with three blows, brought his opponent to his knees. He held out his hand and pulled the man to his feet and within seconds, they were at each other again.

"Your husband acquits himself bravely," Vivian remarked, "and he is exceptionally well-made. You are happy, I think?" This was a question, not a statement and I nodded and felt a faint blush rise to my cheeks as I remembered the scenes of the early morning.

Vivian looked at me and smiled. "Now child, there is no shame in enjoying your marriage bed. It is one of the gifts from the Goddess. And she has blessed you with two daughters?" Once again, I sensed a question behind her words, as if she was not quite sure how many children I had born.

"Yes, I have two daughters living, and one whom the Goddess took from me within an hour of her birth. My eldest Morgause is already promised to the House of Orkney, and she will leave us soon." It was common practice for a well-born girl to leave her family and be brought up in the house of her betrothed, so she would get to know her husband and become accustomed to the ways and manners of his court. This was particularly important for my daughter, who was destined to be the wife of King Lot of Orkney and who would need to be accepted by the wild and independent northern clans if she was to have any chance of ruling by his side.

Morgause was only six years old. When the match had first been made, I had begged Gorlois to let me keep her with me until she had seen at least nine or ten summers. By then, I thought, she would be old enough to understand why I was sending her away from me. It would have given me time to prepare her and to make her understand and accept her duty. But this was one of the occasions when I'd been unable to persuade my lord to let me have my way and Morgause was due to be sent northward next spring, just a few months after her seventh birthday. As always, when I thought of it, a wave of anger rose within me and a tear of impotent and frustrated grief came unbidden to my eye.

"She is young to be sent so far from home." Vivian looked at me with sympathy. "If I remember right, you came to me just before your tenth birthday, and did not venture to your husband's court 'til your sixteenth year."

I nodded. "Yes, but a match had not been made for me when I was in my cradle." I thought about my childhood, the fear and uncertainty of living in a realm torn apart by rebellion and invasion. Many noble houses had lost their lords, killed fighting the Saxon invaders, and lands that had been held fast by one family for generations had changed hands many times during those troubled times as they were lost and won in skirmishes with Vortigern and his insurgents.

"The times were too uncertain; my father and mother were always loyal to Constantine, but they didn't want to risk an alliance with a falling star. I'm sure that's why they sent me to you; not just so I could learn the Craft, but possibly, if no match had been found, to join the Sisters and spend my life in Avalon."

Vivian held my gaze and slowly nodded. "Yes, you're right, Igraine. We talked it through, your mother and I, long before you came to me. So in a way, your life was mapped out as strictly as your daughter's. I promised I would keep you safe, but in return, she promised me a child of noble blood to be devoted to the Mysteries; if not her daughter, then her daughter's daughter." She spoke softly, but there was no trace of question or uncertainty in her voice. "We made such vows as cannot be broken, and now I look to you to honour them."

"I've already spoken to you about my youngest, my little Morgan. I would like to send her to you, but Gorlois…" I stammered slightly. "Gorlois doesn't think we should." Vivian looked at me, one eyebrow raised as if surprised to hear my words.

"The Duke of Cornwall 'doesn't think you should.'" She repeated my words coldly. "Why, pray, does the Duke of Cornwall take it on himself to question the practices of our Mysteries? It is the way, and always has been; the eldest daughter makes a match, secures her house and in time, continues the bloodline. The younger daughter is tutored in the Mysteries and, if she is adept, will find her future in the service and delight of the Goddess and the Craft."

I found that I couldn't meet her eye. "Gorlois has been listening to roadside preachers. The ones who talk about a Risen God and urge us to forsake the Mysteries. He says that Morgan will be happier remaining at home with us until she marries, that a noble woman has no need of the sort of education she would receive in Avalon." I spoke quietly, confused, not wanting to betray my husband, but unable to keep the fear and worry from my voice as I spoke to the Lady who was not only my friend and guardian, but who represented everything I had been taught to believe in.

"Just listening? Is that all he's done?" Vivian now spoke softly, but her hand reached out to touch the edge of my sleeve, betraying the importance of her question.

I shook my head, slowly, knowing that I would have to tell her everything. And in a way, feeling deep relief that I could finally unburden myself.

"No. He has welcomed them into our house and has given them food and shelter. And last year, at Samhain, he would not attend the rites, preferring to spend the evening with the preacher."

"Did he forbid the ceremonies?" Vivian's voice was quick with latent anger.

"No, he wouldn't go as far as that. The people of Cornwall and Lyonesse are loyal to the Mysteries and would have been unsettled and unhappy if we did not celebrate Solstice and Samhain, and light the Yule fires. Last Samhain, we welcomed in the harvest and made sacrifices to the shades of winter, as we have done every year, but the rituals were made more difficult as my lord refused to play his part. We lit the fires as normal, but my maid servant carried out the rituals as my proxy. I lent her my gown, and we placed a glamour on one of the men-at-arms, dressing him in Gorlois' cloak and removing all memory of the ceremony from his mind the next morning."

Vivian nodded thoughtfully. "So the people do not know their Lord and Lady were not present? They think that he is still a true believer?"

"There are rumours," I said. "People know that he spends time with the preachers and even that they are party to his councils. But Elaine, my maid, is true and trusted. You know her Vivian; she was with me on Avalon… My father's child, but not my mother's."

"Ah yes," said Vivian. "I remember her. A pretty girl, but not as beautiful as you." She was silent for a moment and then she raised her hand, lightly caressing my face and placing one finger on my lips.

"You are very lovely, child. And the whole court knows that you have King Uther held in thrall. He couldn't take his eyes from you last night."

I was a little taken aback at the change of subject but was actually quite pleased to stop talking about Gorlois and his spiritual confusions. I loved him and to talk as we had been talking seemed close to a betrayal, despite my deep respect for Lady Vivian and my certainties about the Mysteries. My hope was that he would see the error of his ways if I left him alone and allowed his curiosity to take its course and so I leapt at the chance to discuss another subject.

"No, really?" I lied. "I'm afraid I hardly noticed him last night."

"Yes, and that is one of the things that appears to have piqued his interest." Vivian was smiling again now. "There is nothing like being unattainable and apparently uninterested to make a man like Uther want to rise to the challenge."

I giggled. "In all honesty, my lady, were I still unmarried, I think it likely that I would have welcomed his attentions. No one can deny that he is well-favoured, and what maid would not delight to have a king amongst her suitors? But that is not the case, and so I fear that he must be disappointed. I'm quite happy with Gorlois in such matters thank you."

"I can see you are," said Vivian, once again glancing out of the window where the men had now stopped their practice and were washing themselves at a water trough in the courtyard. Most of them had now stripped to the waist like Gorlois, but I could easily pick him out from the crowd, standing taller than all his men, his hair now released from its plait and hanging in long wet coils across his back and shoulders. I noted with relief that he was not wearing the leather thong on which he had hung the symbol of the Risen God. Such obvious disloyalty to the Mysteries would not be taken lightly here at Uther's court.

Vivian stood up and walked away from the window toward a small table by the fireplace, where a brass bowl full of rose-scented water had been placed to add sweetness to the air.

She continued talking. "But I think you should tread carefully. Uther is unmarried and I have never seen anyone take his fancy the way you have. He can be very persuasive, and I am certain that Gorlois is not the type to stand aside and let his King make him a cuckold." She paused, then said, "I think there could be trouble; indeed, I think it has already begun to brew."

I looked at her uncertainly. Vivian was a priestess and a prophetess. She had the gift of sight, and I was not sure if she spoke words of caution or something more terrible and portentous.

"What do you mean, my lady? What trouble?" As I spoke, I also got up from the window and made my way toward her.

"I am not certain child, but I feel we must know more. I would like to scry this before we go much further. Are you still adept?"

I nodded slowly. As part of my training in her house on Avalon, I had learned to scry the future using water or a burnished surface to bring forth visions of what was to be. I was not very skilled and often could not clearly interpret the images I conjured. It was a gift I used but sparingly, particularly since my husband had voiced his growing discomfort with the Mysteries.

"Then secure the door, for we must have quiet."

I did so, whilst Vivian moved the table to the centre of the room. She now stood beside it, her hands cupping the sides of the brass bowl. She had removed the rose petals and the surface was clear and still. I joined her, my hands overlapping hers as we gazed into the dark shallows of the shadowy water.

Vivian was silent, but I felt the words leave her mind and join with mine as clearly and certainly as if they had been said aloud. "Tell us of Gorlois, of Uther and Igraine… Tell us what is going to befall."

I felt her hands tighten on the sides of the bowl, and I too increased my pressure. The water's surface, which had been flat and motionless, began to churn and bubble. The bronze bowl was heating up, and rose-scented steam began to fill the air, making it hard for me to see Vivian and soon completely obscuring the water in the bowl.

The metal had become very hot, and I did not think that I would be able to keep my hands upon it without damage to my flesh, when the steam suddenly cleared and I was looking down, not into the shallow waters of the bowl, but into my chamber at Tintagel, looking in though the circular window which faces out to sea.

It was dusk, the candles had been lit and the last remaining rays of the early summer sun cast a warm and gentle glow upon the floor. I saw myself, standing by the bed, slowly combing the tangles from my hair. I had on a simple linen shift, reaching to the floor, with a high neck and long sleeves, such as I would wear to bed if my lord was not at home and I had the need for something to keep me warm at night. My eyes were closed, and I seemed at peace as I brushed my hair and then began to divide it into strands so I could plait it and keep it tidy whilst I slept. But before my fingers could begin to twist the strands together, the door of the chamber burst open, and Gorlois, dressed for battle and with a bloody scar upon his cheek, threw himself into the room.

There was no sound; scrying gives only images in its visions of the future, so we watched in silence as Gorlois slammed the door shut behind him and secured it. He pulled off his cloak and armour and flung his sword into the corner of the room. As we watched, I saw myself turn toward him startled, but with great happiness on my face. I ran to him and he grasped me in his arms, kissing me hungrily as if we had been apart for a long time.

I knew what would happen next, for our marriage-bed had been witness to many such scenes of glad reunion. Gorlois had been fighting the King's wars for years, and I had endured the anxiety and loneliness of our separations as equally as I had revelled in the passion and joy of his safe return. I watched as he sought to free me from my nightshift, eager to have me naked before him, my hands fumbling with my laces as I sought to help him with his task.

But I had no desire to share this image with Vivian and so I closed my eyes, breaking the concentration and causing the image to vanish from the bowl. I heard Vivian take a small, sharp intake of breath in disapproval and reluctantly opened my eyes once more. Immediately, the water churned and broiled, the metal once again becoming so hot as to be nearly unbearable as the steam rose once more, enveloping us in its scented haze. But when it cleared, we were no longer looking within my chamber; we were outside, on a summer night, gazing down at a silent and motionless scene. It was just before dawn. The skies were lightening in the east and the pale crescent moon and tiny sparks of starlight gave a dim, insubstantial light.

As my eyes adjusted to the dark, I started to see the most terrible things. Bodies, dead or dying; limbs left where they had fallen and axes, spears and swords no longer needed by their warriors all strewn across the blood-stained earth. We were gazing at a field of carnage, the awful remains of battle displayed beneath us. I saw a horse, its stomach pierced with spears, its blood flowing freely onto the mangled body of a rider trapped beneath it and its eyes open, but sightless. Beyond the horse there was another body, lying on its side, with its legs splayed unnaturally beneath it. There was something about the body, broad-shouldered, slim-hipped, something terribly familiar; we focussed in, moved closer. The fallen man was bare-headed, and his hair was held in one long plait that fell, still proudly, down his back.

I had no need to see his face, to see the wounds upon his much-loved body to know that I was looking at my husband. But Vivian moved us closer, changed the angle of our vision, and there he was below me, his face almost unrecognisable, bruised and bloodied from blows I could not bring myself to contemplate. And as I stared, unmoving, my limbs petrified by the horror of the things I saw before me, I saw his chest was bare, and where his heart had been, there was a vast and bloody hole.

My mind refused to accept the scene that was playing out before me, "No," I stammered, "No, not Gorlois!" I was screaming now as I pulled my hands away from Vivian's and at the same time violently pushed the bowl off the table, breaking our trance and spilling water onto the rushes at our feet.

I fell to my knees, shuddering at the horrors I had seen within the waters of the scrying bowl. I was shaking, sobbing, and almost on the verges of collapse.

"Not Gorlois," I said again and again, wrapping my arms around myself and rocking back and forth until Vivian raised her hand and slapped me once across my face with a force driven by real anger.

"You little fool. Have you become so ill-disciplined? Yes, that was Gorlois, right enough, but we needed to learn more to understand what this truly means."

I looked up at her, at first confused and somewhat angered by her seeming lack of understanding and compassion but then, as my mind began to clear, I became contrite at having failed my lady in so simple a matter as a scrying.

Scrying, or seeking visions, is an old and elemental magic, governed by a few simple but unbreakable rules. The first and most important of these is that each and every vision granted by the Goddess is singular and unique. What is shown within the scrying bowl can be seen but once. When the vision is vouchsafed it will never be repeated exactly. For that reason, we have the second rule: that the seeker must watch until the vision fades and the surface clears before they break the trance. To do otherwise is to dishonour the Goddess and to make a mockery of the gift of vision she has chosen to bestow.

My cheek stung and my eyes were heavy with as yet unshed tears, caused as much by my shame as by the memory of my husband's poor, broken body.

"I'm sorry, my lady," I mumbled, reaching out to pick up the bowl so I could return it to its place upon the table.

"What's done is done Igraine," said Vivian. "You have not made use of the scrying bowl for many years I think?" I nodded slowly. "It was perhaps foolish of me to risk so important a vision to what are clearly clumsy and inexperienced hands." She spoke calmly, but there was no warmth or sympathy in her voice and the eyes that met mine seemed to offer both question and challenge.

"It was the shock of seeing him like that," I repeated. "I am sorry that I failed you," and then, resolving to regain my place in her good graces, I continued, "We can seek another vision if you like, my lady. I promise I will be true to my learning and hold fast this time."

She looked at me but said nothing for so long that I began to fear that I had completely lost her favour, but then her face relaxed and she held out her hand to me, helping me to rise from my place amongst the sodden rushes.

"No, Igraine, now is not the time." She gestured toward the courtyard below which was filled with noise and people. Gorlois and his Cornishmen had gone and in their place I saw riders returning from a day's hunting, knights and their ladies, some with hooded hawks resting lightly on their fists. The castle dogs streamed in behind them, obedient to the commands of the Master of Hounds as he sent them straight to the kennels for their share of the kill. Liveried pages waiting for their masters' return were gossiping with scullery maids sent out on last minute errands to the castle gardens to bring back fruits and vegetables for the cooks in the kitchens below.

"It has grown late and the preparations for Uther's feast tonight are in full flow. There is no time for us to seek further favour from the Goddess and if I am not mistaken, we shall not be left in peace much longer."

She was right, for within a moment, the heavy iron latch was lifted, the door opened and two court ladies who I knew by sight but couldn't name, walked into the solar. We exchanged the pleasantries that courtesy demanded and both ladies dropped low curtsies when they recognised my companion. We did not stay to talk, however, and left in silence. Once we were alone again and walking along the stone-flagged corridor that led from the solar to the Great Hall, Vivian reached out her hand and gestured for me to pause. I saw a look of deep concern upon her face.

"Do not dwell too much on what we saw, Igraine. Remember, not all the Goddess shows will come to pass." I nodded, remembering more of the lore I'd learned during my years beneath the Lady's roof. Some visions are there to warn us of what may be if we do not heed the Goddess' warnings, not to presage things that will inexorably come to pass. Perhaps what we had seen was such a vision. This thought made me even more determined to persuade Vivian to let me scry with her again and as she made to take her leave of me, I reached for her hand and raised it to my lips.

"Lady, I thank you for your care, but I would rest more easy if we could look once more within the waters." Vivian touched my cheek and stroked it gently and then in one sharp and resolute movement, grasped my chin between her thumb and forefinger. She moved my face back and forth, as if looking for something in the set of my jaw or the depths of my eyes. Just as quickly she released me and giving a quick nod, replied, "Yes, I can see that that is true. And I would also like to find out more about the vision we were granted if the Goddess is good enough to send us further enlightenment."

We agreed that we would meet the following afternoon in the solar. But, as fate would have it, I was not to be alone with the Lady for a long time, and by then I would have no need to look within the scrying bowl for understanding.

Chapter Two

I walked quickly through the castle, hoping to reach our chamber before Gorlois, but when I opened the door I found my husband waiting for me and more than a little out of sorts. He had strained the muscles in his shoulder and down his right side during the practice bouts that afternoon; he'd stripped off his tunic and was now sitting, looking rather vexed and more than a little impatient in his bruised and half-naked glory.

During my years at the Lady's house, I had spent some considerable time learning the healing arts, and Gorlois claimed that no one could ease the aches in his joints or unravel the tensions in his muscles as I could.

"I'm sorry I'm late, my love," I said quickly, taking in the situation in an instant. "I was talking with some of the castle ladies in the solar and quite lost track of the time." His mood had not been sweetened by the bruises on his back, and I knew he would be annoyed if he thought I'd sought the company of Vivian. I decided that a slight distortion of the truth was excusable in the circumstances. As I spoke, I went swiftly to my open trunk, rummaging for a jar of the salve I always packed when we travelled in case my physically adventurous husband did something to overstretch himself.

He tutted but made no comment and reached out his left arm to draw me to him, wincing slightly as he bent forward, putting strain on the muscles of his right side. I kissed him gently on the top of his head, nudging him to turn sideways so I could treat his injuries more easily. Coating my hands with the ointment, I began to rub it firmly into his shoulder and onward, feeling the strength of his ribs as I worked downward, following the strong and sculpted curve of his body, right down into the small of his back.

The salve smelled strongly, but not unpleasantly, of lavender and camomile, and these two fragrances hid the smell of the most active ingredient—a strong pepper which served to warm up the muscles and help my practised fingers to relax them. As I worked, I leant into him, my breasts pressing up against his back, my lips almost brushing his shoulders as I slowly rubbed and smoothed the pains away. Neither of us spoke as my hands moved across his stomach and back, up toward his chest, soothing, gently, feeling the solidity of bone and muscle beneath the smooth softness of his skin.

My eyes were closed as I focused all my thoughts on healing, giving my love and strength to the man who sat before me, the man who just an hour before I'd seen dead and mutilated in the waters of the scrying bowl.

Pushing the unwelcome vision from me, I moved around to face my husband and sat astride him. I bent to kiss him on the lips and, almost as a reflex action, his arms encircled me. Softly at first and then, with my arms around his neck, my eyes open and fixed on his, I kissed him with a passion driven by the fear of loss.

THE SUN HAD ALMOST SET as we began our preparations for the feast. Gorlois pulled on his robe and stuck his head out into the corridor, calling loudly for a page to light our lamps and bring us water. When he'd gone, we dressed quickly, preferring as always to help each other with our laces rather than suffer the intrusion of a servant.

Gorlois wore a scarlet tunic and a short cloak, edged with fur and fastened by a golden chain. In my eyes, he looked magnificent. I was still in my undershift, undecided about what I was to wear. Like any woman, I wanted to look my best, but I could not forget what both Vivian and my husband had said about the King and the way he'd looked at me last night. The last thing I wanted was to be accused of wearing clothes designed to further inflame his interest.

I had just picked up my old green gown, one that I had only brought with me to travel in and was holding it in front of me. I looked at my reflection in the glass and thought wryly that I would appear tonight as a real country bumpkin when there was a sudden knocking at the door.

"Who's there?" called Gorlois, striding toward the doorway and gesturing to me to get out of the line of sight. Although my linens were quite modest, it would not do to expose the Duchess of Cornwall in her undergarments to public view.

A woman answered, her voice muffled slightly by the heavy wooden door. "A message from the King, if it pleases you, my lord." At this, my husband opened the door and three women, all carrying bundles, came into the room. By this time, I had pulled my kirtle on over my linens and I walked toward my husband as the women hesitantly placed their burdens on the bed.

"What's this?" asked Gorlois, flicking open the first bundle, which contained something soft and supple, a fabric that shimmered in the candlelight. The women seemed embarrassed.

"'Tis a present, my lord. From the King." The woman would not look my husband in the eye and as she spoke, I noticed the other two moving quickly to the door. Whatever was going on, they were not comfortable with it and at least one of them seemed afraid.

"A present?" Gorlois repeated, "For me? How courteous of his Majesty." But he spoke coldly, his tone belying the gentility of the words. He lifted up the shimmering thing from the bed and looked at it more closely. "There must be some mistake. This garment is for a lady. Pray, take it away."

"Oh, but I canna do that, my lord," the women stammered. "The present is for her ladyship. The Duchess. The King would have her wear it at the feast tonight." She looked at me, and I think I saw a flash of pity in her eyes as I stared, bewildered, at the bundles on the bed.

I could see the anger working in my husband's face as he picked up the rest of the packages, making as if to throw them out of the room. Swiftly, I moved toward him. "Hush, my lord. Be gentle. It's not this woman's fault. She is only doing as she has been commanded."

As I spoke I gestured toward the doorway and with a nod of gratitude, the three women scuttled out and closed the door behind them.

Gorlois flung everything down onto the bed and turned to face me. "Does Uther think I am a knight so mean that I cannot clothe my lady? How dare he insult me by sending this to you!"

"Hush, my lord," I said, smoothing out the creases in the dress. It was truly the most beautiful garment I had ever seen. The cloth looked like woven moonbeams. It shone with a subtle radiance in the candlelight and the pearls sewn with silver thread at the neck and hem gave off an iridescent radiance. More than anything, I wanted to wear it, to feel it soft against my skin. I knew it would suit me better than anything I'd ever worn before.

"It is to honour you that Uther sends it, not to insult you." I spoke carefully, wanting to find words that would appease him, but knowing in my heart of hearts that he was right. No man should send a dress like this to someone else's wife.

Gorlois was silent. Greatly daring, I disrobed and slipped the gown over my head. It was too delicate and fine for any undergarments and I shivered slightly as the cold of the silk touched my naked skin, feeling it settle into place, mould itself around my waist, nestle in beneath my breasts, clasp tightly at my wrists.

I looked down at the other bundles on the bed. In one I found a pair of dancing slippers, made of cloth of silver edged with swansdown. In another, a cloak of gossamer, held in place by a delicate sapphire clasp. Finally, I discovered a silver headdress—a jewelled coronet of roses, exquisitely crafted but still light and finely made.

The beauty of these things entranced me and, without really thinking, I put them on and dressed my hair, weaving the coronet into my curls. Still Gorlois had said nothing.

"How do I look, my lord?" I asked as I turned teasingly toward him, the dress shimmering in the candlelight, my hair loose and streaming down my back.

"How do I look?" I repeated, reaching up to kiss his cheek and knowing as I did so that I looked more lovely than I had ever looked before, feeling the glamour of the silk and silver work its magic.

"You look like a Queen," said Gorlois slowly, a strange expression on his face.

I laughed, seeking to lighten his mood. "Thank you my husband…But I am more than happy just to be your Duchess." I took his hand and looked into his eyes, wanting him to believe me. "I'm certain that Uther only wants to honour his bravest General by making sure his wife is fit to be presentable."

Gorlois shrugged. "I'm not so sure of that…but there is nothing we can do about it now." He glanced out of the window, where the moon was already high above the castle walls; the hour was late and we could already hear the sounds of revelry from the rooms below.

He sighed and stuck his shoulders back with a resigned resolution, just as I'd seen him do so many times when he had an unpleasant but unavoidable duty to perform. "If you don't wear the dress, he'll be offended and who knows where that would lead." He moved toward the door, my hand still in his, but then he paused. "All I ask is that you stay beside me and give Uther no reason to believe his feelings are encouraged." I nodded, and with that we left the room and made our way toward the Great Hall.

By the time we arrived, the feasting had already started, and the hall was full of noise and light. The two vast tables running along the eastern and western walls were piled high with bowls of fruit and loaves of bread. Pages and serfs were bringing in platters of salted fish and roasted vegetables and ensuring each table was well supplied with flagons of ale and tankards of wine filled from the great barrels that rested against the northern wall.

Musicians were playing in the gallery at the far end of the hall, and we could just barely hear the sweet sounds of lute and tabor above the din of conversation. The castle dogs had been brought in from the kennels and were roaming the hall, seeking titbits that fell from the tables and occasionally scuffling with each other over the choicest morsels, their barks and whines adding to the overall clamour.

Most of the seats were taken and we began to walk toward the western wall, seeking Gorlois' Cornishmen with whom we would be seated. The two long boards were joined at the top by a smaller table, raised on a wooden dais. At the centre of this table, seated in a large and ornate chair that I later learned had been carved from a single, ancient oak tree, was Uther Pendragon, the King of Britain. Seated beside him, dressed in a green kirtle with a gold and emerald diadem upon her shining dark hair, was Vivian, looking every inch the imperious, powerful and mysterious Lady of the Lake.

Heads turned as we walked through the Hall, but I was pleased to see that, possibly because of the noise and frenzied activity, neither Vivian nor Uther seemed to be aware of our presence. Gorlois soon spotted Erec, Lord of Madron, a province to the far west of Cornwall. He was a tall, loose-limbed man, also known as Erec the White because of his fair hair and pale eyes. Erec was Gorlois' second in command, his master of arms and best friend since boyhood. As we walked swiftly toward him, Erec caught sight of us and pushed his seat backward, releasing a huge roar of delight before enfolding Gorlois in a clumsy but affectionate bear hug. Erec's wife, Ened, remained seated and smiled rather unenthusiastically at us before returning her attention to her plate. She was the daughter of the Lord of Rheged, in Northern Wales, a vapid and insipid woman with whom I had little in common.

Releasing Gorlois, Erec turned toward me and rather clumsily reached for my hand. As he raised it to his lips, I saw him run his eyes across my body, lingering for a second on the pearls which glowed softly at my breasts. He gave a slow whistle and then winked at Gorlois. "May I compliment you, my lady," he said. "I think there's no doubt who will be hailed as Queen of Beauty at the feast tonight." I wasn't quite sure what he was referring to, so I thanked him with a smile. Ened's expression had become unpleasantly fixed at this exchange. She was a short, fair-haired woman with large breasts and what my mother used to refer to rather disparagingly as "child-bearing hips." She was dressed richly, but unflatteringly in a mauve and gold kirtle that did not suit her complexion and which clung unforgivingly to her stomach. I remembered that her last babe was but six months old and was surprised that she had decided to accompany her husband to Court. When Morgause and Morgan were that young I would have found it hard to leave them.

Erec turned back to Gorlois and nudged him in the ribs. "You always were a lucky dog. I think Uther regrets he gave his consent to your match before he'd seen the lady." Gorlois scowled at this, but Erec seemed not to notice as he gestured toward the two chairs beside his own.

"Not much he can do now, though. Wedded, bedded and two babes to prove it." Erec winked again and raised his tankard, draining it in one go before thrusting his arm out to the pot-boy, who hurried to refill it. From his expansive gestures and the smell of wine that had wafted up to me when he kissed my hand, I was pretty certain that this was not the first tankard that he had downed that night.

It was not to be the last. I became increasingly concerned as I watched Erec down yet more wine, all the while urging my husband to do likewise. Gorlois rarely drank heavily, but there were times when, usually egged on by Erec, his normally sober character became transformed into that of a drunken sot. I knew that he was still angry about the gift from Uther, and I guessed that he was feeling physically exhausted after his over-exertions in the practise yard. This was not a good combination. Soon, Gorlois was leaning back in his chair, his eyes slightly glazed, one arm flung possessively along the back of my chair, his fingers stroking a length of my hair. To a casual observer, he may have looked relaxed. I knew better; he was spoiling for a fight.

Watching my husband's fingers drumming impatiently on the table as he waited for his wine, my heart sank even lower as a young page from the King's household came over to us. In one hand he held a delicate silver goblet, in the other a small, stoppered flask. He bowed slightly awkwardly to Gorlois, who simply nodded curtly, and then, turning to me, he placed the goblet on the table and proceeded to remove the stopper from the flask, and poured out a draft of clear liquid.

"With the King's compliments, D-D-Duchess."

I looked at the goblet and raised an eyebrow questioningly at the stammering youth. "The...the waters of Avalon." The boy's face was ablaze with blushes; I doubt he could have been more than ten years old. "The Lady Vivian suggested to his M-M-Majesty that you might find this more to your t-t-taste than the red wine."

"How thoughtful of the Lady Vivian. Pray give her my thanks." I dismissed the page with a wave of my hand. I had deliberately omitted any word of thanks to Uther, not wanting to further inflame Gorlois, who had observed the exchange through hooded eyes. However, as I raised the goblet to my lips, I couldn't help but notice that the eyes of the King were upon me. He, too, raised his goblet and toasted me, and as he did so, our eyes met. And held.

As if at some unspoken signal, Uther pushed back his chair and stood, clapping his hands for silence. Quickly, all conversation stopped. People eating put their knives down on the table and even the minstrels in the Gallery stopped playing. Gorlois, his tankard now re-filled, continued to drink his wine.

"Welcome. Welcome to you, my true knights, lords and fair ladies. Welcome, brother kings and faithful allies. Welcome to my court." Uther stretched out his arms as if to embrace the entire room. His voice was low and deep, softly modulated and yet commanding. He had no need to shout for all of the assembled host to pay keen attention to his words.

He turned to his left, further along the High Table, where I recognised the banners of King Budic of Brittany, whose court had sheltered the young Uther and his brother Aurelius from the wrath of the rebellious Vortigern.

"King Budic, Prince Ban, you are welcome to my court. My hearth and home are open to you, and my sword and strength are pledged to defend you."

Uther raised his goblet and bowed slightly, paying tribute to his most powerful allies. Budic and his young son, handsome Prince Ban, smiled and raised their goblets to acknowledge Uther's courtesy.

Uther now turned to face the room, welcoming with a smile his liege-men and allies. The Lords of Ulster and Connaught were there with their knights: rough-hewn men, short of stature but powerfully built, with black hair and startlingly blue eyes. They stamped their feet and smashed their tankards on the table as King Uther welcomed them, raising their voices in the wild war-cry of the Irish galloglaigh—the warrior host that had helped Uther to triumph over Vortigern and his Saxon allies Octa and Eossa.

Next to them sat the tall, red-headed lords of Orkney and Lothian, representing their High-King, King Lot. These men did not smile as Uther raised his hand to them, but nodded curtly, as if the homage of the Pendragon was nothing more than their due. I looked hard at the faces of these Celtic lords. Handsome, yes, but aloof and unbending. I felt a slight shiver of fear as I thought of my little daughter, Morgause, not yet seven years old and due to be sent to the court of these cold, forbidding warriors soon after snow-melt next spring.

Whilst I was lost in thought, looking at the men of Orkney in an attempt to find something to allay my worries about my daughter, Uther continued to welcome his guests. He toasted the lords of Northern Britain, Ceint and Mid-Wales, who howled and stamped in a great and ostentatious show of loyalty. The Knights and Lords from my father's kingdom of the Welsh borders pledged their fealty more quietly, rising as one to salute the Pendragon as he welcomed them formally to his halls.

And now, he turned to us, the representatives of Cornwall and Lyonesse, the far western reaches of his kingdom.

"Gorlois, Duke of Cornwall, my friend and ally, I salute you. You are most welcome in my hall." Once again, the King raised his goblet, toasting my husband, his war duke and valued military commander. Gorlois and Erec were now slumped together, and together, they clumsily raised their tankards toward the dais. Their men followed suit, a small number raising a cheer for the Pendragon, but the majority saluting in silence.

That was it. The formalities had now been completed and I assumed that the feasting and revelry would begin again. I took a sip from my goblet. The cool, pure water was very welcome as the Great Hall was now uncomfortably warm. I was secretly wondering how long it would be before we could leave the feast and retire to our chamber.

But even as I was calculating just how soon Gorlois and I could reasonably take our leave, I realised something else was happening. The minstrels remained silent and the pages and pot-boys stood back against the wall as the Lady Vivian rose to her feet.

"This is a most blessed night. The land, for so long rent by war and turmoil, is now at peace. The battle fields are ploughed and seeded with crops to give us bread, and our children can play in the meadows and orchards without fear." The emeralds upon Vivian's headdress glinted in the lamp-light with an unearthly radiance, throwing her face into strong relief. For a moment, she closed her eyes as she stretched out her arms and raised her face to the ceiling.

In strong, sonorous tones, she called out to the Goddess. "I, Vivian, the Lady of the Lake, beseech you to look with favour on this man, our King, Uther Pendragon." She turned to Uther and at her bidding, he removed his crown and knelt before her.

Placing one hand upon his head, she continued to hold the other raised high in supplication.

"Uther Pendragon, do you promise to honour the Goddess and protect her people?"

Uther raised his eyes to hers and speaking loudly now for everyone to hear, he replied. "I do, my lady."

"Do you swear to follow the paths of the Mysteries and bring homage and honour to her shrines?"

"I do, my lady."

"Do you swear to defend Her from dishonour and to oppose with word, sword, and deed those who seek to cast out the Mysteries from the hearths and hearts of your kingdom?"

"I do, my lady."

Vivian now placed the crown upon Uther's head, resting her palm lightly upon his brow.

"Uther Pendragon, may the blessings of the Goddess be given to you.

"May your realm be fruitful, and the bounty of the land keep you and your people in health and happiness.

"Great Goddess give this man the strength to defend his people and the wisdom to rule them. Make his arms mighty, so that he can protect this land and all its subjects. Make his mind clear so he can rule justly and with foresight. Strengthen his resolve to give him courage when the night is at its darkest but make his heart gentle so that he can show mercy in the healing light of morning."

She moved away from Uther to say the final words of the ritual, which I remembered so well from my studies at her house in Avalon.

"May the fire in your hearth burn brightly, the meat and mead on your table bring comfort, and your loins bring forth fruit to keep the land settled and peaceful for this generation and the next."

"For this generation and the next," responded Uther rising to his feet and turning to face his people.

"For this generation and the next," he repeated, crashing his fist hard upon the table as he did so.

"For this generation and the next," came the response from the Great Hall as, with whoops and cheers, Uther's Lords, knights, and allies stood to shout their allegiance as with one voice, beating their fists and tankards on the table as they did so in a pledge of loyalty to their new-made King.

I say, "with one voice," but to my utmost dismay, I realised that one particular voice was very noticeably silent. My husband, alone amongst the lords and allies, was not standing. He was slumped in his chair in a drunken stupor. His head rolled forward limply on his chest and the nearly empty tankard lolled in his lap, the last dregs of wine dripping to the floor in small, crimson droplets. Even Erec had staggered to his feet, his wife Ened's arms around his waist in a not very successful attempt to keep him upright. As I looked on in horror, I saw Ened glancing down at my husband with a look of disgust.

I was not sure if Uther has noticed my husband's dereliction, but I was unable to do anything about it as, within seconds, I was to have the eyes of all the court upon me.

Uther had resumed his seat, but the Lady Vivian was still standing.

"My lords and ladies, the Goddess is good, but she has yet to bless King Uther with a Queen to stand beside him. It is fitting therefore that this place of honour be given to the fairest lady in this Hall, who will sit beside him this evening as a symbol of the goodness of the Goddess."

There was a thrill of interest at this, and I noticed many of the ladies begin to smooth out the creases in their kirtles, or raise their hands to adjust their headdresses, wondering who would be called forward to take the place of honour at Uther's side.

Vivian turned to face the corner of the Great Hall where the Lords and knights of Cornwall and Lyonesse were seated. She smiled at me, holding out her arms in a gesture of welcome. "Come, Igraine, Lady of Cornwall and flower of Avalon. The Goddess honours you this night."

As everyone turned to look at me, I felt frightened and uncertain, unwilling to leave Gorlois' side, but recognising that I could not ignore the request of the Lady, which, though couched in gentle words, was undoubtedly nothing more nor less than a command. As I hesitated, I began to hear faint murmurs of disbelief, followed by the rising buzz of stifled laughter as eyes around the room began to take in the sight of my sleeping husband, shamed now for all to see.

Vivian sensed my hesitation. "Igraine, your duty is to the Goddess and to your King. Come child," She knew me well. An appeal to my duty would always trump any appeal to my emotions; I had been schooled in Avalon and my final and ultimate loyalties had always been reserved for the Goddess.

Now, looking back from the painful vantage point of age and bitter-won experience, I know that it was Vivian who was responsible for so much of what was to befall me and my family, but at that point, I was still a trusting innocent, believing that she had my best interests as heart. So, slowly, I stood and pushed back my chair, moving away from my place at my slumbering, snoring husband's side. I felt Erec's hand pull at my sleeve, as if trying to forestall me, but without even turning to look at him, I brushed it away. Given that I had no choice in the matter, I wanted to move away from my place at the Cornishmen's table, hoping that the eyes of the jealous and the curious would follow me to my new seat on the dais and linger no longer on my husband's sleeping and vulnerable countenance.

As I went toward the dais, I saw Uther push back his chair and turn to me with a look of hunger and longing in his eyes. Once again, I was conscious of the way the dress moulded itself to me, the way the milky-white rounds of my breasts were subtly exposed above the froth of pale lace; the delicate swansdown cloak floating out behind me, displaying the silken curves of my waist and hips to the on-looking courtiers as I slowly walked across the room. At that moment, I would have given anything to be dressed in my old familiar green kirtle, fetching, but modest. How I wished that I'd refused to wear the seductive and dangerous garments the King had gifted me, had not allowed myself to be flattered and enchanted by their beauty.

I reached the dais and noticed that another chair had been placed between Uther and Vivian. Uther bowed to me and, uncertainly, I made him a half curtsey but kept my head down, unwilling to allow my eyes to meet his. He took my hand to his lips and I felt the tip of his tongue delicately insert itself in the space between my fore and middle fingers. The sensation shocked me, and I could feel myself blushing as, involuntarily, I raised my face to his. As his eyes met mine, his tongue once more licked my fingers, and I was unable to prevent myself from gasping at the intimate nature of the caress which had been given shamelessly yet secretly before the eyes of the whole court.

"My Lady of Cornwall, it gives me pleasure to see you here." Despite the little game he'd been playing with me, Uther seemed calm as he handed me to my seat. Once I was settled, he turned to speak to the whole gathering, his voice now resonating with satisfaction and triumph. "I thank the Goddess for her kindness. My table is blessed to receive the Lady Igraine, Lady of Cornwall and flower of Avalon." Like Vivian before him, Uther had not given me my true title, apparently choosing to ignore my status as Duchess of Cornwall, an honour bestowed upon me by virtue of my marriage to Gorlois.

Uther was still speaking. "...and I long for the day that she sees fit to send me my hearts-queen in earnest." There was cheering and shouts from the hall at this, and I could see that Gorlois was beginning to stir. Uther continued. "Now, eat, drink, and please, my lords, follow my example; honour the representatives of the Goddess by doing them the courtesy of remaining awake." This was greeted by a huge roar of laughter, tankards were slammed against tables and, finally, Gorlois woke up.

Chapter Three

Gorlois jolted awake, his wine-stupor making him disoriented as his tankard clattered to the floor. He pushed himself upright, taking in the empty seat beside him, not understanding why I wasn't there. I saw him turn bewildered, bleary eyes to Erec, who slowly gestured with his dagger in the direction of the dais. As he looked at me, sitting in splendour between King Uther and the Lady of the Lake, raised up on the dais before the whole court, I could see hurt and anger replace the confusion in his eyes.

I did not want this. He was my husband and I should be at his side, not sitting beside Uther, this powerful, seductive man who had so unsettled me. As I began to rise, I saw Gorlois push his chair back from the table, but immediately, we both found ourselves restrained: Gorlois by Erec, who had sprung to his feet and was now standing behind my husband, forcing him back into his seat; me by Vivian's hand, which had encircled my wrist with a grip so strong that I knew I would be unable to break free.

"Sit down you little fool," she hissed. "Think what you are doing. You are here as the representative of the Goddess. Would you dishonour her so publicly?"

"But…I don't want to be here. I want to be with my husband… Let me go." I was angry but speaking quietly so only Vivian could hear my words. To my left, Uther was engaged in loud and bantering conversation with King Budic and his son and did not appear to have noticed what was going on. "Let me go, Vivian," I repeated, looking her full in the face and seeing nothing but cold, unbending determination in her eyes.

"No, Igraine. You must stay here in obedience with the Goddess' wishes. Stop behaving like a soft-brained house-girl. You are a princess, court-bred and Avalon trained." She still spoke low and moved closer toward me. There was a smile upon her lips that quite belied the harshness of her tone and the insistent grip of her fingers, hidden beneath the delicate folds of my swansdown cloak. Anyone watching us would have thought we were simply exchanging some spicy morsel of court gossip.

"Think about it. We have finally found peace. Do you want to be the cause of yet another conflict? If you leave the dais, you insult not just the Mysteries but the King and his entire Court. You will cause a rift between Uther and his most powerful commander. Do you want that to be on your conscience?"

"I didn't ask for this, Vivian. I am married to Gorlois. I should be by his side, not Uther's." But as I spoke, I realised that there was no point in protesting. I let myself relax back into my chair and as I did so, I felt the pressure on my wrist subside.

"That's better." Vivian was still smiling and this time there was some genuine warmth in her eyes. "You do look lovely tonight, Igraine, the dress becomes you. I had it made in Avalon you know."

"You had it made?" I was confused. "I thought it was a present from the King."

"Certainly it was Uther who commissioned it. He had heard tell of your loveliness from Lord Merlin, and when he learned that you were known to me, he asked that a gown be made to do justice to your beauty."

This was all a surprise to me. The Lord Merlin was a Druid, a wise but rather enigmatic man. He had indeed visited Cornwall last summer, and we had welcomed him to Tintagel. I had never met him before, although Gorlois had known him from his time in Ireland with Uther. But since those days, Gorlois had become more interested in the new faith; as I cast my mind back to that evening in June, I remembered the way my husband had greeted his old companion with less warmth than I would have expected for someone both so venerable and, to Gorlois, so familiar.

So Merlin had told Uther about me, and clearly in such terms that had piqued both his curiosity and his desire. This was starting to make me uneasy. It was beginning to look as if Uther's interest in me was not some random infatuation; this was something deeper, with roots going back to those days last June when Merlin had been our guest.

I had been thrilled to welcome him to Tintagel and had very much enjoyed his company. The country had still been at war, and this had given Gorlois a reason to excuse himself from the old man's presence. My husband had been constantly busy, overseeing military training, touring his strongholds and garrisons and, on occasion, making time to visit the households of the bereaved. Gorlois was the sort of leader who prided himself on getting to know his men; whenever he could he would visit the homes and families of those who had fallen in battle, making sure that they knew their menfolk's sacrifice had been valued and to ensure that they were not in want.

Despite this, he could have made more time for Lord Merlin had he wished it and I knew, even if the old Druid did not, that Gorlois' non-appearance had as much to do with his growing rejection of the Mysteries as with the exigencies of military command. Still, despite my husband's absence throughout most of Merlin's visit, I was able to make him comfortable, and I think he enjoyed his stay. The weather had been fine, and we had walked in the castle gardens where the soothing rhythms of the summer tides and the calls of the circling gulls had provided a pleasant counterpoint to our conversations. I had not travelled far from Tintagel for several years, and I had been hungry for news. Merlin talked to me of Avalon, and we indulged ourselves, reminiscing about the beauties of the Lake and the island castle, which were so familiar and beloved to us both.

Merlin had also been interested in my girls, and kind to them. Morgan was still not much more than a toddler, so it was my sweet Morgause, who was approaching her fifth birthday, to whom he'd paid the most attention. We spent each afternoon with the girls in their nursery room, high in the western turret of Tintagel. As I sat by the window, embroidering a smock for my younger daughter, Merlin would rest upon a high-backed chair with Morgause upon his knee. He told her stories of the old magic, tales of mystery and enchantment which I think she was too young to truly understand, but which enraptured her, nonetheless. She had come to love him, and she cried bitterly on the day he left us.

I remembered that Gorlois had been irritated by her tears, sending her to her room in a most uncharacteristic display of anger when she refused to dry her eyes. After that, he became irritated and impatient if Merlin's name was even mentioned, so we soon learned not to speak of him. Indeed, I had almost forgotten about his visit until Vivian had spoken of it.

"Merlin spoke to Uther about me... What did he say?... Please tell me," I wanted to find out more from Vivian and was preparing to probe further when I felt the touch of a cool hand upon my arm. Turning to my right, I found the King was looking at me intently, a half-smile on his lips.

His first words were not addressed to me, but to Vivian. "Now my lady, I think you have monopolised my queen for long enough." She inclined her head with a slight smile and turned away to talk with the person to her right, but I was thrown into confusion. I was no queen and had no ambitions to become one.

He smiled at me, sensing my discomfort. "Lady Igraine, you sit by my side, where my Queen would sit, were I to have one." He gave a small sigh and his eyes seemed sad for a moment. "The life of a King is sometimes lonely; it contents me to have you by my side. Please indulge me in this tonight. You are here by the will and grace of the Goddess, it is true, but..." and here he once again raised my hand to his lips. "you are also here because I have a great desire to know you." His lips brushed against my palm and as he released my hand, he gently caressed my cheek, allowing one finger to press against my lips.

Before I could react, the King stood up and clapped his hands, once again calling for the attention of his Lords and Ladies. "Let us have music. I would end this evening with a dance." Immediately, pages and serving women rushed to clear the tables, removing the leftovers of the feast and once again filling tankards and goblets with wine and ale. A space had been cleared in the centre of the Hall and as the minstrels began to play, Uther extended his hand to me and, in front of his assembled court, led me to the dance. As he bowed, my eyes roved urgently behind him, searching the corner of the Hall where the men of Cornwall and Lyonesse were sitting, watching their Duchess with stony and impassive faces.

I looked for Gorlois, hoping to send him some glance, some sign to tell him that this meant nothing to me, that all I wanted was to leave the hall and end the evening in his arms. But as my eyes searched the rows of men, I saw only empty chairs in the place where we had been sitting. Gorlois and Erec were no longer there.

There was a sense of dread in my heart as I curtsied in my turn. Uther and I then held hands and walked to the head of the hall to allow the rest of the court to line up below us in the dance. Part of me was glad that he was gone, glad that he would not have to witness Uther's attentions to me in front of the entire Court. He was a proud man and that would have been hard to bear.

I also took comfort in the fact that he was not alone, that Erec had gone with him. They had been friends since boyhood and although the Lord of Madron had been clearly in his cups, I knew he loved my husband like a brother and would not let harm befall him. As my body mechanically moved through the familiar steps of the dance, my mind was frantically trying to work out where they could have gone. I didn't think that Gorlois would have left the court entirely. His men were still sitting in their places and as I quickly gazed back amongst their ranks I noticed that a few of his knights and their ladies had even joined the dance. I spotted Ened standing next to young Lord Mark of Morwenstow, who was looking both embarrassed and uncomfortable at having to dance in public with a lady nearly old enough to be his mother.

It struck me that perhaps Erec had persuaded my husband to walk beyond the castle walls in search of wine and comfort. The taverns would still be open and at the thought I felt a stab of jealously. I was sure that any of the tavern wenches would be more than happy to provide whatever the two high-born nobles might be seeking and I knew that Gorlois at least had coin enough to pay them. But I stopped myself from thinking this. It was unworthy. I knew that Gorlois loved me, and I had no reason to seriously believe that he would seek consolation and a salve to his wounded pride by laying with some back-room whore.

Taking myself in hand, I decided that the most likely thing to have happened was that Erec had simply guided Gorlois back to our chamber, probably stopping at the buttery for a wineskin on the way. They would be very, very drunk by now, I thought. This didn't please me, but as I could do nothing about it, I decided the best thing to do was to concentrate on the dance and to try to find a way to bring this terrible evening to a close.

UTHER DANCED TWICE MORE WITH me and then, recognising that the King could not dance all night with the same woman without causing gossip and giving offence to visiting dignitaries, he returned me to my seat on the dais and offered his hand to Anna, wife of his ally King Budic.

Vivian was still seated, choosing not to dance, although I had seen more than one hopeful Lord approach her. She smiled at me as I sat beside her. "There, you see, that wasn't too difficult was it? A few smiles, a couple of dances... Was that too much to ask?"

"It has cost me more than a few smiles, Vivian," I replied. "I don't know where Gorlois has gone, and I know he will not be well pleased by this."

"Gorlois should think more about the peace of the Kingdom and the loyalty he owes the Mysteries," Vivian snapped. "Your husband is walking a dangerous path, Igraine, and if you take my counsel, you should warn him that he will not find what he seeks by turning his back on the Goddess and looking for consolation in the rituals of the Risen God."

"My lady, my husband's conscience is his own and I can do nothing to change it," I protested.

She said nothing, just looked at me, with an expression that held both challenge and compassion. The Lady knew the power of silence and how to use it to create a mood of deep reflection, in which the lies we use to distance ourselves from our true doubts and motivations are stripped away and the naked truths that are our fears and dark anxieties are painfully, but honestly, exposed.

We sat together in hushed contemplation for some time, oblivious of the minstrel's music and the raucous shouts and laughter of those assembled in the dance. I realised just how much I had resented, and been frightened by, Gorlois' decision to turn his back on the religion which had always been my comfort and in whose shadow I had been raised. As if she could tell the direction of my thoughts, Vivian laid her hand on mine, but this time in a gentle caress.

"Sweetling, the path the Goddesses sends us is not always easy, but it should be our duty and our pride to set our feet upon it with a strong heart and a good will."

I nodded, slowly. "But I can't choose between them, Vivian; I love my husband with all my heart."

"But you love the Goddess, too, don't you, Igraine?" Vivian's tone was gentle but insistent. "You do, don't you? You were promised to her as a child, just as your daughter is promised. Are you going to break faith with her, Igraine?"

"No, my lady." I spoke softly, hesitantly, but with absolute certainty. "I will never break faith with her."

"Thank you, child," Vivian leant forward and kissed me gently on the brow. "Now, the dance is in full swing and we are unobserved;

why don't you take this opportunity to leave? I will make your apologies to Uther when he returns."

Incredibly relieved to be able to get away, I nodded quickly, dropped Vivian a small, hurried curtsey and swiftly made my way down the length of the room. As I walked through the deserted corridors, lit only by moonlight and the faint, flickering of the torches in the sconces, my one thought was to make my way as quickly as possible to my chamber.

I was not very familiar with the castle and twice I took wrong turnings. I stumbled hard over the threshold of a small, darkened room that in my confusion I had mistaken for the ante-chamber to the Tower. I had fallen, cutting my hand on the uneven flags and hurting my wrist quite badly, and was sitting, wrapped in my cloak, on the cold stone doorstep. I used the skirt of my dress to staunch the blood from the cut on my damaged hand, and was trying to get my bearings when I heard footsteps coming toward me, brisk and confident.

They did not sound like the unassuming, deferential tread of a servant, and the speed at which the person was moving made me think that whoever it was, they clearly knew their way around; perhaps this was some Lord who could direct me to my chambers. I stood up, wincing a little at the pain in my wrist and there, standing before me, was Uther.

"You left without saying goodbye." He stepped closer to me, making me move backward until I felt the stone wall against my shoulder. "That was…discourteous…my lady." His voice, always low, was now quiet and insistent.

"I'm sorry, Your Grace," I murmured, feeling flustered and disconcerted by his closeness. I could feel his warm breath on my neck, and it smelled sweet to me. "The Lady Vivian said she would make my apologies… I was not feeling well and decided to seek the comforts of my chamber."

"I too would like to seek comfort, Igraine." He moved closer to me and pulled me into his arms. His body was different from

Gorlois, lean and long where my husband was muscled and well built. But although he was spare, there was no softness or weakness about him. As he held me close against him, it was like being braced in iron.

"Will you give me comfort, Igraine?" He lifted my chin and brought his mouth to meet mine. For a few seconds I fought against him, but his lips were sweet and soft, and my body responded whilst my mind was still trying to resist. He had one hand on my waist; the other behind my head, his fingers stroking my hair. He moved his fingers to my neck and along my spine, and downward, caressing and stroking me softly through the silk, realising that I was wearing nothing beneath it.

I felt him hardening against me as his hand moved to lift the hem of my skirt, stroking the naked flesh of my thighs and seeking to move higher.

"Igraine, oh, you are beautiful… Igraine, oh, I want you." He spoke softly, his breath light and fast as his expert fingers continued to explore me. Uther may not have been wedded, but there was no doubt that he was experienced in the arts of pleasure. My traitorous flesh was responding to his touch as my mind was trying to work out a way for me to escape.

As his breathing became more urgent, I could tell that he was thinking now of nothing but taking his pleasure; he loosened his hold on me in order to make the necessary adjustments to his clothing and this was enough for me to act. Pushing him hard, I sprang away from him, running down the corridor as he sprawled in inelegant, frustrated surprise on the hard, cold stone flags.

"Igraine!" he called after me. "Igraine… Come back!" I hurtled round the corner, catching my dress, ripping it on a wall sconce and trampling on the swansdown cloak in my determination to get away from him. I could still hear him calling as I opened the door to the ante-room of the Tower. "You can't escape you know; you were chosen for me, Igraine. Chosen by the Goddess."

◆ ◆ ◆

I SLOWED MY PACE AS I mounted the stairs, looking in dismay at the damage to my clothing. The dress was ripped from waist to hem, and the beautiful cloak of gauze and gossamer now looked like a bundle of old and dusty cobwebs.

Hesitantly, I opened the door to our chamber, not sure who, or what I would find waiting for me. Within, all was silent. The room was dark, the candles had all burned down, and the fire was almost spent. In the tawny half-lit shadows, I could just make out two figures sprawled across the bed. Gorlois and Erec, fully clothed with an empty wineskin between them.

I decided that I would not disturb them, so I swiftly took off my ruined finery and pulled on an old linen shift and a woollen kirtle for warmth. There was a low chair by the fireplace and after placing another log on the fire to bring some heat to the room, I wrapped myself in Gorlois' cloak and settled myself down for the night.

TRY AS I MIGHT, I couldn't sleep. My mind was alive with the events of the evening and my flesh still burned with unbidden desire where Uther's knowing, experienced hands had caressed me.

The hours passed slowly as I sat by the fireplace, watching the flames twist this way and that, creating strange, unearthly shadows on the walls. I listened to the soft hissing crackle of sap catching fire as the log eventually fell apart in the grate. I was trying to make sense of the things Vivian had told me, and also, I conceded unwillingly to myself, not liking to cast doubt on my old mentor and teacher, some of the things that she quite categorically had not told me, but which I was beginning to suspect.

Firstly, Uther's infatuation with me was no sudden, random chance. Merlin and Vivian had clearly been talking to him about me, exciting him, feeding his desire and working to foster within his heart and his imagination the idea that he was in love with me. It was Vivian's maidens who had crafted the dress for me, spun moonbeams into samite and swansdown with gossamer to create a garment so beautiful that the wearer could not fail to enchant whoever beheld her. And the enchantment had worked, transforming Uther's dreams of his perfect Queen into a reality that wore my face and form.

And Uther…my King and also the man who had come so close to seducing me with his gentle words, sweet tongue and hard kisses. What were my feelings for him? Now this was a difficult one. He was the King. The most powerful man in Britain. He was the great and terrible warrior who had overcome the Saxons, bringing a hard-won peace to our troubled lands. He was also a man. He had been raised on battlefields and had witnessed blood and betrayal from a young age. He had learned to lead, but had also to keep himself apart, to trust rarely and not to give of himself lightly. What had he said to me earlier? "Will you give me comfort, Igraine?"

And what had I done? I'd rejected him, leaving him sprawled on the floor of his own castle, running away from him rather than submitting to his desires. From what I knew of him, he would not forgive me. Uther was known to be a fierce friend to the few people he trusted, but an implacable, merciless enemy to those who opposed him or lost his favour.

My thoughts were disturbed by a noise from the room behind me. Gorlois appeared to be stirring, but he just shifted his position, gave out a heavy sigh and settled back into his slumbers.

My husband had done himself no favours with the King this night either. We had entered the feast late, a slight which Uther had not mentioned, but which I am sure had not gone unnoticed. I remembered with rising horror how Gorlois alone of all the King's Lords and allies had not stood to cheer his sovereign and offer homage. Instead, he had sprawled on his chair in a drink-sodden slumber.

And how had he behaved when he saw me on the dais? He had left the feast, turning his back on the King's celebrations and insulting his hospitality. As all present would no doubt remember, I had been called there by the Lady as a token of favour from the Goddess. This was an honour enshrined in tradition and if not something all husbands would have welcomed, most would have recognised the right of the Goddess to bestow it.

Gorlois was turning from the Mysteries toward the new religion. I remembered my conversation with Vivian earlier that day, when I told her of his opposition to me sending my sweet Morgan to Avalon to do service to the Goddess, and his refusal to take his proper part in Her rituals. She had been angered by what I told her and that is what led to our experiment with the scrying bowl, where I saw the vision of my husband's bloody, desecrated body.

Now my thoughts turned to the previous summer when the Lord Merlin came to visit us. Gorlois had distanced himself as much as he could from his court at Tintagel, spending time with the old and powerful Druid only when it would have been impossible to do otherwise. Throughout his visit, Merlin had seemed unaware of the slights Gorlois kept paying him, seeming content with my company and that of my daughters, walking in the gardens and telling stories in the Nursery. But what if this had been but a façade of gentility, hiding Merlin's true feelings, his anger at being practically ignored by his old friend and ally, coupled with a righteous indignation at Gorlois' decision to turn away from the Mysteries?

"Oh, Gorlois," I thought, "You have made some powerful enemies. And perhaps, after tonight, so have I."

I was very troubled by these thoughts and found it impossible to sleep.

It was a little before dawn when Gorlois finally woke up. The sky had begun to lighten, and I could see the morning star glinting through the faint pink haze as he raised himself groggily from the bed. Seeing me huddled on the chair by the fire, my finery lying torn and tattered on the floor, he came slowly toward me. He reached down and pulled me up into his arms and as he held me, the tensions of the last few hours washed over me, and I began to cry.

Erec was disturbed by the noise and woke up, making a hasty and embarrassed exit in search of his own chamber. Gorlois' breath stank, and I could tell that his head was pounding. He looked ruefully at the empty wineskin and shook his head.

"This is a mess, Igraine."

"Yes, and you need to be thinking clearly before we can decide what to do about it."

I sent him to the privy to dowse his head in water. When he returned, he still looked awful, but at least he appeared to be awake and capable of coherent thought.

It turned out that his memory of the night before was a little patchy. He couldn't remember much about the feast and had no recollection of falling asleep during Uther's welcoming oration. He groaned and held his head in shame when I told him the whole court had laughed at him as he had sprawled, snoring, on his chair.

"Aye, that was not well done. I was tired and the wine Uther serves is strong." My husband shook his head ruefully.

"But tell me, Igraine, how was it that you were raised to the dais? Sitting beside him, as if you were his wife and queen."

I explained to him what had happened, and told him of my suspicions regarding Merlin and Vivian.

"It was Vivian who had the dress made, woven with enchantments in Avalon." I went to Gorlois, who was standing by the fireplace, and put my arms around him, resting my head on his chest:

"I wish I had listened to you, my love; I wish I had never set eyes on the accursed thing." Gorlois reached down and picked up the dress, which was still lying in a crumpled heap on the floor.

"It is not so beautiful now." He looked at the tattered finery, noticing the rips and tears, the smears and spots of blood. "How now, Igraine? What happened here?"

And so, I told him.

"I got lost trying to find my way back to our chamber. I fell and hurt myself. I was using the dress to staunch the wound when Uther found me."

"But you told me you left the feast early; surely he should have been with his guests?"

"He followed me, Gorlois, and when he found me…when he found me…" I realised I did not know how to tell my husband what had happened, and I was stammering as the guilty memory of Uther's kiss erupted in my mind.

"Igraine, did he…dishonour you?" Gorlois pronounced every word slowly, struggling to keep his self-control.

I was trying hard to regain my composure: "No! Gorlois, no, I promise you he did not."

"Are you telling me true, Igraine? There is blood on this dress, and it has been ripped and ruined. There has been violence here."

"Yes. There has. But I swear to you, he did not get what he wanted." I spoke slowly, trying to keep my voice calm as I gathered my thoughts: "He forced me back against the wall. When he took his hand away to loosen his clothing, I pushed him, and I ran. I ran back here, to find you. That's when I ripped the dress."

Gorlois heaved a heavy sigh. "And I was sleeping like a drunken sot. No use to you. No comfort." He rested his chin upon my head, and I could feel the catch in his voice as he struggled to hold back tears: "Oh Igraine, I am so sorry. Last night, I failed you in so many ways. I let you down so badly."

Gorlois' contrition was palpable, and my own regrets about the evening weighed heavy on me. But I reminded myself that we had done nothing wrong. This was all Uther's doing. I took my husband's hands in mine.

"Gorlois, listen to me. Both of us probably wish last night hadn't happened. I would like nothing more than to forget it. I feel sullied; I wish I could just say: *"let's never talk of this, let's cleanse it from our minds"* but I cannot. Last night, I defied Uther, spurned and humiliated him—he will not let this pass."

By now Gorlois was stone-cold sober: "Call Elaine," he said to me. "Get her to pack your things. I'm going to the stables. We leave in an hour."

At first, I thought he meant that we would leave alone, but that was not what my husband had in mind at all. Gorlois was an efficient and experienced leader. His troops were always battle-ready and once he had roused Erec, it was not long before his knights and captains had the men of Cornwall and Lyonesse marshalled and prepared to leave. We rode out of the city, back toward Cornwall as the sun was rising and before the castle, sleepy from the last night's feasting, had fully woken up.

I had little doubt that Uther would see this as nothing more nor less than a declaration of war.

Chapter Four

Twelve days later, filthy, saddle-sore and exhausted, we rode through the gates of Tintagel. Our flight from Caer-Lundein could not have been a greater contrast to the pleasant and leisurely progress that had taken us to Uther's court. On that trip we had lingered, received as honoured guests by Gorlois' friends and allies along the way. We had been feted and courted, my husband known by all to be the Pendragon's chief general and honoured companion. Now, I reflected ruefully, he would be regarded as a traitor.

My husband was no fool; he fully understood how Uther would interpret our departure, but despite this, he had decided, calmly, clearly and with absolute determination that he would rather risk civil war than give up his wife, or his honour, to his King.

After a hasty discussion with Erec and the other warlords of Cornwall and Lyonesse, we had mounted, bringing with us only what we could carry in our packs and saddle bags. We changed horses twice along the way, trading our exhausted steeds for fresh mounts whose speed and quality declined with each hurried transaction. When we reached Winchester, Gorlois dispatched three riders to travel to my father's court in the Welsh borders, to bring news of what had happened and to ask for his assistance.

My father, King Amlawdd, was old now and tired. It was my brother Gareth who ruled in all but name in the Welsh court, and it was in Gareth that we placed our hopes. There were few others that we might be able to call upon as allies. We had had no time to send messages to Lot of Orkney before we fled the Court. He was promised to our daughter Morgause and we still believed that we could trust him. In my mind's eye I saw again the Highland Lords standing, impassive and unimpressed, as Uther saluted them at the feast. They did not bend before the Pendragon's glamour and his ostentatious display of power and perhaps, if we could hold out long enough, the men of Orkney might send forces to our aid.

We held out little hope that the Lords who had welcomed us beneath their roof but weeks ago would now wish to stand beside us. Uther's Peace had been hard-won, the land was weary of battle and the Lords of the Western strongholds were eager to plant their fields, ride out to hunt with hawk and hound and sport with their wives, both for pleasure and in the hope of siring sons to replace those who'd fallen on the field of war.

In any case, their strongholds would not be willing to receive us. The Lords and Ladies, with the flower of their knights and warriors had ridden east to join in Uther's triumph. Their household stewards would keep doors barred, battlements garrisoned and drawbridges up, admitting no one without warrant from their master. Although the land was now at peace, the memory of the Vortigern's duplicity and the cruel onslaughts of his allies, the Saxon raiders, was still fresh enough to ensure that no one would open up their gates to any they did not recognise as friends and comrades. We knew that to attempt to force admittance would not only waste time and risk unwanted casualties but would also serve to augment Uther's case against us, losing any remnants of sympathy that might have remained in the hearts of our former friends.

From Winchester we journeyed west, mainly sleeping in rough camps beneath the stars. The weather favoured us, and we saw little rain, but it was very cold at night and the ground was hard to sleep on. On the eleventh night, we camped at last on Cornish soil, in the wild moorlands of Whiddon Down. After we had fed and watered our horses, I took coin from my saddlebag and sent several of our men to the nearby homesteads to buy bread and meat and ale. We were on home ground now and could safely ask our people for assistance.

That night we fed better than we had since leaving Uther's court. We built a fire and, after we had eaten, Gorlois stood and called for silence. Up until this point he had refused to talk about his plans even with me. Most evenings, he and Erec had taken themselves away to the edge of our makeshift campsites, out of earshot of the rest of us, and could be seen huddled together in long and serious discussions, sometimes calling for one or other of the knights or lesser warlords to join them in their talk. Now, it seemed, he was ready to share his thoughts.

Gorlois had chosen to stand on a little mound a few feet away from the fire, silhouetted against the sky and visible to us all. He had his hands on his hips, one fist clasping the pommel of his long sword, his feet firmly planted on the Cornish earth that he commanded. Although his head was slightly bowed, his shoulders were thrown back proudly, and the wind played softly with the corners of his cloak. It lifted strands of his hair, which hung long and loose, freed from his war-plait, and the firelight filtered through it, creating an ethereal and otherworldly glow around him.

He waited, saying nothing until the voices all fell silent. He did not have to wait long; some of his men were seated cross-legged on the ground around the campfire, others lounged with their backs against the small, stunted trees that formed the only shelter on this bleak and exposed moorland. I was with Elaine and the other women; we sat close together, huddled in our cloaks for the evening air was growing chilly. But every face was turned toward him, every eye was focused on him, and all were waiting for his words.

Once all was quiet, Gorlois bent forward and dug with his fingers in the rough turf of the moorland. Pulling up a clod of earth and scrubby moor grass, he rubbed the soil between his fingers, covering his hands with dirt and holding them out for all to see.

"This is the soil of Cornwall. Our soil. My soil. It is the soil of the land where I was born, the land I love and have sworn to all of you that I'll protect." He spoke slowly and calmly, but as his words gained force, his voice became stronger and more passionate.

"We have fought many battles to protect this soil. To protect our crops, our homes and hearths, our kin. And we have lost many that are dear to us." He pointed toward the fire, where three of his youngest knights were seated. "Last year, Sir Morwen died at the hand of the Saxons, fighting by my side to win this land its liberty. His fatherless sons are with us now—Mark, Unwin, Erwin, you know more than most the cost of war."

The three young knights stared back at him, unblinking. "But you also know that however high the cost, we will pay it if it means we can retain our freedom. Sir Morwen died because he would not give up his birthright, would not see his sons left landless and his fields and forests overtaken by usurpers. His fight is our fight. And that fight continues."

I looked at the faces of the men around the fire; all were gazing at him and many had, in imitation of him, reached down and taken up clods of Cornish soil, which they were now holding in raised, clenched fists toward him.

"I was a Lord of Uther's, all of you know that. I fought for him and beside him and have given him my fealty.

"Uther Pendragon is the High King of all the Britons, and at this moment, he is still our liege lord."

He paused to let this sink in, and I noticed many of the watching faces seemed confused and uncertain at his words.

"All of you will know that we travelled to his court in honour of his victory and to celebrate his peace. Cornwall, Ceint, the Welsh Lands, the North. The Irish galloglaigh and more. We stood before him, and we bent the knee. And he is, still, our liege lord."

He paused again, looking to his left, where Erec was standing, leaning against a tree, the moonlight glinting on his pale hair. I saw him give Gorlois an almost imperceptible nod.

"But what did this King, this man, this Uther Pendragon, choose to do for one who has stood and fought beside him and seen the blood of his own kin shed to win his battles?

"Did he honour him? Did he raise him to the dais as a symbol of his favour?

"No.

"He tried to rape his wife."

There was a shocked intake of breath, and many people turned to look at me. I felt as if Gorlois had hit me. I hadn't known that this was his intention, to share my shame with everyone, to expose me to their curiosity. I felt an arm around my shoulder. It was Elaine, my handmaid and half-sister and turning toward her, I buried my head in her shoulder as my husband continued.

"Before all the court you saw him raise your Duchess—my wife—to sit beside him on the dais, saw him lead her to dance. You heard the words of the so-called Lady of the Lake, calling her to do this. This was not Igraine's wish nor her desire."

I heard murmurs round the fire and saw people nodding their heads in agreement with their Lord. The men of Cornwall and Lyonesse had not relished seeing their Duchess dancing with the King and their war duke shamed.

"You saw her leave the Hall without him, wanting to get back to her own rooms and me, her own Lord. But on the way, he found her, he trapped her and assaulted her."

At these words, Erec stepped forward, holding out the remnants of my silken dress and tattered cloak for all to see.

"This was his doing. This is why we left his court."

Raising his hand to the sky, he let the final crumbs of Cornish soil fall softly to the ground.

"I am Gorlois, Duke of Cornwall. I will fight to protect my land and my people. I will fight to protect my home and my family.

"I do not want war. We have won peace at a high and bitter cost, and I will not be the one to break it. Uther is still my liege lord and if he will publicly acknowledge the fault he did my wife, the Lady

Igraine, if he will apologise and make due amends, I will hold his peace and remain within his law. But if he will not…"

He paused and looked around the clearing, taking in the faces turned toward him in taut and rapt attention.

"But if he will not, then I will fight." At this, he raised his sword.

Erec, standing beside him, pulled his sword from its scabbard and raised it likewise, joining his voice with Gorlois.

"We will fight," they shouted. And with one voice they turned to the assembled host, which by now was also standing, swords and daggers at the ready.

"Lords of Cornwall, my knights of Lyonesse, are you with us?"

And with one voice, they all responded, "We will fight."

DURING THE COMMOTION, I GOT quietly to my feet and, beckoning Elaine to follow me, slipped away from the fire. I still could not believe what Gorlois had just done, seeking to provide justification for war by having Erec display the dress that I had ripped and ruined.

I did not want to face the looks of pity from the other ladies of Gorlois' court, nor did I relish having to deal with the prying questions that I feared Erec's wife Ened would direct toward me.

We walked away from the campsite toward the copse where the horses were grazing, loosely tied. I had known Elaine nearly all my life. Two years younger than me, she was the result of what my mother had called "an indiscretion," between my father and the widow of one of his lesser Knights. Like Gorlois, my father took his duty to bring comfort to the families bereaved in his service very seriously; however, my father's definition of comfort was rather more self-serving than my husband's.

My mother was a wise and tolerant woman who appeared to regard finding suitable places for my father's by-blows as little more than one of the regular duties of a Welsh Queen. My father appreciated the ease and comfort with which she ran his court, conducted his affairs with discretion, and always treated her with respect. It was not the type of marriage I would have wanted, but it appeared to work for them.

Elaine had been introduced into the royal household just after the birth of my brother, when I was seven and she was five. She had always been a pretty child, with pale skin and auburn hair and dark blue eyes that shone like pebbles underwater. At first, we simply played together, but as she grew older, she spent some time each day with my mother's maid, learning how to care for me and serve me. She was my confidant and my best friend.

When I left the Welsh Court for Avalon, she accompanied me, and together we learned the Mysteries. Despite the two-year age gap, Elaine proved herself far more adept than I was with the scrying bowl. By the time she was eleven and I thirteen, she was able to conjure visions on the surface of glass or water with practised ease and even though we were not supposed to scry without the permission and supervision of the Lady, there had been several times when we disobeyed.

We walked slowly away from the campfire toward the horses; our heads were close together, but we did not speak. I heard a noise in the distance, on the other side of the woodland, and several of the horses whinnied as if disturbed. I raised my head to see if I could discover what had alarmed them, and I was suddenly arrested by the angle of the trees against the skyline and the position of the moon. I knew this place. I had seen this all before.

I stopped walking, unwilling to move any closer to the trees until I had dragged the details of the memory from my mind. I knew that we had not stopped at Whiddon Down on our journey to join Uther at Caer-Lundein, and I was fairly certain that I'd not spent any time here during my years as Cornwall's Duchess. The moorland was a bleak and desolate place which offered little scope for pleasure jaunts or hunting; there were far more captivating places near our Castle of Tintagel for us to fly our hawks. I looked up again at the pale face of the moon, lying low against the treetops, its eldritch light casting long shadows that stretched out toward the campsite. And then I knew. As I realised the truth, my heart beat faster, a chill ran down my spine and my scalp began to prickle. Elaine and I had seen this place, this exact place, with the moon above the woodland, in a vision many, many years ago when we were girls in Avalon.

I think I would have been nearly fifteen, whilst Elaine was just shy of her thirteenth birthday. It was early morning and the dew was still glimmering on the sloping lawns. We had been sent to gather herbs from the castle gardens and our baskets were already lined with bundles of scented thyme and lemon verbena. Elaine was cutting long sprays of rosemary from the bushes which stood as fragrant sentinels at the gateway to the potager, whilst I had been asked to bring back arnica flowers for the infirmary. I was in the middle of carefully snipping the aromatic, daisy-like heads from the delicate stems when we saw riders arriving at the far Lake-side. They dismounted and tied up their horses, waiting for the Lady to send out her silent barge to meet them.

The barge was enchanted, needing neither sail nor oarsmen to propel it swiftly and in complete silence across the still, deep waters of the lake. As the barge neared the shore, a slight breeze unfurled the banner that one of the travellers was carrying, revealing the standard of the Welsh Lords. When I saw this, I was certain that they had come to take me home in readiness for my wedding.

I had been betrothed to Gorlois, Duke of Cornwall at the age of thirteen, but I had never seen him. I was told that a proxy ceremony had taken place at his castle of Tintagel, with another of my father's by-blows, the seventeen-year-old Isabel, taking my place in the ritual as a sign of our good faith. I had asked Elaine to help me scry the ceremony, but she had refused, saying, with what I now recognised as a wisdom beyond her years, that it would only hurt me to see my future husband with another.

I can remember that I was certain that the arrival of the messengers meant that I was being sent for. This time I was determined to have sight of the man who was to be my lord before I met him face to face. After a little bit of pleading and persuasion on my part, Elaine agreed that this was fitting and, after we had taken our basket of herbs to the infirmarian, we crept into the kitchens to find a bowl that we could use for scrying. The kitchens were busy as always; the messengers had arrived unexpectedly, and the Lady had ordered that meat and ale should be prepared for them.

Elaine kept watch at the doorway whilst I slipped into the scullery to steal a bowl. In the end it wasn't difficult, the cook was distracted, and I was able to acquire one of the fine copper basins that were used for puddings on high feast days.

I could almost see us in my mind's eye as we ran toward the shores of the lake, finally stopping at a small sandy beach on the westernmost reaches of the island. It had high banks, overgrown with sedge and rushes that we were certain would protect us from being overlooked from any of the windows of the castle. By now, we were both quite excited, breathing fast and giggling as we filled the bowl with lake water, much of which slopped out as we carried it to a large stone and set it down.

I remembered how Elaine had tutted when she saw how little water was left within the bowl. "I don't think that's enough," she'd said, returning alone to the lake and refilling the bowl. In her absence, I had become calmer and we were now both ready to prepare ourselves for our task.

I cleared my mind as I had been taught, freeing myself to become a vessel for the power of the Goddess. I looked at Elaine and she nodded; she too was ready to open her mind to whatever visions would be sent to us. We both placed our hands on the sides of the bowl, feeling the metal start to warm beneath our touch.

It was Elaine who had said the words. "Tell us of the future, tell us of the husband of Igraine." I spoke them after her and we repeated them softly, chanting together as the bowl got hotter and hotter, the lake water bubbling in the burnished copper, causing steam to rise which stung our eyes and obscured the surface.

As the steam cleared, I saw an empty room. It was a well-appointed bed chamber, richly furnished, with tapestries decorating the wall and floors. As I watched, the door opened to admit two figures: the first was a man, tall, broad shouldered and dressed in green with an opulent black-and-gold cloak flung casually across his shoulders. The visions in the scrying bowl are always silent, but I was certain that he was talking to the second person, a woman I think, although I couldn't be sure because the man had his back to us and was so tall that he all but obscured the other figure.

Then, the tall man turned toward us and I saw his face for the first time, the face that is now more dear to me than any other. This was Gorlois, fifteen years my senior and a warrior in his prime. Handsome and happy on his wedding day, his face was strong and, I realised now in retrospect, without many of the lines of care that fate and war have carved there.

He went over to the fireplace and picked up a large, beautifully engraved pewter jug and poured wine into the cups that had been placed on the carved chest beside the bed. Then, reaching out his hand and laughing, he pulled the other person into view. It was me, dressed in my wedding finery, my hair perfectly arranged upon my head, a coronet of spring flowers at my brow. I remember watching as Gorlois took my future self in his arms and pulled her to him, watching him run his fingers through her hair and reach for the lacings on her dress, and I remember that I almost pulled my hands away from the surface of the bowl, realising at the last moment that I really did not want to share this vision with Elaine.

Perhaps it was that slight shift in concentration that caused the surface of the water to shimmer and the vision to reform as something else. I was struggling hard to bring the details back exactly to my mind. As the bowl cleared, we were no longer looking at a well-lit bedroom. Instead, we were gazing into a bleak, dark landscape; there were few stars visible in the cloudy sky and the moon sat low above a small copse where we could see horses tethered. In the distance, I could make out the dying embers of a fire, with people huddled round it. I saw two women leave the fire and start to walk toward the trees. They went slowly, their heads bent together as if in deep and private conversation.

Then, from the edge of the copse a man came into view. He was tall and cloaked in black. I remember seeing him turn slightly so the moonlight shone upon his face, showing the glint of a snowy beard and a pale green robe beneath his cloak. In one hand, he held a thick wooden staff, covered with strange symbols and letters that seemed to twist and twine in the moonlight. In his left hand, he held a sword.

And then, the vision stopped. Back then when we were girls in Avalon this was the moment that Vivian's anxious voice disturbed us and dragged us back from the depths of our forbidden scrying. The Lady of the Lake had come looking for me herself because the messengers had indeed been from my father's court.

But they had not been sent to summon me to my wedding; they had come to tell me of my mother's death. In the sorrow that filled the next few weeks, the visions by the lakeside were all forgotten, and Elaine and I had not discussed it till this day. But now, as we stood together on that bleak and unforgiving moorland, with the moon setting behind the trees it all came back.

"Do you remember?" I asked Elaine, who nodded, a little fearfully, her hand reaching for mine in the darkness.

"What shall we do?" she breathed. "Shall we go back to the fireside?"

"No," I said, in a whisper. "We go forward. He will be here in a moment." I pointed to the moon which was now almost exactly in the position it had been in our vision. "The vision came to us from the Goddess; she would want us to understand it, to know why she had vouchsafed it."

Holding Elaine's hand to give comfort to us both, I led us toward the edge of the trees. All was still; the horses had stopped whinnying and in the silence we could hear the rustling of the leaves and the distant calls of a night-bird. Then, we saw a movement and a man stepped out in front of us. His black cloak hung heavily upon his shoulders and rested a little wearily on his staff.

Letting go of Elaine's hand I moved in front of her and gave a low curtsey.

"Well met by moonlight, my lord Merlin."

The ancient Druid looked at me, his thin, bloodless lips slowly twisting into a smile that did not meet his eyes.

MERLIN RAISED ME FROM MY curtsey and did not immediately let go of my hand. "You are cold, Igraine, and your face seems care worn; I trust your journey has not tired you over much?"

"We have ridden hard, it's true, my lord. But surely you have ridden harder?" Merlin must have been at least a half a day behind us. He would have driven his horse unmercifully to have arrived on Whiddon Down at the same time as we did.

Merlin shook his head, "You forget who I am, child. I left Caer-Lundein but six hours ago. There are swift pathways for those with knowledge of the ancient magics. I am come with messages from the Lady and must speak with both yourself and the Duke of Cornwall."

I remembered hearing stories of the faery roads during my years in Avalon, secret tracks and byways that allowed those granted access to their secrets the ability to complete their journeys in a fraction of the time it would take a traveller upon the King's roads, but I'd thought them to be just fireside tales. If Merlin was to be believed, he had travelled over two hundred miles in less time than it would have taken us to ride five and twenty.

"Gorlois is in council with his men, and I really don't know when he will be finished." As I spoke I was frantically trying to think of a way to delay bringing Merlin into Gorlois' presence. "This is the first night we have rested on Cornish soil and until tonight, Gorlois has not told anyone why we chose to leave the castle in such a hurry."

"Your husband's knights are loyal indeed to follow him without a word of explanation down a path that could easily be interpreted as the road to rebellion." Merlin's face was expressionless, his voice cold.

"The men of Cornwall and Lyonesse are loyal in truth." I didn't bother to spell it out. Gorlois' men would die for him if they had to; they had fought for Uther because Gorlois had commanded them to, not because they had any innate loyalty to the Pendragon. It was to their war duke that they gave fealty.

"I know he wishes to talk to them of what has happened and what he plans to do." I was thinking quickly now. "I would not wish to disturb him at this time and if you have messages from the Lady, I'm sure she would not care for them to be shared unwittingly with those whose ears are unworthy." I was hoping to get Merlin to agree to wait until morning to speak with Gorlois. After his rousing speeches earlier, I was pretty certain that he and Erec would be fired up and ready for a fight. If Merlin had come with messages from Vivian, I could only think that they would involve asking Gorlois to beg for Uther's forgiveness and to return under what I knew my husband would regard as humiliating conditions of apology and conciliation, in complete opposition to my husband's plainly stated plans and intentions.

Such a meeting could only end badly, and I would do almost anything to avoid it.

"I'm afraid the campsite has little to offer in the way of privacy. We ride for Tintagel at first light. Can your messages be delayed for a few hours longer?" Merlin did not answer, his face, hard and impassive, was as unreadable as a sealed-up scroll.

"It will take but a few hours to reach the castle gates and within are my daughters, young Morgause and my little Morgan. They would be so happy to see you, my lord." This wasn't a lie. Morgause particularly had been very taken with the elderly Druid when he visited us last year, and I knew she would be delighted to see him again.

At the mention of my daughters I saw something in Merlin's face soften and a faint smile played around his lips. "I had not thought to mix any pleasure with my business this night, but I have fond memories of those hours we spent together last summer. It would indeed be good to see the little ones again."

"That's settled then, my lord." I'm sure he must have heard the relief in my voice, but there was nothing I could do to hide it. I'd planned to send Elaine and several of the household men and women on ahead to rouse the castle and make preparations for our arrival. If Merlin could travel with them, then I would be able to speak to Gorlois and at least give him some time to prepare for an encounter which I knew he wouldn't relish.

Merlin was happy with my suggestion; he would borrow a horse and set off to Tintagel with Elaine before daybreak. I think he recognised that Gorlois was more likely to be receptive to whatever it was he had to say within the walls of his own castle. I also suspected that, despite his earlier words, he was tired from his journey and would relish the comforts of a soft bed and warm hearth before returning to Caer-Lundein.

The three of us made our way back to the campsite, where the red glow of the damped down fires cast long shadows over sleeping bodies, huddled together for warmth under the cold, clear skies. Gorlois and Erec were nowhere to be seen. I swiftly woke up the small group of people I wanted to ride on ahead and gave them my orders.

Within the hour, their horses were mounted. I kissed Elaine on both cheeks and wished her good-speed. I knew I could trust her to see Lord Merlin was well looked after until Gorlois and I arrived. I watched them ride away, silhouetted against the sky, cloaks streaming behind them, the tall figure of the Druid easily recognisable from the long staff slung across his back. It was only then that I remembered. In the vision, Merlin had a staff in one hand, a long, gleaming sword in the other. But tonight, there had been no sign of the longsword. Musing on this and wondering if it had any significance, I went in search of my husband.

Chapter Five

As it turned out, it was well past mid-day before we were all seated in the solar of Tintagel's west tower. When I first told Gorlois that Merlin awaited him, he'd been angry, seeing this as yet another example of what he called Vivian's "meddling" in state affairs. At first, he'd refused to meet with the elderly Druid, and it had taken all of my persuasion to get him to agree to at least listen to what he had to say. Despite Gorlois' growing rejection of the Mysteries, he had eventually to acknowledge that the Lady of the Lake had an established and recognised place at Court and that Uther would, to a certain extent, listen to and be guided by her.

If I was honest with myself, I wasn't particularly happy about the way things had turned out either. Throughout our frantic and uncomfortable flight from Uther's court, the one thing I'd held on to was the thought of seeing my two girls again. We had been away for several months, and I was sure that both my daughters would have changed and grown in our absence. I couldn't wait to hold them in my arms again and bury my face in their sweet-smelling hair. As it was, I'd only had chance to give Morgause the tiniest of hugs before Gorlois bore me off to the solar. Morgan I hadn't seen at all; Elaine told me she was sleeping, and I hadn't the heart to wake her and leave her, confused and unhappy as I went to listen to what Merlin had to say.

The solar in the west tower was not a large room and since I had lived at Tintagel had been given over to my exclusive use. The children slept in the room above it, and I had spent many pleasant days there with Elaine and my other ladies, gossiping and enjoying spiced wine and sweetmeats. On more industrious days we would work at our tapestries, the best of which were hung upon the walls. There was a wide window, glazed in roman fashion, its small lozenges of coloured glass casting jewel-like glints on the faces of Merlin and Gorlois, who were seated in high-backed wooden chairs on either side of the fireplace. I chose to curl up in the window seat and had pulled my cloak tight around me. Despite the combined efforts of the early spring sunshine and the logs burning in the fireplace, I felt chilled and uncomfortable as Merlin leaned forward in his chair, his hands steepled in front of him, tapping slowly against his lips as if to emphasise every word he was saying.

"Well, Gorlois, you're a bloody fool." He spoke slowly and without emotion. "You do realise that it is only thanks to the intervention of the Lady, and possibly some small words of counsel from myself, that the Pendragon and his warlords are not already marching against you?"

This didn't bode well. Gorlois always found it hard to take criticism and this sounded like a dressing down from an elderly school-master. "He wished to cuckold me in front of all the court," said Gorlois, pulling himself up, out of his chair and grabbing Merlin by the shoulder. "Did you know that, you doddering old hypocrite?" He was shouting now, and I could see the flecks of spittle landing on Merlin's cheek as he continued to rant. "All that nonsense about gifts of the goddess, just an excuse to take my wife. I won't stand for it. Cornwall won't stand for it."

I had to admire Merlin's restraint. He said nothing, didn't even seek to remove Gorlois' hands from his shoulders, allowing the droplets to remain untouched upon his cheeks. After a moment, the silence appeared to have a calming effect on Gorlois, who held up his hands to the Druid and stepped a few paces back.

"Gorlois' that night, in front of all the Court, the Goddess chose Igraine for a reason." Merlin's voice was low, but was no longer speaking coldly. He was imploring Gorlois, his old comrade and companion to listen to his words. "That is why I've come here, to talk to you about the future of the kingdom and all the realms within it. To share with you the visions that have been granted to the Lady." Here he cast a sidelong glance in my direction. "And to tell you both about the part Igraine must play if we are truly to have peace."

I was startled by this. I'd already worked out that Vivian had been seriously involved in the events that had led to our flight from Caer-Lundein. She had hinted that Uther's interest in me was serious and had used that as an excuse to get me to scry with her. We hadn't found out the answers to the questions she'd asked on that occasion, but from what Merlin was saying, Vivian now had the knowledge she'd been looking for. And it looked like there was no escaping it. This was all about me.

I walked over to Gorlois and took his hand. He pulled me close to him and dropped a kiss upon my brow as we turned to face the Druid. United. Together. Ready to hear whatever he had come to tell us.

What Merlin said next was not what I'd expected. "Igraine, last night, when we met on Whiddon Down, you were not surprised to see me?"

So I had to explain to both of them about the vision granted to myself and Elaine whilst we were girls in Avalon, saying that I had suddenly recognised the scene, the exact position of the moon above the woodlands and then remembered the old man walking toward me with a staff engraved with strange symbols and a pale, gleaming sword.

"Yes. The sword." Merlin nodded eagerly. "You remembered the sword?"

"I did, my lord, and it troubled me last night that you didn't have it with you. Everything else was the same. But not the sword."

Merlin gave a deep sigh. "The sword is not mine to give. Indeed, it has yet to be vouchsafed into my keeping. The Goddess bides her time, and the fates are still uncertain." Merlin paused, considering his next words. The room was completely silent but for the faint crackle of the applewood upon the fire. Gorlois was still holding me tight against him, but I could see that Merlin had his full attention. "The sword is a wonder, an ancient blade, forged in Avalon from faery steel and destined for the warrior who will finally unite our land. I shall be but its keeper for a time."

The Druid got up and made his way to the window and with his back toward us, continued. "Its name is Caliburn, defender of Avalon. Legend says that it can be used only by one who bears it by right, rather than conquest. Whoever wields the blade cannot be defeated in battle." He paused again, and now both Gorlois and I were hanging on his words. "Caliburn is waiting for a warrior. And the warrior it waits for shall be Igraine's only son."

I gasped and heard Gorlois give a sharp intake of breath. Neither of us had expected this.

"What… my… son? But I have daughters, Morgause, Morgan. The Goddess has not sent me a son," In my confusion I was stammering and not really thinking clearly. Gorlois, on the other hand, appeared to have grasped exactly what the Druid was saying.

"I understand now why you're here, Lord Merlin." Gorlois' voice was clipped, unfriendly. "And also, I think, why Uther's forces are not already assembled at the boundaries of my lands."

The Druid turned to face us, a strange half-smile upon his lips. "Gorlois, I serve the Goddess, and I serve the realm."

"And you serve Uther," my husband challenged.

"I serve Uther, certainly," Merlin replied. "Whilst he has the Goddess' favour."

I looked from my husband to the Druid; they both seemed to be speaking in riddles as far as I was concerned.

"I don't know what you're both talking about. I'm not with child and nor am I like to be so if we go to war." I knew from past experience that, loving husband as he was, Gorlois was a commander who fought from the front line. If he needed to take his troops into battle with Uther he would not be doing so from the comfort of his castle and our marriage bed.

"The land has begun to accustom itself once more to peace, Igraine," said Merlin walking toward us and resting his arm gently on my shoulder, "and there is, in truth, little appetite for war."

"You heard the promise Uther made before the court? To honour the Goddess and bring peace and plenty to the realm once more."

I nodded.

Merlin gestured toward the window; beyond the castle walls and the causeway we could see the fields and moors of western Cornwall. "The lands are ripe for planting; our meadows have lain fallow for too long. Our orchards have been drenched with the blood of fallen men and trampled 'neath the feet of marching armies. Now is the time to plant the seeds and prepare for a new harvest. The land wants peace, Igraine."

"And it is a simple matter to achieve it," stated Gorlois. "Tell Uther to admit his sin. To tell his court that he wished to bring dishonour to my wife and the house of Cornwall and Lyonesse. If he does this, there will be no war."

"Gorlois, the court saw Uther dance with Igraine, pay her every honour and treat her with respect. Why should he apologise for that?"

"False words, Merlin," cried Gorlois, his anger beginning to rise. "Uther followed my wife through the castle corridors and attacked her as she was making her way back to our apartments. Is that an act of honour?"

"And was anybody witness to this?" Merlin looked questioningly at both of us. "Could anybody swear they saw the King attack you, Lady?" Gorlois looked at me and I slowly shook my head.

There had been no witnesses. It was my word against the word of the most powerful man in Britain and, although I knew that Gorlois believed me, this was not enough.

"You danced together, in front of the whole court. Not just once, but three times. Igraine, you can't deny you did this willingly and of your own behest."

This was unfair. I thought of the conversation I'd had with Vivian after I'd been called to sit between her and Uther on the dais. The way her fingers had gripped my wrist with bruising force as she hissed at me to take my place and do my duty. "No," I thought, I had not remained there willingly. And then, unbidden and unwelcome, I remembered the terrible, shuddering delight I had felt as Uther's tongue had flicked between my fingers as he welcomed me to his table and I could not deny to myself that, at that moment, I had wanted him.

Flustered, I responded to the Druid's question. "The Lady Vivian reminded me of my duty. I am a loyal servant of the Goddess and what I did, I did to honour her, not from any desires of my own."

"Well spoken, child," Merlin nodded approvingly. "It would go well with you, my lord Duke, if you could view this matter as your wife does.

"Let me be clear. We want no war. Uther is our anointed king, sworn to protect his lands and people. Go to him, Gorlois; bend your knee and declare the fault was yours." I saw my husband start forward, mouth open wide, and fists clenched in protest, but the Druid held up his hand to silence him.

"No, hear me out. Swear fealty and you will once more be honoured as his second-in-command and trusted General. Why should two great lords fall out over inconsequential trifles? Put this behind you and return to spend the summer here in Cornwall, husbanding your estates." Merlin looked at me, his eyes travelling down my body to rest at my waist, encircled by the girdle I wore below my surcoat. He smiled. "By the time the autumn comes, it is likely that the Goddess will have blessed more than just your fields."

At his words, my hands involuntarily moved down to caress my belly, flat within my girdle. I imagined feeling another child quicken there, a brother for my daughters to love and play with, another child to raise within the strong, safe walls of Tintagel.

"And later, when the boy is born, I will come to you and we will raise him to understand the nature of his destiny, to wield the sword the Goddess sends him and to rule our land with justice, strength, and wisdom."

Although I felt angered that Merlin seemed to regard what Uther tried to do to me as trivial, I could see the sense in what he was saying. What benefit would war bring us? Had I been foolish to even tell Gorlois about what had happened that night with Uther? After seeing me dance willingly with the Pendragon in front of all the Court, I thought it was likely that the other lords would not believe me.

I remembered the words Vivian had spat at me when I sought to leave the dais and return to Gorlois' side. *"Do you want to be the cause of yet another conflict? If you leave the dais, you insult not just the Mysteries but the King and his entire Court. You will cause a rift between Uther and his most powerful commander. Do you want that to be on your conscience?"*

I knew that it would be my fault if the hard-won peace was thrust aside.

But Gorlois saw things differently. He was pacing the floor of the solar, unable to keep still, but just managing to keep a curb upon his anger. "You would have me bend the knee to a lecher who sought my wife's dishonour? You would ask me to insult my wife and lady before the whole court, calling her honour into question by pretending that this attack was just a pack of lies?"

Gorlois was standing in front of Merlin now and he reached out and pulled the old man toward him, so their faces almost touched. Speaking slowly, and almost in a whisper he said, "When the rest of the court was feasting, he pursued her through the castle corridors, and tried to force himself upon her. That he did not succeed is testament to the courage of my lady.

"I saw the bruises on her flesh. I will not bend the knee to him again. Never." He released the man who had once been his friend and pushed him backward so violently that the shaken Druid stumbled and would have fallen if I hadn't given him my arm.

"This is the honour of your '*Goddess*' is it?" Gorlois almost spat the words at Merlin. "It sickens me. I will never bow to Uther, and I will no longer allow Her worship in my lands. When my son is born, we will raise him in the new ways.

"Now go, before I whip you from my court, and tell Uther what I've told you. From this moment, we are at war." And with that, he slammed out of the solar and was gone.

For several moments, there was silence.

Finally, Merlin spoke. "And what say you, Igraine?" He had seated himself in the window and his voice was calm. Indeed, he seemed remarkably untroubled by a scene which had left me both disconcerted and afraid.

"He is angry, my lord Merlin; he doesn't mean all he says." But even as I said this, I did not believe it. This was the excuse Gorlois had been looking for to turn his back on the Mysteries and offer the lands of Cornwall and Lyonesse to the sombre, black-robed priests who worshipped the new God.

"Perhaps, child, perhaps. Men often shout words in anger that they come to regret when they have time to reflect. But I think not this time." Merlin's hands rested on his chin, his forefingers rhythmically stroking his beard.

"In fact, I think that Gorlois' feet have been set upon this path for many months. Last summer when I visited, he went out of his way to absent himself from Tintagel, leaving the running of his household and the observance of the Mysteries entirely to you, Igraine. Am I wrong?"

I shook my head but didn't speak.

"And at Court, I saw you dancing with the King, I saw you place your hand in his. I saw you smile into his eyes, Igraine; tell me, can you honestly say that Uther does not please you?"

This made me flustered. Merlin was both observant and very wise, with many years' experience in the ways of men and women. "I did my duty, my lord, as the Lady Vivian instructed."

"Yes, yes, child, but was there more? I need to know because, despite your husband's accusations, the Goddess is both honourable and just. Tell me, Igraine, did Uther truly force you, or would you have given yourself to him if you could have done so without disgrace?"

"I am married to my lord the Duke of Cornwall. I could have no other man and not bring disgrace upon my family and his," I replied, deliberately ambiguous, not wanting to lie to the venerable Druid, but not wanting to admit the truth even to myself.

"I understand you well, child. We shall leave it at that—for now." Merlin was suddenly businesslike, rising from the window seat and arranging his robes around him.

"Well, I must return to court and give tidings of this day to the King and Lady Vivian. I am sorry, child, but the armies will be at your gate by Solstice."

"Please, Lord Merlin, please speak to the King; ask him for my sake to show mercy to the people, to the lands of Cornwall and Lyonesse." I was thinking of the dreadful sights we had all seen in the time of Vortigern's rebellion and the Saxon incursions. Whole villages burned, their fields and orchards blighted, the water in the wells poisoned by the corpses of the dead.

"Pray to the Goddess, Igraine, keep her Mysteries and her rituals and ask for her to intercede. It is her power and not the will of man which will decide our fates."

I knelt before him and asked for his blessing, which he gave willingly, raising me to my feet once he had finished and kissing me upon the forehead.

"Farewell, child. I ask only that you do your duty." And with that, he picked up his cloak from the chest by the solar door and departed. Once he'd left the room, I returned to the window seat and soon I saw him striding purposefully across the courtyard, staff strapped to his back, robes billowing out behind him in the brisk spring breeze. He called to a stable boy to bring a horse to him and once he was mounted he rode out, under the grey stone archway onto the causeway which joined Tintagel to the shore. He rode fast, and did not once look back.

◆ ◆ ◆

ONCE THE LORD MERLIN HAD departed, I hurried to our chamber, hoping to find Gorlois and beg him to do nothing hasty. There was no one there but Elaine, who was still engaged in setting our rooms in order. Her face was pale and, though she smiled when she saw me, her eyes lacked their usual sparkle. I remembered that she'd had no sleep the night before and that, like as not, she'd been constantly on her feet and working since getting back to Tintagel.

I asked her if she had seen Gorlois and she told me that he had been in the room but briefly in search of a riding cloak. I thanked her and urged her to go to bed and get some rest. I realised that Gorlois was probably planning to ride out with Erec to begin work on the castle's defences and if that were the case, that I would see no more of him 'til supper.

I took advantage of my lord's absence to spend time with my daughters, whom I had missed more than I could have imagined. You may think it strange that, at a time like this, with the threat of war upon us and Merlin's words echoing through my mind, I could lose myself in childish play. But you must remember that it was peace, not war, that I was unused to. I had discovered during the years of fear, turmoil, and uncertainty that the only way to live your life, to keep sane amidst the madness, was to seize those brief moments of joy that reminded you of what it was that we were fighting to protect.

After I had told Elaine to get some rest, I quickly made my way to the room high in the Western tower where the girls had their nursery. As I neared the top of the stairs, I stopped. I needed to go quietly. I wanted to observe my girls at play, wishing to gaze upon them before they knew that I was there, to feast my eyes on them before I was enveloped in clumsy hugs and sweet, childish kisses.

Slowly, I crept up the final few stairs, making no noise and leaning close in against the walls so the torches in their sconces wouldn't cast my shadow into the room and betray me. The door was open and I carefully peeked inside. The nursery was a large, light, and airy room, with the wooden shutters thrown open to welcome the spring sunshine. A brisk fire was burning brightly in the grate, scenting the room with applewood; despite the sunshine the room still needed warming. There were always crisp sea breezes playing around Tintagel's walls and their chill fingers could be felt upon your face if you approached the open windows.

There were cushioned benches set against the walls, which were hung with some of my less successful tapestries. One in particular, showing the ancient tale of the capture of the Unicorn by the Lady of the Forest, was Morgause's especial favourite. She loved to stroke the animal's white flank and would gaze for hours into the soft, submissive eyes of the enchanted creature, as it knelt with its head laid meekly upon the Lady's lap. My eldest daughter appeared to not care a jot that her mother had given the poor beast only three legs, having run out of silver thread at the most inappropriate time and not having the patience to put the tapestry to one side until the visit of the next pack-man.

Morgause was now six years old. She was an autumn child, whose copper hair and deep brown eyes would always remind me of the beech woods near St Austell, where Gorlois and I had spent many pleasant nights when we were first married. She was born at the beginning of the tenth month, known to those of us who chose not to use the Roman calendar as *Winterfylleth* (winter full moon). This was a time of beauty and fulfilment, when the woods and forests gloried in their leaves of gold and crimson and the blessings of the Goddess are witnessed daily in the berries of the hedgerow, the bounty of her fruit trees and the crops safely gathered within our granaries and barns.

Like the mellow fruits of autumn, Morgause was lovely to look upon, with a face that betrayed every burst of joy or storm of childish fury. At six years old she had a happy confidence, an assurance she was loved and valued that had not yet been transformed into the blind and selfish assumptions of entitlement and superiority which would dominate her later years. She was a child born of love, wanted and desired by both Gorlois and myself as a symbol of our marriage and proof of the blessings of the Goddess.

Morgan, on the other hand was a winter child, born in the second month that is known to us as *Solmonath* (early seed time), when the soil is just starting to awaken and ready itself to nourish the seeds of new life. Now four years old, my younger daughter was slight of build, with a mass of hair so dark it could have been taken for black. Her eyes, which had always dominated her small and finely drawn face, were a sharp and piercing blue. Quieter and less demanding of attention than her sister, Morgan was often described as "an easy child," but I had learnt early on that just because she didn't wear her heart upon her sleeve and was not prone to those surges of emotion that characterised her tempestuous older sister, it didn't mean that Morgan was not a force to be reckoned with.

As a tiny baby, Morgan had made it very clear that she was not a plaything to be pawed and cuddled like a wooden poppet. I had been taught during my time on Avalon that a mother's milk is important to a child and so, unlike many other high-born ladies, I fed both my daughters for a cycle of the moon before handing them, with some reluctance, to a wet nurse. Morgause luxuriated in the dreamy, milky closeness. She would fall asleep, my nipple still within her tiny baby lips and wake again just moments later, nuzzling for the warmth and comfort of my breast. I think Morgause would have been content to sit within my arms all day, feeding and sleeping, her skin to my skin, my arms encircling her and keeping her safe.

But Morgan would have none of this. She fed swiftly and efficiently and once her tiny belly had had its fill she would wriggle to be put down, to escape the confines of my restricting arms. As a baby, she would lie for hours in her crib, stretching out her hands before her face, gazing in wonder at her own fingers, and protesting most emphatically if her sister, or any other intruder, tried to pick her up and distract her from this fascinating reverie.

At four, Morgan had a vocabulary that was already considerably more extensive than her sister's, and unlike Morgause, who was bright but didn't like her lessons, it was also clear that she possessed a keen intelligence and a mind that was eager to be taught.

The girls were both at play near a low table in the middle of the room. The sunlight made patterns on the floor and Morgause was crawling about beneath the table, playing with her kitten. She was using a piece of ribbon to encourage the tiny creature to chase the specks of flickering light and was giggling and calling out to her nursemaid to watch with her as it leapt and pounced in its efforts to catch the dancing sunbeams.

Morgan was sitting on a little three-legged stool with a wicker basket on her lap. I could see that she was engaged in one of her favourite activities: sorting through my embroidery threads and arranging them into whatever pattern or order her strange little brain had decided was appropriate that day.

Their nursemaid, Avice, was a castle girl, daughter of Gorlois' master falconer and Tintagel born and bred. As I leant further 'round the doorway, I caught her eye and, placing a finger on my lips, rushed into the room, sweeping Morgause up from the floor and swirling her round and round.

"Mama, Mama, Mama," the little girl giggled happily as I drew her to me and held her tight. Laughing, we both fell to the floor onto a pile of cushions near the open fireplace and Morgause snuggled into me as her little kitten, who had been startled by the noise, moved slowly toward us to investigate.

I looked up at Morgan, who had placed the wicker basket neatly on the table and had come to stand beside me. "Hello darling," I said, reaching out to gently touch her nose with the tip of my finger. She bent her head toward me in acceptance of this caress and then, with an elegance remarkable in one so young, arranged herself about a foot away from me on the hearth rug. When she was settled to her perfect satisfaction, she inclined her neck toward me and I leant forward so the very tips of our noses touched. She smiled. "Hello, Mother," was all she said.

Meanwhile, her squirming sister, who was by now getting thoroughly jealous, was pulling at my hair and patting my chin, trying to bring my face 'round toward her. Laughing, I swooped down upon her, rolling her back into the cushions and covering her face with kisses.

It had been many weeks since I'd seen my daughters and I had missed them. Children grow so quickly and I could immediately see changes in both my girls. Morgause's already abundant hair had grown even longer. It fell down her back in a tangle of glossy, burnished curls that I knew caused both Morgause and Avice a deal of pain to brush and braid before bedtime. Her little face seemed more grown-up, with delicate cheekbones becoming visible under the peach-soft childish skin, and she was taller. I noticed that her gown was tight at the elbow and that her skirts now stopped at least three inches away from the floor. The changes in Morgan were a little less obvious. Smaller and more finely made than her sister, her hair was neatly braided with only a few tiny feather-like wisps escaping at her temples; it was hard to tell how much it had grown during my absence, but she too was taller; the sleeve of her dress too short and the bodice somewhat tight even on her tiny frame. It would seem that making new clothes for my daughters' needs must become a priority.

Hugging Morgause to me, I reached out to Morgan and rested my hand on her shoulder. "It is so good to see you, my darlings. I have missed you very much. Have you been good girls whilst we've been away?"

"Very good, Mama, haven't we, Avice? We've not done'd any bad things at all." Morgause threw a quick look at her nursemaid, who smiled at her indulgently and moved toward us, dropping a slight curtsey as she did so.

"Welcome home, my lady. It does my heart good to see you back here in the Nursery."

"I am pleased to be here Avice. And what can you tell me about my little one's progress. It would appear that Morgause is still struggling with her grammar."

My eldest daughter harrumphed at this and shrugged herself away from me. My little Morgause was not good at taking criticism.

"You've not 'done'd' any bad things sweetheart?" I tickled her again as I teased her. "It sounds to me like you haven't done any lessons."

"But I have, Mama; it's just that sometimes I forget things," she pouted at me. "I can't help if I forget things. It's not 'liberate.'"

"She has done her lessons my lady." Avice was quick to come to the defence of young Morgause, whom she utterly adored.

"And how about you, Morgan? Have been a good girl whilst I've been away?"

Her eyes met mine with a look of extraordinary intelligence. "Yes, Mother. I have. But why are you back so soon? You said you wouldn't be back until the apples were ripe in the orchard, yet the blossom is still in bud upon the trees."

"Well, darling girl, I can certainly see that you have been applying yourself to your studies." I was astonished by what Morgan had said to me. Her voice was calm and assured, and she had constructed her words with both grace and precision.

"There was some trouble at Court and your father and I were forced to return sooner than we'd planned."

"Did you bring me a present? You promised you'd bring me a present," demanded Morgause, climbing into my lap and pressing her fingers to my face to get me to look at her.

"I'm sorry, sweetling," I said ruefully, thinking of the great pile of gifts in our trunk at Caer-Lundein. Gorlois and I had taken great joy in collecting little trinkets for our daughters, but in our haste to escape Uther, we hadn't given the trifles and gee-gaws a second's thought. "We left in such a hurry that we brought nothing with us but a few clothes."

"And your weapons, Mother." said Morgan. "I saw Father ride out with Lord Erec and they both had their battle swords."

"Yes, child, your father is a warrior and a great knight and his battle sword will always travel with him."

Morgan didn't appear to be at all bothered by the news that we had returned without the customary bounty of treats and presents, but Morgause was struggling to hold back her tears.

"But you promised me some new ribbons. And some sweetmeats. And I've been so good." I could see tears welling up in her eyes.

Thinking quickly, I unfastened the brooch from my kirtle. It was a silver unicorn and I knew that Morgause had always loved it.

"Hush, sweetheart. See, you can have my unicorn for your very own to make up for it."

Instantly the tears disappeared. "Really, Mama? Truly really?" I nodded and she hugged me before leaping to her feet and running to Avice to ask her to fasten the brooch to her kirtle.

"And how about you, little Morgan? Is there something you would like to make up for the fact I forgot all your presents?"

"No, Mother." She shook her head and bent down to pick up her baskets. I could see she was keen to begin sorting her silks again. But before her small, slender fingers reached out for the next skein she looked up at me, with questions still in her eyes. "But you still haven't told me why you've come back. And why our father has gone away again so quickly?"

"There were just a few problems, darling. Nothing to worry about, but we felt it safer to return home." I hoped that I sounded matter of fact and reassuring. Morgause and Morgan were both just little girls and despite Morgan's quite remarkable precocity, the events that had driven Gorlois and myself from Uther's court and now threatened to engulf us in yet more months of war and conflict were not subjects I wished to talk about in front of my daughters.

Morgan appeared to accept this and settled down once more to her task. Morgause was using her brooch to catch sunbeams, throwing tiny reflections of light upon the floor and the kitten was once again scampering after them. Seeing that both girls were now occupied, I nodded to Avice and left the nursery.

AS I DESCENDED THE TURRET staircase, I looked out toward the causeway and saw three horsemen riding across it at full tilt. From the colour of their livery, I could tell they belonged to the Cornish court, and with a burst of hope I was certain that they were the envoys we had sent to my father's court in Wales.

I quickened my pace down the stairs and just had taken my seat in the Great Hall when one of our heralds entered and announced the new arrivals.

"My lady: Sir Cador, Sir Lowen, and the Lord Madoc."

I inclined my head to indicate my willingness to see the new arrivals, who were in any case striding into the hall. The two knights were young. Sir Cador was a Cornishman, born and bred, with rich fertile lands on the western border between Cornwall and Lyonesse. His companion, Sir Lowen, hailed from the stronghold of Syllan, a large and prosperous fiefdom at the farthest reaches of our territories. Lord Madoc was older and one of my own countrymen.

He had accompanied me all those years ago when I journeyed from my father's halls to wed Gorlois in Tintagel and had been a true and loyal member of our household and court ever since. His lands in the Welsh borderlands were managed by his younger brother, Sir Mark, who I had heard to be a friend and trusted companion of my brother Prince Gareth who was now, by reason of my father's great age and frailty, ruler in all but name in the Welsh court.

"Greetings, my lord, good sirs. You must be tired from your journey and in need of refreshment. Will you take wine?" I gestured to Jago, my steward, who immediately hurried forward with a large pewter jug and three tankards. Cador and Lowen were quick to avail themselves of our hospitality, but the older man waved Jago aside and strode toward my seat on the dais.

"Greetings, my lady." He bowed quickly, his eyes roaming the Great Hall as if searching for someone. "Is Duke Gorlois not present?"

"No, my lord, and I do not expect him until nightfall." In Gorlois' absence, it was up to me to govern the castle and I could sense that whatever Madoc had to say, it was important and should not wait several hours for the telling. "Pray tell me, what news from my father's court."

I could already sense that things were amiss. Both the young knights were hanging back behind the older Lord, silently drinking their wine and not wishing to meet my eyes.

Without speaking, Madoc pulled off his cloak, on which was embroidered his sigil, the white boar. Taking his dagger from his belt, he ripped through the fine cloth, cutting out his badge of honour, which he proceeded to throw to the floor at my feet.

"My lady, I bring grave news. I am dishonoured before you and can hardly bear to tell you of my shame."

I looked hard at the proud man who was now kneeling before me with a look of agonised sorrow upon his face. The hairs on the back of my neck began to prickle.

"My Lord Madoc, you have always been our friend and faithful servant, why this talk of shame and dishonour?"

"It pains me more than I can say to deliver this news to you. My house is betrayed, our kingdom corrupted. I bring you nothing but bad news and ill-tidings from the court of King Amlawdd."

At first, there was a buzz around the room as these words were passed from eager mouth to willing ear, but within seconds the Hall was silent as everyone leant forward, straining to hear what my countryman had to say.

I was sure that the story of our flight from Caer-Lundein was now common currency around the court, most of whom would also be aware that my husband and his warriors had ridden out that morning, having had little rest after our long journey. I would not be the only one making assumptions about what Gorlois and Erec were about. If they were already making plans for battle it would not be long before the whole of Cornwall and Lyonesse knew it.

And the situation was not good. We had few firm allies to call on and much of our hope had rested on obtaining support from my father and brother in the Welsh Lands. Their well-garrisoned fortresses were perfectly positioned to help us defend our borders and, even more importantly, a message of solidarity and alliance from Amlawdd's court could well make the difference in persuading others to stand by us.

As yet, Gorlois and I had had no chance to talk and consider everything that Merlin had told us. We had made no announcement to Court, and I was loathe to allow Madoc to fan the flames of rumour by continuing this conversation in public. There was surely enough gossip and tittle-tattle making its way slyly around the castle.

"Come, Sirs, your words sound grave and I would hear them in a more private place than this."

Without another word, I walked out of the Great Hall into the small private chamber behind it. Lord Madoc got to his feet and, accompanied by his two younger companions, made to follow me. I nodded at Jago to bring wine and, seeing Elaine sitting quietly near the fireside, beckoned her to come with me. If ever I needed a sage counsellor, it was now and I knew that Elaine was not only wise and measured in her considerations, she would also be loyal to me until death.

Once we were seated around the old oak table and Jago had stoked up the fire and poured wine, I asked him to leave, placing a sentry on guard with orders to admit no one but Gorlois or Erec.

Madoc had put his ruined cloak back on again, and he was now worrying the frayed edges of the hole where his sigil had used to be. This time, he had accepted a cup of wine and I gave him time to drink deeply before addressing him.

"Now, my lord, share this grave news with me. What said my noble father when we asked for his assistance?"

"My lady, I bring you nothing but sorrow. King Amlawdd is now very weak and is increasingly confused. His mind dwells in the past and returns but infrequently to the present."

I nodded. It had been five years since I had last seen my father. Gorlois and I had visited the court of the Welsh Lands not long after Morgause had been born, taking our daughter with us to show the King his only grandchild. Even then, it was clear to me that my father was ailing and his thoughts were becoming increasingly muddled. On more than one occasion, he mistook me for my mother and he had difficulty in remembering who Gorlois was.

Over the last few years, my brother had already taken on much of the day-to-day business of the court, the King appearing only rarely. It saddened, but did not surprise, me to learn that my father's condition had worsened.

Gareth, younger than me by some seven years, was a studious man who had never married, a passionately devoted servant of the Mysteries. He had grown up somewhat in my shadow. When we were children, it had always been to me that my father turned to share his laughter and, as I'd got older, he had taken me into his confidence, preparing his oldest child and daughter for her future role—to rule the lands of Cornwall and Lyonesse. And perhaps, he often whispered to me, to succeed him one day as the Queen of the Welsh Lands, uniting our two realms under a single banner.

"But you had audience with my brother, Prince Gareth?" I looked at him questioningly, and slowly, with apparent reluctance, he nodded. "So, tell me what transpired."

"My lady, there is no easy way to say this, so I shall not even attempt to dress things up in fine words and honeyed phrases.

"There will be no help from the Welsh Lands. Prince Gareth has offered his support to the Pendragon and has revoked all oaths of fealty and alliance to the lands of Cornwall and Lyonesse."

"What! He has revoked his oaths. On what grounds and with what authority?" Gareth might have been acting as regent, but he had no legal right to put aside the oaths that bound the Welsh Lands to ours. The pledges we had sworn, myself, Gorlois, and my father, in the presence of the Lady of the Lake and in name of the Goddess, were binding vows that could not be broken without dire consequences.

Madoc's next words shook me to the core.

"With the authority of the Lady and in the name of Avalon and the Mysteries." His voice was low and I could tell how difficult it was for him to frame these words.

"Prince Gareth has proclaimed both you and Gorlois as traitors to the Mysteries, saying that your flight from Uther's court was an act of war and a betrayal of your vows of loyalty. He has set aside all pacts and truces and has declared that he will seize Tintagel, in Uther's name."

At first, I could not speak. To be betrayed by a brother, by one who shared my blood and in whose face I could see the likeness of our mother. My brother, whom I had played with and protected from the more boisterous of our father's by-blows and who had often crept into my bed at night, hoping for a story to settle his mind and bring him sleep.

Madoc had stopped speaking, and the room was silent. I was conscious of someone standing beside me and turned to see Elaine. She was now standing close to me, saying nothing, but giving me strength and comfort by her very presence. I gathered my thoughts.

"And does my brother speak for the Welsh Lords? What of your lands and fiefdoms, Lord Madoc? Have they also joined him in this abomination?"

At this, Madoc bowed his head and it seemed as if he had no strength to carry on. Wordlessly he gestured toward the younger knights and it was Sir Lowen who continued.

"My lady, it would appear that all of the Welsh Lords have rallied to Prince Gareth. Lord Madoc's lands have been seized, those loyal to him captured and…" At this the young knight faltered. "…his brother executed."

I gasped in disbelief, not quite able to take in what I was hearing. "Can this be true?"

"Aye, my lady. We saw his head upon the walls. They said it was a warning. A warning to everyone of what would happen to those who defy the Goddess."

"But I am loyal to the Goddess, I told Vivian that I would always honour her and keep my vows. How has Gareth done this? Who has allowed it?" I was speaking to myself, barely conscious of my audience. This could not be happening. But Madoc raised his head and spoke to me in slow and saddened tones and his words drove a dagger into my heart.

"The Lady of the Lake was there, in the Great Hall. We saw her. She blessed Prince Gareth and his actions and said that the curse of the Goddess would fall upon us if we did not immediately renounce you and swear loyalty to Uther."

"She granted us our lives so that we could return to you and tell you. What will you do, my lady?" Sir Cador had finally found his voice and he sounded lost and terrified. He was so young, he looked little more than a boy, with tired eyes and a grey, drawn face. I realised that all three of them had probably been riding non-stop for days in order to get word to us.

"What will I do, Sir Cador?" I tried to speak lightly, to hide the fear and panic that his words had brought me. What game was this? What were Vivian and Merlin doing? Only this morning, Merlin had promised us a peaceful future if we bent the knee to Uther, but all the while the Lady of the Lake, my former mistress and adviser, was working with my brother, whose love and loyalty I had been certain I could depend on, to betray us.

I could make no sense of it and knew that any hint of my panic and confusion would only serve to further alarm our already exhausted and bewildered knights. Summoning up all the self-control my years at Avalon had taught me, I kept my tone light and set a smile on my face. "What will I do? Why, I will order you some supper and a good warm bed. You have ridden far and fast and I am sure they will be welcome. Elaine, be so good as to instruct Jago to guide these good Sirs to their chambers."

She nodded, and unseen by the others, gently squeezed my hand.

"I will await my lord and we will consider the tidings you have brought. You have my thanks and the thanks of Cornwall. Please, go now and rest. And I beg you, keep your counsel. I would not have word of these tidings spread around the court before my lord and I have had chance to consider them."

Lord Madoc and his two companions nodded in agreement and followed Elaine from the room.

Once they had gone I sank back into my chair and, resting my head upon my hands, began to weep.

Chapter Six

Gorlois did not return that night, so I went to bed accompanied only by fears and unhappiness, finally falling into a fitful and uneasy sleep as the stars began to fade. I had left no instructions about the morning and Elaine had chosen not to wake me, allowing me to sleep until the sun was high in the sky. After a hurried breakfast, I dressed and made my way to the battlements. I wanted to look out across the causeway, to search for the first signs of riders, as if my ability to see them from a distance might somehow hasten the return of my husband and his companions. I was not alone. Morgause was playing with her kitten in the orchard, under the watchful and loving eye of Avice, but Morgan had accompanied us up the steep turret stairs and was now sitting calmly, looking into a small hand-glass as Elaine patiently brushed the tangles from her long, dark hair.

"I said, tell me about Avalon," Morgan's low, determined and precise tones penetrated my concentration. I hadn't been listening to anything that my daughter and Elaine had been saying as my eyes ranged back and forth, scouring the empty horizon, looking desperately for the glint of sunlight upon a sword or bridle—anything which I could possibly interpret as the approach of Gorlois and his riders.

I turned and saw that Morgan and Elaine were sitting side by side. They were now both holding the looking glass, and they were staring into it. Elaine's face seemed empty, as if she was in a trance, but Morgan's eyes were focused, and her features were set in an intense and determined expression which made her seem much older than her years. As I looked, I saw the delicate metal edges of the hand-glass begin to shimmer and glow with a strange greenish-yellow light. The polished surface of the glass lost its sheen as mists began to form within it. I watched with disbelief as I realised what I was seeing. She was scrying. My four-year-old daughter, untaught and unprepared, was scrying. I watched uneasily, knowing from experience that by now the metal at the edges of the glass would be almost too hot to touch and yet that my small daughter appeared to give no heed to the discomfort this must be causing her.

She spoke again, this time with fierce certainty. "Tell me about Avalon." At her words, the mists began to roll back and in the dulled surface of the mirror, images begin to form. I saw the castle, the lawns leading down to the lake and at the lakeside, on the jetty, stood a woman with her back to us. This image clarified, and as we closed in I was left in no doubt as to who it was. She held herself proudly and was dressed magnificently in a dark green samite gown, embroidered with flowers. Her black hair fell over her shoulders in a long, shining wave, held in place with a delicate golden net. Vivian raised her arm in a gesture of welcome that was both elegant and commanding and I could see that visitors were approaching.

The enchanted barge made its swift, silent way to the edge of the lake, where unseen hands secured its moorings. A tall man I didn't recognise bent down into the boat and with a display of great deference and care lifted something up and placed it on the jetty. My view was obscured by the folds of his cloak and it was only when he returned to his place on the barge that I was able to see exactly what it was that he had brought to Avalon.

It was a child, small and slender and cloaked in a soiled and tattered travelling cloak. There were spatters of mud at the hem, and the dark hair that emerged from the edge of the hood was tangled and unkempt.

As I watched, Vivian went down on one knee so that she was now the same height as the little figure standing in front of her. With infinite gentleness, she eased back the hood of the travelling cloak and caressed the cheek of the unknown child. There was a look of tenderness such as I had never seen before in her brilliant blue eyes, but the smile that played upon her lips was one of triumph. As I watched, the perspective shifted, and I was now seeing as if through Vivian's eyes, directly into the face of the dishevelled but oh-so-familiar little girl standing calmly on the jetty. I saw the Lady's finger reach out and gently touch Morgan's nose and with disbelief, saw my daughter press her cheek against Vivian's. I was now gazing on both faces, side by side, staring into two almost identical pairs of piercing blue eyes.

Why had I never seen it before? Morgan, my winter child with her long dark hair, delicate bones and pale, pale skin, looked more like Vivian's daughter than my own.

"Stop it," I yelled, rushing toward them and pushing the looking glass to the floor, where it shattered on the flagstones. Elaine at once fell forward and would have hit her head on the rough stone walls if I hadn't caught her and pushed her back against the turret.

Morgan was looking at me accusingly. "That was very clumsy, Mother. You didn't let me see what was going to happen."

"What on earth do think you're doing, Morgan?" My young daughter had wrong-footed me, and it made me feel both shaken and angry. "You have no idea how dangerous it is to call on the power of the Goddess without the proper training."

Morgan looked at me calmly, her great blue eyes unblinking. "I don't know what you mean, Mother; I didn't call on anyone. I just wanted to look. I've always been able to do it."

Momentarily stunned by this, I was unsure how to respond when the door to the turret was flung open. Ened stood there, flushed and panting. The stairs to the battlement were steep and unforgiving and Ened was no lightweight. Before she had fully caught her breath she started gesturing wildly toward the causeway.

"Riders, Igraine. There are riders. But it isn't Gorlois or Erec. You must come at once." She spoke desperately, forcing out the words as she struggled to regain her breath.

I turned to look out across the causeway. I had no idea how long we had been staring into the mirror watching the vision that Morgan's scrying had called forth, but where before there had been nothing but empty moorland and tall, desolate clifftops, there was now an army riding resolutely toward us.

With rising concern I looked toward Elaine and was relieved to see that she had got to her feet and seemed none the worse for her recent experience. Realising that now was not the time or the place to find out more from my strange, precocious daughter, I simply instructed Elaine to find Avice and Morgause and take both girls to their nursery. She gave one glance at the line of warriors assembling on the edge of the causeway and nodded, taking Morgan by the hand.

"Come, Ened, you are right; we must not tarry." We both moved toward the doorway, Ened walking ahead of me as I had the keys to the turret on my chatelaine and needs must lock and secure the door. As I was pulling it closed behind me, my eyes lit upon the pieces of the broken scrying glass. I thought, for just a second, that I could still see Vivian's triumphant, mocking smile.

WE MADE HASTE TO THE courtyard, where I was pleased to see that Jago was mustering the household guard, swiftly distributing mail, helmets and weapons from the armoury and deploying our men to pre-arranged defensive positions throughout the castle. Despite his cool efficiency, I could sense that fear and panic were in danger of taking hold, not helped by Ened and her ladies, most of whom were sitting uselessly in a corner of the Great Hall, wringing their hands and wailing.

I saw some of the younger pages and kitchen maids had huddled together in the doorway, white-faced and seemingly on the verge of tears. "Get about your work," I scolded. "What will my lord say if he returns and finds there is no meat to place before him?" They looked at me as if astonished by my words, but hurried to obey me, dashing off toward scullery and cellar.

"And as for you, Ened, just be quiet. Compose yourself and provide an example to your ladies. We do not know who these soldiers are and it may yet be that they are friends."

Ened looked at me as if I had just slapped her around the face, and indeed, I would have had no compunction about doing so if she did not do as I advised.

"But the banners, Igraine. I don't recognise the banners. What if these are Uther's men come to destroy us?" Her voice was once again verging on frenzy.

"And what banners are they?" In my haste to get down to the courtyard, I had not had a chance to study the banners of the men assembled across the causeway.

Ened looked at me blankly, her round, still, pretty face flushed. "The crow, it's a crow, flying above a battlefield."

This surprised me. The flock of crows was the banner of the Ceintish Lords, all of whom were undoubtedly loyal to Uther, but I would not have thought they could have assembled in such numbers and made the long march from their Eastern strongholds in such a short time. Merlin has warned us to expect warriors at our gates before the month was out but it was less than two days since he had ridden forth with Gorlois' insults still ringing in his ears.

"I will see for myself before leaping to any hasty conclusions. Will you join me, Lady Madron?" I hoped that by giving Ened her formal title, I would be issuing her with a reminder that she was the wife of a great warlord who was also Gorlois' second in command, and that she should begin to comport herself as such.

No such luck.

"I don't think so, Igraine; I don't feel well. I think I'll retire to my chamber." Frowning at her refusal to use my formal title, I dismissed her with a nod. The remaining ladies now looked toward me uncertainly, as if not sure what they should do next.

"Ladies, any of you who wish to join me are welcome to do so, but if this is not to your taste, I suggest you repair to your chambers and seek counsel of the Goddess."

At my words, one of the younger women rose to her feet and came toward me, pleased, I think, to have something to do. She was, I assumed, the wife of one of Gorlois' officers who had marched with us from Caer-Lundein. The rest picked up their belongings and made their way in ones and twos toward their chambers.

With my new companion in attendance, I made my way across the courtyard toward Jago. He was now standing in the shadow of the locked-down portcullis, instructing his men on the final elements of the castle's defences. Up on the battlements, I could see men beginning to light the braziers which would be used to send flaming pitch-tipped arrows amongst the horses of the assembled host if it began to march across the causeway.

As I approached, Jago stopped talking and bowed low. "My lady, the castle be as ready as it'll ever be. What's your orders for us?"

Tintagel born and bred, Jago had worked hard to get our defences in order and his men had obeyed him without question. Like all of Gorlois' most trusted officers, our house steward was the veteran of many a battle, and those men who had fought side-by-side with my husband had a loyalty and devotion to him that was deep and unswerving. In his absence, that devotion was now mine to command.

"You've done well. Tintagel is now as well defended as she has ever been." He nodded, pleased that I had been appreciative of his hard work and efficiency. I continued with a question. "Do you recognise the banners? My Lady Madron has told me that these are Ceintish men on our doorway."

"I cen't be sure, my lady," replied Jago. "There be no wind and the banners ain't unfurling. There be a great black bird on the shields of them standing close in to the shoreline, but whether 'tis the Crow of Ceint or some other sigil, by the Goddess, I cen't be certain."

"I wish to find out more about these warriors before I give any orders, either to attack or defend."

He looked at me uncertainly. I knew he would obey me, but I wanted him to understand what I had decided to do and why.

"Think about it, Jago; how could these warriors have marched here from Ceint? They would have needed the chariot of the Goddess herself to have covered so many miles so quickly. I intend to ride out myself and seek parley. I will need your men to guard me and keep cover from the walls."

He looked horrified. "But you never can, my lady. My lord would kick me out the castle if I let you put yoursen in such danger."

Remembering all my father had taught me about statecraft and the art of war, I pulled myself up to my full height and assumed a haughty and commanding expression. "Master Steward, you forget yourself. In Gorlois' absence, I am in command here and I am not going to authorise anything until we know for certain exactly whose forces have assembled at the end of the causeway." I took a deep breath. There was no going back now, and I had to sound absolutely confident and in control as I gave him my instructions. "Find me some armour, get my horse saddled and instruct the archers to provide cover from the battlements."

"But you cen't go alone, my lady; for mercy of the Goddess, let me give you an escort to ride with'ee at the very least." Jago was distressed, and I was sorry to be the cause of it, but he had at last seemed to recognise that he would not dissuade me. And when I thought about it, I accepted that I would feel safer if I had three or four of his finest riding beside me.

"Yes, do so." As I spoke, I felt a slight touch on my sleeve and the woman who had walked with me from the Great Hall came forward.

"Please, my lady, may I ride with you?" She was young, no more than three and twenty, with a strong, fine-featured face, and intelligent eyes. Her dark-blonde hair was held neatly and securely in a long plait that fell over her shoulder, reaching almost to her waist.

"My name is Bennath of Syllan. I can shoot a bow as well as any archer should you need protection, and I would rather ride by your side than cower within the walls of my chamber."

"Who is your husband?" I asked, feeling a little ashamed that I didn't know already.

"Sir Lowen," she replied. "He returned yesterday from the Welsh borders and if I call to him now, we will both ride out together at your side."

I nodded slowly. "You keep the old ways in Syllan?" I asked her, recognising the light of battle in her eyes and glancing appreciatively at her lean, well-muscled body which her simple linen kirtle did nothing to disguise.

"It is the job of the Lord and his Lady to hold the land, to protect it and keep it," Bennath replied. "Lowen and I are Syllan born and bred. His mother was my mother's sister, and we were both raised in the ways of the Mysteries."

"Then I thank you, Bethan of Syllan," I looked once more at Jago. "Come, let us waste no more time."

Within half an hour, Jago had found me a breastplate and helm and had saddled horses for myself and Bennath. Beside us rode Sir Lowen and Sir Cador. Our party was completed by a third knight, young Sir Unwin whose father had been killed by Vortigern's Saxon allies and who rather hero-worshipped my husband. He had volunteered for the task as soon as Jago had put out the call to Tintagel's garrison and despite the gravity of the situation, I smiled with pleasure to see his young, ardent face, slightly shadowed by an ancient helm that was really much too big for him.

"It was my father's, my lady," he said, by way of explanation

"He would be proud to see you wearing it this day," I replied as Jago opened the small gate at the base of the portcullis and the five of us rode out of the castle onto the long, exposed track that ran the length of the Tintagel causeway.

◆ ◆ ◆

THE CAUSEWAY WAS TOO NARROW for us to ride comfortably more than three abreast. Sir Lowen placed himself at the front of our small party; I positioned myself behind him between Sir Cador and Bennath, who rode with her bow at the ready, leaving young Sir Unwin to guard the rear.

Tintagel is an island, joined to the mainland by a narrow strip of land which can be quite impassable during the winter storms. Today, however, the sea was calm and the sky almost cloudless. There was practically no wind and the seagulls, who would have loved to swoop and glide upon the air currents in more blustery conditions were sleepily bobbing on the gentle waves or strutting in a rather haphazard fashion along the rocky shore.

Looking over my shoulder I could see Jago and his men upon the battlements. Smoke was rising from the braziers and I was certain that whoever was waiting for us on the shoreline would already have recognised that Tintagel was well-defended and would not prove to be an easy conquest.

Sir Lowen was carrying a white banner, indicating that we wished for parley; we rode at walking pace, to show that we were neither fleeing nor intending to attack. On the mainland, I saw three of the mounted warriors move slightly to the front of the assembled soldiers, as if preparing to greet us. Out of the corner of my eye I also noticed a small band of horsemen had just come into view and were riding hard toward the causeway.

As we passed the halfway point, the wind began to rise and the banners to unfurl. I saw a red griffin on a white background, a black boar impaled on a broken spear, both of which were unknown to me; but, then, the largest of the proudly swelling banners unfurled and there, flying high above the silent warriors was not the crows of Ceint but the single raven, sigil and standard of the Northern tribes.

I called out to Bennath, who was also studying the banners with close attention. "But that is Orkney's banner. And Orkney is our friend, or was when last we met." King Lot of Orkney was betrothed to Morgause, and Gorlois and I had sworn vows of friendship with him during the ceremony which had pledged our eldest child to the Northern kingdom.

At almost the same time, the riders I had seen approaching reached the shoreline and reined in their horses as they neared the three mounted men and their banners. As I watched, all three of them dismounted and bent to one knee in front of the first of the newcomers who I now saw, to my surprise and relief, was none other than Gorlois.

Filled with a new sense of hope, I spurred my horse onward and rode past Sir Lowen, leaving the rest of the party to follow in my wake. We raced the remaining length of the causeway, only pulling up to a more sedate pace when we were within a few yards of the shore.

I called out to him. "Greetings, my lord husband. I had not thought to find you here, but it brings me joy to welcome your return."

Gorlois was clearly unsettled by my presence and was looking at me and my small band of followers in confusion. He had not expected his wife to have ridden out to meet an army of unknown warriors accompanied only by a woman archer and three young and relatively untried knights. I recognised the expressions passing across his face as a mixture of disbelief, incredulity, and, finally, a grudging sense of pride.

Wishing to ease the situation, I turned to the leaders of the Northern knights. "Welcome, my lords of Orkney. In my husband's absence I took it upon myself to meet with you. Until the wind came to our aid and unfurled your banners we were uncertain who you were. I did not wish to act with force and fury against those who are our friends and so came in peace to greet you and establish what has brought you to Tintagel."

I saw a look pass between Gorlois and Erec, who had, of course, been one of the riders that I had seen racing across the headland. He had now dismounted and was allowing his chestnut cob to graze on the rough seagrass. He said something to Gorlois, which I couldn't quite catch, but it was clear that they now understood why I'd brought my ragtag band out on to the causeway, and I could see that they approved.

"'Twas well done my lady." Gorlois rode to my side and raising my hand to his lips, kissed it, holding it tight as he turned to speak to the Northern Lords. "Please allow me to present Urien, Prince of Rheged and younger brother to King Lot. Urien, my wife, Igraine."

The man my husband had addressed removed his helm and I recognised him as the leader of the tall, silent, red-haired men who had attended Uther's feast at Caer-Lundein. I remembered the dignified, almost disdainful way in which he had acknowledged the greetings of the High King and was amazed to see his eyes crinkle into a smile as he extended his arm toward me.

"Weel met my lady, ye are as brave as ye are bonny, a fitting wife for my auld friend Gorlois. I can only hine your daughter, uir future queen, will follow in her mother's footsteps."

I smiled in acknowledgement of his words and Urien went on to introduce me to his companions, his uncle Angmer, the Duke of Moray and his cousin Einar who was also his squire. Einar was little more than a boy, and I learned that he hailed originally from the distant shores of *Noreg* (Norway). He was King Lot's ward and had lived at the court of Orkney since his fifth birthday.

Urien was accompanied by a force of over two hundred knights and I knew that we would not have room for all of them in Tintagel. However, when I mentioned this to Gorlois, he smiled and told me that the men of Orkney would be happy to make camp upon the shoreline, if we could but furnish them with meat, mead, and firewood.

I asked Bennath and her husband to ride back to the castle ahead of us to give word to Jago and to prepare rooms for Prince Urien, Duke Angmer, and the young Einar. Once this was done, Cador and Unwin led us back across the causeway and in through the castle gates, which had been opened wide to welcome our allies.

Ened and her ladies were waiting in the courtyard, all smiles now they knew that it was the Raven and not the Crow that camped out upon our shoreline. Deciding that it was time she did something to make herself useful, I asked her to look to the comforts of our guests and, not waiting to deal with her fluttering protestations and ridiculous questions, Gorlois and I made haste to our chamber.

THE ROOM WAS EMPTY AND I shut the door to the antechamber behind me with relief. Walking through into our bedroom, I found that the fire had been lit and there was a jug of wine warming beside it. Silently blessing Elaine, who I was certain had been the one to see to our comforts, I poured out a cup for each of us and went over to the window where Gorlois was standing, looking out onto the courtyard and struggling with the fastening of his cloak.

"Let me help you," I said, reaching up to ease the leather fastenings, which had become twisted. "Is this Erec's?" I asked. I didn't recognise the cloak, which was old and heavy. I had originally thought it to be black, but on closer inspection, it was a dull, dark green, similar in colour to bladderwrack, the seaweed I had been taught to cleanse and prepare for medicinal uses during my time on Avalon. Although it was old, the cloth was still supple and smooth, and it smelt of lavender and chamomile as if it had been cared for and well-laundered.

"No, I found it in the stables," Gorlois replied as I folded it and hung it neatly over the settle at the end of our bed. "I was so angered by what that old bastard Merlin had to say that I forgot to take my cloak with me. I was not going to make myself look an idiot by coming back for it."

I remembered Gorlois storming from the room after Merlin had put his proposals to us: that we acknowledge Uther as our overlord and apologise for our transgressions; that we bow in submission to the man who had tried to take me for his own. And, in return, Merlin promised that we would live out our lives in peace and our child, my son, would inherit Caliburn, the sword gifted by the

Goddess which offered victory in battle and whose owner could not be defeated.

I passed Gorlois his cup and he drank deeply, reaching out his other hand to draw me to his side.

I remembered how Merlin had reacted after Gorlois had left us. He had not seemed angry or surprised. On the contrary, I think my husband had behaved exactly as the old Druid had expected, as if the argument and rejection of his proposal had been an unpleasant but necessary hurdle that he had to overcome. He had been calm when he left, simply collecting his cloak from the chest by the solar door and departing without further ceremony.

But I now realised that the cloak had not been his, it had belonged to Gorlois, and I did not think that Merlin could have taken it by accident. I was not sure exactly what this meant and at the time, I had other things to distract me, giving me little time to ponder its significance. I was eager to hear what my husband and Erec had been up to that had kept them absent from the castle for nearly two days.

"Yes, I can see that it could have been embarrassing to come back for your cloak. But where have you been Gorlois? It was not kind of you to leave without telling me where you were going, or to send message to let me know when to expect your return," I refilled his cup and took a sip from mine, trying to ease myself away from him and let him see that I was not well pleased.

"I'm sorry, my love, but in war there is often no time for niceties. I knew that Merlin would make haste to take tidings of our decision back to Uther and that witch queen Vivian. My first thoughts were for my land and my people, to ready and prepare them for the war that is to come."

I nodded, understanding that what Gorlois was saying was right, but still not quite ready to forgive him for leaving me alone, with no word of where he was or what he was doing, to deal with the news of my brother's betrayal and Vivian's decision to place a curse on us and those who support us.

"…and so, we have alerted our garrisons and set up our beacons…" My husband had continued talking, but I hadn't been listening. He now put down his cup and turned to face me, trying to take me in his arms, his mouth seeking mine. I pushed away angrily.

I was upset and unsettled, and a few kisses were not going to placate me.

"No, Gorlois, this is not the time. I am the Duchess of Cornwall, your wife and a princess in my own right. Whilst you were gone, it has been up to me to run this castle, to deal with messengers, calm our household and to decide what to do when an army turns up at our gates."

He put out his hand again, but I slapped it away. "I am not like Ened; I'm no silly girl cowering in her chamber at the first hint of war. I am Avalon-trained and my father's daughter. Do you realise that if I hadn't intervened, your men would have sent soldiers to attack Prince Urien and the troops from Orkney, and we could well have lost our one and only ally?"

By now I was shouting, the fear I had bottled up inside me turning to violent rage.

"Hush, sweetheart, you did well, but you exaggerate, you must calm down…," Gorlois was standing behind me now, his hands on my waist, trying to turn me to face him.

"…Orkney is not our only ally. We have your father and brother and the Welsh Lords…"

This was too much. I turned toward him and slapped him hard across the face.

"We do not have the Welsh Lords. Gareth has turned against us, calling all who join us traitors. Lord Madoc's lands are seized, and poor Sir Mark's head has been placed upon a spear, as a reminder, for any who need it, of what Uther's troops will do to those who stand beside us!"

I would not weep. My rage now burnt with an incandescent heat; in all our years together, Gorlois had never seen me like this before.

"Why are you so proud, my lord? Why have you done this? Do you want to see our people slaughtered? Our rivers run with blood? Merlin was right. Peace is more important than false pride. Why can't you see that?"

"Because I love you and I love my country." Gorlois' voice was calm, but it had an edge that was as hard and unyielding as the granite cliffs of Cornwall. "Don't you see, Igraine; if I submit to Uther in this matter, my people will not respect me, I will lose all honour and you, even you, will start to hate me?

"I fought beside Uther to restore the rightful King, but Uther swore to rule justly. He promised peace and vowed that all of us, his friends and allies, would be allowed to hold our lands and rule them as we wished. But what has he done? He has tried to steal my wife. To take you from me. To turn me into a cuckold, a horned fool who all will laugh at. This is not false pride, Igraine. It is all that we have left."

There was a catch in his voice and I could not bear it. I went to him and kissed him, smoothing his cheek where my fingers had left a livid weal.

"I'm sorry. I should not have struck you."

"And I should not have ridden off in anger, without talking to you and telling you of my plans."

His mouth sought mine and I returned his kiss, which was sweet and gentle. His clothes smelt of lavender, like the cloak he had been wearing and I could feel him begin to grow hard and urgent as he pressed against me.

But before we could use our passion to set a seal upon our mutual forgiving, there was a loud rapping on the door of the antechamber and without waiting for an answer Erec, followed by Lord Madoc and Prince Urien, came into the room. A flushed and flustered Elaine followed them, throwing me a glance of supplication. I imagined that she had tried to prevent them from entering and had been overruled.

"What mean you by this Erec? Prince Urien? Am I not to be allowed some privacy to reacquaint myself with my wife?"

Erec apologised. He had only just found out about the dreadful tidings from my father's court and felt that Gorlois needed to talk to Lord Madoc without delay. He had found Prince Urien, who had been deep in conversation with Sir Lowen and his warrior wife Bennath, and decided that it would be a good idea to bring him along as well.

"I tried to stop him, my lady," whispered Elaine, who was now pulling chairs around the old oak table and fetching more cups and an extra flagon of wine from the settle.

"It's alright, don't worry. These are extraordinary times, and we must accept that some of the usual courtesies' needs must be put aside."

She moved toward the door as if to leave, but I shook my head and gestured toward the seat beneath the window. I wanted her to stay and listen. I respected my half-sister's counsel, and I was certain that there were matters to be discussed that night that I would welcome the chance of talking over with her later.

GORLOIS AND I CHOSE TO sit next to each other, and, beneath the table, I felt his hand reach for mine. When the others were seated and the wine poured, Gorlois began to speak.

"Lord Madoc, we have heard your story with the deepest sorrow. Not only is it clear that we no longer have an ally in the Welsh Lands, our heart is saddened by the cruel fate meted out to your brother at the command of Vivian, the witch queen of Avalon."

"That is an act that cannot go unpunished," flared up Erec. "He may be your brother, my lady, but blood calls to blood and I will see justice. I will have vengeance for Mark's murder." I remembered that Erec and Lord Madoc were related, they were cousins on his mother's side. More than that, Erec and the murdered knight had fought together, winning their spurs beneath my father's banner in the early wars against the usurper Vortigern, before Uther had returned from Brittany.

I said nothing. I still could not believe the depths of my brother's betrayal and did not trust myself to speak of it.

Lord Madoc reached across the table and grasped Erec's shoulder. "'Twas murder right enough. My brother was a good man, and loyal. My grief runs deep and believe me, I will make Gareth pay a blood price for his vile and traitorous act." Madoc leaned back in his seat, letting go of Erec's arm and looking at each one of us in turn, catching, and holding our gaze.

"But what's done is done. We must concern ourselves with the living, rather than the dead. Uther's men are but days away from our borders and we must ready ourselves for the fight."

I felt Gorlois' grip upon my hand tighten, then he loosed my fingers and raised his cup to his lips, taking a long draught before getting up from the table and walking to the window. He gazed out toward the mainland, where the usually dark shoreline was now illuminated by the flickering glow from a number of small cooking fires. Urien's men were clearly making themselves at home.

"You are right, Madoc," my husband said. "We have enemies approaching, and few friends to stand beside us in our hour of need." He gestured toward the shore saying, "Urien, your men are well-fed and are now resting. We will have need of them in the morrow."

Pacing the room, my husband paused in front of the northern prince. "Orkney is our friend and ally, and that will not be forgotten when the time comes to make a reckoning. And I think you know, Prince Urien, that it will not just be Cornwall who will take note of the stance you have taken. We honour the faith and loyalty of the Northern Lords. Uther, I think, will see it differently."

"Aye, yer nae wrong thare," said Urien, his voice low and measured. "Uther's pride haes nae fun' favour wi' King Lot and Orkney does nae forget th' promises made whin oor king promised his haun 'n' hert tae yon queen's fair daughter. We wull fight beside ye, bit thare is yin condition, 'n' if ye cannae swear tae it, then oan th' morrow, we mist leave ye."

"What condition? We have already agreed Morgause's dowry, and a generous one at that." I was taken aback by Prince Urien's words and could only think that he had come to ask for more Cornish silver in exchange for his support. "It does not become King Lot to use our current ill-fortune as a bargaining tool. Surely the men of Orkney are not warriors for hire like the Irish galloglaigh?"

The expression on Urien's face hardened; I had insulted him. "Na mah Lady, we ur nae swords fur hire lik' th' Irish. Th' men o' Orkney honour thair vows 'n' dae nae betray thair friends. Na, oor condition is one ah think yer laird wull find pleasing. Ye 'n' yer daughters mist lea' immediately fur the Northern Isles."

"What?" I turned toward Gorlois, who had stopped pacing and was standing behind my chair. "I'm not leaving Tintagel. I am Cornwall's Duchess and Gorlois' wife. I will not run away like a craven kitchen maid."

"Hush, Igraine," said Gorlois. "No one who saw you ride out this afternoon could doubt your courage. I think I understand what Urien is asking. Flowing in your daughter's veins is the blood of one of the oldest and most noble families in Britain. You were a Princess long before you became a Duchess. King Lot is seeking only to protect the girl he has sworn to marry. Am I right Prince Urien?"

The northerner nodded and his brow cleared. Gorlois' perspicuity had gone some way to easing the smart I had inflicted when I implied that he and his warriors were mercenaries, on sale to the highest bidder.

"Aye. Ye ken that King Uther does nae fight in hauf measures. His pride haes bin wounded 'n' he is keening fur revenge." Urien looked at me and I was surprised to see a softening in his eyes, as if he wished he did not have to say the things that he was saying.

"Ah kin ainlie say it lik' ah see it, Gorlois. Uther's aim is tae tak' yer wife 'n' kip her." I stared at him in horror. "If things gang badly fur ye, dae ye think he wull think take guid care of yer daughters? Send Igraine 'n' her young ones tae Lot's court 'n' thay wull be protected."

At his words I remembered the stories of Uther's conquests that I had tried my hardest to forget; women raped and murdered, their babes killed in their cradles. One tale still made me feel sick to my stomach. Toward the end of the war, Uther and his men had laid siege to one of the Saxon strongholds, home of a young Thane who had killed one of Uther's warlords in battle the previous year.

Uther ordered his men to poison the water supply by throwing the carcases of slaughtered cattle into the river upstream. They laid waste to the fields, orchards, and vineyards that surrounded the impoverished hamlet and burned the crops to charred stubble. After three weeks, the village surrendered, sending out the young wife of the Thane as an emissary for peace. If they had believed that Uther would treat her kindly, they soon learned that the Pendragon was not a man to treat his enemies with forbearance.

The Saxon woman was brought before him as a supplicant, carrying her child, a babe in arms who was, I was told, no more than three months old. Placing the child on the ground in front of Uther's chair, she knelt before him and undid her hair, which was a rich, deep gold and fell almost to her waist. Taking a small flask of precious oil from her belt, she poured it on his feet, massaging in the sweet-smelling unguent before proceeding to dry him with her hair. I'm told that she raised her eyes to his, hoping to see mercy, but finding only cold and unrelenting hatred. Without addressing a single word to her, he ordered her to be stripped and sent out to his soldiers, who were told to do with her as they would. The child he instructed to be strangled and thrown to the dogs.

I shuddered, thinking of my sweet Morgause, so beautiful and full of life, and my delicate, clever Morgan. If we lost, if Gorlois was defeated, is that what Uther would do to them? Strangle them and throw them to his dogs?

I looked in panic at my husband. "Gorlois, he can't do this, he must not have the girls. Urien is right. We must protect them."

"And will you go too, Igraine? Will you leave me?" my husband spoke quietly so no one else could hear his words.

"No, I cannot leave you. I will not leave you. But Morgause must go. We can send Avice with her; she loves her and she is old enough to leave me." Strange to think that but a few short weeks ago, I had not wished to send my daughter away from me, had argued with Gorlois that next summer was too soon, and that now, I was making plans to send my firstborn on a sea voyage that would take her hundreds of miles away.

"And Morgan?" Gorlois looked at me questioningly.

I considered. "No, not Morgan; she is but four years old. She is too young to go." I still had not had chance to talk to my small, strange youngest daughter about the vision she had seen in the scrying glass. I had seen her take the enchanted barge to Avalon, to be greeted with great affection by the Lady. My thoughts regarding Vivian were confused and complex. From what Lord Madoc had said, she had made a stand against us, had supported or perhaps even instructed my brother in his defiant acts of treachery. But she was still the Lady of Avalon and I was sworn to honour and obey her. Without saying a word to Gorlois, I resolved to seek out Elaine the next morning and see if we could find out any more about the Lady and her plans.

"Morgause must go." I continued, "Orkney is to be her home and King Lot to be her husband. It is right that she should seek sanctuary at his court. But my place is here, in Cornwall with my people. And if it is also your will, my lord, I will keep Morgan with me and we shall see what fate befalls us."

Gorlois briefly squeezed my shoulder. "I think my lady has the right of it, Prince Urien. She will not leave her duty and her youngest child is too young to travel on such a journey without a mother's care. But Morgause, your King's intended, we shall intrust to your protection. Will this meet your Lord's conditions?"

Urien looked first at me and then at Gorlois and slowly nodded. "Aye, my lord, it wull."

We agreed to have our largest ship made ready. Although Gorlois had no war vessels at his command, our Cornish mariners were all skilled in combat, being well used to sharing the open seas with both battle-ready Phoenician tin traders and the Breton and Irish pirates that bedevilled the farthest shores of Lyonesse.

We decided that Morgause would be accompanied by Avice and a small number of servants from the Tintagel household. Urien said that he would send fifteen of his warriors with them, and that they would also take young Einar, Urien's cousin, who had been acting as his squire. I began to feel that within such a company, my pretty little daughter would be as safe (or even safer) on her sea voyage as her sister within the high stone walls of Tintagel.

"And now, my lords, I suggest you retire to your chambers. The night is no longer young and tomorrow we must begin the work for our defences in earnest," Gorlois spoke these words with courtesy, but I could see that he had had enough of talking. At a slight nod from me, Elaine got up from her window seat and cleared the wine jug and cups from the table. Urien and Madoc got to their feet immediately and made their departures, followed more slowly by Erec, who paused in the doorway. "Good night, Erec," said Gorlois. "Tomorrow we ride. We ride long and hard. Make sure you are ready."

"I'll be ready, Gorlois." Then Erec turned to me and smiled an odd half-smile. "This is a lost cause you know. We cannot win."

I looked at my husband, expecting him to bluster or respond in anger, but he just shrugged and pulled me to him without saying a word.

"I understand why you're doing it. And I would do the same. Good night, old friend. Good night, my lady," and with that, Erec left the room.

We undressed slowly, moving stiffly like people twice our age and went to bed in darkness. We did not speak. The campfires on the shoreline had nearly all gone out and the moon hung low on the horizon. There were very few stars.

I made my way into my husband's arms, and he held me gently, my ear to his chest, breathing as he breathed, nestling as close to him as I could.

Chapter Seven

I slept fitfully, unlike Gorlois whose long years of soldiering had taught him to snatch sleep when he could find it, in even the most uncomfortable and trying of circumstances. I rolled away from him carefully, not wanting to disturb his rest and dressed myself in the old white shift and blue kirtle that Elaine had left out for me.

As I made my way through the still half-slumbering castle, the muffled noises from the kitchen and courtyard below told me that Jago's army of cooks, pages, scullery maids and grooms were already hard at work. Within minutes I was at the foot of the Western Tower and as I climbed the stairs to the nursery it soon became clear that any thoughts of surprising my daughters by being with them when they woke was already doomed to failure.

"I'm not goin' away. I'm not. You're horrible and I hate you." Morgause's angry words were followed by what sounded like a slap and the noise of something—or someone—falling to the floor.

"But you are. Mother is sending you away and there is nothing you can do about it... Stop it, STOP IT, STOP IT!" It was Morgan's voice this time, accompanied by the ominous sound of something being pounded against the wooden floorboards.

I moved quickly, running up the last few stairs and flinging open the door to see Elaine trying to pull a tear-stained and furious Morgause off her younger sister, whose hair she had grasped in both hands as she attempted to bring her head down yet again on the floor.

"Stop this at once," I yelled, rushing toward Elaine and the still struggling Morgause. "What on earth do you think you are doing? My daughters are not Saxon savages; how dare you behave like this!" As I spoke, Elaine finally managed to release poor Morgan, who had stopped screaming the moment I had entered the room. At the same time, Morgause hurled herself at me, throwing her arms round my waist and sobbing as if heartbroken.

"Mama, oh Mama, don't send me away. Please don't make me go…please…please… don't." Her words were lost in incoherent sobs and I looked questioningly at Elaine over my distraught daughter's head.

But Elaine was none the wiser. She simply shrugged and continued helping Morgan to right herself. Her night shift was torn and her face was bloody from the sharp scratches of her elder sister's nails, but otherwise, she was already regaining her composure. I sank to the floor and took the still-sobbing Morgause in my lap. "Come now, sweetling. Calm down. Tell me what happened."

"It's very simple, Mother." It was Morgan, not Morgause who answered me. "I only told her that she would be leaving soon. In a boat. But she didn't believe me."

"It's not true is it, Mama? You're not sendin' me away are you? I don't wan' to go."

I looked at my two daughters, one calm now and looking at me with a measured confidence, as if seeking assurance that she had mastered yet another difficult lesson, the other tear-stained and unhappy, her arms tight-wrapped around my neck. I was desperate to talk to Morgan, but I knew that at this moment, it was Morgause who had need of me.

"Hush now." I stroked Morgause's hair, smoothing out the copper curls and looping one wayward strand behind her ear. "Elaine, will you please get Morgan washed and dressed and put some salve on her face. Perhaps you could take her to break her fast in my solar? I will join you there presently." Elaine nodded, gently taking an acquiescent Morgan by the hand and leading her from the room.

As soon as her sister had gone, Morgause relaxed against me and began to suck her thumb. This was a childish habit that Morgan had never even started, but one which I was finding hard to break in my eldest daughter. I put my arms around her and slowly rocked back and forth, holding her close to me until I could feel her heartbeat slow down and her breathing settle to a pace that matched my own.

My sweet Morgause, firstborn, and still so young. Could I do this? Could I send her from me, to travel a thousand miles away, on a small boat, protected only by a nursemaid and a handful of Northmen?

"I'm not goin' away am I, Mama? Morgan's just a horrid liar?"

"Shush, sweetheart." I ran my finger gently along her cheek, tickling her behind her ear, making her squirm with pleasure. "Let me tell you a story.

"Once upon a time, there was a princess. She had long hair that shone like polished copper in the autumn sunshine."

"Like mine, Mama?"

"Yes, sweetling. Like yours."

And so I told her a tale of the beautiful princess, who was promised in marriage to a noble King who loved her very much, and who would make her very happy. But then, I told her, a bad King came to threaten the castle where the beautiful princess lived and she had to be sent away on a wonderful boat with milk-white sails, far across the sea to join the King who one day would be her husband.

"Was the boat pretty, Mama?"

"Oh so pretty. The princess had her own cabin, with a tiny little bed and a porthole so she could look out across the sea. And when the sun shone, the light danced in through the porthole, onto the floor of the princess's cabin where she was playing with her kitten."

"Like my kitten, Mama?"

"Yes darling. Just like your kitten."

"Can I go on a boat like that, Mama?"

"Would you like that, Morgause?"

"Yes, Mama."

"Well, if you are a very good girl, you can go on a boat like that, with your kitten and Avice and sail far away to a place where you will be safe until I come and get you."

"I won't be going forever?"

"No, sweetheart." And when I said those words, I meant them. I truly meant them. "Not forever, I would miss my girl too much."

Morgause looked at me, her cheeks still wet, but her eyes now clear and free from tears. "Is there a bad King really?"

"Yes, there is. And I need to keep you safe. Can you be a big girl and understand that?" She nodded slowly as if not quite sure, and then another thought struck her.

"But what 'bout Morgan. Is she going away too?"

"Yes. Yes, she is," And as I said those words, I knew that it was true. I would have to send both my daughters from me, and I didn't know how I would be able to bear it.

"Morgan is going away, too. But not on the boat with you."

Morgause seemed satisfied with this and I realised that she was probably quite pleased to be going somewhere where she would be the petted darling, the undisputed centre of attention and would not have to compete with her precocious and most unusual sister.

We sat there in silence for a little while longer until Avice arrived to help Morgause dress and break her fast. I thanked her and told her that it was the wish of Duke Gorlois and myself that she accompany my daughter on a voyage; I asked her to attend me later that morning to discuss it. Avice simply curtsied in agreement and, taking Morgause by the hand, led her away.

I now went in search of my younger daughter and found her, as I had hoped, sitting on a cushion on the window seat in my solar, eating bread and honey. She looked up and smiled at me when I entered the room but made no move toward me. When I looked more closely, I could see that my thread basket was open beside her and she had once again begun to sort out my embroidery silks.

I saw that Elaine had prepared a plate of bread and fruit for me and had poured me a cup of ale.

"Thank you, Elaine, but I have a fancy for warmed milk this morning. Would you fetch me some from the kitchen?" I wanted to speak to my daughter alone, and this seemed the perfect way to achieve it. Elaine nodded and went out.

"How are you, Morgan? Does your face still hurt from your sister's scratches?" I moved toward the window seat and sat down opposite her, being careful not to touch even the hem of her robe. I knew of old how much she disliked uninvited physical contact.

"I am alright; thank you, Mother. How is Morgause? I am sorry that what I said upset her. I was not telling lies, you know."

"Yes, I do know. But what I don't understand is how you knew. Your father and I only discussed it late last night, long after you had gone to sleep."

Morgan said nothing, but put down her plate, being careful to avoid the rows of brilliantly coloured silks lined up beside her. Reaching into her pocket she took out a small, shiny object and held it out to me. I put out my hand and she dropped a carefully polished silver locket into my palm. I looked at it, not recognising it at first, but then when I saw the tiny broken clasp, I realised it was an old necklace of mine that I thought I had thrown away several months ago. Then, it had been battered and tarnished; now it shone with a burnished gleam that spoke of many hours of dutiful polishing.

"I found this in your chest, Mother. When I was looking for your silk basket. You don't mind do you?"

"No, Morgan, you're welcome to it. And you have polished it very well. It looks beautiful. But why are you showing it to me?" I thought I knew the answer to my question, but I needed my daughter to tell me about what she had been doing in her own words.

"I thought you knew, Mother. I use it to see things."

"Like the looking glass?" I realised that I had not had a chance to talk to either Morgan or Elaine about what had happened yesterday morning, when I had watched Morgan conjure images of Avalon as Elaine sat behind her, combing her hair.

"Yes," she smiled, clearly relieved that I was not being difficult or stupid.

"And you saw Morgause being sent away? In a boat?"

Morgan nodded and reached out her hand to take back the locket, as if everything was now clear and she could dismiss me from her thoughts and get back to the things that really mattered to her. But I was not yet satisfied. There was still much that I needed to know and so I pulled my hand away from her and once again made to examine the locket.

"I need you to tell me more about this, Morgan. Do you understand what you are doing when you see pictures, in the glass or in the locket?"

"What do you mean, Mother? I just see them. I always have."

This was exactly what she had said to me yesterday, and once again her words threw me off balance. Learning to scry was a difficult and demanding task. It took years to learn how to summon the visions, to form the right words that would bring forth images from the future and to understand how to command and interpret them. Many scryers, and I counted myself amongst them, never advanced beyond the basics. It was rare indeed for even an adept to be able to distinguish between *prophecy* goddess-sent foretelling of what would indeed come to pass—and what was simply *possibility*—a warning to be heeded, or a chance to be taken.

"Tell me more about it. Do you know that it is very unusual to be able to see things like you do? I learned about it when I was at Avalon, but I was not able to do it before I went there."

Morgan looked at me with what I was astounded to realise was rather a pitying look, as if I had just revealed an embarrassing weakness.

"It is actually quite easy, Mother; all I need to do is look deep into a shining surface and ask a question. And the pictures just come.

I can use water as well you know, but I prefer your locket, it doesn't move about as much."

"And what question did you ask last night, when you saw your sister going away in a boat?"

"Oh, that's easy. I just asked what was going to happen to Morgause when I went to Avalon."

"When you…go to Avalon?"

"Yes. I do want to go, Mother. It looks very beautiful. Did you like it when you were there?" Morgan looked up at me with an air of positive but calm expectation, as if we were simply discussing a trip through the caves to the beaches on the other side of the Tintagel causeway, a favourite and familiar outing for both girls.

"Well, yes, I did. But I was much older than you when I went there. Wouldn't you rather wait a little while?"

"Oh, but I will, Mother. Morgause will leave first. I had thought that I would leave before her, because I've been seeing pictures about it for such a long time now and I've never seen anything about Morgause before. But last night, the pictures were clear. Morgause has to leave now, in the next few days. I won't be going until Samhain."

Completely at a loss to know how to respond to these words, I meekly handed the locket back to Morgan, who tucked it back into her pocket and resumed her work with the coloured silks. The door opened behind me and Elaine came in, carrying a pitcher of milk, which she put down on the table, noticing as she did so that I had not touched any of the food she had laid out for me.

"Now, my lady, you must eat something. The Duke is up and about and has been asking for you. He and Lord Madron are breaking their fast in the Great Hall. Those others are with them, and I think they are keen to be off." Elaine bustled about me, pulling out a chair and helping me to sit down. She cut a slice of bread from the loaf and passed it to me. Obediently I took it and reached for the cup of cold milk she placed before me.

"Elaine, please would you take Morgan to the nursery and leave her with Avice? And then come back to me here. There are things we must speak of."

She looked at my plate, noticing that I had yet to eat. I gave her a faint but reassuring smile. "Please, Elaine, you don't need to watch over me." My half-sister was sometimes more than a little bossy if she thought I was not being sensible. "Take Morgan to the nursery, and make sure she doesn't say anything else to upset her sister. And come back to me as soon as you can. I would see my husband before he rides out today."

Elaine nodded and went to the window, where she carefully helped Morgan pack away the silks in the particular and precise order she insisted on. When it was done, Morgan came to me and, most unusually, turned her face toward me to be kissed.

"I'm sorry if I worried you, Mother." Gently, I reached out and stroked her soft, shining hair. She was so lovely, my daughter.

"It's alright, sweetheart. I was just a little unsettled. I had not realised I had so talented a daughter."

Morgan smiled briefly, her eyes lighting up with pleasure at the compliment before she followed Elaine silently from the room.

Mindful of my promise to Elaine, I finished my milk and ate the slice of bread with some berries. I did not really want them, but I had a feeling that it was going to be a long and difficult day, and it would go better for me if I was not faint with hunger by noon time.

WHILST I WAITED FOR ELAINE to return, I looked out of the window, observing what was going on in the courtyard below. Two people were already practising at the archery butts at the far end of the castle green and I watched with pleasure as the shorter of the two unleashed arrow after arrow, each one hitting their mark with speed and certainty. I was even more delighted when an unexpected gust of wind lifted the cap from her head, revealing a long, coiled plait of dark-blonde hair. It was Bennath, and the man beside her I took to be her husband, young Sir Lowen of Syllan.

I saw Jago walking briskly toward the stables, talking all the while to a man I felt certain was Tom Lidgate, constable of the castle and Gorlois' master of horse. All of a sudden one of the young pages ran out in front of them, arms outstretched as if begging them to stop. He said something and they both turned, looking back toward the inner courtyard, and beginning to hurry back in the direction they had come.

I had no time to consider what might be happening as Elaine was now entering the room, shutting the door behind her quietly, with her usual grace.

"Are my daughters behaving themselves for Avice? No more trouble from Morgause?"

Elaine smiled. "They are pretending your old oak chest is a boat and are sailing together on a voyage across the ocean. Avice is being the captain and Morgause is a beautiful princess."

"And what about Morgan?" I asked

"She is being the Goddess," answered Elaine, with a wry smile. "When I left, she was sending winds to fill the sails and commanding the sun to shine." This surprised me slightly as Morgan did not often relish the sort of make-believe that Morgause so enjoyed. Still, I was not going to question what was going on if it meant that my daughters were at peace and Elaine and I had some time to talk.

I motioned to my half-sister to join me in the window; she sat down and immediately reached out to take my hand.

"I am glad to find you calm, Igraine." Elaine was far more mindful of propriety than I was and would never call me anything but "my lady" if there was anyone else present. On our own, I'd entreated her to call me by my name, as she had done when we were girls together in Avalon and at my father's court.

"Oh, Elaine, I may appear calm, but I honestly do not know what to do for the best. Morgause is very young and the court of Orkney is many leagues away. But you heard what Prince Urien had to say last night. I can't risk her falling into Uther's hands." As I spoke, I realised what a relief it was to be able to share my anxieties with this woman, whom I had known nearly all my life, and who I trusted implicitly.

"She's not much younger than you were when we went to Avalon."

"I was nine, Elaine, and I had you with me. She is only six years old and will have no one to travel with her and guide her but a servant."

"Avice loves her, Igraine. And would you have liked it if your husband had behaved like your father? Populating the nursery with his by-blows just to create a companion for your eldest daughter?"

I heard no resentment in her tone; Elaine had always accepted her status as my illegitimate half-sister, but she was quite right. What my mother had appeared to tolerate with great forbearance, I would have found unacceptable. To the best of my knowledge, Gorlois had remained true to me throughout our marriage, and I had never had to deal with the humiliation meted out to my mother on more than one occasion; watching one or other of the court ladies grow large with a child that had been fathered by her husband.

"I just can't bear to let her go. The journey is perilous, and she will be so far away from me. Once she is established at Lot's court, I don't know when I will ever see her again."

"That's true, Igraine, but don't be so despairing. We who know the ways of Avalon are always able to find out what is happening to those we love, no matter how many miles there are between us," She paused and took my other hand in hers, fixing her eyes on mine. "And if Morgan is anything to go by, it may be that your daughters have a great potential for the Mysteries."

I considered what she said. "Morgan frightens me. Did you know that she could scry?"

Elaine shook her head. "Ah, so that was what she was doing. I wasn't really certain. The first I was aware of anything to do with Morgan's unusual abilities was yesterday, and to be honest, I'm a little uncertain about exactly what happened."

She let go of my hands, and gently massaged her forehead with her pale, slender fingers, as if hoping to rub some clarity into her recollections. "I was combing her hair and she was holding the looking glass whilst asking me about Avalon. Next thing I knew, I was on the floor, the glass had shattered and you were yelling at Morgan about the dangers of abusing the powers sent by the Goddess."

I told Elaine about what I had seen in the scrying glass, and also about the conversation I had just had with my little daughter, who, it appeared was already so gifted in the Mysteries that she could summon scrying visions at will.

I was at first surprised to find that Elaine was less concerned about this than I was, but then I remembered that my half-sister had always been a far more talented seer than I was. She told me that she could remember many strange things that had happened to her when she was a young child, long before she went with me to Avalon and received tuition in the Mysteries. She remembered seeing peculiar visions and had sometimes been absolutely certain that she knew what was going to happen long before it actually took place.

She told me that on one occasion, just after she had come to court, she had seen a vision of our father falling from a horse, only to be fatally trampled underfoot at a tourney. He had been wearing my mother's favour, a delicately made shawl of the brightest blue. She had seen, quite clearly in her mind's eye, the shawl, ripped and torn and covered with blood as my father's body was carried from the joust.

Four days later, at a tournament held in honour of my brother's birth, she had watched in horror as my mother fixed her bright blue shawl to my father's lance. As he prepared to make his way toward the lists, Elaine had run to him and begged him not to wear the favour, but he would not listen and eventually, she pulled it from his lance and ran away with it.

"And what happened," I asked.

"Your mother had me whipped," she replied matter-of-factly.

"And the shawl?"

"I gave it to Sir Beorn."

I gasped. I could remember this. It was one of the most unpleasant memories of my early life at my father's court in the Welsh borders. It was also the first time I had seen someone die. "Sir Beorn… You mean that young knight, the one who…"

"Yes, the one who died; trampled by his own horse on the last day of the tourney held to celebrate the birth of your baby brother."

"And you saw it, you knew it was going to happen?"

"No," Elaine corrected me. "I didn't see exactly what was going to happen. In this case, the Goddess vouchsafed me a warning. I saw a man boasting a bright blue favour tumble to the ground, only to be trampled underfoot. When I saw our father attach the silk shawl to his lance, I knew that I did not want it to be him, so I gave the scarf to Sir Beorn and—"

"And sent him to his death…" I finished her sentence.

She nodded. "I was only five years old, Igraine… Not much older than Morgan is now."

"And you sent a man to his death?"

"I saved the life of our father."

I considered Elaine's words. Clearly, Morgan's gifts were not quite as uncommon as I had thought. Just because I had had to work hard to achieve even a reasonable competence at the Mysteries, it did not follow that this would be the case for my daughters. Elaine had always been a gifted seer and Morgan's abilities by now could not be doubted; perhaps Morgause, too, had talents that I was not aware of.

I decided not to push Elaine any further on the circumstances surrounding the terrible death of young Sir Beorn; rather, I wanted to discuss with her the notion she had hinted at earlier—that we could use our knowledge of the Mysteries to teach both my girls to scry.

As I had hoped, Elaine was of the same mind and we decided that we would begin that very day. It was likely that the ship that would take Morgause from me would be ready within the week; we had but little time to teach my sweet but not-so-clever daughter to learn an art that her younger sister appeared to have mastered with the greatest of ease.

We agreed that it would probably be best if Elaine spent some time alone with Morgause; she was the more gifted scryer and had a deep wellspring of patience which I knew myself to lack. I determined that I would use the hours that Elaine was planning to spend tutoring Morgause with Morgan; instructing her in some of the more formal rites and rituals of the Mysteries, in the hope of giving her more control over the powers she had inadvertently acquired.

I requested Elaine to bring both girls to my solar at noon, before either of them had broken their midday bread. I would tell them of my plans and we would make a start at once. It was best to fast awhile before scrying and I was certain that both girls would be more alert and ready to learn if they knew they would not be served their dinner until their lessons were finished.

Elaine nodded in agreement and we both left the room, she in search of my two young daughters, whilst I made my way toward the Great Hall, and, I hoped, my husband.

AS I HAD EXPECTED, THE Great Hall and the courtyard were a frantic muddle of noise and activity. Last night Gorlois had warned Erec to be ready to ride out and I could see that he had not been joking; Tintagel was preparing to march. There was no sign of Jago, our steward, but I could see Tom, the Master of Horse, hard at work in the yard, inspecting the horses. He and the grooms were examining each of the great creatures with care, checking their hooves with meticulous attention and sending any that needed to be reshod over to the castle smithy. Each beast would be given a clean bill of health before Tom would have it saddled in readiness.

I caught sight of Gorlois and Erec, deep in conversation with Prince Urien and Duke Angmer. Lord Madoc was making his way toward them and within minutes of his arrival, all five of them appeared to reach some sort of agreement. They nodded to each other briskly before Erec, Madoc, and the northern Lords dispersed, moving out of the Great Hall into the courtyard. Gorlois had now seen me and began to walk unhurriedly toward where I stood in the doorway, stopping now and then to clap this man or other on the back, or to answer a question from one of his household.

"Well met, my love." Gorlois bent and kissed me lightly on the cheek. Unlike some of the war dukes, he had never felt the need to hide his affection for me in public. "How goes it with our daughters?" I saw a look of concern in his eyes. "Have you told Morgause that she will be leaving us?"

"Aye, my lord, and she and Morgan have now turned my old oak chest into a boat to sail the oceans and wish for nothing but to drift away across the waves," I answered him lightly, wishing to spare him the pain of Morgause's earlier distress.

Gorlois chuckled, amused by the picture I had painted for him. "I sent Jago to the harbour this morning, with instructions to have our most steadfast vessel made ready for my daughter and her companions." He paused, smiling down at me. "It is my belief that he was not best pleased to be sent away, with all this going on," Gorlois gestured around the Hall and courtyard. "But Tom Lidgate is perfectly competent, and the comfort and safety of my daughter must be Jago's priority."

I now understood what had made Jago and his companion return so hurriedly to the Great Hall earlier this morning. I was deeply moved that Gorlois was going to so much trouble to make sure that the preparations for Morgause's voyage would be scrupulously managed. He was about to go to war with a man who had set himself up as his rival for my affections, yet still his thoughts were for the comfort and safety of my child. I moved closer to Gorlois and put my arm round his waist. "Thank you," I whispered.

"And what of Morgan? Does she relish the chance to rule the roost in the nursery?"

"I think she has done that for some time," I replied. "Indeed, I believe that Morgause is looking forward to going to a place where her little sister will not overshadow her."

"Morgause will be a beauty; she takes after her mother. She need have no fear of anyone overlooking her once a few more years have passed."

"Fie, my love; there are many who don't share your partiality, many who would prefer the looks of our little Morgan, who I think is also growing up to be a beauty."

Gorlois frowned. "Aye, I can't deny that she is fair to look on, but I'm afraid she has too much of a look of the witch queen for my liking."

"You mean Vivian? The Lady of the Lake?" I had yet to talk to him about his recent habit of referring to her as "the witch queen." I did not like it myself, and I knew that many of our Cornish people still felt a deep allegiance to the old ways. To disparage the Lady in this way would not go down well with them.

"You know who I mean. And do not talk of her if you wish me to preserve my temper."

I decided to hold my tongue. "And when do you ride, my lord?"

"Prince Urien and the men of Madron will be on their way within the hour, taking with them the Northern Army and one third of the Tintagel Garrison." Gorlois moved slightly away from me now, assuming once again the air of military commander rather than husband and father. "I will await news from Jago regarding the commissioning of the ship to take Morgause and her household to Orkney and will then set out myself, with Sir Lowen, the men of Lyonesse and another third of our Tintagel warriors. The remainder I leave here, under the command of Lord Madoc."

"You do not leave them to my command, my lord?" I rejoined, a little put out that he did not have sufficient faith in me to manage the affairs of the castle in his absence.

"You will have enough to do, managing the household and looking to the demands of our daughters." He put up a hand to silence my mounting objections. I was Avalon-trained and prepared for leadership. I knew myself to be more than capable of command. This was but one more example of the influence of the travelling preachers, who spoke out against the priestesses of the Goddess, arguing that a woman's place was little more than hearth and home.

"Now is not the time or place to talk of this." Gorlois could see that I was unhappy with his decision, but he was not prepared to listen to me. "I needs must see Tom Lidgate about the horses and armoury and I would talk with Erec once more before he departs. Meet me in our chamber presently. I should not be more than three hours." And then he pulled me close to him, this time kissing me full on the lips.

"And I would fain say goodbye to my wife properly," he whispered so only I could hear, "so I have some memories to keep me warm in the nights ahead."

Despite my irritation, I clung to him then, breathing in his scent and feeling the warmth of his body; refusing to release him. In the end, he had almost to prise himself free from me, and as he pushed me gently but purposefully away from him, I turned and ran from the Great Hall. I would not look back at him, not wanting to see him move from me and disappear amongst his men, preparing for a war that was of my making, and one from which I knew he might never return.

Chapter Eight

I made my way back to my solar, which was now empty. Someone had cleared away the milk and bread Elaine had brought for me to break my fast and had placed a jug of cold water on the table. The room was filled with the delicate scent of mint and camomile, plants that I knew from my days in Avalon would help refresh the mind and bring clarity of vision. As I looked around, I noticed small bunches of the herbs lying on the dresser and scattered by the fireside. The water had also been infused with them and I poured myself a cup, looking out across the causeway as I drank, wondering how best to help my daughters.

Although the sun was fully risen, it was not warm. The wind was up, whipping the surface of the waters around Tintagel into frenzied waves that dashed the edge of the causeway. Great gushes of cold salt-spray rushed into the path of the men toiling across it leading packhorses carrying stores and supplies over to Urien's encampment on the mainland.

The seabirds were gathering, white wings diving in low over the clifftops, only to rise again with harsh, triumphant cries as the currents lifted them high above the castle battlements. From their windswept nests deep in the granite crags, I could see small clusters of red-beaked, black-winged choughs flying purposefully toward the causeway, hoping to feed on the small specks of grain that spilled from the sacks as they jolted their way across the wave-lashed narrow track.

As I watched the birds swoop and glide, riding the currents with pale wings outstretched to take the maximum they could from the flurries and gusts of air beneath them, I felt my mind moving toward them, out of my body. This was another magic, one which I had learned to harness as a girl in Avalon, but which I had not ventured to make use of for many years. As my eyes focused on the rhythmic swoop and turn of the seabirds' flight, I concentrated on finding one mind that would open to me, a mind I could control. Within seconds, I had it.

It was a mature female, who had been using all of her concentration to hover low above the waves, where a shoal of fish were feeding. Smoothly, I entered her. She did not immediately notice my presence and I was almost overwhelmed by the intensity of her focus on the small, silver creatures flicking and darting beneath us. Her desire to hunt, to dive beneath the waves and satisfy her hunger was so single-minded that she put up no resistance as I overpowered her, causing her to lose control over her pinions as she was plucked skyward by the next gust of wind.

After that, it was easy. Her mind was simple, made up of basic impulses: to hunt, to feed, and to protect her chicks. But as I probed deeper, I found something else as well, something I hadn't found in the minds of the smaller birds and animals I had temporarily inhabited before. She also took a fierce delight in the glory and power of opening her wings and letting the wind take her—and for a minute or two, I indulged her. We rode the wind, screeching in triumph as our wings flexed and tipped with beautiful precision. As I took my bearings, I was surprised to realise that unlike other birds whose body I'd commanded, her eyes could move in their sockets, making it much easier for me to take in my surroundings. I cast to left and right until I spotted what I had been looking for. Out along the harbour arm, a vessel was being made ready.

The bay was full of ships, coracles, and small, colourful fishing boats that were often passed down from father to son. Many were patched up and rather ramshackle in appearance, but I knew that all of them were seaworthy. The fishermen of Cornwall did not underestimate the power of the waves and would spend the winter months, when the high winds and cruel storms made it difficult for them to venture out to sea, mending their nets and caulking the timber of their vessels, paying particular attention to the paintings on the prow, designed to ward off the evil eye and ensure the protection of the Mother.

There were also larger boats moored up in the sheltered harbour; I spotted a longboat and two Phoenician galleys. Even after the Romans had left Britain, Gorlois had encouraged trade with the sailors from the southern seas and we owned several vessels capable of the long journeys to trade our Cornish tin for fine glassware, wines, and pottery. The largest of these was the *Llyr's Daughter*, a sleek, three-masted merchant ship of Roman design. Swooping in toward it, I landed silently on the main mast and looked down at the hustle and bustle below.

Although the ship had sails, it was also equipped with a galley for fifteen oarsmen, but unlike the Romans, we did not use slaves. Duty at the oars would be taken in turn by the ship's crew, who would be supplemented on *Llyr's Daughter*'s next voyage by hand-picked warriors from our household garrison.

I watched as stores were unloaded from ox carts and stowed safely away on board. Bags of flour, dried fruits, casks of wine and fresh water. I was also glad to see the strong oaken trunks which, I assumed, contained my daughter's clothes and belongings and several bundles that I thought could only be blankets and soft bedding to keep her warm whilst at sea.

Then I caught sight of Jago, the castle steward, on the quayside. From his gestures and what I could make out of his face, he seemed to be having an animated and apparently one-sided conversation with a tall, leathery-faced man who standing impassively by the side of the gangplank.

Wanting to hear more, I opened my wings and glided down toward the quay, where I alighted on a pile of rope just yards away from the unknown sailor.

He was tall, with a confident bearing and a handsome face seasoned by wind and wave. He also had his arms folded implacably across his chest, his feet firmly positioned about two feet apart, and his chin lowered; all in all, he was a picture of stubborn determination.

Jago had stopped speaking and was scratching the back of his head as if he really did not know what to do next. One of his men came up to him, carrying an ornately carved chair, embossed with silver; I recognised it as one of our gifts to King Lot. He looked questioningly at the steward, trying to find out if he needed assistance, but Jago simply shook his head and gestured him to continue up the gangplank and stow his valuable burden securely away.

Still the leathery-faced man said nothing. Jago heaved a sigh, and turned to him, arms outstretched as if pleading.

"Now lookee 'ere Clem Trevenna. We go back a long while, man and boy. Your ma was loike a mother to me. You know that."

The leathery man shrugged, remaining silent but despite this, his face softened and he uncrossed his arms.

"Have I ever asked ye to do summat wrong? Summat that your mother would be ashamed on. Have I, Clem?" Jago moved closer, his arms reaching out to gently touch the other man's shoulder.

At his touch, the man flinched and pushed him away, but it was clear that the impasse was now broken. "You don't know what you're askin', Jago. Are you grown so high and mighty, workin' up at castle that you've forgotten what my old ma taught us? Have you forgotten the old ways?"

He moved away from the gangplank toward the ship's prow where a golden crescent moon overlaid by a great blue eye, were painted. He pointed at them, his hands shaking a little in anger.

"Do ye think my men will sail without the Mother's blessin'? Without the protection from the Goddess? It don't matter how much you pay us nor what promises your Master makes, this ship b'aint leaving the harbour without Her mark upon it."

He turned and looked contemptuously at a little bundle on the quayside that I hadn't noticed before.

"An' if you think that bunch of sticks can take its place, you have clearly lost what little sense you ever 'ad, Jago."

Jago moved protectively toward the bundle, picked it up, and opened it, revealing a large but clumsily made wooden cross.

"It's only a bit 'a wood. That's all it is. The Duke… He's angry with the Goddess, angry with the Lady… He says he doesn't trust 'is daughter to her protection," Jago spoke pleadingly, and I could tell the words were costing him dear.

"You don't need a get rid of the Goddess' mark, I won't tell the Duke you kept it…but he made me promise you would sail under the blessin' of the Risen god."

The leathery man, who I now knew to be called Clem, looked as if he was about to turn his back once more, but this time Jago did not hesitate to reach out to him.

"Clem, whatten I to do? He's my lord, and he's a good master. He's sending away his little daughter and wants to keep 'er safe." Wanting to make sure I missed nothing of this, I flew up and perched on the gangplank, just feet away from where the two men were standing.

"You know I keep true to the old ways, but I 'ave to do his biddin'… Come now, what would it hurt to take these on board, to nail them to the prow? What would it hurt, eh Clem?"

I was quite unable to believe what I was hearing. Whilst Gorlois' infatuation with the new religion had become even more pronounced as a result of Vivian's activities in the Welsh borderlands and her apparent decision to brand both of us as traitors, I had assumed that he would have known better than to impose his rejection of the Goddess on our people. The men and women of Cornwall and Lyonesse held fast to the old ways and however much they loved their war duke, they depended on the rites and rituals of the Mysteries to provide certainty and security in their daily lives.

If Jago tried to force Gorlois' ridiculous decision upon Clem and his sailors, I thought it highly likely that it would not only jeopardise our one chance of sending Morgause to safety but could also lead to a more general mutiny throughout Gorlois' forces.

I watched as the steward moved forward toward the ship's captain. As he spoke, he put the bag containing the ungainly wooden cross down on the quayside and once more held out his hands, imploringly. Instantly, I saw my chance. Jumping down from my perch, I strutted toward the two men, who took no notice of me. Why should they? Seagulls were all around us, flying, balancing on masts and exploring every aspect of the quayside for leftovers from the morning's catch.

When I reached the hessian sack, I tore at it with my beak, ripping it open and exposing the contents. Then I walked forcefully toward it, pushing it insistently with my flank until the bag rolled over the harbour wall, the wooden cross tumbling into the water, where the waves caught it and began to bear it swiftly out to sea. It was the work of a moment, completed before Jago and Clem had time to realise what was happening.

Both looked aghast as the bag and its contents tumbled into the ocean. It was Clem who was first to regain his composure. Slapping his friend round the back, his face broke into a smile. "Well there's your answer... Everyone knows the seagulls are the Mother's messengers. Llyr's chickens, we calls 'em. And they've made it pretty clear what the Mother wants for *Llyr's Daughter*."

Jago nodded slowly. "Aye... I think you're right Clem. I'll tell the Master that your ship is well protected. The Goddess must be watchin' over her to send that seabird. I don't think I've ever seen the like..."

"You see many a queer thing at sea, let me tell you, Jago. Things that you soft-livin' castle fellas would never believe." Clem's good humour had clearly been restored to him by the seagull's fortunate intervention. "My ship has alus been lucky; we've honoured the Goddess and put our trust in her. Come now, let me take you aboard,

I want to show you the quarters we've prepared for your young Lady and her smart companions."

And with that, the two men made their way up the gangplank, any hostility between them consigned to the watery depths, alongside Gorlois' ill-judged and ill-fated offering.

Thanking my stars that inspiration had come to me in time, I looked upward and realised with a start that the sun was now nearly midway across the sky. Opening my wings, I flew swiftly toward the castle, knowing that if I did not make haste, Elaine and my daughters would arrive in my solar only to be greeted by the lifeless, unresponsive husk of my physical body.

I pushed thoughts of Gorlois and his folly to the back of my mind, knowing that I would need to find a way to deal with this later. The wind was with me and I was able to make the most of the gusts and flurries, soaring on the updrafts, up and away from the harbour and out across the causeway. I made good time and the seagull whose mind I had been controlling for the past hour or so soon landed on the stone ledge outside my room.

I must admit that it was with some regret that I unbound myself from her consciousness; it had been a great joy to fly freely across the sky and to feel the power of the wind rushing through her pinions. Still, I consoled myself, now I had bound her to me, it would be an easy thing to recall her, and this, I reflected, would now also give me a means to keep watch over my eldest daughter on her long voyage north.

Smiling, I watched the great bird as she flew away, heading back toward the edge of the causeway and the little shoals of fishes that had captured her attention earlier. As I refilled my cup with the sweetly scented water, I heard the sound of muffled voices and the ring of footsteps on the stairs; a few seconds later the door burst open and Morgause tumbled inside, followed more sedately by Morgan and Elaine.

Morgause ran toward me and flung her arms around my waist. As always, she looked enchanting. Someone, probably Avice, had tamed her unruly tangle of chestnut curls into two long plaits, which hung to her waist. She was wearing a shift of dark green linen, belted at the waist with a copper-coloured girdle, and had on an overdress of fine tawny samite that I instantly recognised as having been cut from one of my old court gowns.

"Mama, I'm hungry…have you got any food for us?" Morgause began to search amongst the bowls and dishes on the table, rooting around under bunches of herbs and dried flowers and overturning the pile of small clothing that I was embroidering for her to take with her on her journey.

"No, darling; please stop that and listen to me. There is something very important that I need to talk to both you and Morgan about."

Morgause continued to half-heartedly turn over the bowls and dishes laid out on the table, although I think she knew by now that she would not find so much as an oat cake concealed there. In the meantime, Morgan had settled herself comfortably on the bench by the fireside, wrapping her skirts neatly around her. She was dressed simply that morning, in a bleached linen smock and an old pale blue kirtle that Morgause had outgrown several summers before. She said nothing, just looked at me expectantly, her head held slightly to one side, chin cupped in her hands.

"Now both of you, please listen to what I'm going to tell you. You are both rather young for me to be talking to you about Avalon and the Mysteries, but these are difficult times and I need to do what I can to prepare and protect you for the future." My tone was serious, and I did not smile. Morgause moved away from the table and went to sit beside her sister, as if seeking comfort. I noticed that, unusually, Morgan did not push her away, but instead put her arm around her sister as if to protect her.

"Morgause, you are soon to leave us, to journey far away to the North, where one day, you will be a Queen." At these words, I noticed a small complacent smile flutter involuntarily at the corner of my eldest daughter's mouth as her hand went up to stroke her hair at the base of her neck.

"And you, Morgan, you will also be leaving me, although the date for your departure is, as yet, unknown to us. You are going, as I did, to Avalon, to seek the favour of the Goddess." Morgan too gave a small smile when I said this, but unlike her sister, her hand went to her chest, and rested above her heart.

"I was nine years old when I left my parents' court and, if truth be told, I had hoped to keep you with me for longer still than that."

"Why can't you then, Mama?" asked Morgause, her brow slightly furrowed and a look of uncertainty on her face.

"Because we are at war, my darling, and I need to keep you safe," I said, unthinkingly. Morgan nodded sagely, as if this was an obvious and well-known fact, but I could see Morgause's bottom lip start to tremble and the glisten of tears at the corner of her eyes. I cursed myself inwardly. Why had I said that? I had worked so hard to keep her calm, to make her voyage seem like a lovely and fascinating adventure, and here I was, stupidly sabotaging my own handiwork.

It was Elaine who came to my rescue, kneeling down before the two girls. "This is why we are going to teach you about the Mysteries of Avalon. You know your mother and I were there when we were not much older than you are now." Both girls nodded.

"Well, we learnt many things there; how to make potions and medicines, how to tell fortunes and interpret dreams." Both girls were looking at her raptly; she had their full attention and, I was glad to see, had managed to stem the flood of tears that had threatened to overwhelm Morgause.

"And we learned to scry. You know what that is?"

Morgan nodded eagerly, whilst Morgause looked a little uncertain.

"To see visions, to tell the future, in a scrying bowl or mirror," Elaine explained.

"And to read the will of the Goddess?" asked Morgan.

"Yes, Morgan," Elaine replied, "to read the will of the Goddess."

Both girls now turned to me, keen now to know just exactly what it was I had in store for them. "We don't have much time. You, little one, will be leaving us before the month's end," I touched Morgause lightly on the head. "So I have decided it is best if we teach you individually, so that you can each learn as much and as quickly as possible. Morgause, you will work with Elaine, and you, Morgan, will work with me."

I could see that neither of my daughters were happy with this suggestion. Morgause had always preferred Avice (who adored her uncritically) to Elaine, and I felt certain that Morgan had already worked out that Elaine had a greater mastery of the Mysteries than I. Still, they could tell from my voice that I would brook no argument and, at a nod from me, Elaine took Morgause by the hand and led her from the room.

"The first lesson should last no more than an hour," I reminded her. "Take her to her meat when you have finished. I think she may have need of it." The door closed behind them and I turned to face my younger daughter, who was now standing by the fireside, hands behind her back, as she looked intently at the bowls and serving dishes arranged along the mantle.

"That one I think, Mother," said Morgan, pointing to the largest of the serving vessels, a shallow copper serving platter that was beautifully engraved with vine leaves, but which was so heavy and cumbersome that we rarely made use of it. I looked down at her, frowning slightly. "But why Morgan? Surely one of the smaller bowls would do just as well?"

My daughter simply shook her head and crossed her arms in front of her narrow chest, a sure sign of youthful determination. Her response irritated me somewhat, but recognising that I did not want to waste time, I simply reached for the huge platter with both hands and, not without difficulty, lifted it down from the mantle and placed it gently on the floor beside the fire.

Cooperative now, Morgan fetched the jug from the table and carefully poured in the herb-scented water, filling the shallow platter almost to the brim.

"Now child, take care, the water should rest at least a finger's breadth from the rim." I kneeled down next to the bowl to demonstrate what I meant and then used one of the stone cups to scoop out what we did not need.

"Why, Mother?" Morgan had moved close to me, resting her chin against my shoulder and staring into the scrying bowl with fascination, her voice little more than a whisper. I realised that despite her uncanny abilities, Morgan had never seen anyone else scry before and was unaware of the formalities that usually accompanied the ritual.

Saying nothing, I placed my hands on the flat edge of the platter and nodded at Morgan to kneel down and do likewise.

"Now, clear your mind. Keep silent and fix your gaze upon the bowl." She looked up at me at once, her mouth starting to frame a question, but she must have caught the seriousness of my intent, for her lips remained closed and her eyes returned to the surface of the water.

Together we stared into the shallows, our fingers just touching, warm flesh against cool metal. Clearing my mind, I opened myself to the Goddess, seeking her guidance before framing the question that would determine the visions I hoped she might grant us. I closed my eyes, preparing my mind to receive her, but before I could complete my ritual preparations, I felt the surface of the scrying bowl warm beneath my fingers and sensed the disturbance in the water as it began to ripple and roil. I felt Morgan's hand move closer to mine. Her thumb gently twined itself across my little finger, but not for a second did we take our palms away from the vessel's surface which was now becoming almost unbearably hot.

Clouds of dense, herb-scented steam rose from the water which was now churning violently. I could see shapes and figures beginning to form just below the surface of the waters. I had no idea what we would see when the mists cleared; this was a vision the Goddess was sending to us unasked.

We were looking down on a rocky moorland crag whose harsh granite cliffs pitched unforgivingly toward the open sea. The moon hung low in the sky, illuminating the waves with a long pathway of light, stretching out toward the horizon. The sky was clear and the stars shone cold upon the desolate clifftop. A half-formed track wound through the rough grass and gorse bushes toward a dense coppice of ancient beech trees whose dark, spiky outlines were but little softened by the buds of new leaves.

Because the scrying bowl was so large, we could easily see across the wide emptiness of the scrubland. As we continued to watch, unspeaking, our viewpoint changed and we were drawn in closer, down toward the far side of the beechwood until we were able to make out a rough encampment. There were horse lines and several large, rudimentary structures of roughly tanned hide stretched over wooden frames. We saw carts pulled closely together to provide protection for provisions and weaponry, and everywhere there were soldiers, keeping guard, checking supplies, or putting the finishing touches to the makeshift battle tents.

Through the trees we could see the dim glow of the campfire, small flames flickering low between the gnarled and twisted trunks of the ancient trees. My mind was racing. This was an army, but whose? There was little wind; the banners stuck haphazardly into the ground around the edges of the campsite hung limply in the still air and we were not close enough to see the sigils on the soldiers' breastplates or helms. I could tell that the scene we were watching was set in early summer; the red planet that the Romans held sacred to the God of War was still visible, near to the horizon in close conjunction with the moon. But had the Goddess granted us a vision of what was happening now, in one of Gorlois' border outposts, or even Uther's battle lines? Or were we scrying somewhere in the future, being granted sight of things that were to come?

THE SURFACE OF THE BOWL was so wide that, as our eyes became accustomed to the darkness we were able to see the encampment stretched out in a long, straggling line along the far edge of the coppice and beyond. We saw foot soldiers and archers lounging together in the firelight, casually sharpening their blades or fletching new arrows. Every fifty yards or so we noticed clusters of mounted warriors searching for a place on the horse lines before dismounting, tossing the reins to their squires and moving off to find a safe bed for themselves. There was activity all around us as the camp cooks called for the scullions to feed the cook fires and keep watch over the spit-roasts. Pages ran hither and yon along the battle lines, looking for their war dukes or carrying messages. As always, no sound issued forth from the scrying bowl, but it was easy to imagine the noise and commotion that must have accompanied the scenes we were watching in the still, clear waters of the vast copper bowl.

It was clear to me by now that these could not be Gorlois' men. Cornwall and Lyonesse could not muster a force this size; there must have been near three thousand men gathered together in the bustling, well-organised camp, and I knew that my husband's forces would scarcely equal one-third of that number. As if to confirm my conclusion, our vista shifted once again, and we were now looking down into a great clearing. At its centre was a deep and apparently well-established fire pit whose tawny flames burned brightly in the still night. Around the fire lounged a number of still-armoured warriors, sitting on stumps of the recently felled trees; torches had been placed at regular intervals around the clearing, and I was able to make out the sigils on shield and breastplate with little difficulty.

This time, it was indeed the black crow of Ceint that was blazoned across the chests of many of the men talking together around the campfire, but I also spotted other emblems. A short, powerfully built warrior standing to the left of the fire pit sported a snarling wolf's head on both chest and helm—sigil of the men of Ulster and Connaught, the mercenary warriors or galloglaigh whose forces had been instrumental in the final defeat of Vortigern. As I watched, he turned to engage two other men in conversation. Taller and more athletically built, they each wore a pair of black spears emblazoned on their breastplates. As the nearest one turned toward me, I recognised the face of young Prince Ban, eldest son of Uther's most powerful ally, King Budic of Brittany.

I could no longer have any doubt about what we were seeing. This was the battle camp of Uther Pendragon and if any further confirmation were needed, the scene shifted once again and we moved away from the fire into the heart of the command tent that had been erected at the southerly edge of the clearing.

We could see two people inside the tent, which was lit only by a flickering oil lamp and the muted glow of logs burning in a small brazier. One of them, the larger of the two, was seated on a rough carved chair in the centre of the shelter. His broad shoulders were hunched, and he held his head in his hands, elbows resting on a table in front of him. The second person, a small, slender woman, was standing behind him with her hands on his shoulders. I could see that she was using her thumb and the palm of her hands to gently apply pressure to the muscles at the base of his neck, perhaps hoping to release some of the tension that was obvious in the taut lines of his shoulders and the hard set of his chin.

Of course, I recognised both of them instantly. In front of me was the man I had last seen sprawled in angry confusion on the stone floor of Caer-Lundein, calling out to me as I ran from him to find my husband—but with the taste of his mouth on my lips and the feel of his hands on my body. This was Uther Pendragon and behind him, starkly elegant in a simple tunic of dark green linen, was Vivian, the Lady of the Lake.

Beside me, I felt Morgan's fingers twitch as she too recognised the Lady. Up to this point, my daughter had observed the visions unfolding before us with a detached, almost analytical interest but now, as we watched Vivian move nearer to Uther, shifting her hands from his neck to the pressure points at the base of his skull, she leaned closer and closer, until I feared she would actually touch the water and inadvertently draw our scrying to a close.

She had also completely blocked my view. I gave a slight gasp of annoyance and, ever quick to understand, Morgan moved back to her original position, her gaze fixed on the scene in front of us, but now we could both see what was happening.

Vivian's fingers continued to work their magic and Uther's shoulders were now visibly less tense. He had taken his head from his hands and was now leaning back in his chair, listening to whatever Vivian was saying to him. The conversation continued for a minute or so, and as we could not hear a word that was being said and, because nothing of any moment appeared to be happening, I was on the verge of telling Morgan that our lesson was over for the day. Just then, Uther pushed back his chair and got rapidly to his feet, making a sharp gesture with his hand that could have been a signal of either anger or denial.

Instantly, Vivian responded. She was talking fast, her eyes focused on the King's face and her hands making insistent, chopping gestures emphasising each point she was making. She gestured toward something small on the table, half-hidden in the shadows of a pewter wine jug. It was too dark to make it out, but that was of no matter as Uther leant forward, grabbed whatever it was from the table, and hurled it into the brazier, where it exploded in an intense flare of green light.

When Vivian saw this, her eyes blazed with anger and, without saying another word, she pulled her cloak tight around her and stormed out into the darkness. When he was sure she had gone, Uther walked slowly to the brazier, which now burned pale green, throwing out a faint and rather eldritch light. He looked inside, as if wanting to make sure that whatever it was he had thrown in was well and truly destroyed. When he was satisfied, he nodded grimly, his lean, sculptured face taking on an unearthly pallor in the soft green half-light and then, without a word went back to his seat.

Now, our view had shifted, and we were facing him. We watched as he reached inside his cloak and drew out a small pouch that he had been wearing on a chain around his neck. He held it to his face and kissed it, and then, with great care as if handling a precious relic, he took from it something small and delicate, flimsy like gossamer and shining with a strange, milky whiteness.

He held it in his hand, smoothed out across his palm and stroked it gently, as he had once caressed my cheek before we danced together in front of his entire court. I knew then what Uther held so tenderly between his fingers; I recognised exactly what it was that he was stroking like a talisman, with a look of such longing and sadness on his face that my heart was troubled.

It was a small piece of fabric torn from the moonbeam dress he had had made for me. The dress that I had worn against my husband's advice and my own better judgement; the dress I had torn and trampled to the ground in my haste to get away from him.

I remembered the feel of his arms around me, the way my traitorous body had been unable to resist the pleasure his hands and mouth had brought me. I remembered what he had said to me as he drew me to him and kissed me. "Will you give me comfort, Igraine?" And I had rejected him, pushed him from me to sprawl in a bruised, humiliated heap on the floor of his own castle.

Yes, I loved my husband, but Uther stirred something in me that had long been dormant, and its intensity frightened me. Merlin had guessed this; his words to me before he took his leave on his last visit to Tintagel had made it clear that he had seen through me.

And Uther Pendragon, King of all the Britons, had broken the peace, declaring war on his own right-hand man, sworn ally and friend—because of me.

I watched him as he kissed the small piece of cloth before putting it back in the pouch around his neck. As he did so, he looked up, as if he had heard something stir in the darkness and, as he did so, he appeared to stare straight at me. I knew that he could not see me, but still, I gazed into his eyes with an intensity that startled me. As I did so, I saw an expression of desire and disbelief begin to emerge on his face as if, despite everything I knew to be true about the way a scrying vison works, he could see me as clearly as I could see him. This lasted but seconds.

Uther dragged his eyes away from me, needing to attend to whatever had previously disturbed him. He was now looking expectantly toward the entrance of the tent. Was it Vivian, returned in a more amenable or supplicatory mood, or could it be a deputation of his war dukes, wishing to discuss plans for the morrow? I dismissed both of these ideas when I saw him get to his feet, arms thrown wide in welcome as a tall figure made its way toward the table and the warmth of the brazier. Even before he threw back the hood of his travelling cloak I knew him. Lord Merlin, Druid, enchanter, and trusted advisor to the King.

Merlin returned the King's salute of welcome, and the two men embraced before seating themselves at the table, where Uther snapped his fingers and a page scurried forward bearing cups and a fresh flagon of wine.

Merlin removed his travelling cloak and handed it to the page, who placed it carefully on an oak chest some feet from the brazier. The two men talked, Uther sitting back in his chair, with Merlin leaning close into him. After a moment, Uther pushed his chair backward. I saw him shake his head firmly, folding his arms tight across his chest and looking away from the Druid as determinedly as he had turned from the Lady but minutes before. But Merlin played his man with greater skill than the more tempestuous Vivian; rather than responding with anger at Uther's rebuff, I saw Merlin lean back into his chair and take something from within his robes. It was a small flask, made of silver, or some other burnished metal. He began to turn it slowly in his fingers, letting it catch the flames, sending small patches of light dancing across the walls. All the while his lips moved slowly as he continued to talk, his face calm and untroubled.

As we watched, the expression on Uther's face changed from anger to uncertainty; he unfolded his arms, shrugging his shoulders and holding his hands out to Merlin in a gesture of despair. At that,

Merlin leaned forward, taking the king's hands in both of his own, bringing them together and then wrapping Uther's fingers around the small, shining flask he had been playing with in the firelight. Uther looked down at the flask, then up into the patient, kindly eyes of the wise old Druid, who nodded, giving him a half smile. Slowly, Uther took the flask in his right hand and pulled out the stopper. He looked once more at Merlin, half opening his lips as if to say something, but then thinking better of it, he raised it to his lips and drank.

I was utterly absorbed in what I was watching, but Morgan had clearly had enough. Before I could see what would happen next, I heard my small daughter's quiet, very precise voice saying. "This is rather boring, Mother; can we see where the Lady went?" and the scene in front of us rippled and vanished, leaving us both staring into the clear, shallow water, our eyes blinking as we became re-accustomed to the harsh mid-day sunlight.

I was disappointed that we had been pulled so abruptly from the vision in the scrying bowl and was also more than a little disorientated, so I spoke more harshly to Morgan than I would normally have done. "Child, you have much to learn. You should never speak before the Goddess chooses to end her message to us. It shows disrespect and must be atoned for."

Morgan, who was not used to harsh words from me, got to her feet and backed away. "I didn't like that man, Mother. He made Vivian angry and she is the Lady of Avalon."

Her defence of Vivian angered me. "Vivian is not always right, my girl, and there are many things that you are still too young to understand."

"I don't care. I don't like him and I wish the Goddess had never shown us that vision."

Her words shocked me. It was not for us, the handmaidens of the Mysteries, to question the wisdom of the Goddess, but as I looked at my small, angry daughter, I remembered just how young she was and that this was the first time she had received any instruction in the arts of Avalon. "Hush, child." This time, I spoke gently. "There are still many things for you to learn even though you have travelled the path farther and faster than any other I have known." My words of praise gave her pleasure and I saw the cross expression begin to melt away.

Always sensitive to atmosphere, Morgan came back to my side and touched my sleeve with one small, slender finger. "I'm sorry, Mother. Will you teach me more tomorrow?"

"Yes, sweetling, I shall. Now let me take you down to your sister and Elaine in the Great Hall. It is past noon time, and you must be hungry." I gently touched the tip of her nose with my finger and she placed her small hand trustingly in mine.

We descended the stairs quickly and in silence. Once I had left her safely at the table, I made my way swiftly back to my chamber to await my husband, desperately aware that despite my best efforts, I was unable to stop thinking of Uther, his face desolate and my torn finery cradled against his heart.

Chapter Nine

All in all, I was not in a very good mood to greet my husband. Gorlois had promised to be with me a little after noon, but the mid-afternoon sun was starting to move toward the horizon before he finally showed his face at the door of our chamber, and what warmth I felt toward him had dwindled with its rays.

I had little but my thoughts to occupy me whilst I waited. Morgan had once again requisitioned my box of embroidery threads and although my small harp had been recently tuned and re-strung, I did not have the stomach for music. Instead, I watched the gulls swoop and soar across the causeway. I was still able to sense the bird-mind I had commanded earlier that morning. After I'd released her, she had fed well and had now flown back to her nesting ground on the cliff tops. She was sleepy and needed to rest, but I knew I could summon her to my window in an instant if I so desired.

I smiled, remembering how I had exulted in the joy and freedom of flight, vowing to myself that I would bind my mind with hers once more before many days had passed. But as I allowed my mind to dwell on what I had learned down at the harbour that morning, I no longer felt like smiling. I remembered what I had heard of Gorlois' plan to remove the Goddess' protection from the *Llyr's Daughter*, his intention to send Morgause on a long and perilous voyage without the protection of the Mysteries—and my anger began to build within me.

I have never been very good at doing nothing, but I was loathe to leave our chamber as Gorlois had particularly asked that I wait there for him. Much as I knew that he would have many things to attend to, I resented the way that he seemed to accord no value to my time, which he clearly thought I could just squander, waiting aimlessly for him.

In fact, I had much that needed my attention around Tintagel. The herb gardens and potagers had been sadly neglected during our absence and I had already noticed that our stocks of medicinal herbs was running low. Elaine and I would need to work hard if we were to prepare a good supply of salves and potions to treat Gorlois' men when they returned—as I knew many would—wounded from battle, feverish, or maimed. I also needed to give thought to plans for the mid-summer rituals, which would soon be upon us and which would be doubly important this year, with fighting on our borders and the blight of the Lady's curse hanging over our homes and harvest. I could not hide it from myself. I was frightened. We were at war, and it was a war that I knew in my heart of hearts we could not win.

There would be many empty spaces around the summer bonfires as Gorlois and his men sought to secure and hold the borders of Cornwall and Lyonesse. Those of us that remained—the women, the young, the aged, and the infirm—would have to do what we could, to do honour to the Goddess and to beg for her favour for our fields and orchards.

And by Samhain, many of those men and boys who were, at this very moment, saddling their horses and strapping on their sword belts to fight under the banner of their war duke would lie, still and cold, in the silent earth. And for what? To allow my husband to vent his anger and to bolster up his pride? Surely, this was nothing but folly.

If I am honest, my anger was also tempered by my sense of guilt. Despite everything I had done to bury it, I could not deny the strength of my physical response to Uther, and I had yet to fully consider the implications of the scene Morgan and I had just witnessed in the scrying bowl. I had no way of knowing if the things we had seen were going to happen soon, or at some distance in the future, still yet if they were a glimpse of actions the Goddess had decreed would come to pass, or a vision of a potential future—which could be helped or hindered by the decisions I would make.

As I stood by my window, waiting for my husband and watching the shadows lengthen, I felt myself grow heavy with resentment, anger and guilt at the futility of our situation. When finally, the door opened and Gorlois stood before me, I would neither look at him, nor smile. At first, he did not notice, wrapping his arms around me and seeking to pull me to him in his warm and strong embrace, but as I kept my face turned resolutely from his questing mouth and refused to allow myself to melt into the familiar contours of his body, he pushed away from me, a matching gleam of anger beginning to fire in his eyes.

"How so, Igraine? This is cold comfort indeed." He took my chin in his hand, holding my face so that he could look into my eyes, and I was unable to turn away.

"Do you not have a kiss for me? Something to warm me on the cold nights without you?"

"There is no need for this, Gorlois. You do not have to have 'cold nights without me.' You do not have to go." I pulled away from him and moved back toward the centre of the room, wanting to make sure that he would hear me out.

"You don't need to fight Uther. People do not have to die because of this." I was determined to have my say, to tell him that I was not prepared to have the lives of our people on my conscience simply to salvage his pride and my reputation.

He looked at me and to my surprise and irritation, I saw a small smile twitching at the corner of his mouth. "Igraine, my dearest love, I know why you are saying this, and believe me, it does you credit. But you do not understand the ways of war. I can no more back down now than the seas outside Tintagel can cease to beat upon the rocks.

"Uther has threatened to take you from me. To unman me and humiliate me before my people. Do you not see? If I turn back now,

I may spare a few lives, but I will lose everything. We will lose everything."

"No, Gorlois. That is not true. Merlin showed us another path. If we bow the knee in this, not only will we keep our people safe, but our son, Cornwall's son, will one day be mightier even than his father."

Gorlois shook his head fiercely. "No, Igraine; Avalon-trained you may be, but you have no part in this. I will have no truck with the Druids and their evil magics. When the war with Uther is over, I have taken a vow to clear them from our land. Cornwall and Lyonesse will no longer strain beneath the cursed sorceries of Merlin and the witch queen, and our people will be free to hear the truth."

I stared at him in horror. Was he mad? Did he really think that there could be any defeat of Uther? Were his pride and arrogance so great that he would set himself up against the Goddess herself?

"Like you tried to make Jago listen to 'the truth'? When you tried to force the captain of the *Llyr's Daughter* to carry Morgause without the protection of the Goddess?" I was shouting now, forgetting that I had sworn to myself that I would not reveal to my husband that I had uncovered his plans to replace the mark of the Mysteries with the wooden cross.

"How dare you lie to me, to make me think that you'd done all you could to keep her safe, when all the time you schemed to take away the one thing that would protect her.

"Listen to me, Gorlois. There is still time. We have time. But not if you keep up this mad obsession, and not if you leave me to wage this war." I looked at him, standing still and silent as he took in what I had just said to him.

My heart turned over. This was my husband, the father of my children. Despite everything, I loved him and wanted nothing more than to return to those easy days before we had travelled to Caer-Lundein, before I had dressed myself as a queen and danced with Uther in the presence of his sworn allies and courtiers. Before I had touched his skin and felt the taste of his lips upon my mouth.

Gorlois moved toward me, and I braced myself, expecting him to pull me to him, to force a kiss on me, to try to mend our quarrel in the flames of passion as had happened so many time before. But he did not.

"I'm sorry. I don't understand how you discovered what I'd asked Jago to do, but no matter, I did what I did to guard our daughter." His voice was quiet and resigned as he continued. "There is no going back this time. I must fight Uther, and it will be for the Fates to decide which one of us will be the victor.

"I had hoped to leave with your blessing and the memory of your kisses on my lips, but with or without your favour, my men will ride within the hour. And I ride with them."

At this, he turned and walked toward the door, pausing to give me one last look before closing it behind him as he went to join his men.

I said not a word as I watched from the window. I saw him put on his helm and mount his war-horse, taking his place in the vanguard behind his herald and standard bearers. I felt a touch upon my shoulder and knew without having to turn my head that Elaine had come noiselessly into the room. I took her hand and gripped it tight as, together, we watched Gorlois and the men of Cornwall ride out across the causeway to join Prince Urien and the soldiers from Orkney who waited, armoured and battle ready, on the shore.

With Erec now mounted in his customary place beside him, Gorlois looked back across the causeway. I saw him lift his hand to his brow, scanning the castle walls and shading his eyes from the sun, which was now low on the horizon. Perhaps he had hoped to see me and the children up on the ramparts, but if so, he would have been disappointed. Seeming to realise this, he gave up on his search and, raising his hand in farewell salute, wheeled his horse and rode hard away from Tintagel.

AND NOW THE DAYS PASSED swiftly. There was much to do to complete the arrangements for Morgause's departure and the day after Gorlois left I summoned Jago to my solar. I gave our steward very precise instructions about everything that I required my daughter and her companions to take with them. In addition to clothing, gifts for the Lords and Ladies of Orkney, and rugs, blankets, and other household items that would add to her comfort in the cold Northern lands, I also gave thought to more pressing needs.

I knew that it was highly unlikely that the *Llyr's Daughter* would have reached its destination by Solstice and I wanted to make sure that Morgause and her ladies would have what they needed to do honour to the Goddess. I instructed Jago to cut and prepare a supply of wood from the four sacred trees—Ash, Elder, Willow, and Oak— and to make sure it was stashed securely in a place where it would not get confused with more common kindling. Even on board the ship, Morgause need must ensure the Solstice fire was lit and the rituals attended to. If the steward was surprised at my orders, which were so different from those he had received but a short while ago from my husband, he gave no sign of it, simply nodding to show he understood before taking his leave with his usual courtesy.

I knew that Morgause was as yet too young to take a leading role in the Solstice rituals, but in time she would be called upon to do honour to the Goddess just as I had. My daughter was destined to be a Queen, and as such needed to be well versed in the sacred rites and duties that would become both her privilege and her responsibility. I was very conscious that even before I was sent to Avalon to receive instruction from Vivian I had spent years observing my mother as she led the worship of the Mysteries at my father's court. My daughter would not have that advantage.

Last year had been the first time she had been permitted to take even a minor role in the celebrations. She had relished the fact that she was allowed to stay up long after Morgan had been sent to bed, and she had loved being allowed to take small sips of sweet, spiced Cornish cider as we stood together on the battlements, watching the Solstice fires on the beach at Tintagel. But when the fires began to dwindle and the moon reached its zenith, I signalled to Avice to take my now sleepy daughter to her bed as Gorlois and I crossed the causeway to the shore. And there, as we had done every year since we had ruled Cornwall and Lyonesse, we took our part in the ancient rituals by which a Lady and her Lord pay homage to the Goddess and bring blessings on the land.

That was the last time Gorlois had agreed to participate in the Mysteries. At Samhain and at Yule last year his growing allegiance to the Risen god had caused him to refuse to take his part in the rituals, despite all of my pleading. I remembered how, in desperation, I had persuaded Elaine to take my place. As half-sisters, we were of similar colouring and build and in the dusky half-light of the winter bonfire, we were both sure that the people would not be able to tell the difference. On both occasions, I had kept out of the way, knowing that if anyone had seen me it would have exposed my deception and could even have called into question the sanctity and power of the rituals. Staying in my chamber with Morgan, I had entrusted Morgause to Avice and her ladies, who I'm sure would have done all they could to keep her safe and entertained—but do nothing to enlighten her about the deeper meaning of the bonfires, the sacrifices, and the dancing.

This was one of the problems I had wished to discuss with Vivian on that ill-fated afternoon at Caer-Lundein: the afternoon when she had taken up the scrying bowl and I had seen a vision of my husband's death, the afternoon when I had told her of Gorlois' growing disenchantment with the Mysteries, the afternoon when all of this began.

And now, because of Gorlois' war with Uther, Morgause was being sent from me, before I could prepare her for her duties and give her at least an elementary schooling in the arts of queen craft. The *Llyr's Daughter* was due to set sail when the tides turned with the new moon, and I determined that I would do what I could in the short time we had left to us to try to prepare my pleasure loving, scatter-brained, and sadly rather selfish eldest daughter for the disciplines and responsibilities that I knew would lay ahead.

I decided that I would need help in this undertaking if I was also to carry on initiating Morgan into the Mysteries. Both tasks required time, patience, tact, and perhaps most importantly, an understanding of the roles my daughters would be expected to undertake as women grown. I needed to enlist the assistance of another woman, someone gently born and raised in the old ways as I had been, and as I broke my fast in the Great Hall on the morning after Gorlois' departure I cast about my mind for someone I could trust.

I had always thought Tintagel quite small by the standards of my father's court or that of Uther's, but after Gorlois and his men had left the castle suddenly seemed a vast and empty place. With far fewer mouths to feed, the kitchen maids and pages were no longer to be seen scurrying hither and yon doing the bidding of Jago's cooks and cellarers, and the courtyard and practise butts were quiet, with only a few warriors left to take their daily turns at practice.

Those of us left behind had by unspoken consent begun to take our meals together, ostensibly to make life easier for the kitchen, but really because we sought comfort from the presence of others when we broke our fast each morning or sat down to sup together after sunset.

It was on the evening of the second day after Gorlois' departure that I found the solution I'd been seeking in a quite unexpected quarter. I had nearly finished eating when Ened and two other women came and sat themselves at my table and I greeted them politely. I did not know Ened's companions well; their husbands were both knights who owed their fealty first to Erec, the High Lord of Madron, and they had come but recently to Tintagel.

"And how are you, Igraine?" Ened smiled at me warmly enough, but her eyes were hard and cold and her tone seemed to me to be almost accusatory. "We never seem to see anything of you these days...you are always down at the harbour or closeted away with your daughters and your servant girl." She reached across for some bread, taking several hunks for herself before passing the basket to her companions.

"I was saying to Hild and Epona here only this afternoon that Tintagel feels like it has been deserted." This time there was no mistaking it. Her voice was hostile, and I now noticed that the two women sitting beside her were also looking at me with set expressions and anger in their eyes.

"Our men have gone to war on your account you know, Igraine," she hissed at me, leaning forward so her strong, heavy forehead was but inches from me. "It wouldn't hurt if you were to spend a little more time with those of us who face widowhood because of your wantonness."

"What?" her angry accusation had taken me completely by surprise. "I don't know what you are talking about, Ened. Gorlois has made his own choices, despite my counsel to seek peace with the Lady and the Pendragon. This quarrel is not of my making."

"But we all saw you dancing with Uther, in front of the whole court," said the woman sitting next to Ened. She was no longer young, with a narrow, lined face and a plait of long, greying hair that fell over her shoulder almost to her waist. She was thin, verging on scrawny, and dressed in clothes that, though well-cut and well-laundered, were old fashioned and had been darned at neckline and sleeve.

"Your husband had drunk himself into a stupor and you chose to flaunt yourself in front of the high-king. We all saw you." She turned to Ened and the other woman, who both nodded and moved even closer to me. "And because of you, my man has had to go to war. My sons have gone to war. And there is no one left to bless the fields and tend to them."

As she looked at me, I saw fear in her eyes and knew that, if I was not careful, the fear would soon turn to hatred. I was also quick to realise that the hostility that Ened, in her jealous stupidity, had been quick to lay before me might also be simmering within the breasts of others who were more subtle or more circumspect.

"Ened, why don't you introduce me to your friends? I recognise both of you, of course, but I would formally welcome you to our court," I smiled warmly, and beckoning to one of the pages, asked for a jug of wine to be brought for us.

Ened presented her companions; the scrawny woman in the darned gown was Lady Hild, wife of one of Erec's vassals, who hailed from a large farmstead on the edges of Heamoor. She had four sons, all of whom were full-grown and marching under Gorlois' banner. She also had a daughter, a girl of nearly ten years old, who had accompanied her to Tintagel.

The second woman was younger and not ill-favoured. Her hair was unusual, rich and golden, and she wore it in two long braids twisted round her head in a sort of crown. Her dark blue kirtle looked both new and lovingly made and it flattered her strong, somewhat angular frame.

This, I learned, was the Lady Epona. She was married to a wealthy man who had recently inherited lands on the border of Erec's territory, running from Tredarvah to Penzance on the coast and her story was an interesting one. She had been born a Saxon, her father one of Vortigern's warlords, and had been captured during the early years of Uther's wars. Growing up in the seaside hold-fast, she had been treated well and had grown to beauty. The young Brendan Tredarvah had fallen in love with her and, defying his father and mother, they had married. Banished by his family, they lived for several years in exile in Brittany, at the Court of King Budic. Here Brendan met Uther and his elder brother Aurelius, and some years later, returned to England with them to join the fight against Vortigern and the Saxon usurpers.

When his father died and peace was restored, Brendan and Epona made their way back to Tredarvah with their children, two young boys who I learned were now in Penzance with Brendan's mother, as Epona felt that the castle by the sea was a safer place for her children than the large, but poorly garrisoned stronghold on the edge of the moors.

"And what of your lands, Lady Epona? Do you still have men in Tredarvah to work the fields and manage your harvest or do you share Lady Hild's concerns?"

"Many of our men have ridden to war beneath the banners of Madron, Cornwall, and Lyonesse, but my lord agreed with Lord Madron that the levy would be reduced so our harvests would not suffer. Our fields will be worked, my lady, but my worry is that they will not bring forth fruit."

"And why is that, may I ask," said a forceful voice behind me. I turned and was pleased but a little surprised to see Bennath of Syllan. Her lovely face was slightly flushed, and I could smell sea-salt and the crisp chill of a sea breeze upon her cloak. I realised that I had not seen her since the morning of the day that Gorlois and his men had left the castle and wondered where she had been hiding.

She smiled uncertainly at me and curtsied slightly, as if to apologise for her intrusion, but I shifted along the bench to make room for her and gestured to the page to bring another cup.

I introduced Bennath to the others and once more, she put her question. "Why, pray, are you concerned that your fields will not bring forth fruit?"

Epona looked first at Hild and then at Ened, but neither of them appeared prepared to speak.

"They say the Lady of the Lake has placed a curse upon you. They say the Goddess is displeased and has taken away her favour." Epona spoke slowly, her voice low and her dark blue eyes looking steadily into mine. "They say that the lands of Cornwall and Lyonesse will be blighted if we do not turn away from you. My husband…he wouldn't listen. He is a man's man, Gorlois' man. They fought side by side for Uther, and Brendan says that he would follow your husband wherever he commanded.

"But I am a woman. I care not for battles, blood, and glory. I seek a peaceful harvest, the blessings of a full granary and the comfort of our crops safely gathered in.

"Have you brought down a curse upon us, Lady Igraine? Will the crops in the fields wither and die and our children all go hungry because of you?"

Once again, I saw the fear in her eyes, and I understood it. Had I not pleaded with Gorlois to swallow his pride and make peace, to allow his people the time to tend their fields, raise their crops and nurture their families? I understood exactly why these women were looking at me as if I was the harbinger of disaster. And I did not know what to say to them.

"What a load of craven nonsense. Igraine is not cursed, Cornwall is not cursed. You have been listening to scandal-mongers and tittle-tattle and you should be ashamed." At the last word, Bennath slammed her wine cup down on the table and turned to look challengingly at each woman in turn.

Ened refused to meet her eyes and moved closer to Hild, who cowered a little at the other woman's words. Only Epona was willing to face Bennath's anger and return her gaze.

"Yes, we have all heard that the Lady of the Lake has placed a curse upon Cornwall," Bennath said. "She encourages the Welsh Lords to slaughter our allies and will do everything she can to turn our people against us. But remember, the Lady is not the Goddess."

"What do you mean by that Bennath?" I asked. "Surely the Lady is the Goddesses, representative and the mouthpiece of her Mysteries." I had been raised, as I'm sure all the women seated round the table had been raised, to view Vivian as the living embodiment of the Goddess, to do her bidding unquestioningly and to always honour her with our loyalty.

Bennath shook her head. "Let me tell you where I have been and what has passed since our men left us. When Lowen told me he was going to ride with Gorlois rather than return home to Syllan, I supported him and told him he was right to honour his vows of loyalty to Gorlois and the Cornish duchy.

"But I knew that our lands had been leaderless for too long, and I determined to return. We rule our lands in the old way, Lowen and I, and if the Lord is not there, the Lady will take his place and govern the people in the name of the Goddess to ensure the peace and prosperity of the land.

"So, when Lowen and his men rode east, I set out to the west, toward Syllan and Lyonesse. I rode for hours without stopping, driving my horse onward through the night, and by daybreak, I had reached Treliggan." Bennath paused and took a sip of her wine before resuming her tale.

"By this time, I was exhausted...I ached all over and was fairly sure that my horse felt the same; she'd stumbled twice as we made our way across the clifftop. I dismounted and led her to the edge of the headland, to the House of the Goddess where I planned to seek shelter. Do you know the place I'm talking about, Igraine?"

I nodded. In fact, there are many such Houses, home to wise women and healers, under the leadership of a priestess who must have served her time on the Lake Isle. Some of them are large, and grand, with a household of servants and extensive grounds, but the House of the Goddess on the Treliggan headland is small and simple, occupied by only a handful of women, who provide care and comfort to the remote homesteads and farms scattered around the bay.

Bennath continued. "I took my horse into the paddock and set her free to graze with the other animals and made my way over to the House to see if I could find someone to give me food and water. I was in luck. Although it was only just after sunrise, the House was already awake and I recognised one of the women who were already at work in the kitchen garden."

Bennath said that she had been welcomed warmly and after she had broken her fast, was taken to the solar to speak with the leader of the Treliggan household.

"As you may remember, her name is Yseult," Bennath told us, "and I know her well. Like me she is Syllan-born and I was pleased to see her. She poured me a glass of spiced wine, and begged me to keep her company for a while. I could see she was eager for news, and I wished to give my horse time to rest herself before we rode onward, and so I was more than happy to oblige her.

"She had heard of Gorlois' quarrel with Uther and wished to know how many of the men of Cornwall and Lyonesse had answered the call to follow the war duke. I told her that hundreds had answered the call, including my husband. I explained that was why I was making my way back to Syllan, to take my rightful place as ruler, and to keep the land peaceful and the fields fruitful until my lord and I are reunited. She nodded when I said this, but didn't comment; instead she told me that she had lately had news from Avalon and knew of the Lady's curse on all those who fail to bow the knee to The Pendragon."

"And yet she helped you?" I asked. "Even though she knew that you and your household are loyal to Gorlois and have taken arms against Uther?"

"Yes. She helped me. And not only did she help me, but she spoke words of great foresight and wisdom, and told me to return to you and share them."

By now, we had all turned toward Bennath and no one, not even Epona, seemed to have any desire to interrupt her.

"Yseult is a priestess and a seer. She is old now and has seen more summers even than the Lady. There is no other to equal her skill at reading the signs and portents in the stars or the scrying bowl. Many times she has been granted the gift of prophecy. With her gifts, she could have been the leader of one of the larger Houses, living a life of great comfort, but she has chosen to live away from the world on the barren headland of Trevose."

At this, I nodded, remembering the stories I had heard of Yseult, who I now recalled was known by many as "the Lady of Treliggan." This was an affectionate and completely unofficial title, and one which I was sure angered Vivian. The Lady of the Lake, I felt certain, wished to be perceived by all as the unrivalled mouthpiece of the Goddess. Yseult had never chosen to take part in high politics, contenting herself with healing, meditation, and the affairs of her own community, but despite this, her reputation had grown, particularly amongst the people of Cornwall and Lyonesse who loved and respected her with an almost territorial pride.

Bennath continued with her story. "When I told Yseult of my intention to return to Syllan and govern my people, she nodded, as if in agreement, but then she asked me, 'And do others do as you do, Bennath?' I wasn't sure what she meant, and my confusion must have shown on my face, for next time she spoke, she left me in no doubt.

"'Do other women do as you do, Bennath?' she asked me, quietly. "Have they accepted their responsibility to the land, to the woods and fields, to the homes and hearths?

"'The Goddess has given this land to us in trust, and expects us to care for it; it is our duty to see it is fruitful.'" At this, she got up from her chair and walked to the window that looked out onto the paddock and gestured for me to join her. Outside, I could see my horse peacefully grazing, side by side with a handsome chestnut cob.

She pointed at them saying, "Our horses work together, mare and stallion, to plough our fields and carry our burdens. Both are equal in the sight of the Goddess. And so should it be for us. As Man and Woman, we were created to cherish the land the Goddess has given us and, in return, to take our livelihood from it. The earth brings forth all that we require, but we needs must give of our own labours in equal part if we are to truly earn our right to the enjoyment of her blessings." She took my hand in hers and turned me to face her and her eyes just seemed to bore into me. She said, 'The Goddess has spoken to me, Bennath, and I know these words to be true. She does not want her land to lie fallow, her fields untended and her crops strangled by weeds.'"

Bennath paused and I pushed her wine cup toward her. She took another sip and then continued.

"I wasn't sure if I really understood what she was saying to me, so I asked her if she meant that the Goddess doesn't want our men to follow Gorlois. Was she saying that Vivian is right? Did she mean that the curse of the Goddess will fall on all of us who refuse to bow the knee? But she smiled gently and shook her head."

"'No child,' she said, 'The Goddess has granted me many visions and has chosen to share much with me, but she does not reveal everything, and we, her children, must have faith in her wisdom. But I know that the war between Uther and Gorlois is but one part of a larger tapestry, one which I cannot see in its entirety, but one it is certain the Goddess is weaving.'

"'But what of the Lady?' I asked her. 'What of the curse she has laid upon all who refuse to follow Uther?'

"'The Lady Vivian serves the Goddess, just as I do, and I will say nought against her,' she replied. 'You must remember child that we are here to do the will of the Goddess, not the other way round. We all should seek to walk the path that She has prepared for us, and should not question the deeds of others, if done honestly in her name, even if they do not make sense to us. But believe me, Bennath, this war between Gorlois and Uther is part of a wider plan, a greater destiny—so how can anyone taking part in a plan that has been willed by the Goddess be cursed by the Goddess?

"'I cannot see what will happen as a result of this conflict, but I know what must come to pass for the decrees of the fates to be fulfilled. Uther and Gorlois must go to war, and only one of them will survive. The Goddess has shown me that we will not have peace in the land until then.'"

As she said this, I heard Ened tut under her breath. Her lips were pursed and she clearly did not much like the tale Bennath was telling, but as I quickly scanned the faces of the other women, I was pleased to see that Epona and Hild were both looking at Bennath with open, eager faces, and hanging on her every word.

"And then Yseult smiled at me," said Bennath. "She said that the Goddess had told her that She does not want Her fields to lie untended and her harvests ungathered. She said that was why the Goddess had guided my steps to the House of Treliggan and that my job is to be Her messenger, and to take her words to the women of Cornwall and Lyonesse.

Yseult told me that I must implore the women to return to their Halls, their farmsteads, and houses. To take up the tools their men have cast aside for weapons and armour, and to work on the land together. She said that this is the old way, and it is the right way. She said I must tell them that the rituals must be observed. The fires must burn at Solstice and the ancient sacrifices must be offered. She said that if they do this, the land will be fruitful and that this is the will of the Goddess."

Bennath finished speaking and reached for a piece of bread. For a moment, there was silence as each one of us took time to consider the implications of what she had told us.

I knew that I could turn Bennath's most welcome words to my advantage, and so before either Epona or Hild could speak, I rose to my feet.

"Well, ladies, it would seem that there is much for us to do. The Goddess wishes to see our lands fruitful, and I for one am happy to do her bidding."

I looked down at the four seated women. Ened did not meet my eyes. She had always been lazy, and I'm sure she dreaded the idea of spending her days doing anything other than gossiping in her solar and toying with her embroidery. The other three, however, were made of sterner stuff.

"There is much to do, here at Tintagel and across Cornwall and Lyonesse. We must school our girls and young women, teach them field craft and husbandry, and ensure that in every farm and in every castle the rituals are observed and the Goddess honoured.

"Bennath, we will need to school our girls and young maidens if they are to take on this task. Are you willing to assist me?"

"Willingly, my lady," replied Bennath, who had risen and now stood by my side.

"And I, too, would help," said the Lady Epona, whilst Hild nodded slowly, her eyes now gleaming determinedly in her gaunt, unlovely face.

And so, we organised. Within two days, Bennath and I had brought all the women of the castle and the surrounding houses together. I enlisted the help of Jago, our steward. There was no one who knew more of farmcraft and land management and soon he, Epona, and a surprisingly enthusiastic Hild could be found working together in the Great Hall, planning their campaign.

I even found work for Ened, who refused to get involved in anything that might get her hands dirty. She grudgingly agreed to work alongside Elaine, teaching the young women of the castle in the rites and rituals of the Goddess, viewing this as a task that she could perform without demeaning herself. Despite the fact that I despised her for her ridiculous snobbery, I was also grateful to her, as I could now ensure that Morgause would get the instruction she so badly needed. This also enabled me to divide my time between making detailed plans for my daughter's departure and to help Bennath, who we had agreed would now ride farther afield, taking the words of the Lady of Treliggan to strongholds and farmsteads across Cornwall and Lyonesse. I also devoted at least two hours every day to Morgan and her increasing mastery of the Mysteries.

Time passed quickly. On the morning of the third day, Bennath set out with a small party, planning to ride across Bodmin and down toward Fowey. If all went well, she would find help in the larger of the Houses of the Goddess, who could then send word out to the western promontories and the Isles of Syllan and Lyonesse. We had agreed that she would then ride east to Polperro and Saltash, before heading North through the Tamar Valley, and the long ride back across the moors to Tintagel, speaking to all of the Houses of the words of Yseult the seer and preparing the women of Cornwall to do their duty by the land.

AND SO, THE DAYS PASSED. Morgause and Morgan saw very little of each other. My elder daughter spent much of her time with the older girls and young women, learning from Ened and Elaine about the Mysteries and the rites and rituals they would be called upon to lead. I was reassured to know that she would be prepared for what would come at Solstice and the role that she, as my daughter and a future Queen in her own right, would be called upon to perform.

On the afternoon of the last day before Morgause was due to set sail, she and I made our way along the causeway to the harbour to where the *Llyr's Daughter* was moored. The sky was grey and cloudy and threatened rain. The wind whipped the waves up onto the causeway and we pulled our cloaks tightly around us as we walked in single file through salty puddles toward the now fully loaded vessel.

The quayside was crowded. I spotted Jago deep in conversation with the tall, broad-shouldered man I knew to be the ship's captain, Clem Trevenna. They were overseeing the loading of the last few bales and a great barrel of Tintagel barley-ale which I knew Jago had been quite loathe to part with. Despite all our efforts, I knew that the Tintagel steward still doubted that the women of the castle would have the skills and determination to work the land and grow the crops he would need to harvest in the autumn if he was to replenish his supplies and provision us for winter.

Making a mental note to take him with me next time I rode out to inspect our fields and orchards, I simply smiled at Jago and indicated that I wished to accompany my daughter on board.

I had become a regular visitor to the *Llyr's Daughter* and walked confidently to the small cabin I had fitted out for the use of Morgause and her guardian Avice. I saw with pleasure that the unicorn tapestry that my daughter had always loved had been successfully cut down to size and neatened by a hand much more adept than my own; I suspected that Elaine had been at work here. It was now hanging on the side wall and I hoped that Morgause would look upon it before she went to sleep and be comforted by its warm and shabby familiarity, which gave this small space a sense of both luxury and ease. The two tiny beds, tucked away in what could only be described as small, narrow cupboards to the left and right of the door, had been made up with linen sheets fragranced with dried herbs from the castle gardens and topped with soft woollen blankets which I had dyed a delicate crimson using the roots of the local wild madder which grew so abundantly in the woods and hedges around Tintagel.

I pulled Morgause gently into the cabin; she had been hanging back, uncharacteristically silent. I think it was only just dawning on her that the result of all of the plans and preparations was about to be realised and that she soon would be on a voyage that would take her far away from nearly everyone and everything that she had ever known. At first, she stood beside me, one small hand brushing against my skirts, but then I watched delightedly as she ran across to the unicorn and stroked his soft foam-white nose.

"Is this really for me, Mama? Have you really given me your unicorn?" Her eyes were wide and bright in her small, beautiful face, and I moved toward her and knelt down on the floor, pulling her into my arms and cuddling her on my lap.

"Yes, sweetling. It is yours for always, but I'm sure you will have many finer tapestries when you are a queen in the Orkneys."

She looked at me, a small smile beginning to form on her lips. "And will I have jewels and pretty dresses like you, Mama? And be a truly great lady?"

"You shall be a great queen, Morgause. I have heard that King Lot is a kind man, and I am sure he will want to make you happy and comfortable. But you know, my darling, there is much more to being a good queen than sparkling jewels and fine dresses." She looked at me uncertainly, but I pressed on. I knew that I would not have much more time with her, and I was still very aware that my pretty but rather spoilt oldest child still had a lot to learn and, unlike myself, would not have the advantages of an education on Avalon.

I leaned back against the cabin wall and moved Morgause so she sat astride my lap, her face almost level with my own.

"A good queen must think of the needs of her people. Remember what Ened has been teaching you. As queen, you are the hand-maid of the Goddess and must do everything you can to care and protect the land she has chosen you to rule over. What do you think that means little one?"

She gave a pout and a small shrug as she prepared to recite her lesson. Speaking in a fast sing-song, she began to declaim by rote the words the Lady of Madron had taught her. "Ened says that 'a-great-Queen-must-make-sure-the-wells-are-sweet-and-the-granaries-full-that-the-orchards-bear-fruit-and-the-fields-are-fertile-that-the-hearths-are-warm-and-the-roads-are-safe-for-travellers,'" she paused for breath.

"'She-must-ensure-the-Mysteries-are-observed-and-the-sacrifices-offered-with-piety-and-obedience-so-that-the-earth-bears-fruit-and-the-Goddess-is-honoured-and-all-is-safe-and-well-within-the-land.'" She gave a great, panting sigh as she finished her declamation, shrugged her shoulders and smiled at me, looking for a word of praise for a lesson so well learned.

"That's very good, sweetling. But do you understand what that really means?"

"Ened said I must wear the green gown and lead the sacrifice at Solstice. That means I'm the most 'portant one doesn't it?" Morgause squirmed delightedly in my lap.

"Well, yes, you will one day be a queen, but that doesn't mean you should forget about the people and the lands that the Goddess has given you to rule." I reached out and lifted my daughter's face toward me, holding her chin gently, but firmly between my forefinger and thumb.

"As queen you must not eat your fill if your people go hungry. You must not hide away in fear when your lands are threatened but must show courage and do all you can to keep your people safe." I saw her eyes widen and pulled her close to me, smelling the sweet, fresh scent of her newly washed hair and whispering in her ear as I rocked her gently. "It is not easy being a queen, my darling, but I know that you are my beautiful daughter and I know that you will be brave."

"Can you not come with me, Mama?" Morgause whispered, her voice heavy with un-shed tears.

"I cannot come this time, my darling, for I have the people of Cornwall and Lyonesse to take care of, and I must keep Tintagel safe whilst your father is away."

I stroked her hair and spoke again, making promises I wanted to believe in, but which a sense of deep foreboding told me I would never be able to keep. "But I will come soon, my love, I will come next summer, before the blossom turns to fruit on the trees in Orkney."

"Before the blossom turns to fruit," she repeated, and to calm her further, I helped her to her feet and showed her round the cabin, revealing the little treats and trinkets I had stored away for her to help make the parting easier for both of us to bear.

As she was carefully re-packing the beads and baubles I had given her from my own jewel chest, there was a knock on the cabin door and, after I had called to bid whoever it was to enter, the door opened to reveal Elaine and Avice.

"Look at the unicorn, Avice; isn't he lovely?" shouted Morgause as she hurled herself toward her beloved nursemaid, catching her hand and dragging her toward the tapestry.

"You have improved it, I think," I said quietly to Elaine. When she had cut the tapestry to fit the much smaller wall of Morgause's cabin, I noticed that my half-sister had not just neatened up the edges but had added in the animal's missing fourth leg that I had been just too lazy to complete. Elaine smiled at me and looked around the cabin with quiet satisfaction.

"We should be getting back to the castle, my lady. There is much to do before nightfall, and those who set sail on the morrow have an early start ahead of them." Elaine moved toward the door and held it open for me to pass though, followed by Morgause and Avice, who I could see was well pleased with the comfortable quarters she was to share with her charge on the long voyage North.

As I walked out on deck, I was pleased to see that the weather had changed for the better. The sky had shifted from dismal grey to a soft, pale blue and the dark clouds that had seemed to promise an unpleasant downpour had moved eastward overland, where I had no doubt the rainfall would be welcomed by the women I had sent out to husband the fields.

There was a small group of people huddled together around the gangplank. I recognised Urien, Prince of Rheged and brother to King Lot, and behind him the Norwegian boy Einar, who was his page and a ward at Orkney's court. Einar was still very young, possibly not having seen more than eleven or twelve summers, but he was gazing at my daughter with a look of frank admiration and she, little minx that she was, was very clearly aware of the fact. I watched with a mixture of annoyance and amusement as she smoothed down her curls and looked at the young lad under long dark lashes until he blushed and moved hurriedly down the gangplank to the harbour wall below.

Urien turned toward me and bowed. "Weel mit mah Lady, it seems th' goddess has sent us guid weaither after aw."

"Indeed she has, my lord," I responded, smiling at the tall, dignified Scotsman who I had learned to both trust and respect in the short time I had known him. "Let us hope that the seas remain calm and the winds kind for my daughter's journey to your brother's court."

When Gorlois and Erec had ridden to war, Urien had remained behind with a small band of warriors, most of whom he pledged to send on the *Llyr's Daughter* to act as a bodyguard and protection for Morgause and her ladies. I knew that he and his remaining cohort of hand-picked soldiers were eager to join my husband on the battle lines and planned to break camp at daybreak.

Urien offered me his arm and we walked together down the gangplank. As I was about to move away from the ship, I noticed Jago, still deep in conversation with the ship's captain. "Jago," I called to him, beckoning for him to come closer. He did so, the other man following a little uncertainly behind him.

"Yes, my lady?"

"Have all the preparations for the Solstice been carried out as I instructed?"

Jago nodded and gestured toward his companion.

"This y'er is the Cap'n, my lady; he'll tell ye that 'tis all prepared, is it not Clem…?" Jago looked beseechingly at the ship's captain; I was fairly certain he was hoping that his earlier attempt to prevent the *Llyr's Daughter* from sailing without the protection of the Goddess would go unmentioned.

The other man nodded and, making me a reverential bow, proceeded to tell me in some detail, and with great pride, exactly how the Solstice would be celebrated. I was soon satisfied that everything that would be needed had been taken on board, including a certain small wooden chest that I had asked to be entrusted to his keeping. I also had a very particular request to make of him, and was pleased when, after a short moment of reflection, he agreed to my entreaty. I thanked him and, after I had made sure that all of my party had safely reached the harbour, set off to walk back along the causeway with Urien. Elaine and Avice walked a few steps behind us, followed by Morgause and Einar, who seemed to have overcome his embarrassment and was talking animatedly.

That night I slept little. Morgause had asked to spend her last night in Tintagel with me and she snuggled down to sleep happily, her small hand held trustingly in mine. For what seemed like hours, I lay beside her, watching the passing of the moon and the brightening of the stars and wondering how I could bear to send my precious girl away from me.

All night my thoughts chased each other around my mind. I knew that it was not safe for Morgause to remain in Tintagel, that she would be much safer in the remote court of our ally King Lot, who I was sure could be depended upon to cherish my daughter, not just because of her sweet face and tender ways, but because of the royal blood that flowed within her veins.

But she was my baby, my first child. I had grown large with her and delivered her here in this castle, had suckled her and watched her take her first steps in the orchard within these walls. How could I even consider parting from her?

And then I remembered the very words I had heard Morgause repeat by rote in her childish voice that very afternoon. "A queen must ensure the Mysteries are observed and the sacrifices offered with piety and obedience, so that the earth bears fruit and the Goddess is honoured and all is safe and well within the land."

This, then, was to be one of the sacrifices demanded of me. That I give up my child and send her on her way to a land of strangers, in a small boat on a large and storm-tossed sea. But even as I thought those words, a peace came upon me and I slept. And in my sleep, I dreamed.

I saw Morgause sitting in splendour on a wooden throne, and in my dream, she was a woman grown. All the early promises of beauty had been most splendidly fulfilled: her skin was clear and fair and her hair fell in rich tawny curls about her shoulders. She was not alone. Behind her stood a tall and upright figure, some years older than my radiant daughter, but still handsome and commanding in appearance. This must be the King of Orkney, Lot himself, I thought, and as if to confirm my supposition, he put his arm around her, leaving his hand to rest lightly on her shoulder. She turned and smiled at him and then, as if responding to a sound I could not hear, they both looked toward an open doorway through which walked five figures. Five boys, all good to look upon, all hearty and well-made.

This then, was the reason for my sacrifice; this was the future, my sleeping self decided. I must let my daughter go so that she, too, can find happiness in her marriage and bear children of her own.

As my slumbering mind began to sink toward the hope of welcome, dreamless sleep, the five children walked toward the throne and took their places around the king and queen. Two of them stood to the right of the throne. They were red-headed and strongly built and when they raised their faces, I saw they had their father's eyes of bright sea-green. Another pair took up their places to the left of their mother. Although they, too, were redheads, unlike their brothers their hair did not flame within the torchlight, but glowed richly like their mother's. Like her they were of a slender and graceful build and the eyes that stared at me from their small, untroubled faces were of the warmest, softest brown.

And then the fifth child raised his head and stared at me. Smaller than the other boys, his hair was black as the sky at midnight and the eyes that bored into mine were the mocking, implacable, all-seeing flame-blue eyes of Vivian, Lady of the Lake.

My screams woke Morgause and we spent the last watches of the night cuddled together, my daughter returning to her slumbers soon enough, whilst I, fearful by now of dreams, forced myself to remain awake.

THE FIRST FEW HOURS OF the next day were all hustle and noise as what seemed like half of Tintagel made its way across the causeway to take their leave of Morgause and her household.

I had set out before sunrise with my daughters and Elaine. None of us had any appetite for breaking our fast and we reached the castle gates before the rest of the household was ready to leave the tables in the Great Hall.

As we passed out toward the causeway, I heard the sound of running footsteps and turned to see Bennath of Syllan racing toward us. Jago had told me that she had returned to Tintagel very late last night and I was surprised to see her up so early. She was carrying a leather pouch and was out of breath, the colour high on her usually pale face.

"I'm sorry, my lady, I hope you don't mind, but I thought you might be thankful for a little company this morning." She spoke quietly and her voice was gentle, but she looked at me uncertainly when she saw how close I was standing to Elaine. Like many of the women in Tintagel, she would have heard the tales of Elaine's origins and known her to be one of my father's by-blows, but few, if any, knew just how close my half-sister was to me or how much I depended on her.

"I thank you, Bennath. The thought was kind, but I am not alone, see..." I gestured toward Elaine, who had now moved a few yards away, my children's hands in hers. "I have my daughters and my half-sister to accompany me."

Bennath's face fell and I could see she felt both foolish and rebuffed. My heart warmed toward this open-hearted woman from the far-off Isles of Syllan and I knew that I didn't want to cause her hurt.

Impulsively, I reached out and took her hand. "Truly, I'm grateful to you for your thoughtfulness. Come, please join us, we shall walk to the harbour together and get Morgause on board before the rest of the castle is properly awake."

I caught Elaine's eye, she smiled at me and nodded and together the five of us walked silently, but companionably, toward the ship.

Within the hour, we had settled Morgause in her cabin. Morgan had been very quiet as we walked along the causeway and, uncharacteristically, she stayed close to her sister and even on one or two occasions reached out to take her hand. My eldest daughter had cried a little as we kissed her and made our final goodbyes, but fortunately Avice chose this moment to arrive with the kitten in its basket and we took advantage of the distraction to remove ourselves.

The jetty was full of Tintagel folk, saying farewell to the sons and daughters who would be travelling to the Northern Isles as part of my daughter's tiny household. I saw Avice's father, one of the older men who had remained at Tintagel as part of its defending garrison, comforting his wife. They were both crying as their daughter rushed out on deck to wave a final goodbye. Like me, they had no idea when, if ever, they would be reunited with their daughter.

Urien arrived with the fifteen men he had sent to guard the *Llyr's Daughter*. They marched on board, followed by young Einar who was also being sent back to King Lot's court. He was a valuable ward and, in any case, too young to fight in battle against the Pendragon.

I could see that Morgan was getting disturbed by the noise and bustle of the harbour and so, not wanting to return to the castle until we had seen the ship set sail, we walked inland, up onto the headland, where we could look far out to sea, and keep watch on the sails of the ship until they disappeared over the horizon. Elaine and Bennath accompanied us and when we had settled ourselves comfortably on the grass, Bennath opened her pouch and took out freshly baked rolls, fruit, and a flask of wine.

"I knew you had not broken your fast my lady," she explained, and indeed, by this time, the sun was quite high in the sky and all of us suddenly discovered we were hungry.

As we ate our simple meal, we watched the ship make ready. One by one, the ropes were cast off, the anchor weighed and the sails unfurled to catch the early morning breeze. Down in the galley, I knew that the men of Orkney must have taken their places at the oars, for they dipped and swooped into the waves, driving the great ship forward as with great cheers and shouts from the crowd assembled on the Harbour arm, the *Llyr's Daughter* set off to sea carrying my first born, my darling, my Morgause, so very, very far away from me.

I turned to my younger daughter, lifting her into my lap and holding her close. For a few seconds she snuggled into me, wishing, I soon realised, to give me comfort, rather than because she needed it herself. After a short while she wriggled free from my arms and went to stand a little way away from me, her eyes fixed on the horizon. I was crying unashamedly and behind me Elaine and Bennath had placed their hands on my shoulders, comforting me with their love and understanding.

I could not take my eyes away from the ship as she moved away from Tintagel, getting smaller and smaller, the white sails soon shrinking to the size of a cloud, a seagull, a tiny dot…and then they were not there at all.

Pushing up from the grass, I got to my feet and turned away from the sea toward the others, trying to put a brave face on my grief. "It won't be long before I see my girl again…maybe next summer, when all of this is over? What do you think? Shall we all travel northward together?" Bennath said nothing, but reached for my hand and squeezed it, reassuringly.

I looked toward Elaine and Morgan. They were staring out to sea, their eyes vacant, their expression fixed.

"No, my lady," said Elaine in a strange, hollow voice. "You shall not travel northward and Morgause will not return to Cornish soil." She turned to face me, her empty eyes staring deep into mine, her mouth twisted into a strange parody of a smile as she spat out her next words.

"You will never hold your daughter in your arms again."

And at that, she crumpled, falling to the ground, dragging the silent and senseless Morgan down onto the grass beside her.

Chapter Ten

Elaine regained consciousness quickly with no memory of what had just taken place, but it took some time before Morgan came back to us. I sat beside my daughter, holding her small hands in mine and waiting for the colour to return to her cold, pale face. I knew what must have happened. Morgan had tried to harness the ocean itself as her scrying bowl, and the magnitude of the forces she had unleashed had been too much for her still-untrained mind to master.

I had worked hard with her, trying to pass on to her in a matter of days the wisdom it had taken me years to acquire and she had responded eagerly, desperate to learn everything Elaine and I could teach her. But there are some things that can only be learned by experience—and as my clever, independent and slightly arrogant younger daughter had just discovered to her cost, one of these is an understanding of your own personal limits and span of control.

Even an adept of Vivian's stature would have thought twice before casting her mind out, alone and unsupported, upon the vast depths of the ocean. To be safe, such a ritual would take much planning, calling upon the support of others well-tutored in harnessing the magics and able to channel the power the ceremony would unleash. Morgan had clearly managed to direct Elaine's mind to join with her, so she had not been entirely unsupported, but my half-sister, experienced though she was, had not been prepared for Morgan's meddling and would not have been able to do much to protect herself.

During my time on Avalon, I had once been part of such a scrying, and even though the ritual had been well-planned and twelve of us had participated, it had left me weak and unsettled for many hours.

I had no idea how long it might take Morgan to recover and was beginning to think that it might be sensible to carry her back to Tintagel when her eyes opened and she sat up, gently but insistently removing her hands from mine, then turning to be violently sick on the grass at the edge of the cliff.

"That was disgusting. I'm sorry, Mother." Morgan got to her feet, moving away from the cliff edge to stand in front of me with an unexpected look of contrition on her still pale face.

"What were you trying to do, Morgan? That was very foolish indeed." My concern for her made me angry and I took her firmly by the shoulders, thinking to shake some sense into her. "You could have been really hurt. And how dare you make use of Elaine like that?"

"But I didn't do anything. It just happened." Small tears were beginning to form at the corners of her eyes and her lip began to tremble. "I don't like it, Mother. Why did it do that? I just wanted to know when we would see Morgause again and it just happened." This disconcerted me. Morgan had always been a most resilient child, not given to hysterics and never, unlike her more emotional and manipulative sister, the sort of girl who would use tears to avoid dealing with the consequences of her actions. Rather than shaking her, I pulled her gently toward me, cradling her in my arms as she sobbed, stroking her hair and rocking her until, within a very short time, her crying ceased, and she regained her composure.

As I held her, I looked toward Elaine and Bennath who were sitting a few feet away. They were talking quietly; I guessed that Bennath was telling Elaine about what had just taken place. I hoped that my half-sister would not be too distressed when she learned the truth about what had just happened and the prophecy she had made.

I was certain that she had not been a willing participant in Morgan's foolhardy experiments, but this was the second time I had witnessed her in thrall to my daughter's magics, and I was concerned that she seemed to be unable to protect herself. I had been standing just as close to Morgan as Elaine had been, but I had felt no commanding force pulling at my mind, subjecting me to its will and compelling me into the deep trance that Bennath and I had witnessed. If what Morgan said was true, and she had not willingly invoked the scrying, then why was it Elaine's consciousness that her mind instinctively melded with, rather than mine?

The events of this morning had raised some very worrying questions, not least of which was how to progress with Morgan's training. My daughter appeared to have emerged unscathed from what could have been a very damaging experience, but next time she might not be so lucky. I wanted some time to think before I discussed any of my concerns, and I was not really sure who I wanted to discuss them with.

It was true that I had warmed toward Bennath, but I hardly knew her, and besides, she would not be staying long in Tintagel. I knew from my conversation with Jago that it had only been by chance that she had arrived just before Morgause' s departure. She had been despatched to bring news and messages from some of the Great Houses she had visited and would stay with us only until I had time to answer them. Was it really fair to burden her with my worries and concerns when she already had so much to occupy her? And as for Elaine, my half-sister, whom I loved and had come to depend on, how could I voice my worries to her when she now loomed so large within them?

I decided that now was not the time to discuss these concerns and instead opted for practical action and, calling Bennath and Elaine to me, we returned to Tintagel, Morgan walking steadfastly beside me, looking tired and more than a little drained, but refusing all offers of assistance.

As soon as we reached the castle, I took Morgan to my solar, instructing Elaine to fetch a sleeping draught from the kitchens.

Despite her protestations that she did not want to go to bed, Morgan's pale, drawn face and eyes still red from crying told a different story. By the time the sleeping draught arrived I had dressed her in her night shift and tucked her up in the small truckle bed that stood in the corner of the room, beside the fireplace. She did not take much persuading to drink the warm milk flavoured with honey and soothing herbs, and soon began to yawn. As she fell asleep, I covered her with a soft woollen blanket and watched her face smooth into the calm tranquillity of what I hoped would be a dreamless slumber.

Elaine was still there, standing quietly just inside the doorway in case I had need of her. But I was not ready for the conversation she clearly hoped to initiate. I needed more time to reflect on the events of the morning and to consider what they might mean before embarking on any discussion of them; so, rather than gesturing for her to join me, I walked to the doorway and asked her to find Bennath and bring her to me. I could tell that she was both surprised and unhappy at being dismissed. "The lady of Syllan has much of import to discuss and needs to be on her way before the morrow," I reminded her.

She moved toward the doorway, then turned to ask, "Would you like me to watch over Morgan so you can talk without interruption?"

"Do you think that would be a good idea, Elaine?" I responded, looking swiftly from my half-sister to the sleeping child tucked up so innocently in the small truckle bed.

It was true that Morgan had been exhausted by her experience and I had put her to bed as any good mother would if she was mindful of the care and comfort of her child. But if I was being completely honest with myself, I had been very disturbed by the powers I had seen channelled through my daughter, and I knew that, for the time being, she was safer fast asleep.

I also knew that, without realising it, I had come to a decision. I was not going to leave Morgan alone with Elaine. If Elaine was unable to resist whatever magics my daughter was experimenting with, who knows what dangers they both could be exposed to, and I could not take that risk.

Looking at her closely as she considered my question, I saw what looked like fear awaken in my half-sister's eyes. Perhaps she was also worried about what had happened that morning and her seeming inability to resist Morgan's mind control. I reached out and gently touched her cheek. "You've had a tiring morning. After you have found Bennath and given her my message, why don't you try to get some rest?"

She gave me a small, rather hesitant smile and then nodded. "Thank you. That is very kind. I do feel unsettled." She left the room, and I moved toward the window, gazing northward across the vast expanse of rolling, white-topped waves, wondering how Morgause was faring on the *Llyr's Daughter* and trying to prepare myself for whatever news Bennath of Syllan was going to bring me.

IT WAS NOT LONG BEFORE Bennath entered the room quietly and alone, closing the door behind her. She looked toward the truckle bed where Morgan was sleeping soundly and stood for a moment, uncertainly, as if not sure where I wanted her to go. Putting my finger to my lips, I gestured toward the table beneath the window, at the farthest end of the room. Moving the heavy chairs with caution to minimise the noise, we took our seats.

"How is she?" Bennath nodded toward the bed.

"Sleeping soundly. She'll be fine when she wakes up."

Bennath was still looking in my daughter's direction. "I hope you don't mind me saying so, Lady Igraine, but your daughter is…most unusual…"

I said nothing.

"I've never known a girl so young have so much power. To be frank with you, I found it quite frightening."

"That surprises me, Bennath," I said, speaking lightly and trying to force a smile. "I thought you to be quite fearless," I had seen her outdo all comers at the archery butts and knew her to be completely at home in full armour, mounted astride a warhorse. I had not expected her to be as unsettled as I was by my daughter's recent exploits.

"My mother always said that only the very stupid and those who care no more for living are truly fearless. I was taught to fear the Goddess and respect her power." Bennath looked at me a little uncertainly. I nodded, indicating that I was happy for her to continue. "Your daughter has been given great gifts, but, forgive me, my lady, I do not think she knows how to manage and control them.

"What I saw this morning…that voice that spoke through your servant girl…it was a dreadful power. Not the voice of the good Goddess, but something darker. Something terrifying." I considered for a moment, a little unsettled by the fact the conversation had moved so swiftly into territory I was not sure I was ready to explore.

"Oh come now, Bennath, you exaggerate. Surely those of us who know the Mysteries have all had strange experiences, particularly when our minds were young and relatively untrained. But enough of this. My daughter is asleep, and all is well…Now, I want to hear about what you have been doing." As I spoke, I poured two cups of spiced wine and passed one to Bennath, making it clear that the subject had been changed and that I was now only interested in hearing her news.

What I heard heartened me greatly; Bennath had done her work well. She had first visited the great House of the Goddess on Bodmin Moor, where the ancient stone circle bore witness to worship and practice of the Mysteries that dated back long before the memories of man. She was welcomed with courtesy by Jowanet, the chief priestess, a Cornish-woman born and bred. I had met her several times at Tintagel and knew her to be a strong, straightforward sort of woman, now in her prime middle years. She ruled her House and her priestesses with practical common sense and when Bennath told her of her visit to Yseult, Lady of Treliggan—and the call for all the women of Cornwall and Lyonesse to return to their halls and hearths to work on the land—she had smiled broadly and began at once to send messages and instructions to the moorland's isolated farms, small hamlets, and secluded homesteads.

Bennath fared equally well at the smaller House situated at the mouth of the river in Fowey. The chief priestess here was a younger woman; as luck would have it, we had studied at Avalon together, and I counted Matilda as a friend. Between them, Jowanet and Matilda had agreed to rouse the Western coast and central moorlands. They told Bennath that they would send messages to the Houses in Mevagissey and Truro and, between them, would do all they could to ensure that the vision of the Lady of Treliggan was heard and the fields and orchards of Cornwall and Lyonesse would ripen and be bountiful this harvest.

I was relieved that the Houses of Bodmin and Fowey had so willingly adopted our plans. I had hoped that Jowanet's pragmatic intelligence and Matilda's personal loyalty to myself would work in our favour; indeed, it was for this very reason that I had selected these Houses for Bennath to approach first. But these were dangerous times, and I knew that not everyone would be prepared to accept the words of the Lady of Treliggan in the face of Vivian's damning proclamation.

My fears were justified by Bennath's next words. "The news from the borders is not so good, my lady. The priestess Matilda told me that the Houses of Tamar and Metherell have already declared allegiance to Uther and the Lady of the Lake and she fears that most of the other Houses to the North and East will do the same."

I nodded grimly; I had feared that this would happen. "That does not surprise me. Remember the words of Hild and Epona? Their fear and anger that their men would die and their lands would lie barren because of this war. Vivian has cursed me, and many will not dare to defy the orders of the Lady of the Lake."

"Aye, my lady, but that does not mean that we should be silent and bow down to them," replied Bennath. "The priestess Jowanet believes that the Houses that are loyal to you and to the words of the Lady of Treliggan should stand together at Solstice. She and the priestess Matilda have proposed that there should be a Great Gathering at Tintagel, to witness the rites and to honour the Goddess. It was to bring you this message that I returned to you rather than carrying on with my quest to the other Houses. If you are in agreement, I will send word to Bodmin and Fowey and set out as planned to visit the Houses at Polperro and the Southern coastlands to see if they will stand with us."

I considered. A Great Gathering would be costly and use far more of our resources than Jago would be pleased to part with. Our steward was a cautious man and although our cellars and storerooms were well-stocked, I knew he would not be happy if supplies fell below the level he regarded as prudent. On the other hand, a gathering such as this would send a strong and positive message to all Cornwall and Lyonesse—a message of hope, determination, and loyalty to the Goddess and her Mysteries. That decided me. We would have a Great Gathering at Solstice, and if I had anything to do with it, it would be a triumph.

I smiled. "That is indeed a good idea. I agree." I looked at the young woman sitting across from me; I could see signs of tiredness and strain; there were dark shadows beneath her intelligent grey eyes. "Thank you, Bennath; you have worked hard and must be very tired. Drink your wine and relax a little; there is much to do I know, but I think you can wait until the morrow before you ride out again."

Bennath took a sip of her wine and, grinning at me, leaned back in her chair. She stretched like a cat and lifted her face to the warm sunlight that was now streaming in through the open window. She gave a little grunt of pleasure. "Thank you, my lady. It will be good to sleep in a soft bed again. 'Tis only a shame that my Lowen is not here to share it with me."

"You love your husband, I think?"

"Yes, and I miss him. But we are bound to the land as much as we are to each other and neither of us will shirk from doing our duty." She looked at me, a wicked smile playing about her mouth.

"Still, I have an itch to scratch and a soft bed to scratch it in. If he is not here, I needs must find someone else to accommodate me."

"And what would Sir Lowen have to say about that, if he found out?"

"He would no more begrudge me a stable boy than I would object to him tumbling in the hay with a tavern lass. The Goddess has made us as much for pleasure as she has for war. As I said when we first met, my lady, Lowen and I keep the old ways." With that, she drained her wine and stood up, clearly eager to be on her way.

"With your leave, my lady?"

I nodded. "If I do not see you this evening, please join me tomorrow morning to break your fast before you set out."

She closed the door behind her and I poured myself some more wine. I envied her. I too would like to lose myself in the arms of a lover. To forget everything but touch and taste and the wild heat of desire, skin upon skin. When was the last time that Gorlois and I had loved like that? As I thought about it, I realised that it had been months ago, at Uther's castle of Caer-Lundein, the night that Uther sent me the dress of moonbeam gossamer and all this terrible madness had begun.

Since then, our love-making had been at best, merely comforting and at worst, perfunctory. We had not even said goodbye to each other with the passionate affirmation of our love and need for each other, as was our usual custom, but had instead spent our last moments together in conflict—and he had left without my kiss of blessing.

Thinking of Gorlois, my thoughts flew, unbidden, to that other man, Uther. I remembered the way he had held me to him, the force of his body pressed against mine and surprising softness of his lips. Like Bennath, I realised that I too had an itch to scratch, but unlike Bennath, I could not simply find a stable boy to satisfy me; Bennath hailed from the isles of Syllan, where the old ways still held sway and the right to rule was passed down through the mother's line, not the father's. If her roll in the hay resulted in a swollen belly, the child would be accepted, but I was the wife of Cornwall's war duke, who was a jealous man, disenchanted with the old ways and possessive of what he regarded as my honour.

Heaving a sigh, I pushed aside my wine and stood up. Morgan was still sleeping soundly. The effects of the potion combined with the natural exhaustion created by her scrying experiment should ensure that she would not wake for several hours yet. I decided to go in search of Jago, for I knew my steward would not be happy about the scheme I had agreed to with Bennath, and I wanted to discuss plans for the Great Gathering with him as soon as possible.

Making my way through the Great Hall, I saw Ened sitting at the table. She was working her way through a large trencher of cheese and cured meats, whilst at the same time talking animatedly to Hild and Epona, neither of whom seemed able to get a word in edgeways. I took great pleasure in informing her that I needed her to go to my solar to keep watch over my daughter. I knew that she hated making her way up the great, steep staircase, and I had not yet forgiven her for her attack on me.

She grudgingly agreed, asking if her friends could accompany her, a request I refused, saying that the Lady Morgan was sleeping and their chatter was likely to disturb her. I don't think it was my imagination, but both Hild and Epona appeared to be quite relieved by my decision. I asked to see all three of them the following morning, to discuss plans for Solstice, and continued on my way.

I was making for the buttery, a small room next to the kitchens where the great casks of ale were stored and which Jago had made his stronghold. My steward had an open face and a lean, wiry frame; he was a few years older than Gorlois and his thick shock of black hair was now thinning and beginning to silver. Jago was not a tall man, but he had an air of competence and certainty that commanded immediate respect. Born and bred in Tintagel, his father had been castle steward before him and had raised his only son with but one ambition—that he succeed him in service to the castle and the

Dukes of Cornwall. No one knew more about Tintagel and the lands that surrounded it, and no one was more loyal to Gorlois—and by extension—to me.

I found him at work. I guessed from the number of scrolls and tally sheets piled up behind him that he had, until recently, been employed in checking inventories and supply lists, but he was now engaged in an uncharacteristically heated conversation with another, much younger man who I did not recognise. When they saw me in the doorway, both men stopped talking and got to their feet.

"Af'noon, my lady. How can I be of service?" Jago's voice seemed strained, as if he was not best pleased by my visit, but he bowed with his usual courtesy and gestured for me to enter and be seated.

The other man made as if to leave, but before he could do so, my steward grabbed hold of his sleeve. "Not so 'asty young Cubert. I got meat that needs salting and ale over-brewing. I needs to know when them barrels will be ready, and you're not going anywhere until you've given me an answer."

"Like I told you, Mester, there's only me an' Tom now. You can't expect two men to do the same work as four. It just ain't possible." The young man shot me a nervous look. "We're behind on all of our orders, and we can't do nothing in our orchards. That's what happens when you go to war. The land suffers. People suffer, begging your pardon, my lady, this war b'aint a good war. I'm loyal to you and the war duke, but I can't make you no promises about them barrels. It just ain't possible."

"And can women not make barrels?" I asked.

Both Jago and young Cubert stared at me as if I had taken leave of my senses. Neither of them responded, so I repeated my question. "Barrel making is not particularly heavy work I think, no more so than managing the castle's laundries or brewing the beer." Jago looked at me, and nodded slowly, but with a troubled expression on his face. "You're not wrong, my lady, but Cubert here…him and his family have always made the barrels and casks for Tintagel. It's always been man's work."

"And if we leave it to Cubert, the meat will rot in the kitchens and the ale will need to be thrown away," I responded tartly. "I am minded to call a Great Gathering for Solstice and we will need everything to be plentiful and in good order.

"Listen, the Goddess has spoken to us, through Yseult, the Lady of Treliggan. Despite what you may think,"—and here I noticed a blush rise on young Cubert's cheeks—"this war is not of my desiring. I wish to keep Cornwall safe, peaceful, and prosperous, and the Goddess has shown us a way. Women must work and take the places of the men who have gone to war. Women must husband the land, tend the orchards, and, if needs must, make the barrels."

In stunned silence, I instructed Jago to send three of the most dextrous of Tintagel's kitchen maids and laundresses with Cubert to be instructed in the ancient craft of cooperage. I told Cubert to send all of his finished barrels to the castle immediately and to ensure that the full order would be completed by the end of the week. If he required more help, he would get it. I had to be certain that nothing would get in the way of my plans for the Great Gathering; we would need meat and ale aplenty if Tintagel was to hold a Solstice that would truly honour the Goddess and send a message of hope and unity to all of Cornwall and Lyonesse.

I waited impatiently whilst Jago hurried to the kitchens to select the most likely young women to accompany Cubert. In less than half an hour he had returned to the buttery, and I told him what would be needed. Although I saw his brow furrow more than once and he appeared several times to be on the verge of speaking, he did not interrupt me to gainsay or list arguments to oppose my plans.

"And so, Jago," I concluded, "now more than ever, Tintagel must proclaim its loyalty to the Goddess for all to see. In Gorlois' absence, I am ruler of Cornwall and Lyonesse, and I will not spend Solstice cowering behind the battlements. The Goddess has shown us what we need to do to ensure the land is fruitful, and in return, we must take the lead, setting an example to all the Great Houses in doing her honour and praising her name."

♦ ♦ ♦

THE NEXT FEW WEEKS PASSED quickly; messages were sent inviting all who owed fealty to Tintagel to attend the Great Gathering, and most had responded to say that they would come, although, as Bennath had predicted, many of the border dwellers, the Houses to the North and East of our domain, had either sent curt refusals or not replied at all.

The kitchens buzzed with activity from first light until dusk. There was no longer any space in our cellars and storehouses. Sturdy parcels of fresh-made cheeses—tightly wrapped in dark, deep-veined green cabbage leaves to preserve them—rested on shelves above Cubert's newly made barrels, some containing salted meats and fish, others brimming with the strong malted ale that Jago was inordinately proud of.

I had instructed Elaine to prepare rooms within the castle for the mistresses of the Great Houses, and to see that there would be sufficient straw in the barns and fresh water in the butts for those visitors who must make do with more humble quarters. I expected many of our visitors would pitch camp on the shoreline, as Prince Urien had done, and I made sure that Jago had taken into consideration the need to provide meat and ale for all our guests, not just those housed within the castle walls. I was pleased to learn that he had already thought of this and had instructed that several rough tables be fashioned and carried across the causeway tomorrow—which was Solstice Eve—so as to be ready for the feast.

I smiled as he told me, with a slightly disapproving grunt, that these tables had been made by the women Cubert had instructed in barrel making who, it now appeared, were far happier to engage in carpentry and metalwork than the kitchen skivvying and housework that had previously been their lot.

"And do you have anything to complain of about their work?" I asked him, knowing that the three young women had also been doing their fair share of their old domestic duties.

"No, my lady, it just seems odd to see a maid with a hammer in her hand. Not natural-like."

"It is what the Goddess has commanded, Jago. And if Bennath of Syllan can wield a sword and fire an arrow as well as any man can, I don't see why the maids of Tintagel cannot be as skilled with an axe or a hammer as they are with a fish knife or darning needle."

Bennath had returned the day before, and as I spoke with Jago I could see her through the window, practising her swordcraft in the courtyard. Her face was set in a grim line as I watched her teaching a group of boys too young to have gone to war with Gorlois how to stab and parry. With them I noticed a number of young women wearing breeches and jerkins, their hair tied securely in plaits. All of them were armed and, like Bennath, seemed to handle their weapons with the confidence and skill that speaks of years of familiarity. These were the warrior maids of Lyonesse, who had travelled here from the ancient house of Ynas Bray eager to show their loyalty to the Goddess and also, I had been delighted to learn, to me as their liege.

Bennath looked older and more care-worn than she had when she had ridden out to spread the news about the Great Gathering just a few weeks before. I had greeted her with affection when Elaine had brought her to my solar and urged her to sit down.

I had been discussing preparations for the rituals with Hild and Epona, whilst Ened sat at the far end of the room with Morgan, practising the roles I had asked them both to play for their part in the Solstice celebrations. We would set bonfires ablaze on the cliff top and along the causeway, leading toward Tintagel. At sunset, Morgan, Ened, and I would light the sacred fire, or "litha," and begin the Solstice rituals.

I was worried about the more serious role that I would be called upon to play in the rites that honoured the Goddess and sought to bring life and fruitfulness to the fields and orchards. Part of me was also thinking of Morgause, on her long journey North to Orkney.

This would be the first time I had not been with her at Solstice and this year she, too, had an important role to play.

Twice I had called to me the seabird whose mind I could control, and twice I had journeyed far out across the waves, following the path of the *Llyr's Daughter*. I was anxious just for a glance of my beloved girl, to know that she was in good health and the vessel she sailed in made firm progress and was safe. On both occasions, all had been well. The seas had been calm and the winds gentle but strong enough to aid the rowers and the little ship was now well on its way North.

She had passed through the dangerous waters off the coast of Wales, where I had feared attack from those whose loyalty lay with my brother and who would be likely to take heed of the curse laid upon me by Vivian. But no attack had come, and the last time I had seen my daughter she had been standing on deck laughing with Einar, King Lot's ward.

I had made my seagull perch on the mast, as close to them as I could get. The wind took their words so I could not hear what they were saying, but Morgause's face was animated and beautiful, her copper hair whipped around her face by the sea breeze, laughing with delight as Einar pointed out to sea where three dolphins had just leapt from the waves.

Returning to Tintagel, I released my seabird, who I was certain felt exhausted from the flight, which had taken more than four hours and had put great strain on both her body and her mind. I knew the distance meant I could not safely make use of her again and I had been vexing myself for some days as to the best way of making sure Morgause was ready and prepared for Solstice.

As Bennath sat down beside me, I decided that I had to talk to her. I asked Ened and the others to leave us, saying I needed to hear Bennath's news. Elaine, understanding why I needed to be alone with the woman from Syllan, asked me if I would like her to take Morgan for her supper and get her ready for bed. I nodded, but then, as they were leaving the room, I called her back, telling her to join us when she was finished and to bring with her a flagon of spiced wine. I knew that this Solstice I would need my half-sister to help me as she had done before, and I also needed to take Bennath, the warrior woman who remained true to the old ways, into my confidence.

Whilst we were waiting for Elaine, I asked Bennath to tell me of her travels. She seemed to have lost the light-hearted confidence that had previously always sat so easy on her, and I was anxious to know what had befallen her.

She told me that, as planned, she had gone South and, as we hoped, she was met with kindness and a warm welcome. As she travelled, Bennath saw that the words of the Lady of Treliggan were already being heeded. Women were working in the fields, sometimes with their children beside them, helping to pull weeds or fetch water. In the smaller villages, she noticed that many little dwellings stood empty; families had moved into the larger buildings, better to work together and care for the elderly or the infirm who could do little without assistance. But even they did what they could, mending the fishing nets or patching the field clothes, or even tending the tiny babies so their mothers could go out to the fields.

Everywhere she went, people were working together, contributing what they could so everyone could benefit. And the land was being cared for.

The Houses at St. Austell, Fowey, and Polperro had rallied to her. They had agreed to send messengers farther West and South, to Mullion, Pendeen, and Porthcurno, and it was with a glad heart that she set forth on the last leg of her journey, riding east toward the Tamar and the great house at Metherell.

"We knew Metherell was quite close to the border, but the last word received in Polperro was that all was quiet, that there had been no sign of Uther's soldiers. We thought he had been concentrating his forces higher up, on the more northerly edges of the border. We were wrong."

Bennath described what she had seen as she rode onward, along the Tamar Valley. She had met people fleeing the wrath of Uther's army. They travelled in small groups, mainly women and children, dirty, hungry, in rags. Frozen-faced, with blank eyes, they told Bennath their tales.

Farmsteads and villages had been laid waste. The small chapels and wayside shrines set up to honour the new religion had not escaped the force of Uther's armies and many were destroyed. Crops had been burned in the fields and the livestock that had not been taken to feed Uther's army had been slaughtered and left to rot.

It would seem that the soldiers had a pattern. When they entered a village, they would muster, usually on the green or by the well and call all the villagers together. Anyone who did not come voluntarily was dragged from their homes and whipped. When they had searched every building and were satisfied that no one was left in hiding, the villagers were ordered to stand in silence and to listen to the words of Uther, their High King and liege lord.

One woman told Bennath that her daughter, a little child of not quite three summers, would not stop crying. A soldier came and dragged her from her arms. He took her into one of the buildings and the crying stopped. The woman never saw her daughter again.

The message from Uther's heralds was simple. The people of Cornwall were rebels, taking up arms against their sworn king, who had the favour of the Goddess. Disobedience would not be tolerated.

In some villages, the men, excepting the old or sickly, had been dragged from their families and beheaded by the soldiers, their corpses piled up into large and stinking bloody piles, and set alight as both a sacrifice and a warning.

"But that is sacrilege," I'd said, "The Goddess would not want such offerings to be made to her." It was true that sometimes the Mysteries demanded the ultimate sacrifice of a human life—ritual blood spilt to feed the earth and guarantee fertility—but these demands were rare and sought a willing victim.

Bennath's tales of mass slaughter disgusted me. We were not strangers to the atrocities of war; during the years that Gorlois had fought by Uther's side against Vortigern and his marauding Saxons, I had seen much to turn my stomach. But that had been necessary: We had been fighting to retain our lands and freedoms.

The stories Bennath told me seemed very different. This was Uther Pendragon slaughtering his own people, and not even soldiers, but civilians, farmers and blacksmiths, ordinary working men who probably did not even understand why there was a war, let alone what it had to do with them.

Once again, I was wracked with shame and anger. Was all this my fault? I had begged Gorlois to humble his pride, to listen to Merlin—but to no avail. But what was done, was done, and I was doing the best I could. This was no time to listen to my demons.

"And the women?" I asked Bennath. "How are the women?"

As she told me, I came to understand that not all weapons are made of wood and iron.

Many of the women who had spoken to Bennath regarded what had happened to them as simply part of war. They had been able to survive the degradation, the violence, and humiliation of being raped in front of their children, seeing their own mothers stripped naked and jeered at by Uther's soldiers by removing themselves from it, seeing it as something they had endured, but had survived. But some were not so resilient. Bennath told me of the young girls with empty faces and haunted eyes, terrified that a child could be growing inside them, whilst they were still but children themselves.

And there were worse cases. One evening, seeking shelter in a small hut by the Tamar's edge, Bennath met a slender, grey-eyed woman, with dark hair and a face that was frozen into a grim mask of fear and desperation. Her name was Eseld, and she had spoken not a single word.

She was travelling with her husband, one of the few men to have survived the soldiers' slaughter. He had been away from his small farmhouse on the morning when the soldiers came, foraging for duck eggs by the river, and had managed to remain hidden in the sedge and reeds. He had stayed in hiding until he saw the smoke rising, black and greasy from the place where his home had been and heard the furious sound of the soldiers' horses riding on to the next village.

Terrified of what might await him, he dragged himself from the mud and rushes and ran back along the silent pathway. In the yard outside his homestead, he found Eseld. She was lying face down on the ground next to the headless body of his son. At first, he thought his wife was also dead, but when he touched her, she was still warm. When he turned her over, he could see her chest rising and falling in shallow, hesitant breaths and he would have taken her in his arms had she not pushed herself away. He heard someone call his name and saw his mother emerge slowly from the ruins of his still smouldering homestead. Her face was bruised and bloody, and she was limping. She told him that the soldiers had slain his son. At fourteen, he was no longer a child, and now would never grow to be a man.

They had forced themselves upon Eseld, each one of them taking her until she collapsed, riven with grief and pain onto the ground beside the headless body. They had not raped his mother. One of the soldiers had told her that she was too old and too ugly, and it would be an insult to the Goddess to even think of bedding her. He pointed to the mutilated body of her grandson and told her that was the price of disloyalty.

When Bennath told me this, she looked up at me, her face twisted into a cold, white rictus. "And they say they have the Goddess on their side. That she would order men to despoil women in this way. That she would countenance such senseless slaughter." She stood up and moved away from me.

"Do you know what happened? Eseld hanged herself." Her voice was shaking, as she fought to master her anger. "The next morning. I got up early and decided to be on my way. And I found her, hanging from a tree at the water's edge. She had taken my reins and bridle and made a noose. She was cold by the time I got to her. Cold, and still."

I reached out my hand to touch Bennath's elbow, but she shrugged herself away from me.

"This must stop, Igraine. We can fight, but we cannot win."

"We must do what we can," I told her. "We can't end this war; Gorlois would not listen to me when I begged him to lay down his arms. I doubt that even if I could get a message to him that he would listen to me now. All we can do is work to keep our people and the land safe. And that is what you have been doing, Bennath."

"It's not enough."

"It's all we have. And now, we must come together to celebrate Solstice and pray that the Goddess knows what she is doing. Our lives must be in her hands now."

Bennath slowly sat back down again, her shoulders bowed, her head cradled in her hands.

"I have always followed the old ways. I've had no doubts, no uncertainties. I knew who I was, deep down inside, in my very core. I trusted in the Goddess to bless and guide us.

"But now, after what I've seen…Igraine…how can I have faith?"

Once more, I reached out my hand, and this time she did not thrust me away. Instead she turned toward me and I held her in my arms as she wept.

I remembered then how young she was, no more than three and twenty, but she had borne the burden of my commands like a seasoned warrior. I said nothing, and for a few seconds, we sat in silence, until she pushed slightly away from me.

"I'm sorry, my lady."

"Don't be. To have seen what you have seen and remain untouched would be the mark of a heartless fiend. I remember something I was taught in Avalon, when I was grieving for my mother. Vivian told me to use my pain to strengthen myself. To forge my spirit in its depths as a sword is melted, moulded, and strengthened by the flames. What you have seen can give you power if you allow yourself to use it.

"I need that power," I said. "I need you to use it with me this Solstice. Will you help me?"

She looked at me mutely, and uncertain. I held her gaze until she nodded, and the faintest flicker of a smile played around her lips. At this moment, the door opened, and Elaine walked quietly into the room. She put down the flagon of spiced wine and, once she had poured for each of us, took a seat on the other side of the table.

Calmly and quietly, I told them what I needed.

Chapter Eleven

And now, the day before Solstice Eve, I believed we were ready. Leaving Jago to his preparations I walked out into the courtyard and made my way to the kitchen garden. Elaine was already there, and I could see that she had gathered much of what we needed. Her basket was filled with freshly cut bundles of sage, bettony, camomile, and rue. All that was missing was comfrey, which I knew my half-sister disliked collecting because of her sensitivity to the little hairs along its hollow woody stems, which always made her skin itch.

Fortunately, I am not similarly afflicted and so I made my way to the far end of the garden where the comfrey and borage grew. I used the small silver sickle that I always carry at my waist to cut a handful of the pale green stalks, making sure that I selected stems that were firm and blemish free, rich with lush silver-green leaves, but no flowers. The plant is at its most potent before its delicate blue bells emerge and although it can still be used in healing once it blooms, it is by then almost completely useless for any form of ritual purpose.

Elaine had now finished collecting the other herbs and was now waiting for me at the gate. Together we walked back across the courtyard where Bennath was just drawing the afternoon's training session to a close. Many of the young warriors, both male and female, had stripped themselves of their tunics to wash the sweat from their bodies at the well. The sunlight dappled their skins as they be-sported themselves beneath the ancient willow and ash trees that grew around the castle well. They were laughing and flicking water at each other, their weapons sheathed and placed at a safe distance along the far wall. Several of the older lads were paying very particular attention to the newcomers from Ynas Bray who in turn now seemed much more relaxed and appeared to be actively encouraging the boys' interest.

"I think there are some here who may well find this Solstice brings its sweetness early," I said to Elaine, swerving slightly aside to avoid being splashed by one of the Lyonesse girls, who had just filled her tunic with water and thrown it, with rather more strength than accuracy at one of the Tintagel lads. He was a good-looking, muscular fellow and a typical Cornish man, with red hair and green eyes. I remembered that he was apprenticed to the castle blacksmith and as we watched, he swooped in on his tormentor. Taking advantage of her raised arms, he lifted her skyward as his companions whooped and egged him on. At first she struggled, but then, as we watched, we saw their eyes meet. They stared at each other, skin pressed against skin as she slowly sank down into his arms and he pressed her to him, her breasts held close against his naked chest. They must have been able to feel each other's hearts beating.

The yard fell silent and then, blushing and a little flustered at being the object of everyone's attention, they separated. She picked up her tunic and began to wring it out before pulling it, still dripping, over her head. Without a word, she joined her fellows who were by now making their way into the Great Hall in search of bread and ale. He made to walk back to the stables, but I noticed that he did not take his eyes from her and was still watching as she walked in through the stone gateway only to be swallowed up by the shadows.

"Let them take their pleasure while they can," said Elaine. "If they are old enough for sword craft, then they're old enough for love."

"She's got good taste, that girl from Lyonesse," said Bennath, who had walked across to join us, her sword now strapped to her belt and her bow in its usual place across her back. "I'd spotted your young smith myself, Igraine, and had a mind to take a step in that direction this Solstice." She smiled. "I won't now, of course, unless I plan to bring the wrath of Ynas Bray upon my head."

"Did you not find someone to scratch your itch the last time you were here, Bennath?" I asked.

"Well, yes, and he was fine and good enough. But I do not like to return to the same spot twice if I can help it. I must needs cast my net a little wider if I'm to do the Goddess her due honour. And I am, as you know, the most dutiful of her servants." She grinned, and Elaine and I laughed with her. It was with a surprisingly light heart that I went into the castle, the three of us making our way up the stairs to my solar.

AS I HAD EXPECTED, THE room was quiet. Morgan was sitting at her favourite place, my silks aligned in rows on the table in front of her. Ened was slumped, drowsing on the settle by the fireplace, a half empty flagon of wine on the floor by her feet. To be fair to her, this was not her fault. When I had left her alone with Morgan earlier that afternoon, I had told Ened to help herself and she had done so, not knowing that Elaine had added a generous helping of poppy seeds to the spices she had used to enhance the flavour of the rich Phoenician wine.

I walked over to the settle to make sure she really was asleep. Her head was resting at an odd angle, so I positioned her more comfortably, covering her with a blanket. As I did so, she grunted a little and turned herself to face the wall. I picked up the flagon and smelled the wine. It was strong and heady.

"She will sleep for hours," said Elaine. "You need not worry."

I thanked her and went to sit beside Morgan, whilst Elaine and Bennath busied themselves around the room: Elaine fetched down the large burnished copper mirror that usually hung above the fireplace, whilst Bennath began to prepare the herbs.

"What are you doing, Mother?" asked Morgan. "Are you going to make a magic?"

She was not stupid, my daughter. She had shown absolutely no curiosity in what had befallen Ened, who had been her guardian for many weeks now and who was lying drugged and snoring in the corner of the room. That she took in her stride. However, she was clearly very keen to know what we were doing and hoped that she could be part of it.

"I hope you don't want me to leave." My daughter looked at me with unblinking eyes, her mouth set in a determined line.

"You told me that I needed to learn the rituals if I was to manage my powers."

"Yes, my darling, I did. And no, I do not want you to leave. This is an important ritual and one Elaine and I have not done for many years. Not since we were girls in Avalon."

"Did Vivian teach it to you, Mother?" Morgan's eyes had that eager but irritating gleam that always seemed to be there whenever Vivian's name was mentioned.

"Yes, Vivian taught us both, and Bennath learned it when she was a girl under the care of Yseult, the Lady of Treliggan. We need you to help us, but you must do what you are told. Do you agree?"

Morgan nodded, looking serious, but also pleased to be included. She said nothing, waiting for me to explain the ritual and tell her what I needed her to do. As always, I found my daughter's composure quite unnerving. Unlike her sister, who would by now have been dancing from one foot to the other and pestering me with questions at the thought of learning another magic, my youngest daughter simply rested her chin upon her hands and gazed at me in calm, expectant silence.

The ritual that I had asked Bennath and Elaine to help me with was an old magic, brought to our shores many centuries ago. Vivian told me that the ancients, who lived far away, farther even than the homelands of our Roman conquerors, had discovered it. It is called the psychomanteum, and we were going to use it to raise a taibhse.

◆ ◆ ◆

FOR THIS MAGIC, I NEEDED much more than scrying. Rather than just seeing a vision of Morgause, I needed to actually be with my daughter. I had to be certain that she and those around her were prepared for what they must do to ensure that on this Solstice, above all others, they were able to give the Goddess her due. The *Llyr's Daughter* had now travelled too far north for me to use the mastery of a seabird's mind to fly out to her—and even if I could, I would not be able to talk to Morgause or Avice, who had full charge of her. No, for what I had in mind, I needed to use a deeper, darker magic.

The psychomanteum is an old and dangerous ritual. It can be used to raise the spirits of the dead, but that was not what I had in mind that day. One of its other purposes is to raise a taibhse—a spectral vision of a living person—that can then travel freely and with speed to the side of a loved one.

To call the spirit forth requires dark and perilous magic. The person who's taibhse is summoned will be held in thrall, hovering just this side of death, caught in limbo between the land of the living and the realm of departed souls, whilst their essence roams free across the world. The trance cannot last too long. The longer the taibhse is at liberty, the less inclined it is to return to its fleshly prison, so I knew that we had to work speedily if I was to accomplish what I needed to do and return safely to Tintagel to celebrate my own Solstice.

When I had first proposed the ritual, Bennath and Elaine had been loath to fall in with my plans. Both had offered to go to Morgause in my stead, but, as I had eventually convinced them, this really would not work. The taibhse will go only to the side of a beloved, and although Elaine was fond of Morgause, she did not love her as a mother loves a daughter, whilst Bennath hardly knew her.

Also, I knew that both Bennath and Elaine's skills in magic were greater than my own, and that I needed them to hold me safe so that my taibhse would return unscathed to my body by daybreak on Solstice Eve. And that was also why, after much argument and discussion, I had allowed Elaine to persuade me to include Morgan. I did not doubt that my youngest daughter was immensely gifted in the craft. Indeed, from what I had seen of her forays in the magics, Morgan had more power than any of us, more power perhaps than any I had met, excepting Vivian, the Lady of the Lake. But she was still very much untrained.

Nonetheless, Elaine had argued with truth that Morgan was gaining an increased mastery of the Mysteries. I knew myself from the hours I had been spending with her daily that she now had much greater control over the powers the goddess had bestowed upon her. She no longer summoned random visions or sank unbidden into trances. Her powers of concentration and control were remarkable, and I recognised that her involvement in the psychomanteum would very much increase my chances of success, however much I disliked the idea of exposing my beloved child to a ritual so dangerous and demanding.

Bennath had now finished preparing the herbs and had lit a fire of willow wood. Above it, she had placed a small cauldron filled with spring water and thrown in sprigs of camomile, bettony, and sage. I could tell from the thin mists of faintly astringent steam that the water was very nearly at boiling point.

Whilst I had been preparing my mind for the ordeal that lay ahead, Elaine had been quietly speaking to Morgan, explaining the ritual and telling her what we needed her to do.

Bennath had placed the mirror on the hearth behind the willow fire and, through the clouds of steam, it seemed to shimmer with an otherworldly radiance. In front of the hearth was a pile of furs taken from my bed; I sat down on them, straight-backed and cross-legged, and at a word from Elaine, Morgan positioned herself neatly on my lap. We both held out our hands, palms upward, to Elaine, who took the silver sickle from her belt and made a small incision, first in my left palm, then Morgan's.

As the blood began to flow, Bennath came forward and caught it in the small mortar she had been using to grind leaves of rue and comfrey. When she had enough, she nodded at Elaine, who reached across and touched our hands with the dull edge of her sickle. The blood ceased to course and our wounds healed. There was no pain.

Bennath returned to the fire and poured the contents of her mortar into the cauldron. The flames surged upward, turning from tawny orange to green, then blue, and finally to a burnished silver. The pot bubbled and thick, moist steam billowed upward, covering the surface of the mirror and shrouding it from view.

Elaine and Bennath took up their places behind me. They placed their hands upon my shoulders and looked beyond me, into the depths of the mirror, where we could see strange, swirling shapes, obscuring our reflections.

Up until now, the room had been almost silent, the only sounds the faint crackling of the willow fire and the gentle bubbling of the cauldron. But now, first Elaine, then Bennath, and finally Morgan, began to hum. It was a low, thrumming sound that filled the air, vibrating in the stillness until I felt it deep within me. And now, the mists began to clear, and I could see four shapes, sitting still as death, deep within the mirror. I was looking at four faces, but only one looked back at me.

Morgan, Bennath, and Elaine all had their eyes closed, their heads down, motionless except for the slight rise and fall of their chests as they continued to send forth their mesmerising, resonating music.

I stared into my own eyes and held their gaze. Deeper and deeper I stared, until all I could see was the inky darkness of the depths of my own soul. And from deep within myself, I called her to me. My soul, my spirit, my taibhse. I called her from the depths, to come to me.

And then, I saw her. The face that was my own, but not quite my own, death-pale and spectral and looking back at me with such intensity that for a second I recoiled with a shudder and almost took my eyes away. But as I did so, I felt the reassuring touch of Elaine's hand upon my shoulder and the weight of Morgan nestled on my lap and I lost my fear. The strength of my desire intensified, and I gazed hungrily upon her and called her to me.

In the mirror, I saw one of the four shapes rise and begin to move toward me. It was my own self, slowly approaching, walking with a slight, uncertain step, closer, closer. And then she was there, emerging from the mirror into the misty darkness, reaching out toward me as she stepped hesitantly into the room. She stretched out her cold, slim fingers, and I felt a chill as they touched my forehead, insubstantial, and uncanny. Raising my eyes to hers, I stared at her, unblinking as her lips, my lips, began to curl into a smile.

She moved closer, bending forward as if to kiss me. Her lips brushed against mine, chill like the touch of a shadow on a summer day. I felt the cold darkness enter me and then there was nothing, as I fell backward into a black, silent void.

THE LIGHT WAS BRIGHT AND hurt my eyes. I moved away from the fireside, into the dark corner of the room. Around the fireplace, the women were busy. "Cover her, keep her warm," said one of them; at her words, the other moved quickly to the settle, fetching blankets to drape across a third figure, Igraine, who lay on the floor, senseless, motionless but not dead. I could see her chest rise and fall, slowly but evenly in the tawny firelight. I knew who she was because I was her spirit, her taibhse. She had called me, and I had come.

As my eyes adjusted I noticed there was a fourth person in the room. She was smaller than the others and as she walked toward me, I realised that she was a child. "Hello, Mother," she said. "Are you a taibhse now?"

I said nothing.

"What is it like?" asked the child. Her eyes were pale and piercing like the blue heart of a flame. I felt a rush of recognition; I knew those eyes. "Vivian?... Are you Vivian?" I felt confused. I had not been to this place before. I did not know these people. The last time Igraine had summoned me had been years ago, in Avalon. Vivian had been there, and they had called me together. On that occasion,

Vivian had instructed me, told me why they had called me and what they would have me do. I had listened and obeyed, bound by the magics to serve the Lady of the Lake.

The child smiled. "No, I am not Vivian, although I am of her kind. I am Morgan, your daughter, and I will tell you why we have called you and what it is that you must do."

"You are young to talk to spirits, child."

"I am young," she replied, "but my mother has placed her trust in me, and we have great need of you tonight."

I nodded and beckoned her to come to me and she explained quickly and calmly why Igraine had called me from the realm of spirits. As Morgan she gave me her instructions—who I needed to find and what I needed to tell them—I studied her, this child who called herself my daughter, and as she talked, I began to recognise her, to feel myself loving her, catching up on the years that had passed since I had last crossed the void. I knew that I was married, that I loved my husband, although I also sensed that something within the marriage had gone awry.

But that was not tonight's business. I had but a few hours to visit Morgause to ensure that all that was needed for this Solstice was prepared. If I failed to pass back through the mirror by sunrise, I would be trapped forever in the realm of the living and Igraine would remain a lifeless but still breathing corpse.

"I will take the message to your sister, and if you continue to play your part, all will be well. Did Igraine instruct you on what you must do to keep the portal open and to ensure my safe return?"

Morgan nodded. "I must sit beside my mother and keep watch throughout the night. I must keep the willow fire burning and not let a soul enter this room until you have returned, and my mother is herself again."

When Morgan had finished speaking, I smiled and reached toward her, wishing to place a parting kiss upon her brow, but she shrank away from me, backing toward the women by the fireplace and the body of Igraine.

And so I turned away from her and went to the open window, the waves crashing below me as the thin, horned moon lit me on my way. I travelled swiftly through the darkling skies, faster than any seabird, faster even than thought. Beneath me were fields and ragged forests, vast mountains and wide rivers, barren heathlands and busy townships, and then, the sea, boundless and roiling.

There were few ships to be seen out on the blue-grey depths. Most had sought safe harbour before sunset and it was not hard to spot the lights of the *Llyr's Daughter*, as she navigated the rocky coastline of the Muir Eireann, heading north. Sailing at night could be treacherous and I was pleased to see that she was not making her way recklessly through deep waters, but rather was staying closer in, whilst keeping a safe distance from the rocks and reefs that fringed the shoreline. When I spotted her, she was skirting the headland that would take her on, beyond the old Roman forts of Hardknott and Ravenglass, making her way carefully toward Whitehaven and the wide mouth of the Solway Firth. Even without the lights to guide me, I felt a pull, a call of recognition, drawing me toward the boat. I knew that the other child of my body was there. I could feel her.

Even at night, the deck of the *Llyr's Daughter* was alive with activity. Sailors were checking the ropes on the wide central sail, others were scouring barrels and preparing fish for salting. Below deck, men were still at their posts, wielding the oars that drove the ship forward, making sure the vessel would make progress even when, as tonight, there was little wind.

Most of the crew slept in the bulkheads, where they would rest if they were not working on deck or manning the oars, but there were two small cabins toward the stern of the ship, and I was certain that I would find Morgause in one of them.

Alighting, I knew that I would not be visible to any of the sailors. The most sensitive of them might experience a slight chill as I passed them, or feel the hairs rise along their shoulders or the back of their necks. No one would see me unless I chose to reveal myself.

The door to the first cabin was open. It was empty and lit only by moonlight, but I guessed from the charts scattered untidily across the battered wooden table and the empty flagon of what had been good Roman wine, that this was the captain's cabin.

The other door was closed. I passed through it as though it were made of mist rather than seasoned cedar-wood and instantly knew that I was in the right place.

The cabin was small, but bright and welcoming with a number of candles held in small metal sconces along the walls. To the rear of the cabin there hung a cleverly wrought tapestry depicting a maiden and a unicorn. Opposite was a small circular window through which I could just make out the pale stars. There was not much furniture, just a small table, an old wooden trunk that could double as a settle. One of the truckle beds had been made up and on it sat a woman I did not immediately recognise, but I knew must be Avice, my daughter's nursemaid and companion. She was combing the hair of a young girl with a beautiful but sullen face, who did not appear to be enjoying the experience. She gave a shout of annoyance and pulled away as the comb caught in her long, tangled hair. Avice reached out a gentle hand and stroked her cheek, before retrieving the comb and beginning her task once more.

Sprawling on the floor at their feet was a boy of perhaps ten or twelve summers who was playing with a small tabby kitten, teasing it by darting lengths of ribbon backward and forward, always just out of reach of its swift, darting paws. None of them gave the slightest indication that they were aware of me as I studied them with interest.

Morgause did not resemble her sister. With her deep brown eyes and rich tangle of tawny hair, she looked more like her mother. Despite this, I did not feel the same rush of recognition that I had experienced when I had looked into Morgan's eyes. But as I watched her, submitting with what seemed to be very poor grace to Avice's ministrations, I knew that Igraine had seen this scene unfold on many an evening back in Tintagel and felt a sudden surge of love for this petulant, pretty child.

Her hair now neatly plaited into two braids, Avice put her hand out to the boy, who handed her the ribbons and sat back to look at Morgause, his head on one side.

"I like you better when your hair is untied," he said, "You look too neat and tidy like that."

"I told you I look horrid with these stupid plaits." Morgause turned an angry face at Avice, who I could see was trying, without much success, not to laugh. "Why do you want to make me look ugly?"

"I couldn't make you look ugly if I shaved off your hair and painted your face blue," the nursemaid replied, "which I may well do one of these days." She winked at the boy, who grinned back at her. "I've heard that they paint their faces at King Lot's court; en't that right, Einar? So maybe we should all try it; have you got any of that woad-dye with you?"

"I've some in my pack, Avice. Shall I go get it? I'd like to see Morgause with a blue face. We could pretend she was a mermaid."

"Aye, or maybe one of your pictish warrior women…"

"Oh no, Avice; we don't have women in our armies. And Morgause isn't brave enough to go to war anyway; she'd only run away."

"No, Einar, I wouldn't, but I don't want to anyway. Being a soldier is stupid and boring. And I don't want you to paint my face blue." Morgause hated being teased. "Why are you both being so horrid?" There were tears welling up in her eyes as she flung herself face-forward onto the mattress. Instantly Einar looked contrite. He knelt beside the bed and stretched out his hand to pat her small, shaking shoulders.

"I'm sorry, Morgause." She said nothing, only buried her face deeper into the coverlet.

"Morgause, I didn't mean it. Don't cry." The boy reached up and clumsily stroked the braid that fell across her trembling shoulders.

Instantly, she twisted beneath him, a wicked smile on her face. She leaped from the bed, pushed him onto all fours, and jumped onto his back.

"I don't want to be a soldier. I'm going to be a queen like Mama told me. And you can be my pony. Giddy-up, pony." She kicked at his sides none too gently, but Einar, clearly very pleased that she was no longer sulking, obligingly trundled round the small room with the now utterly contented little girl on his back. Avice clapped her hands together after watching the pair bump twice into the settle and send the kitten scurrying for shelter under the bed.

"Enough now; it's time for Morgause to go to bed." She looked quickly through the window, noting the position of the moon. "Einar you have stayed here far too long; are you not supposed to be with the captain? Did he not promise to teach you to navigate by reading the stars?"

Einar made once last circuit of the room, ending by the bed where he stood up slowly, catapulting a giggling Morgause backward onto the mattress. "Yes, but it seems unfair that I have to do lessons at night as well as during the daytime."

"One day, I'll warrant that you will want to leave King Lot's court and go back to your own home. I think you'll be glad then that you took the time to learn about the night skies. It is kind of Captain Trevenna to give up his time for you."

"I think he'd much rather be under the stars with you, Avice," the boy said. "I watched him yesterday when you and Morgause were sewing, up on deck. He couldn't take his eyes off you."

"Get on with you, lad," said Avice, turning away from him to plump up the pillows, and perhaps to prevent him from seeing the blushes which had suddenly appeared on her cheeks. "Now say good night to Morgause, and mind you pay attention to your lessons."

Einar planted a quick kiss on the top of Morgause's head, bade them both good night, and left the cabin.

"Now then, young lady, into your nightgown and straight into bed." As she spoke, she began to help Morgause to undo the laces of her over-dress and soon she was tucked up in the truckle bed as Avice folded her clothes and packed them neatly in the trunk. As she went round the small cabin, tidying away Morgause's work box and playthings, she sang softly, in a low sweet voice. At the end of each verse, she blew out the candles until only one remained alight and the child was fast asleep, with the kitten curled up on the bed beside her.

Avice took a cushion from the end of the bed and sat down on the trunk. It was too dark for her to sew, but I saw that she had a large hank of washed lamb's fleece and a pair of small, flat brushes. She was clearly going to occupy her time carding the wool, possibly in preparation for spinning it the next day.

She settled herself back against the cabin wall, and I knew that now was the time for me to approach her. Stepping forward into the faint flicker of the candle flame, I touched her lightly on the shoulder, and then placed my finger first on my lips and then on hers, betokening her to silence. I saw her eyes widen in shock as she recognised me, and it is to her credit that no sound escaped her.

I spoke quietly, my voice little more than a whisper. "Avice, you know what I am?"

"I th-think so, my lady. You are my lady's taibhse, sent hither from Tintagel?"

"Yes, I must speak with you, and I do not have much time. Where can we talk?"

Her eyes darted first to the bed, where Morgause turned in her sleep, burrowing deeper into the soft mattress, and then to the door, which Einar had not closed completely. "Clem…the captain. His cabin will be empty for some time yet I think."

I nodded and we left the room, Avice taking with her a candle to lighten the gloom in the captain's cabin. She propped the door open with her carding brush to make sure she would hear if Morgause woke up and called for her. There was something about the gesture that seemed practised, almost habitual, and I wondered if Avice had been leaving her cabin at night on other occasions.

Remembering Einar's words and the blush they had raised on her cheek, I thought that perhaps the handsome captain and my daughter's nursemaid had struck up something more than a professional friendship during the voyage. If so, it would be a good thing as it would make what I must ask of her perhaps a little more palatable.

The summer Solstice is a celebration of life, of fertility, of the Goddess' goodness in making our fields and bellies fruitful. It is a festival of fire, warmth, love, and desire as we honour the power that has brought us into being and taught us that our time on this earth is not just about duty and hardship but also about pleasure.

Morgause was but a child, and no one would expect her to complete the most sacred element of the Solstice rituals until she was a woman grown. Nonetheless, her position as the soon-to-be Queen of Orkney meant that, as the most high-ranking person on board, she must participate. I needed Avice to act as her proxy, and to do so willingly and in full understanding of what the ritual would require.

The young woman tutted at the mess of papers strewn across the table and immediately began to tidy them, putting them into orderly piles before folding the jerkin that had been left in a heap by the bed and placing it over the back of the wooden chair. She clearly felt very at home here, and equally clearly was doing these tasks as a way to avoid looking at me and finding out what I had come to say.

Suddenly I remembered that a taibhse often visited its loved ones at the point of death, and perhaps Avice feared that this was why I had come.

"Avice, stop doing all that and listen to me. What I have to say to you is important and I need to you to hear and understand me."

Avice nodded, raising her eyes to mine for a second, before casting them downward. "My lady…are you…"

"No," I interrupted. "You have no need to worry, I'm not dead. I have not come to Morgause to say goodbye, but to make sure that she will do what I need of her this Solstice." At this, Avice nodded and met my gaze with a little more confidence.

"Have you been preparing her, teaching her of the rites and her role within them, as I instructed you back in Tintagel?"

"Yes, my lady I have…when I can…" She paused and looked up at me somewhat shamefacedly. "You know Morgause…she doesn't like her lessons; she prefers playing with her kitten and talking with Einar."

"It really is irrelevant what she likes and dislikes, Avice; she is my daughter and will one day be Queen of Orkney. She has a duty to undertake and this year it is more important than ever that we honour the Goddess and show her our love and our respect."

Avice nodded. "I'm sorry, my lady. I'll make sure she understands what she has to do. It helps when Einar's there; he's a good boy and Morgause loves being with him."

"Whatever it takes, Avice. The rituals must not only be observed, they must also be seen to be observed. Lot's men will be watching Morgause, child though she is, and it is important that they carry good reports of her back to his court."

I looked around the cabin, seeking the small wooden chest Morgan had told me I would find there. Finally, I spotted it next to a small pile of branches, boughs from the hallowed trees that had also been entrusted to the ship's captain. It seemed that Igraine had judged him well. He was a man loyal to the Goddess, and keen to keep his word.

I asked Avice to bring the chest to the table and open it. Inside were a number of small jars and muslin bags containing the herbs, salves, and potions that would be needed for the ritual. There was also a beautiful box, made from polished copper, engraved with the symbols of Solstice, the sun, moon, and sacred flame.

"Open the box," I instructed. She did so, revealing two beautiful amulets hung on strong but delicate chains. One, made of gold, depicted the Solstice fire, the other, cast in silver, showed the Sun and Moon entwined in an embrace of perfect balance and symmetry.

Avice gasped in recognition. "But my lady, these are yours, you can't give these away, not even to your daughter. Surely you will need them for the rituals in Tintagel?"

"They are copies Avice, exact and perfect, as Igraine's amulets are exact and perfect copies of her mother's. You must hold them in trust for Morgause until she is old enough to claim them. Until then, they are for you to use, at my bidding and with Igraine's blessing."

I looked out of the window at the blue-black sky. The moon was still high in the heavens, the stars shining keen and clear in the cloudless sky. I gauged the hour to be still some way before midnight, but I did not know how long Einar would remain at his lessons, nor how soon after that the captain would decide to return to his cabin. I knew I might not have much time.

Avice was still preoccupied with the amulets, turning them this way and that, smiling as they caught the light from the candle, sending small shimmers of light dancing across the walls of the cabin. I think she felt the intensity of my gaze for she suddenly replaced them carefully in their box and turned to face me.

"What will you have me do, my lady?"

"You are to lead the rituals this Solstice on the *Llyr's Daughter*. In the years to come, you are to be Morgause's proxy at the court of King Lot, until my daughter is old enough to claim her rightful place."

At this she gasped but said nothing. I was reassured by her silence. Avice had been raised at Tintagel and was well versed in the ancient ways. What I asked of her was not completely unknown. Many noble girls were sent to live with their intended husbands long before they were old enough to join them in the marriage bed, and it was accepted that an alternative had to be found if the rituals were to be celebrated during the years before the marriage could be consummated. Indeed, I knew that many would regard what I asked of her an honour, but still, I was pleased that she did not protest.

"Morgause will take the lead in the ritual. She will wear the silver amulet, and Einar, as Lot's ward, shall wear the gold. Together, they will light the litha fire and say the ritual words. You must coach her until she is word perfect. You say she works better when the boy is present, so teach them together tomorrow." Avice nodded, still saying nothing.

"When the fire is lit and the ritual blessings are complete, you will kneel before Morgause, and she will anoint you and present you with the amulet. You will then be acknowledged by all as the representative of Cornwall and of Avalon. But for the rites to be complete, you will also need a partner to channel the flow of life and power that is at the heart of Solstice."

I looked at her, a faint smile on my lips. "We have chosen the captain to play Lot's part in the ritual." At this she started. "I think that you and Clem Trevenna are already more than friends. Am I right?" Avice nodded, and once again, a blush rose upon her cheeks.

"Are you lovers?" Again, she nodded, not looking me in the eye.

"There is no shame in it, girl; you have given yourself freely, and that simply honours the Goddess. It many ways, it makes this easier for you, as I am merely asking you to do through duty what you are already doing through inclination."

I decided at this point to say nothing further about the future Solstice rituals, where Avice would act as Morgause' proxy with King Lot until my daughter reached an age where she could be a wife to him in truth. Avice had accepted the charge I had laid upon her, and at this moment, my only real concern was this year's ritual. Worrying about the far distant future was not a luxury I could afford to indulge in.

"When you have received the amulet from Morgause, the captain must kneel before Einar and be anointed and receive the gold amulet in his turn. The final part of the ritual will then begin. Sky-clad, you and your lover must hold your hands fast and swear, on behalf of Cornwall and of Orkney, to honour the Goddess and do her bidding so that she will bestow her blessings on our lands. Then, you must both leap the flames. Do you understand?"

Avice nodded. "And then…the final part of the ceremony…must it be in front of everyone?" I could see the worry in her eyes.

"No child, there is no need. You may then retire here, to this cabin, to complete the ceremony. Use the salves within the box to prepare your bodies and to enhance your pleasure, which you must offer up as a final gift to the Goddess."

"I will do so, my lady. I give you my word." She paused and I could see questions forming in her mind. "But what about Clem… who will instruct him? How can I tell him about the part he will be called upon to play? He may refuse me…if he does, what will I do?"

"Hush, child; he agreed to play his part before the ship set sail." Morgan had told me that her mother had discussed this with the handsome captain the day before the *Llyr's Daughter* sailed from Tintagel harbour. He was a loyal servant of the Goddess, and it had apparently taken but few words to persuade him. And that was before he had been bewitched by the shy smile and pale green eyes of the pretty nursemaid.

"So all of this has been planned for weeks…" Avice's tone was hurt and resentful. "Is everything he's said to me a lie? Has it all been just because of Solstice?"

I could see that she was about to cry and wished that I could take her in my arms to reassure her, but I could no more embrace her than I could loosen the kerchief from her waist and pass it to her.

"Hush, child; no, if all he cared for was his duty, I doubt he would be mooning after you in front of Einar and his crew. I heard what the boy said earlier—that the captain 'couldn't take his eyes off you.'" The girl sniffed and rubbed her eyes. "Listen, Avice; perhaps Igraine should have spoken to you of this before you set sail, but she did not want to burden you. Take it from me, whatever Clem Trevenna has said to you is genuine. He is a good man and an honest one."

This seemed to comfort her. I just hoped that she would not begin thinking about what would happen when she and Morgause arrived in Orkney, and she would be parted from her lover. It had been agreed the *Llyr's Daughter* would continue on from Orkney on a trading mission to Einar's homeland, and it would be many months before she would have any hope of seeing him again. Still, that moment was several weeks away, and my instinct told me that Avice was young enough to think little of anything but the moment she was living in.

Suddenly we heard noises from the deck. Voices and snatches of laughter. Einar and the captain had finished their lesson, and both would be wanting to turn in for the night. It was time for me to leave Avice to the tender mercies of her lover.

Once again, I looked at the sky, where the moon now rode high upon the heavens. I calculated that I still had several hours before I needed to go back to Tintagel. This decided me.

"Avice, I thank you with all my heart. I've a little time before I go, and I would spend this with Morgause. I'll watch over her whilst you tell Clem all that I have told you. I think you may have much to discuss." I smiled at her. "Put away the amulets, they are very precious and mustn't come to harm. It would be a difficult task to replace them if they were to be lost or damaged. I entrust them to both of you, to keep them safe."

"Yes, my lady." She bowed her head, and I went toward her and touched her lightly on the brow, my cold fingers brushing her soft skin almost imperceptibly. She shivered involuntarily as the door opened and the ship's captain strode into the room. His face lit up when he saw her standing there and in a heartbeat he had pulled her into his arms.

I made my way back to Morgause' cabin, feeling certain that, at least on board the *Llyr's Daughter*, the Solstice ritual this year would be performed by true and loving souls.

ALL WAS AS IT HAD been when we left her and Morgause was snuggled deep beneath her blanket, the kitten curled up beside her. The single candle had long since burned out, but there was a narrow track of moonlight falling on the pale wooden floor of the cabin, casting sufficient light to show me the soft curve of her cheek and the delicate sweep of her lashes. I stood beside her, silent and unmoving, conscious only of her gentle breathing and the passage of the moon across the sky, marking the hours.

As the sky to the east began to lighten, I knew that I would have to leave her. I bent toward the bed, meaning to place a single kiss upon her sleeping forehead, but as I did so I felt a wrench within my chest. The searing pain was sharp and violent; if I had been corporeal, it would have been akin to someone pulling my heart, still beating, from my body.

Then I heard a voice shouting, a cry turning into a scream of anger and despair. In an instant, I recognised the voice. It was Gorlois. At the same moment, I felt a force pulling me backward, away from the bed and out, through the walls of the ship, into the ever-lightening sky. Faster and faster I flew, heading southward, onward, onward, until the lands below me were nothing but a blur.

And still I heard the screams, but now there were more voices joining those of the war duke. I heard commands and battle cries, the terrified whinnying of horses and the clash and batter of sword, axe, and shield.

I could not make sense of this. Armies did not wage war at night, but I could not doubt that there, below me, a battle was taking place. As the speed of my flight lessened, I began to recognise my surroundings. This was the fort of Demelihoc, after Tintagel, Gorlois' strongest fortified castle. But the moat, ramparts, and sturdy oak portcullis had not prevented the castle from falling to what must have been a surprise attack.

As the sky at the horizon began to turn a deep dusky rose, I could make out soldiers sporting the snarling wolf's head of Ulster and Connaught and the pennants of the black crow of the Ceintish men ranged around the walls. Out on the wide plain before the castle, the battle was seething. I could see that Gorlois' men were completely outnumbered, and there, at the furious, hopeless heart of the fray, I saw a horse, dragged to its knees, pierced on one flank by an arrow and, on the other, a long, deadly spear.

There was something terrifyingly familiar about the scene I was watching. I felt that it had been seared with a dark and fierce pain upon my memory. And then I had it. Igraine had seen this, or something very like it, in a scrying bowl, with Vivian by her side, in the castle of Uther Pendragon.

As I got closer, I could see that the rider was a tall man, well-built, with broad shoulders. His head was bare and down his back tumbled a single war-plait. I saw three soldiers pull the rider down and engulf him as he continued to scream out his war cry.

Was it Gorlois? I still was not near enough to be sure. I willed myself forward, but as I did so, I felt the grip of small hands upon my shoulders, pulling me, shaking me. I tried to resist. I needed to go onward, deeper into the battle. I had to see what was happening, but the pull was too strong.

Gradually, the sounds of the skirmish faded, the screaming stopped, and I could hear only the soft voices of Elaine and Bennath, murmuring words that were calling me, entreating me, begging me to come back. And overlaying this, less regular, but more insistent, the voice of Morgan, commanding me to return.

Within seconds, I was back in the chamber in Tintagel. It was much as I'd left it. The body of Igraine lay still, unconscious on the floor, and the fire of willow and herbs continued to smoulder in the grate. The room was heavy with their scent and a heavy, fragrant haze hung around the hearth. The moon had vanished from the sky, and there was but a single star, shining above the horizon.

Bennath and Elaine smiled in relief when I appeared before them, but Morgan had nothing but fury in her fierce blue eyes. Before I could say a word, she pointed to the mirror, still balanced at the back of the hearth, half shrouded in the mists.

"We have no time for questions. It is nearly sunup and you must return to the place where you belong." Morgan threw a handful of herbs upon the fire. The twigs flared tawny red and orange for an instant and the smoke billowed up, once again obscuring the copper surface.

"Elaine, Bennath, help my mother to sit up." Instantly they obeyed her, Elaine sitting behind Igraine's limp body supporting her whilst Bennath raised her head so that she appeared to be looking deep within the mirror.

"It is time," Morgan said. "Thank you for your service, but now you must depart."

I could do nothing. I had no time to tell them what I had been called to witness, what had distracted me and caused me to endanger Igraine's life. Had I just been present at the moment of Gorlois' death, as it had appeared to her and Vivian so many months before in the scrying bowl at Caer Lundein? I did not know, and there was no more time. If Igraine were to survive this night, I had no choice but to walk toward the mirror.

I passed through Igraine's body, feeling as I did so a shiver of reawakening as that part of me which was her inner essence found its normal resting place. Her eyes flew open and watched me as I walked back into the mirror, back through the mists; back into nothingness.

Chapter Twelve

"Mother, wake up, mother… Come back to m," I heard Morgan's voice calling me, but it was muffled and distant, as though from a long way away. I was cold and my body felt heavy and unresponsive. I tried to speak but did not seem to be able to make my mouth move, and when I attempted to sit forward, I found I couldn't. I was completely reliant on Elaine's supporting hands keeping me upright. I wanted to scream, to tear my hair, to run from the room to the stables. I wanted to saddle a horse and ride to Demelihoc to find out what had happened, to seek the truth about what my taibhse had just seen. But I could do nothing.

I looked at myself in the mirror, my eyes wild, full of panic and anger. I willed myself to move, but nothing was happening. Then, I felt a touch, soft fingers rubbing something cool and sweet-smelling onto my hands, working the ointment slowly upward, past my wrist, toward my elbows. It was Bennath. Gently, and with sure, measured movements, she was urging my blood to flow and my energy to return to me. As she worked, I began to feel warm again, and I could sense a tingling beneath my skin as my body reawakened.

Soon, I could raise my arm. I reached out and touched Bennath's shoulder. She looked up at me, and smiled, but did not cease her work. She was now sitting in front of me, rubbing salve into my feet and legs, with firm, practised fingers. I tried again to sit up and this time I managed it, shifting slightly away from Elaine, and pushing myself forward until I was sitting upright and unsupported. Still, I could not speak.

"Morgan, please get your mother some wine, it will help to revive her," said Bennath, and without a word, she obeyed, half-filling a small beaker from the pitcher of spiced wine on the table.

"What's wrong with her?" asked Morgan. "Her eyes are strange, she looks frightened…no, she looks angry Do you think something happened to her when she was a taibhse?"

"I don't know, sweetling," said Elaine. "I won't lie to you. Though you are but a child, you kept vigil with us all night, and it would be wrong to pretend that I have no concerns. It always takes a little while for the body to recover after the ritual. We expected that. Your mother's essence has been apart from her body. That normally only happens on death, which makes everything stop. The blood ceases to flow, the heart to beat, and the lungs to draw breath. We made sure that Igraine's body still retained the tiniest flicker of life, but dawn was almost breaking when she returned to us. We will need to wait for Bennath to finish her work before we will know for certain that she will be well."

Morgan stood beside me and offered me the wine. I raised my hand to take it but found I could not make my fingers grasp the cup with sufficient strength. It would have fallen to the floor had my small daughter's fingers not closed around my own, helping me hold the wine and raise it to my lips. As I took a few small, hesitant sips, I looked into Morgan's eyes. She stared at me steadily, unblinking. Had I just been a witness to the death of her father? If Gorlois was dead, what would become of us? Would Uther show mercy to the daughter of his enemy? From what I knew of him, I doubted it. At this moment, I cared nothing for myself, feeling only an overwhelming sense of grief for what I feared I had lost, and a rising sense of panic about what would happen to my daughter. I had no fears for Morgause; she was on her way North, to the court of King Lot where she would be cared for and protected. But Morgan…what would happen to Morgan?

The wine warmed my throat; my mouth no longer felt dry. I felt my heart beat more strongly and my lungs fill with air. Pushing the wine away, I pulled myself to my feet and began to scream.

It was several minutes before I was calm enough to speak and, even then, my words came out in shuddering gasps that made little sense either to Bennath or Elaine. They were expecting me to tell them of my visit to Morgause on the *Llyr's Daughter* and could make neither head nor tail of my distraught and incoherent half sentences describing Gorlois and the battle at Demelihoc. I was aware of Morgan sitting by the fire, which by now had dulled down to a faint tawny glow, giving very little of either heat nor light to the cold morning. She stared at me fixedly, with an appraising gaze that appeared to be more intrigued than disturbed by my obvious distress. It was her composure that eventually allowed me to regain my own.

Elaine was standing beside me, trying to put her arms around my shoulders, but I pushed her away. Walking to the settle I picked up my old shawl and went to wrap it round Morgan. I could see the gooseflesh on her slender arms, and her face was pale, her eyes huge and blue-rimmed with tiredness.

"No, Mother, I don't need it. You take it," She held out the shawl to me and I suddenly realised that I too was frozen with cold. "What happened, Mother? Why were you so late returning you to us?"

"Did I frighten you, darling? I'm so sorry, but the night did not turn out as we had planned." I wrapped the shawl around me and motioned to Bennath to stoke up the fire with logs from the wood basket.

As she did so, I sat down beside my daughter and accepted the beaker of milk warmed with honey that Bennath had just fetched from the kitchens,.

I told them about my journey to the *Llyr's Daughter* and all that had happened. When Elaine heard about the romance that appeared to be blossoming between Avice and the ship's captain, she smiled, saying, "Well there's a match that will please her parents." Avice was the daughter of Gorlois' master falconer, and he and his wife had always lived within the castle walls. "I know for a fact they were worried that she'd up and marry one of the men of Orkney and never feel the need to come back here to Tintagel. If Avice weds Clem Trevenna, like as not he will bring her back here when Morgause is a woman grown."

Bennath nodded, but clearly had little interest in the affairs of a woman she had never met. "And the Solstice…is all prepared? Does Morgause understand what she must do—and is Avice ready to play her part in the ritual?"

I told them that all was well and that nothing ill had befallen me on my journey to the Northern seas. And here I hesitated, very conscious of my small daughter sitting beside me. She had allowed me to wrap the ends of the shawl around her shoulders and the soft wool and the glow from newly re-kindled fire had warmed her. Whilst I had been speaking, I had seen her eyelids drooping, and as she leant in to me, nestling close in a way she almost never did when awake, I could see that she had fallen into sleep. Gently, I moved away from her, lowering her softly onto the pile of furs that lay in front of the hearth. I covered her with the shawl and putting my fingers to my lips, gestured to Bennath and Elaine to join me on the other side of the room.

Quietly, I told them about the scream that had pulled me from Morgause's cabin and sent me flying in desperation to the battleground at Demelihoc. Tears came unbidden to my eyes as I told them what I had seen, and what I now feared—that Gorlois was dead, the war lost and the vengeance and fury of Uther Pendragon was about to fall upon myself, my children, and all of Cornwall.

When I had finished, Elaine and Bennath were silent. I could see that both of them were thinking hard about what this would mean and how best they could advise me. It was Bennath who spoke first. "My lady, we must first establish if what you have seen is true, or if it was merely a trick of the psychomanteum. You say that you had seen this scene before, in the scrying bowl?"

I nodded.

"Perhaps your taibhse did not wish to return to the land of shades. Perhaps she decided to play a cruel trick on you, to keep you occupied beyond daybreak. Perhaps she took you onward, into the future, to see something that might happen, but as yet, has not."

Elaine seized on this idea eagerly. "Yes, Igraine, this could be true. We called upon rough magic this night and it does not always deal gently with those who summon it."

Bennath took up her cloak. "I will send riders to seek news. Demelihoc is not so far from here. If they leave now, they should be back by noon tomorrow."

"Do so," I replied, reaching out to touch her cheek, grateful that this woman stood beside me, adding her strength and determination to my own. "But a word of caution, choose only riders who know how to keep their counsel. Until we know the truth of it, no one else can know what might have happened."

Bennath nodded. I drew her to me and held her, feeling her warmth and strength. I kissed her brow, released her, and she was gone.

"Elaine, send Jago to me; I must tell him what has happened. We needs must make ready."

"And what of the Solstice, Igraine? What of the Great Gathering?"

I had almost forgotten the Solstice. The sun was now risen on Solstice Eve, and Tintagel and the villages on the headland were thronged with those who had journeyed to us, to take part in the ritual and to pledge their support to me, to Cornwall, and to the Goddess. I thought quickly.

"I must speak to the leaders of the Great Houses. Bring them to me in my solar after I have spoken with Jago. Whatever has happened, Uther's forces cannot reach us for several days. Our riders will be fleet of foot, an army cannot move as quickly."

She nodded. "Aye. And like as not, Uther will also wish to celebrate the Solstice. He will not think of battle until the rituals are done."

This was true, and it bought us time. I was certain that both Vivian and Merlin were with Uther. For both of them, the need to publicly proclaim their loyalty to the Pendragon as the favoured of the Goddess would mean that the rituals would be held with great pomp and ceremony—perhaps, I thought, amid the ruins of Demelihoc, a place where Gorlois and I had often kept Solstice in the early years, before Morgause and Morgan had been born. I did not want to think of those nights, where we had offered up our love as a tribute to the Goddess. It was too painful and distracted me from what I had to do.

After Elaine had gone, I carried Morgan to her chamber and put her to bed. She did not stir as I loosened her kirtle and covered her with a warm blanket, closing the shutters so the sun would not wake her. I returned to my solar to find Jago waiting for me, a look of concern upon his face.

Not wanting to disclose the full truth of our activities the previous night, I simply told him that we had been sent a vision in the scrying bowl. When I told him of the battle scene, and the rider that could have been Gorlois being unhorsed and pulled to the ground, he turned pale and sank to his knees, a look of horror on his face.

"Jago, we do not know if what we saw has happened. The Goddess sometimes sends us visions to prepare us for what must be, or to warn us of what may come to pass. We have sent riders to find out more and until they return to us, we cannot know for certain what has happened."

"That's as mebbe, M'Lady…but I can tell that you're afeared that my lord is dead and all is lost."

"Jago, whatever has happened, we must be ready. There is no time for debating over niceties. We must do everything we can to prepare for the worst, whilst all the time hoping that Gorlois is unharmed, and Uther and Vivian are not calling their forces down upon us."

Jago nodded slowly, biting his lip, his eyes closed. He gave a deep breath that was almost a sigh and got to his feet. "What would you have me do?"

"I need you to prepare the castle. My husband left Lord Madoc in charge of the garrison, please can you go to him and tell him what we fear. I must talk to the Great Houses about our plans for Solstice. They must be given the chance to leave today if they wish to do so."

My steward saw the sense of my words and took his leave. I asked him to invite Lord Madoc to the feast in the Great Hall at sundown. For the rest of the day, I was busy.

As the sky began to darken I finally left my solar. It had been a hard day and although I had changed my work-stained robe for a formal kirtle and overdress of sapphire-blue samite, I still felt tired and sullied. I made my way to the Great Hall.

The room was full. Apart from the table on the dais, every seat was taken, and many people stood around the walls or perched on the ledges of the high stone windows. As I walked in, Bennath got up from where she had been sitting with the warrior maids of Ynas Bray and came to stand beside me. Elaine, holding Morgan by the hand, joined us and, together, we walked toward the high table.

I saw Ened, sitting beside Hild and Epona, looking scared and uncertain. At the far end of the room I spotted the young Tintagel smith and the girl from Ynas Bray. They were standing close together, her head just resting on his shoulder. Although they looked relaxed and secure in each other's company, they were not smiling.

Jago, now dressed formally in his steward's robe, with a battle axe at his belt, was standing by the steps that led up to the dais. Next to him was Lord Madoc, my old friend and countryman. He took my hand to lead me to my seat, and I motioned to Bennath and Elaine to follow me, Elaine lifting Morgan up the high steps and placing her on the chair next to mine. I took the High Chair at the centre of the dais and Bennath ranked herself behind me. Elaine took her place behind Morgan and Lord Madoc seated himself on the remaining chair to my left.

The Hall was silent. Although I had instructed Jago to say nothing and had requested the representatives of the Great Houses to hold my words in confidence, I could sense the fear and apprehension in the room. Solstice Eve was usually a festive occasion, a chance to laugh and make merry before the more formal rituals took place.

I had managed to speak to the Priestesses of the Great Houses—Treliggan, Fowey, Bodmin, Ynas Bray, Polperro, and Mevagissey—and had been greatly heartened that all of them had decided to remain in Tintagel and celebrate our Solstice together as a symbol of our unity.

"We stand together, Igraine," said Matilda, priestess of Fowey and companion from my days in Avalon. "What will be is the will of the Goddess, and if we hold fast to her wisdom, we have nought to fear." I had embraced her when I heard these words and was delighted that Matilda's thoughts were echoed in the other conversations I had held throughout the day.

I had been honest with each of the priestesses about my adoption of the psychomanteum and the summoning of my taibhse. Unlike Jago, these women were adepts, daughters of Avalon, and learned in the Mysteries. They understood why I had made use of such a dangerous ritual and agreed that the need to prepare Morgause had justified the risk.

They could not agree, however, about the true nature of what I had seen. Yseult of Treliggan felt certain that I had been called to witness an actual event and it had been the dying screams of Gorlois that had summoned me to his side. But Jowanet of Bodmin saw things differently, putting forward an argument very similar to Elaine's and citing other occasions where vengeful and unhappy spirits had refused to return quietly to the shadowlands.

As we could not agree about what had actually happened on the previous night, we decided the wisest course was to say nothing and to carry on with our arrangements for the Solstice. I reassured the Priestesses that Lord Madoc and Jago were actively engaged in preparing the castle and our dominions for defence against an attack by Uther's forces, but that nothing was likely to happen for several days. Several of the Houses declared that they would change their plans and make ready to leave on the morning after Solstice, but I was delighted that the Houses of Ynas Bray, Fowey, Truro, and Mevagissey would stay and join with us if it came to battle.

The noise and chatter in the Great Hall had fallen away and I looked down the tables at the faces turned toward me, all waiting to hear what I would say. I raised my goblet in welcome as Bennath pulled back my chair so I could stand and address them. My mind had been troubled all day about what I would say, but now I knew with certainty that the right words would come. I smiled, took a sip of my wine, and saluted them.

"Friends, guests, good countrymen, thank you for being here in Tintagel on this Solstice Eve. Our lands, Cornwall, Syllan, and Lyonesse are most precious to us. Our fields bring forth crops; our orchards bear fruit. We harvest the fish from the seas and the deer from the woods and forest. All of this we have because of the Goddess and her goodness. All this we have because we love our lands and care for them.

"This year, we are at war.

"Many of our warriors cannot be with us and that is a sad and terrible thing. We miss them and wish that they were here with us today."

I heard a muffled sob, and, looking around the room, saw Ened, tears rolling down her face, being rocked in the bony arms of Hild, whilst Epona hurriedly filled a goblet and passed wine to her distraught friend.

"Lady Ened, we all share your fears. But we must not be consumed by fear. We have heard the words of Yseult, the Lady of Treliggan. She has been blessed with a vision and she has told us that this war is part of a wider plan, a greater destiny—so, how can anyone taking part in a plan that has been willed by the Goddess be abandoned by the Goddess?

"Tonight, let us make merry, let us eat and drink and enjoy our pleasures." My eyes roamed around the room, looking for the girl from Ynas Bray and her blacksmith conquest.

"There are some here who are discovering these pleasures for the first time." I raised my wine in their direction, and when their eyes caught mine, they smiled, blushes on both their faces. She took his chin in her hand and kissed him hard and sweet and the room erupted in cheers and laughter. When it fell silent, I continued.

"Tomorrow, we rise early to celebrate our Solstice, but until then, my friends, my guests, my countrymen, may the blessings of the litha fire be upon you and the hospitality of Tintagel bring you joy."

I took my seat to resounding applause and Jago signalled to the scullery boys and maids to bring in the feast. "What think you, Lord Madoc, will all be well tonight?"

"Aye, my lady, that was bravely done. You are your father's daughter. He would have been proud of you tonight." The old warrior smiled at me, and taking my hand, raised it to his lips. "I salute you, Igraine. But, please, heed a word of caution from one who has known you long and loves you well." He was no longer smiling, and his pale grey eyes stared unblinkingly into mine. "You must know that we cannot defend Tintagel from Uther's forces. If what you saw was true and Gorlois is defeated, you must leave. You must take Morgan and you must go."

"But where could I go, even if I had mind to? I cannot go back to my father's court, not after everything my brother has done. He has declared himself against me. And I cannot return to Avalon. The Lady Vivian has made it plain that I will find no welcome there. No, Lord Madoc, my place is here. I will not run. I will keep my faith in the wisdom of the Goddess and will dance my steps to the music that she plays."

The old man gave my hand a final, gentle squeeze and let it go. "Igraine, brave words are easy said when there is a fire in the grate and food on the table. Things do not always look the same when the enemy is at the gate. Please, think about it. You should prepare to leave. If Uther marches on Tintagel, it will not go well for you and your daughter."

I knew that he was right, but I was not prepared for discussions of this nature. I had succeeded in lifting the mood in the Great Hall, and I did not intend to risk this by engaging in an argument on the dais. I looked down at my daughter, who was toying with the food on her plate. She yawned ostentatiously and turning to me said, "Mother, I think I would like to go to bed. Will you take me, please?" I saw Elaine was about to speak, most likely to offer to take on this task herself, but I shook my head slightly to dissuade her.

"Lord Madoc, I know that all you have said is said from care of me and mine, and so I thank you. I must get young Morgan to her bed. Please, stay, enjoy the feast. We will meet tomorrow."

I stood, and Morgan uncharacteristically held up her arms to me to be carried. I picked her up and she snuggled up against me and, looking the picture of doting motherhood, I slowly made my way out of the hall, with Bennath and Elaine following behind.

As soon as we were away from the Great Hall, Morgan wriggled in my arms and said, "Please put me down, Mother. There is no one watching us now." I did as she asked. My daughter suddenly seemed very wide awake. I smothered a giggle.

"That was very naughty, Morgan," said Elaine. "Pretending to be tired so that your poor mother had to leave the feast."

"Oh, I think that Mother wanted to leave. And I was very happy to oblige. I was getting very bored."

I smiled down at my marvellously intuitive little daughter. "Morgan, you are a clever sprite, and I thank you for your invention. I did want to leave. Truth be told, I am tired; I have had little rest these past two days and I would be early to my bed."

I turned to Bennath. "And you, lady, are you tired, or would you like to re-join the feast?" I had seen the way Bennath had been looking at one of my men-at-arms, and I had a feeling that she had some unfinished business that last night's activities had prevented her from attending to.

"With your leave, my lady. I am still a little…hungry," Bennath winked at me and I smiled as she made her way back into the Great Hall.

"Elaine, will you stay with Morgan and see her to her bed? I will look to myself tonight." Elaine nodded her assent; I could tell that she was tired and was grateful that I did not require her to help me ready myself for sleep.

We mounted the stairs together and I said good night at the door of Morgan's chamber, making my way up the last set of stairs to my own room.

The candles had been lit and the last remaining rays of the early summer sun cast a warm and gentle glow upon the floor. I was tired and wanted nothing but to ready myself for sleep. A bowl of hot scented water stood upon the settle, and I undressed and took pleasure in washing myself with soap that smelled of roses. Elaine had left out one of my simple linen nightgowns, and I pulled it over my head, loving the feel of its cool folds against my skin.

Sitting on the bed, I reached for my comb and began to ease the tangles from my hair. I closed my eyes, breathing in the scent of applewood burning in the hearth. I would not think of the things Lord Madoc had spoken of. I would not allow my mind to be dragged back to a place of fear and uncertainty. Slowly, rhythmically, I combed my hair, calming myself and allowing a gentle peace to descend upon me. I began to twist my hair, to divide it into strands so I could plait it and keep it tidy whilst I slept when I heard a noise upon the stair and the door of the chamber burst open, and Gorlois, dressed for battle and with a bloody scar upon his cheek, threw himself into the room.

I could not move. The comb fell from my fingers. Gorlois pushed the door shut behind him and shot the bolt home. He said nothing as he threw off his cloak and then undid his sword belt, flinging both to the corner of the room. He began to unbuckle his breastplate as I stared, bewildered and uncertain, desperate to believe that what I was seeing was indeed my husband and not some revenant, a phantom conjured from the grief that was welling deep within me and which I had tried so hard to push away. If this was Gorlois, then the vision I had seen, the battle, the slaughter at Demelihoc, could not have taken place. Perhaps it had been a warning, like a vision in the scrying bowl. A warning I would heed if I wished to keep my husband safe.

"Gorlois?" I spoke his name and moved toward him, slowly at first, but then his eyes met mine and I ran toward him, into his open, welcoming arms.

At first we kissed with a hard hunger that, for me at least, still held within it the memories of our last parting. He had left me when I had begged him to stay, to bow down to Uther and to value the lives of our people more highly than his vainglorious pride.

I had been angry and refused to give him the reassurance he had asked for, had rejected him and sent him from me without my blessing. But then, today, on the battlefield of Demelihoc I'd seen a man so like to Gorlois it could have been his twin, dragged bleeding from his horse to what I'd thought was certain death. That sight, that fear of all I thought I'd lost, had once again woken within me the strength and certainty of my love.

Gorlois was not dead. He was here. In my room. In my arms. And I knew I loved him. I kissed him now with a passion that held no anger, only joy and a desire made even sharper by my awareness of what I'd thought I'd lost. I closed my eyes, and felt his hand cup the back of my head, his thumb gently tracing my cheek, his fingers moving downward, tracing my collarbone, moving toward the neck of my nightgown and the gentle swelling of my breasts.

Softly, I closed my mouth and moved away from him, placing my finger on his lips, to tell him that we needed no words. I pulled my nightgown over my head to stand naked before him in the flickering firelight. The room was warm, but I felt a faint shiver as the night air from the casement touched my skin and my nipples hardened as I felt his gaze upon me. I wanted him to know that all I had was his and that this night—I was giving myself to him, freely and with love. I went to him, easing first his tunic and then his shift over his head, noting that he winced with pain as he raised his right arm. Tomorrow, I would put salves upon his abused and beaten body, but now, there were more important wounds for me to heal.

I knelt before him, removing his battered deerskin boots and then loosening his belt and the cords that held his breeches. Weeks of marching and surviving on a meagre diet of soldier's rations had hardened my husband's muscles and worked away any spare flesh. He stood before me now, his beautiful, familiar body pale and lean. There was a new scar across his chest, still livid and inflamed, and mottled blue and yellow bruising patterned his ribs and back.

"Am I not a thing of beauty, Igraine?" he smiled ruefully, his voice low and soft.

I did not reply, simply reached out toward him to lead him to our bed. Pulling back the coverlet, I lay down upon the sweet-scented linen sheets and took his hand, drawing him to me. He moved slowly, with a shyness, an uncertainty that I had not known before; perhaps, like me, he was remembering our parting and the bad blood that had grown between us. Seeking to reassure him, I raised his hand to my mouth, kissing the tips of his fingers and flicking them with the tip of my tongue. I heard his breath quicken and I looked at him, meeting his eyes, gazing deep, deep within them as I placed his hand upon my breast, showing him that I welcomed him, that I wanted him.

"Let me look at you, Igraine," he spoke softly, but I could hear the desire within his voice, and it pleased me.

"As you wish, my love," I whispered, taking his hand once again and leading it downward, opening myself to him, never taking my eyes from his face, watching him as he explored the secrets of my body, as if discovering them for the first time.

And then he lay beside me and held me tight and kissing my lips, my face, my neck; his tongue gently licking, flicking, his mouth sucking, his fingers stroking and caressing until I was nothing but desire, shuddering beneath his touch with a pleasure that was more overmastering and intense than any I had known before.

When he too had spent, we lay together as we had done so many times before on his return from battle. He cradled me in his arms, my head resting softly on his chest, his fingers entwined in my hair, which had long ago escaped from its constraining plait.

"I'm sorry that I sent you away without my blessing. Do you forgive me?"

"Aye, Igraine," he said softly, almost on the verge of sleep, "you have given me comfort now, my love, and that is all that matters."

His eyes closed and his breathing was now slow and steady as he readied himself for slumber, but suddenly, I was restless. There were questions I had to ask that would not wait 'til morning.

"Gorlois, don't go to sleep yet, please tell me what has happened. How did you get here? Where are our soldiers? Where are Uther and his men?"

"Hush, sweetling," he murmured, not opening his eyes and clearly not wanting to rouse himself from slumber. "I came to you for Solstice. Because I love you." And with that, sleep took him. Gorlois had the soldier's ability to sleep anywhere and that, combined with his obvious physical exhaustion and the exertions of our love-making had sent him into a sleep so deep that I knew I would be unable to rouse him.

It was different for me. Despite my exhaustion and the need for sleep which had almost overwhelmed me earlier that evening, I was now wakeful, my mind full of worries and confusion. I eased myself from Gorlois' arms and, pulling on my nightgown, made my way to the window.

The sky was clear. The night was hushed and gentle and the stars and the horned moon shone out upon the water, making a silver pathway across the darkling waves. All was still. At night, the seabirds are quiet, and no sounds disturbed the dusky air as I looked out across the causeway to the headland.

The trees and shrubs cast long shadows across the scrubland, and I could see nothing moving. I had been looking for tents, for soldiers and horses, resting up after a long ride, but there was nothing. Gorlois must have come alone.

Feeling cold, I picked up my shawl and, wrapping it tightly around me, went to the hearth where a few embers were still glowing. Taking some peat from the basket, I built up the fire and sat down beside it, looking deep into its flickering heart.

Gorlois was here, in my bed; I could not doubt it. My mouth was still warm from his kisses and when I raised my hands to my face, I breathed in the familiar rich, musky smell of him.

There was a noise from the bed. Gorlois had stirred and rolled over and was now lying on his side with his face toward me. I noticed that the rawhide throng with its wooden symbol of the Risen god that he had been wont to wear despite my protests was no longer there. Instead, around his neck was a thin chain from which hung a small leather pouch, of the sort I had made in Avalon to hold herbs and amulets to bring calm or ward away bad dreams. I remembered that I had made just such a necklet for Gorlois when we were newly married, and he was leaving me to go to war for the first time.

"Promise me you'll wear it," I'd said, as I hung it round his neck, "It will bring you sweet dreams and will protect you, so you come home safely to me." I remembered that he had smiled and tucked the little pouch for safety inside his tunic. I had refilled it many times over the years, re-sewing the seams when they wore thin, and he had never left me without it safe in place around his neck until his growing disillusionment with the Mysteries had caused him to set it to one side, replacing it with the plain, unlovely wooden cross.

I knew that the necklet he wore tonight was not the one I'd given him. I had wrapped it in linen and tucked it away in my jewel-box for safekeeping, hoping that one day he would ask for it again. I knew not who had given him the chain he wore around his neck, but however he had come by it, I could not doubt he now wore a token that honoured the Mysteries and had set aside the wooden cross.

He had told me that he'd returned to Tintagel to celebrate the Solstice because he loved me, but I found it hard to believe that he had lost all his doubts concerning the Mysteries. Our arguments on the subject had been too long-established and destructive for me to accept such a transmutation.

My mind was filled with questions as I gazed into the fire, staring deep into the black heart of the tawny flames that shimmered and twisted in the hearth. I thought back to that afternoon in Caer-Lundein when Vivian had called upon the Goddess to show us the future. We had seen the battle, the horrifying death of a man I had taken to be my husband, and I had seen that self-same scene again this morning as my taibhse was dragged from the *Llyr's Daughter* by the terrible screams of a dying man.

But She had also granted us another vision, that of Gorlois returning to me, as he had tonight. It had been exactly the same. Me, dressed in a simple gown, combing my hair as my battle-worn and injured husband burst into my chamber. We had watched for but a few seconds before I broke the spell, not wishing to share my most intimate moments with the Lady. It had only been after I had done that, and we had cleared our minds for a second time that the vision of my husband's death had unfolded in the waters of the scrying bowl.

These visions do not always presage what will take place. Sometimes they are a warning, a foreshadowing of a fate we may yet avoid if we can recognise the signs and turn ourselves toward the path the Goddess wishes us to tread. If that was so, then I had been sent this portent twice and I must not now ignore it.

As I watched the fire, the peat logs collapsed in upon themselves, extinguishing the flames and sending small sparks darting around the hearth. The fire was dying, its flames now dancing the final, slow measure that signifies the revels are close to ending. The more I thought about it, the more certain I became. Gorlois had been returned to me, and it was for me to make an end to the madness that had started when I had danced with Uther.

If I wished to avoid the fate that I had seen within the scrying bowl, I must persuade my husband to lay down his arms, swear allegiance to Uther and the Lady, and sue for peace.

Getting to my feet, I walked once more to the window. The moon now lay low, at the very edge of the world where the sea touches the sky. There was but one star still shining, the morning star, beloved of the Goddess. It was Solstice morn, and I had much to be thankful for. Smiling, I undressed and slipped into bed beside the man I loved.

I DID NOT SLEEP LONG and when I opened my eyes, I saw Gorlois, wide awake and looking at me, his face close to mine and smiling. I smiled back, and then frowned as I looked more closely at the raw, jagged edges of the inflamed scar on his cheek.

"How came you by this, my love?"

"It is nothing, Igraine. Nothing matters to me now that I am here with you. I truly thought this day would never come, that I would never hold you in my arms again." He bent to kiss me, but I moved away, sitting up in bed and resting my head against the wooden headboard.

"Tell me about it, Gorlois." I sat up, reaching out my hand for his. "We have had little news since you left us. Bennath has told me of the terrible things happening on the border, the atrocities carried out by Uther's soldiers, but we have heard nothing of you and your armies."

"Atrocities happen in war. You know that, and this war was not of my doing. I would rather have had the realm at peace than waste yet another summer on the battlefields when we could be caring for our lands." He untangled his fingers from mine and rolled over onto his back.

"Our lands are being attended to, as are the needs of our people. Tomorrow, after the rituals are done and we can rest, I will show you. We have not let the fields lie fallow. I have taken care of Cornwall whilst you have been at war."

He looked at me in astonishment. "Tell me of this, Igraine; what have you been doing whilst I have been away?" I told him everything, of Bennath's visit to Yseult of Treliggan, of the Goddess' command that the women of Cornwall and Lyonesse should take their place upon the land, ensuring it was cared for and brought forth fruit, of the messengers we had sent to call our people to action and, finally, of the summoning to the Great Gathering for the Solstice.

When I had finished he was silent for a moment, as if weighing up everything he had heard. Then he smiled. "My Igraine, you are a wonder. As clever as you are beautiful and as brave as you are compassionate. There never was one to compare with you. You are worth everything I have done, everything I have risked." He leaned toward me, and this time, I could not have avoided his kisses even if I had wanted to.

I felt exultant. My love had been returned to me, and the anger and bitterness that had eaten away at us during the days before he went to war now seemed to have vanished. I pushed him back upon the bed, moving on top of him and taking him deep inside me, where I wanted him to be, where I had need. I watched his face, his eyes closed, his mouth slightly open. I could see the pale pink edge of his tongue pressing against his teeth as his breath came faster and his pleasure rose. Suddenly, his eyes opened, and he pulled me to him, kissing me, drinking me in as though to slake a raging thirst. He shuddered, calling out my name. And then was still.

I lay upon his chest, quiet now, feeling our heartbeats beginning to slow down, in step with each other, joined to each other. I licked his skin, tasting the familiar salt and put my hands to his lips so he could taste me. His tongue flickered, licking between my outstretched fingers. I don't think I have ever felt so at peace, so close and connected to another.

I closed my eyes and would perhaps have drifted back to sleep had there not been a noise from the corridor, the sound of the door handle rattling, then a loud knocking and two voices speaking simultaneously. "My lady, Igraine, are you well?" "Mother, why have you bolted the door?" It was Elaine and Morgan, one sounding worried, the other simply annoyed.

I giggled. "Shush, say nothing, lie back and cover yourself. Let us give our daughter a surprise." Gorlois nodded and did as I suggested. I pulled my nightgown over my head and made my way to the door.

The knocking continued, and someone was twisting the handle furiously. "Be calm, all is well; there is no need to shout, Elaine, you will waken half Tintagel." I drew back the bolts and stood to one side as the door was thrown open.

Elaine was holding a tray laden with fruit, fresh bread, honey, and a pitcher of water whilst Morgan carried bunches of wildflowers, the dew still wet upon them. They must have been out early, picking them from the castle gardens. Elaine looked at me, her face an unspoken question, but said nothing as she placed the tray upon the table. Morgan walked across to the settle and laid the flowers out in a neat row. Columbine and honeysuckle, kingcups, cornflowers, and sprays of dog roses, still in bud, but which I knew would shed their petals before the day was done.

"They are beautiful, Morgan, thank you."

"They are for your hair. Bennath said she would come and help you. She will do mine too. We need to get ready. Why was your door locked?"

"Well, sweetling, last night I had a visitor. Can you guess who it could have been?"

Morgan looked at me, her fierce blue eyes large and serious in her small, pale face. "Whoever it was seems to have made you happy, Mother. You are smiling like you used to before you went away to the King's court."

At her words I turned involuntarily and looked in the mirror. She was right. My face glowed; there was a rosy blush across my cheekbones; my eyes were bright and my lips, fuller than usual and reddened from Gorlois' kisses, had relaxed into a smile. I had not looked like that for months.

"A visitor? But there are no new horses in the stables and Jago said nothing of this. I was with him but an hour ago." Elaine looked troubled; if the castle Steward was not aware of my visitor, Elaine assumed that something had gone awry.

"My visitor saw no need to make himself known to Jago. His business was with me." I held out my hand. "Now come here, Morgan; come closer, I have a surprise for you."

She walked toward me, and as she did so, I pulled at the bedsheet. Gorlois understood the signal and sat up, letting the sheet fall forward and opening his arms.

Elaine stifled a scream and then ran forward to embrace me. "Oh, Igraine; he's come back, he's not dead; I am so happy for you." I kissed the top of her head and returned her hug. Letting her go, she made a curtsey to Gorlois. "Welcome home, my lord."

"Thank you. It does my heart good to see you again." He smiled briefly at Elaine, before turning back to look at Morgan, who was still standing by the settle, a look of disbelief upon her face.

"Morgan, come here," he spoke quietly, and beckoned her to him. Still she did not move.

"Who is that man, Mother?" She spoke quietly, but I could sense the fear in her voice as she looked at Gorlois, with his newly scarred face, livid cuts and bruises disfiguring his ribs and chest.

"Sweetheart, this is your father; he came back to us last night."

"That man is not my father." She stepped backward, knocking the flowers to the floor as she did so, and made for the door. "I don't know who he is, but that man is not my father."

She ran from the room as Gorlois threw back the sheets and made to follow her. I caught his arm and pulled him back into the room.

"Gorlois, let Elaine go to her. You are not dressed for a chase around Tintagel."

He grunted, wrapping the sheet around himself as a makeshift robe, but did not sit down, preferring to pace around the room.

"How dare she say I'm not her father; who does the little minx think she is?" He was angry, hurt that our youngest child had not thrown herself upon him, seeking hugs and kisses. But Morgan was not like that. Had Morgause been here, I felt certain that by now she would be sitting cuddled on her father's lap. But Morgan had never been a demonstrative child.

"Think about it, Gorlois; she hardly saw you when we got back from Caer-Lundein and before then you were often absent, doing Uther's bidding. She has seen little of you in her young life, and perchance you look very different from the father she remembers. Your hair has more than a touch of silver now you know, and there is a scar upon your face that was not there before."

"Hmmm. Perchance you are right. I must have become a very fearsome fellow for her to run away from me." He looked in the mirror and grinned ruefully. "This scar does nothing for my looks, Igraine. I have become a ruffian indeed."

I went to him and touched his face. "I think it becomes you well, my lord. But we have things to do and now is not the time for dalliance." I turned to my half-sister.

"Elaine, find Morgan and take her to Bennath. If anyone can calm her, she can do it. When you have done that, please ask Jago to prepare a bath for my lord and lay out his clothes for Solstice, then come help me to get ready."

She nodded and left the room. Gorlois was now seated at the table and making short work of the bread and fruit Elaine had brought me. I joined him, breaking off a crust of bread and coating it with honey. I poured us both some of the cool water.

"Are you still upset about Morgan?"

"No, I'm sorry I was angry. All I have dreamed of these many weeks has been to join you here, in Tintagel, and I wanted it to be perfect."

"It is perfect. You are here." I hesitated, knowing that I did not have much time before Elaine would return, accompanied, if I knew him at all, by Jago, who would be overjoyed to hear of the return of his lord and war duke.

"Gorlois, this morning you said that this war was not of your doing, that you would rather spend the summer making our lands strong and peaceful than on the battlefield." He nodded, his mouth too full of bread and honey to reply.

I chose my words carefully. "I noticed that you no longer wear the symbol of the Risen god around your neck." His hands went to the chain around his neck, as if he had forgotten it was there. I continued, "And last night you told me that you came back because it is Solstice. And because you love me."

"I do love you, Igraine. There is no one like you. No one could ever mean more to me than you do."

"Then, please, for my sake if not for your own, please bring an end to this war."

The words hung between us in the silent room. I had begged him not to start this conflict and each time he had argued with me, refusing to listen, determined only to defend what he thought of as his honour, not caring about the cost to himself, to me, or to his followers.

The world was still. We could just hear the shrill calls of the seabirds as they circled the causeway and the cliffs beyond Tintagel. Voices drifted up from the courtyard where the kitchen maids and pages were beginning to make ready for the celebrations. I said nothing more but continued to hold his gaze, and he did not look away.

"What would you have me do, Igraine?"

I had my answer ready. "Celebrate the Solstice with me, as Lord and Lady of this land, honouring the Goddess and swearing to protect and cherish Cornwall, Lyonesse, and all our people."

He was silent for a moment, his head bowed in thought.

Finally, he said. "Yes, I can do that. Over the past few weeks, I have felt the power of the Goddess, and she has been good to me. I am happy to pay tribute to her as she deserves." As he spoke, I saw his hand return once more to his neck, to touch the little pouch that nestled there. I was certain that it contained an amulet, something that had been given to him as a benison and protection. I knew not who had given it to him, but in my heart I blessed them.

"Gorlois, when the Solstice is over and we have time to talk, please tell me how this change has come about. It delights me that you and I are no longer in conflict. It is the thing I have hoped for above all others."

"Aye, Igraine, I too have longed for us to be as one." He raised my hands and kissed them. "And yes, there is much to tell and too much to do today. Tomorrow, we shall ride out, and I will tell you all that has befallen me." He paused. "But I think that is not all, there is more that you would have me do."

"Gorlois, this war will destroy you; it is already destroying Cornwall. Our people are being slaughtered in their hundreds, women ravaged, children orphaned. Our farms and fields are being laid waste. We cannot win. You know that. Uther is stronger, better equipped, with allies who will not fail him."

He was silent and would not meet my eye.

"You told your men that Uther had tried to rape me. Had dishonoured me, and in doing so, had dishonoured you. That is why we fled from Caer-Lundein. That is why we went to war.

"But was there really just cause? He kissed me, yes. And I was frightened, but I pushed him away and ran back to you, ruining that beautiful, cursed dress in the process, and yes, I was angry.

"Angry with Uther for making a spectacle of me before the court, furious with Vivian for trying to make me her puppet and yes, I was angry with you too, for your false pride, for getting drunk, for behaving like a boor rather than a noble war duke."

Gorlois reached out for me, placing his hand upon my arm: "Igraine, I understand your anger and truth to tell there is much about that night that shames me."

I looked away, gently removing his hand as I busied myself by pouring out more water and passing it to him. He seemed calmer, more accepting. Perhaps this time he would let me speak.

"Gorlois, please listen to me. Uther tried, yes. But he did not succeed. All that happened was a squalid little fumble in the castle corridor. And because of this, we went to war.

"And so many people have suffered, because of this war, because of me. Because of what Uther tried to do to me. Men killed; women despoiled. I do not want another child orphaned in my name.

"If you love me, listen to me. I cannot bear to be the cause of so much bloodshed, so much destruction. I do not matter. Cornwall matters, Lyonesse matters. Please, Gorlois, swallow your pride. Make peace"

Gorlois was sitting very still, a strange expression on his face. "Oh Igraine, you are hard upon yourself. I know that Uther wanted you. I am certain that he would have done anything to have you.

"I knew this war would come when I saw you walk toward the dais in Caer-Lundein, wearing that silver dress and looking more beautiful than any woman on earth. You could have done nothing to prevent it." I opened my mouth as if about to speak, but he raised his hand to silence me.

"Listen Igraine, I will heed your words. There will be peace. I will make my right and proper oaths, and you must, too. Will you swear loyalty to Uther? Recognise the Pendragon as your liege, overlord of Cornwall and rightful king of all the Britons?"

I felt a swell of relief begin to build within me. He had listened. He had agreed and now there would be peace. "Oh yes, I will bend the knee at your side. Today, during the Solstice rituals we will make our pledge for all to see," He leaned forward and kissed me lightly on the lips just as the door opened and Elaine, followed by Jago, made their way into the room.

Jago had tears in his eyes as he bowed low to welcome home his lord. The Steward had never faltered in his loyalty and had done all he could to serve me over the past months, but I knew that he was Gorlois' man through and through. For him, the world was out of kilter when Gorlois was absent from Tintagel. My husband used his good arm to pull his old servant upright and embraced him, an informality that I had never seen before, and which took Jago by surprise. Somewhat flustered, the steward assured him that hot water had been prepared and the ceremonial robes and golden chain I had never thought my lord would wear again were laid out in his chamber.

As they made to leave, I handed Jago a pot of salve and instructed him to treat Gorlois' bruising. I would have preferred to do it myself, but there was not time. "Apply it to his face as well," I told him. "It will help the wound to heal and make the scar less livid."

"And less frightening to my daughter," said Gorlois, smiling. "I hope that once I am once more presentable she will give me the welcome I desire."

"I'm sure she will, my love. Were Morgause here, I think you would have had all the kisses and affection any father could desire, although she would have been disappointed that you had not brought her back a present."

At the mention of our older daughter, I saw a look of slight confusion in my husband's eyes, but it cleared almost immediately,

"And what of my sweet Morgause…she is not here in Tintagel?" This disconcerted me. Surely he had not forgotten our plan to send our eldest child to the safety of King Lot's court, let alone our terrible argument caused by his attempt to remove the Goddesses symbols from the *Llyr's Daughter*.

"No, do you not remember? We agreed that she should be sent away for her own safe-keeping. By now she will be halfway to Orkney."

He nodded and rubbed his head. "How could I forget…Now, Jago, let's away. You will have your work cut out with me, but you must do your best to make me presentable if I am to be worthy of my lady."

With that, they left the room. Elaine was beginning to fuss about my own preparations and from the sounds drifting in through the window, the Great Gathering was already getting underway.

Chapter Thirteen

I undressed and washed quickly in the warm water Elaine had prepared for me; I felt quite giddy, my thoughts at sixes and sevens as I told my half-sister all that had happened. I could not doubt that Gorlois was here, returned to me with but a few bruises and another battle scar, but his sudden change of heart about the Solstice and the Mysteries was something I found difficult to understand however much I rejoiced in it.

As I pulled on my simple white underdress, I noticed Gorlois' sword and cloak lying in the corner, where he had thrown them last night. Picking up the sword, I stowed it carefully away in the settle. His cloak I hugged to me, breathing in my husband's familiar scent. I would know it anywhere. Closing my eyes I let the smell of him envelop me, finding both strength and comfort in the knowledge that my husband was back where he belonged, here in Tintagel. I allowed my mind to wander to the previous night and the sweetness of our reconciliation, only to be pulled from my reverie by a knock at the door and the sound of voices.

I opened the door to find Bennath and Morgan, both wearing their ceremonial gowns. Morgan's robe was deep red, cut open at the front to reveal a samite underdress embroidered in gold. They had originally been made for Morgause to wear the first time she had participated in the Solstice rituals and she had long ago outgrown them, but despite this, we had needed to shorten the kirtle and adjust it at the waist and shoulder to make a comfortable fit for my younger daughter's delicate, narrow frame. Her long dark hair fell in a glossy mass beneath her shoulders, and I could see a gleam of excitement in her pale blue eyes.

She went immediately to the flowers, which were still lying on the floor and began to choose the ones she wanted Bennath to weave into her hair. Bennath went to help her and soon they were sitting together in front of the old copper mirror.

"Is all well, my lady? Morgan has told me that you had a visitor this night?"

"Aye, Bennath; my lord husband has returned to me, to celebrate the Solstice."

Bennath's eyes opened wide and she looked at me in surprise. "He came alone? Where are the rest of the warriors? How goes the struggle?" I could see that Bennath had a thousand questions. Her husband, Sir Lowen, was with Gorlois' army, and I knew she was anxious to have word of him. Although she kept the old ways and was not averse to honouring the Goddess with one of my handsome men at arms, Bennath loved her husband and I knew she longed for their reunion. She had also witnessed first-hand the savagery with which Uther's troops had treated the people of Cornwall and I could tell that, like Elaine and Jago before her, she was a little bemused that Gorlois had risked the journey alone.

"There is much that I still don't understand," I said, realising just how little Gorlois had actually told me. I had been so determined to tell him the truth about what had happened in Caer-Lundein and to find a way to bring this conflict to an end that I had asked him very few questions. "Something has happened to change Gorlois' mind and he felt that he could travel more swiftly and in secret if he made the journey here alone. The one thing I can tell you with certainty is that he is here; he will join me in leading the rituals and afterward, and we will make oaths of loyalty to Uther and the Lady and the war will come to an end."

Both Elaine and Bennath turned to me in astonishment. Bennath dropped the flowers she was weaving into Morgan's hair and got to her feet.

"Igraine, what are you saying? Are we suing for peace without seeking reparation for all the destruction Uther's troops have wrought upon our land?"

At first, I did not know how to reply. I could see the shock and anger on Bennath's face. She was a warrior, trained and skilled in the arts of war. She wanted those people who had lost their families, their homes, and their livelihoods to be avenged. I understood that. But that was too simple a reaction. I was raised in a royal court, where I'd learned that the first duty of a ruler was to protect the land and its people, sometimes at great personal cost. I had been schooled in Avalon and had been taught to be far-sighted in both thought and deed, to consider my actions, and to think through their possible consequences. Gorlois, on the other hand, was a war duke, a man of action, but also a man who was not always willing to listen to wise counsel. His temper had long been his undoing and his determination to challenge Uther had led to the war and the brutalities and devastation that now haunted Bennath.

Elaine was now holding out my kirtle, which was the palest of greens, embroidered with summer flowers. It had been my mother's, and every time I wore it, I remembered her calm dignity and measured acceptance of the sorrows and indignities that marriage to my father had often brought her. I thought of her, sitting by the fire in the Great Hall embroidering the flowers of summer, cornflowers and columbine, poppies and campion, as the winter storms besieged the castle's stone walls. She was a queen who had understood that sometimes it was necessary to compromise in order to keep the peace. I slipped my arms through the sleeves and Elaine began to tie the green and gold laces. "Nothing we can do will bring back those who have died. What we can and must do is to prevent any more suffering."

"But Igraine, my lady, Uther's troops have not contented themselves to slaughter on the battle field. That is war, and a warrior goes into every battle knowing that it may be their last.

"They have raped and tortured, murdered young children and civilians, people who have committed no crime and who now have no home or livelihood. This must not go unpunished."

"Bennath, trust me. When we have peace, I will discuss this with Vivian, the Lady of the Lake. I've known her since childhood. She will listen to me."

"Have you forgotten that she has cursed you? She is not your friend. To negotiate peace is one thing. To surrender without making terms is at best foolhardy and at worst the actions of a coward." Bennath's lips were taut and thin in her narrow, sculptured face; her anger had caused her cheeks to flush and I could see that she was struggling to control her fury. "I will take leave of you, my lady."

She did not wait for my permission and left the room in silence.

Elaine had finished tying my laces and now motioned me to sit so that she could dress my hair. She did not meet my eyes. I grabbed the comb from her hand and began to drag it through my unruly, tangled hair.

"And do you think the same? Do you agree that I was wrong to persuade Gorlois to bring this war to an end?"

"I think it strange that he was so willing to agree. How many times did you ask him to swallow his pride and ask for forgiveness? But he would have none of it." Gently, she took the comb from my fingers and gestured once more for me to sit. This time I did so. "Igraine, he rode to war knowing you were unhappy, but it didn't bother him. He wouldn't listen to any of your arguments then. I know what you said to him before he left—and it fell on completely deaf ears. But he comes back to Tintagel a changed man. What's happened to make him listen to you now?"

"I don't know…maybe he's seen enough of war and death, maybe seeing our Cornish villages razed to the ground has sickened him, made him want to bring an end to it."

Elaine's fingers worked gently, easing the tangles, beginning to separate my hair into long strands for braiding. "But Igraine, Gorlois knows more of the brutality and cruelty of war than we can even imagine. He's been a soldier all his life. He knew what he was doing, he knew what Uther's troops would do. He went into this with his eyes wide open, prepared to pay the price. For him, dishonour was far worse than death."

"I know all this. To be honest, I'm as surprised as you are. But something has happened. Something has changed his mind." I told Elaine about the necklet and that Gorlois was insistent that he had come back at this time because he wanted to celebrate Solstice with me. "I believe he has been visited by the Goddess and that this is her work."

"You are right, Mother," said a small, confident voice from the corner of the room. I had completely forgotten that Morgan was with us. She had said nothing in response to Bennath's angry outburst and had been sitting quietly all this time, gazing into the mirror and weaving flowers into her hair.

"I saw you, Mother, kneeling before Merlin and the Lady. She was smiling. You had roses in your hair." As she spoke, she picked up the roses, which she had worked into long, beautiful garlands. She handed one to Elaine. "Just like this. See, they look lovely."

"When did you see this, Morgan?"

"Just now. In the mirror."

"And did you ask the Goddess for this vision?"

"No. It just came to me. Very quickly. I saw you, in the courtyard, here in Tintagel. You were wearing that dress and kneeling to the Lady. You had flowers in your hair and she looked so happy to see you."

"Thank you, sweetling." I smiled at my daughter and looked into the mirror she now held out to me. I knew that what she had seen couldn't possibly be a real vision. Vivian and Merlin were with Uther's army, far away from Tintagel. The foreshadowing sent to Morgan was surely more symbolic in nature, suggesting that what we planned to do today did indeed find favour with the Goddess. Perhaps, I thought, it would help bring about a reconciliation between myself and Vivian, allowing me to make a claim for reparation for the victims of the war, just as I had suggested to Bennath.

As I reflected on Morgan's words, Elaine quickly twisted the roses into place. They did indeed look lovely, with an exquisite simplicity that added the perfect final touch to my Solstice robes. Morgan was standing beside me, and our reflections smiled at each other. "You look very charming my darling, and your hair looks beautiful, even without Bennath's help." Morgan had threaded cornflowers and columbine into her braids and had made herself a delicate coronet that sat well upon her slender brow.

"Let's hope that everything goes well today." Elaine held out her hand to help me stand up. The ceremonial robes were heavy and the great panels of embroidery made them more than a little stiff. She helped me fasten the silver crescent moon around my neck. "You have never looked more beautiful, Igraine. Gorlois will be delighted."

I smiled at my half-sister and bent to kiss her. "And you are not disappointed, not sad that you will not be taking my place in the ceremony today?" I was teasing her, but Elaine did not respond to the twinkle in my eye.

"I would have done it for one reason and one reason only, because I love you. You know that Igraine. You are the Duchess, the Lady of Tintagel and it's your place to lead the ritual. I'm happy to play my part, but I've often wondered if the troubles of the past year were caused by our deception at last year's harvest rituals. Did we anger the Goddess by what we did?"

"We did what we had to. It would have been worse if we had not held the celebration at all. But today, all will be well, and before all of Cornwall, Gorlois and I will celebrate it together."

Elaine squeezed my hand and there was a knock upon the door. Before I could answer, it opened and Gorlois strode into the room. I smiled at him, and he paused, standing still and staring at me as if he could not quite believe his eyes. He said nothing.

"What is ill, my lord? Does something displease you?" Still, he was silent. Then, with all the grace of an experienced courtier, he went down on one knee before me and raised my hand to his lips. He kissed my fingers, one by one, and then placed the palm of my hand to his forehead, as if asking that I give him my blessing.

"Everything that has passed, everything I have done these last few months; I have done for you, Igraine. Never forget that." He looked at me, unsmiling, his eyes holding mine as if there was no one else in the room, no one else in the world. I stroked his cheek, gazing at the face of the man I loved, the man I'd thought was lost forever. I still did not know what happened to bring him back to me, what sights he'd seen and what compromises he'd had to make. And I didn't care.

"Whatever you have done, we will face the consequences together." I raised him to his feet, reaching up to smooth his hair and position his coronet of flowers more securely in place. "Come, my lord, our guests await."

Together we descended the stairs and made our way to the Great Hall.

THE NEWS OF GORLOIS' RETURN had clearly travelled far beyond the castle walls. I had thought that the Hall had been full last night, when we welcomed the representatives of the Great Houses to feast with us on Solstice Eve, but today it was crammed beyond anything I had ever seen before. The courtyard was also packed. Looking out toward the mainland I could see a stream of travellers trying to make their way toward the castle, but unable to make any progress because of the sheer number of people who had also decided to find out if there was any truth in the rumour that their war duke had returned.

Gorlois beckoned to Jago, who was standing at the foot of the stairs, clearly watching out for us. Our steward was looking flustered and unhappy; the crush within the Hall and the melee outside in the courtyard had not been part of his meticulous planning for the Great Gathering. Gorlois was quick to understand the nature of the problem.

"Send messengers out at once to clear the causeway. We will need to make our way to the mainland to light the first bonfires and this hurly-burly is like to make that impossible."

"Tes true, my lord, but folks 'ave heard that you've come back to us. They want to see you. To see if the truth on it with theirn own eyes."

"And see me they will; I have much to say to them. But first I have business here, with my guests. I need the courtyard cleared. Tell them to return to their homes and wait for me on the mainland."

I could tell that Jago did not think that Gorlois' suggestion would hold any water with the anxious villagers who were thronging the courtyard. They would be anxious for news of their loved ones, the sons, fathers, and lovers who had marched into battle and who, unlike my husband, had yet to return. But the noise from the Great Hall was getting louder and louder. The Priestesses and Seers from the Great Houses were within, as were the representatives of Cornwall's vassals and liege men, all of whom had travelled here today to celebrate Solstice and affirm their loyalty to their Lord.

Gorlois needed to address them. But I didn't. "Jago, please accompany my lord to the Great Hall. Our guests will be anxious for news. I will go talk to the people in the courtyard. I know them; they will listen to me."

Jago, who had become accustomed to taking orders directly from me, nodded gratefully and, turning to Gorlois said, "Shall I give orders for the herald to announce 'ee, my lord? Lord Madoc has a place waitin' at the Dais." But Gorlois looked uncertain.

"Igraine, are you sure? There are many people out there, they may not all be happy to be just turned away. I like not to send you out there alone."

"Nonsense, Gorlois. These are our people. I have nothing to fear. They have come here to find out the truth, and I will tell them all they want to know. Do not fret about me." I reached up and brushed my lips against his cheek. "I will ride with them, back across the causeway and await you on the headland. Now make haste to bring the glad news of your return to our guests." But before he would let me depart, Gorlois pulled me into his arms and kissed me, not caring who was watching. My eyes closed and I held myself against him, dizzied by the joy I felt at his return.

"You are a wonder, Igraine." With those words, he nodded to Jago and walked toward the Great Hall. I stood listening for a moment. First, I heard the triumphant blasts of the bugle as the herald led the great war duke into the packed gathering. Next, there was silence, as each person stopped talking in order to look at the man now making his way through the Hall to the Dais. Finally, with increasing strength and fury, came the hullabaloo. Shouts and cheers, the stamping of feet, the clanging of pots and pans and the banging of tankards upon tables. And then silence. As I made my way to the courtyard, I could just hear Lord Madoc's voice as he began to welcome my husband home.

Elaine and Morgan were still with me. I could tell that Morgan was finding the noise and confusion unpleasant. She was standing very close to Elaine and, most uncharacteristically, was holding her hand. It would be unkind to ask them to accompany me. The next few hours were likely to be busy and full of clamour and commotion. I saw no need to subject my daughter to the experience.

Thinking quickly, I suggested Elaine return with Morgan to my solar. It was quiet there and Morgan had things to occupy her whilst they waited for the uninvited throng to leave Tintagel. Elaine would be able to keep watch from my window as I urged people back across the causeway and could judge when things had calmed down sufficiently to set out. I asked her to join us on the headland later that afternoon, and to ensure Morgan was calm and prepared. For the first time Morgan had a part to play in the Ritual. It would be her task to light the first of the litha fires that would encircle the headland, celebrating the power of light, the blessings of the warm sun and the all-consuming power of the Goddess.

Chapter Fourteen

I stood on the threshold for a moment, wishing to compose myself. There was no sign of Bennath. I had hoped to speak with her, to reason with her, and to convince her to stand with me as I addressed the crowds that were gathering in their hundreds in Tintagel's courtyard. Bennath had a calm, strong presence; people trusted her, and despite my earlier words to Gorlois I would have felt more comfortable if she had been by my side. But that was not to be. Bennath was gone—I knew not where—and I had a job to do.

I thought of the accusations she had thrown at me that morning. That I was foolhardy, a coward, and, most damning of all, ignorant and blind to the feelings of my people. It was true that, unlike Bennath, I had not seen my country's burning fields and farmsteads or witnessed first-hand the cruelty and destruction brought by Uther's soldiers, but that did not mean I was naïve or uncomprehending. Over the past few weeks many people had found their way to Tintagel, seeking sanctuary and shelter. I had spoken with them, listened to their stories, and promised them a place within the castle walls or in the farms and homesteads of the villages beyond. These people had lost everything and now they looked to me to protect them and keep them safe.

One thing Bennath had said struck home. Uther's soldiers had not confined themselves to the battlefield but had taken their brutalities into the towns and villages of Cornwall, killing, raping, and maiming innocent people whom they had regarded as friends and allies, but a few months before. For this, I now determined, we would seek justice and reparation. When Bennath returned, I would tell her this, make her see that my craving for peace was not born out of weakness, but from a desire to protect my people, and that I would not allow their suffering to be forgotten or ignored. Feeling stronger now, I raised my head high, straightened my shoulders, and walked through the castle doorway into the courtyard.

The sun was now high in the sky; it was past noon and there were very few shadows. There was little wind and I could see that many people were flushed from the heat. I also noticed that the barrels of ale and cider that Jago had prepared for the feast had already been broached. Despite the crush, the mood was festive, people were talking, and I caught snippets of song and laughter floating through the warm mid-summer air. Looking down I caught the eye of the kitchen maid who was serving cider from the nearest barrel and gestured to her to pass some to me.

Although I had not made a sound, I could see that my presence had not gone unnoticed. As I took the cider the voices raised in song faded into silence and the hum of chatter stilled. I raised the wooden mug high in the air, in welcome and acknowledgement.

"Good people, welcome; may the blessings of Solstice be upon you."

I drank, and the crowd cheered and whistled.

"It does my heart good to see you here in Tintagel. This is truly a blessed day."

Most of the people were silent, listening to what I had to say, but there was a disturbance at the back of the crowd, near the gates that led out to the causeway. I could not quite hear what was being shouted, as the voices were faint and did not carry well in the still air.

"Hush, good people: I cannot hear what is being said." I saw the people in the crowd begin to shift to one side to allow the speakers to move closer. Two men began to walk toward me. From their clothes and bearing, I guessed them to be soldiers. They looked battle-scarred and weary. One appeared to have lost an eye, his face bloody and half covered with a stained bandage. The other was limping badly, using both a stick and his comrade's shoulder for support. As they reached the front of the crowd I recognised them as two members of the castle garrison, the riders we had sent forth the previous morning to find out what, if anything, had happened at Demelihoc.

"Bran, Drustan, I am sorry to see you in this state. What has befallen you?"

It was Bran, the older of the two soldiers, his face bruised and raw, who replied.

"My lady, we have no tidings from Demelihoc. We got no further than the copse on the outskirts of Trewalder. We were set upon as we rode inland, attacked, and left for dead."

"Who did this?" I was angered and although I did not show it, not a little afraid. If Uther's troop had penetrated so far inland, it would be but a matter of hours before they were at our gates.

"Brigands, shadowpads, and thieves," answered Bran. "A ramshackle group if ever I saw one." I felt relieved. I knew that the roads had become more dangerous this summer, with displaced men and deserting soldiers roaming the roads looking for easy pickings, but I wanted to be certain that this attack had not been the work of the Pendragon's outriders.

"Not soldiers," I persisted. "You caught no sight of Uther's army?"

"Nay lady, these were scoundrels seeking to fill their own pockets. Once they had stripped us of our weapons and stolen our horses, they bound us and left us on the side of the road to die. Uther's soldiers would not have done that. They'd have finished us off for sure."

The crowd were murmuring now, restive and unsettled. This news was worrying. But as Bran spoke, I saw the other man falter. His face was pale, his body wounded in many places. Slowly, silently, his eyes closed and he collapsed, sinking onto the cobbles in a bedraggled heap.

Without hesitation, I gestured to the maids and pages standing at the edges of the crowd. "Quickly, these men need help. Take them to the infirmary and see that they are cared for." As people hurried to do my bidding, I turned back to Bran, who I could see was also but a hair's breadth from collapse.

"Bran, you have my word that the men who set upon you will be found and punished. There is no place for brigands in Cornwall and Lyonesse. Once Solstice is over, I will speak to Jago and we will send a band of soldiers from the household garrison to hunt them down.

"Go now, rest, sleep. But before you go, there is something I would tell you."

I stood back, high upon the castle steps above the courtyard. Once again, the crowd fell silent. I raised my arms, outstretched, as if to embrace the crowd.

"Good people, today is Solstice, the day on which we thank the Goddess for her bounty and honour her for the gifts she bestows upon us. This year, perhaps it seems that we have little to look forward to. We have had a hard few months and many of us have lost much that we love and hold dear."

I gazed down into the courtyard at the people now turned trustingly toward me. I looked at the faces of the old men and women, squinting slightly in the sun. How many of them had seen their sons march to war behind Gorlois' banner, not knowing when, if ever, they would return? I saw children who had lost their homes and families and young women who had taken up the challenge of replacing their men in the fields and workshops. My people, all of them, and they had all sacrificed so much because of me. But today, that would end.

"But now, today, I have such news for you... The Goddess in her goodness has sent me a sign, proof positive that all that has happened has been her will. And how do I know this? I will tell you. Last night, on Solstice Eve, my husband was returned to me."

I heard gasps and whispers from the crowd.

"Yes, you heard me right. Gorlois is back, here in Tintagel. Our war duke has returned, and I believe that, soon, the war will be at an end."

There were cheers and shouts, a babble of voices and although I could not make out what anyone was saying, I guessed that many people were shouting questions, seeking more information and reassurance.

I let the noise grow, not seeking to shout above it, knowing that they would soon be still if they wanted to hear the rest of what I had to say. As I waited, I drained my mug and passed it down to be re-filled, relishing the strong Cornish cider that warmed and refreshed me like a draught of sweet sunlight. Then, once more I held up my hand, letting them know that I had more to say to them.

"My lord is with our guests in the Great Hall, welcoming them to Tintagel. He is here to celebrate Solstice with you, as is his right and duty." I saw faces turn toward the windows of the Great Hall and was suddenly worried that if I did not intervene the crowd would surge forward, desperate to have sight of their long absent liege-lord.

The sun had now begun its afternoon descent toward the sea and the shadows were lengthening in the castle courtyard. "See, good people, as we stand here talking, the hours are passing and the time to light the litha fire will soon be upon us. We should not be here, in the castle courtyard. Our place is on the mainland." I gestured across the causeway, still crowded with people, toward the headland, where I could just make out the silhouette of the first of the bonfires rising tall against the pale, cloudless sky.

I heard a voice say my name and, looking down to my right, saw that Jago had appeared, leading my palfrey. I smiled at him in thanks.

"It is time. The Goddess is calling us. Shall we go together across the causeway? Will you join me?" And with one voice, the crowd roared their ascent. Jago helped me mount my horse and, slowly, I made my way through the crowded courtyard.

◆ ◆ ◆

THE LITHA FIRE HAD BEEN built high on the headland; at its centre were two huge branches cut from the ancient oaks from the sacred grove to the west of Tintagel. Only two a year were taken, cut as part of the Beltane rituals that herald the Spring, and kept safe until Solstice. Above the oaks, the villagers had built a pyramid of ash and elder, interwoven with willow wands, and now the pyre stood tall, dominating the skyline, a beacon that would be seen for miles along the western seaboard.

Morgan and Elaine had ridden out to find me soon after I had led the crowds away from the castle and we were now waiting for Gorlois and our guests to make their way across the causeway. Morgan seemed calm and composed and looked very pretty. She was carrying a slender willow wand and was using it to flick away the small insects that hummed around her pony's head.

The late afternoon sun was warm, but not unbearably so, and the sky was flecked with small clouds. Far below the clifftops, the sea was calm; small waves creased the deep blue water and tiny flecks of foam lapped the shore. I thought of Morgause and her companions on the *Llyr's Daughter* and sent a silent prayer to the Goddess, asking for her blessing. My thoughts were interrupted by Morgan, who tugged at my sleeve, pointing toward Tintagel. Together we watched as the gates opened and a great mass of people streamed out across the causeway. At their head was Gorlois, wreathed in flowers and mounted on the great grey stallion that had been my gift to him at Yuletide.

As the people began to gather in a large semi-circle around the litha fire, Gorlois dismounted and made his way to my side. With him were the three women who would lead us in the day's ceremonies: Yseult, Matilda, and Jowanet, High Priestesses all. They were richly robed and wore ancient coronets of Cornish silver. Yseult, as the most senior, carried an oaken staff, whilst Matilda and Jowanet held wands of ash and elder.

We took our places and Gorlois planted a swift kiss on my brow, whispering in my ear. "I have told them of our decision, all will be well." I had no time to say anything in return, so I simply squeezed his hand and then gestured to Elaine to bring Morgan to us.

The three priestesses stood together in front of the litha fire, Yseult slightly in front, Matilda and Jowanet ranged behind her. Gorlois and I stepped forward and knelt before them, with Morgan and Elaine kneeling just beyond us, to my left. The crowds ranged around the bonfire also knelt or sat upon the ground, until only the three priestesses were standing, proud and tall against the great wooden pyre. All was still, even the seagulls had ceased their cries and the sky, at last, was cloudless.

At a signal from Yseult, the three women raised their arms toward the heavens and the Lady of Treliggan began to speak. "Great Goddess, Holy Mother, we greet you. We thank you for your bounty and seek your forgiveness for our transgressions.

"We thank you for your wisdom, which has helped guide us through these past months of conflict, and for the strength that you have given us, your children.

"Strength to bear the grief of loss and the pain of parting, strength to shoulder unaccustomed burdens to care for the land we hold in trust from you.

"Today, we come to seek your blessing, for heath and hearth and home. To ask that our fields and farms be fruitful and that your goodwill be granted to us, helping to heal us and bring peace once again to the lands of Cornwall and Lyonesse."

The time had come for Gorlois and I to make the first of our three pledges—to honour the Goddess and keep Her laws. Yseult placed her hands on our bowed heads in benediction. Her calm, strong voice rang out as she called upon the Goddess, using the words of a ritual that I had last heard when Uther made his vows to the Lady of the Lake so many months ago at Caer-Lundein.

"I, Yseult, the Lady of Treliggan, beseech you to look with favour on this man and on this woman." Keeping her hand upon Gorlois' head, she raised the other high in supplication.

"Do you promise to honour the Goddess and protect Her people?"

Gorlois raised his eyes to hers and, speaking loudly so that everyone gathered around the litha fire could hear, replied. "I do, my lady."

"Do you swear to follow the paths of the Mysteries and bring homage and honour to Her shrines?"

"I do, my lady."

"Do you swear to defend Her from dishonour and to oppose those who seek to cast out the Mysteries from the hearths and hearts of your lands?"

"I do, my lady."

She now turned to me and repeated the ritual. When I had made my final response, she raised us to our feet and kissed us thrice, upon brow, cheek, and lip.

Although the sky was still a brilliant clear blue on this, the longest day, the sun had started its downward journey toward the western horizon. It was time for the great litha fire to be lit. Matilda and Jowanet took Morgan by the hand and led her toward the bonfire where Yseult awaited her. Although small beside the stately priestesses, Morgan had a dignity and composure that drew all eyes to her. She walked proudly, her shoulders back and her braided hair, glossy and garlanded with flowers, fluttered lightly behind her, catching the sun and surrounding her with a strange and ethereal nimbus of light.

She stood before the bonfire and should have knelt in fealty to the High Priestess; instead, I was astonished to see Yseult pause, a slight frown on her otherwise dignified countenance. She then bowed her head to my tiny, self-possessed daughter and slowly knelt before her. I gasped and tried to get to my feet, but Gorlois grabbed my wrist and gestured that I should remain where I was. I could see people in the crowd turning to each other, expressions of shock and even anger on their faces, and I heard the murmurings of surprise. Why was Yseult, the Lady of Treliggan and High Priestess second only to the Lady of the Lake herself, kneeling before a small child?

Morgan smiled and bent to kiss Yseult gently on the brow. As she did so, she raised her head and looked at me, a smile of exultation on her lips and a flash of delighted excitement in her pale blue eyes. I could not hold her gaze. Recoiling involuntarily as I realised once again how like Vivian she looked, I glanced away and, when I raised my eyes, I saw that Yseult was no longer kneeling. She and Morgan stood side by side, but now it was my daughter who held the oaken staff. I saw the older woman look questioningly at Morgan, who nodded, and as if at Morgan's bidding, Yseult began to speak the ancient words that began the next part of the ritual.

"Great Goddess, Mistress of the Sun and Moon, Lady of the Harvest and Mother of the Fields, we light the Solstice fire in your honour." At these words, Morgan stepped forward. She was silhouetted against the sky, but instead of the willow wand, she raised the great oaken staff toward the sun as if to steal its flames. Although fire magic is dramatic and always impressive, it is technically quite simple and Morgan had mastered it with ease. Nonetheless, she had only practised in my solar with twigs taken from the fireside kindling, and I was suddenly worried that her decision to use the heavy oak staff might prove challenging.

Her chin had a determined set; I was certain that even my apparently poised young daughter was nervous about the role she had to play, displaying her powers so publicly and in front of such a large assembly. But she had insisted on doing so. Unlike her sister, she had spurned the offer of a wend fire to help her set the litha pyre alight. Morgan had been resolute in her desire to play her part in the rituals and had forcefully asserted her right to do so by making use of the talent for magic the Goddess had bestowed so abundantly upon her.

"Great Goddess, Mistress of the Sun and Moon, grant me the gift of fire." Morgan's voice, though child-like still, was strong and surprisingly rich. She said the words again, then thrice more, each time more loudly than the last. Her voice rang out across the silent headland, resounding across the cliffs and rocky causeway, and as the last echoes died away, the tip of the ancient staff began to glow with a tawny orange flame. Soon, it was burning fiercely. Morgan turned toward the litha pyre and raised the torch on high in salute to the gathered crowds who until now had watched in silence. And they took her to their hearts, cheering and calling, whistling and clapping as the small, fragile figure thrust the burning staff into the heart of the bonfire, which immediately burst into flame.

The fire lit, I knew that many of the people who had gathered to celebrate Solstice would choose to remain upon the headland. They had witnessed our vows to the Goddess and would now be content to complete their revels under the midsummer sky. The litha fire would burn deep into the night, sending tiny specks of flame dancing upward toward the horned moon and some would wish to honour Her with their private rituals, sky-clad beneath the stars. I knew that Jago had more than amply provided for the festivities and was certain that none would go hungry or thirsty.

But for Gorlois and myself the rites of Solstice were not yet complete, and we needed to return to the shelter of Tintagel. Hazy banks of cloud were gathering at the horizon where the pale orange sky melted into the sea. The bats that roost in the caves below the headland had just started to emerge, swooping and darting over the causeway. I mounted my horse, looking round for Gorlois, Morgan, and Elaine, but they were nowhere to be seen. Instead, I found myself riding beside Yseult.

The High Priestess seemed preoccupied; she nodded to me in acknowledgement but did not want to talk, and we started our ride across the causeway in silence. But as we neared the gates to Tintagel and our horses' pace slowed to little more than a walk, she turned to me, saying. "Your daughter is destined for Avalon, is she not?"

"Yes, although I think she is still too young to be sent from home." I wanted to mention the ceremony on the headland, to apologise for her humiliation at the hands of my daughter, but I really did not know what to say. I was still very uncertain as to what had happened to compel this shrewd and dignified woman to kneel down in submission to a four-year-old child. What we had witnessed had been extraordinary, but I could not in all honesty say that Morgan had done anything wrong. Before I could begin to frame my thoughts, Yseult spoke again. "You should send her without delay. Your daughter has great strength, perhaps more concentrated ability than I have ever seen before, but she needs to be taught how to control it."

I was silent, not knowing quite how to respond.

"Come, child; don't tell me that you are ignorant of her power. You were Avalon-trained yourself were you not?" I nodded.

"Then you know that, whilst all can learn a little of the Mysteries—to weave a charm and brew a potion—only few are chosen to wield the deep magics. Morgan's powers are already far greater than my own, but her mind is untrained."

"Yseult, my lady, what happened out there? Why did you kneel?"

"I knelt before a magic greater than my own. The power of the Goddess, working through your daughter, commanded me. I had no choice but to submit." She said this calmly, as a matter of fact rather than emotion.

"Igraine, Morgan is but a child, but she is a strange and unusual child, unlike others of her age, unlike any I have met before. The rules and principles that would normally come to bear are just not appropriate for her.

"I believe she is destined for greatness. Power such as hers is given rarely and—do not doubt me—those who wield it will always make a mark upon this world, for good or ill. Morgan is only just beginning to experiment with the gifts she has been given and we owe it to her, and to the Goddess who has chosen her as a vessel, to teach and guide her"

I could not disagree: "Morgan has always been different, more complex, more self-possessed than her sister ever was, but until this year, I had no idea that she could do the things she does. I have tried to teach her, but…" My words trailed off, knowing that the older woman was right. I had neither the knowledge nor the skill to instruct my daughter in the Mysteries.

Yseult continued: "She must learn that discipline and control are needed to temper the powers she has been given, so that she seeks the will of the Goddess, rather than indulging her own untrained curiosity"

I smiled ruefully, thinking of the hours I had watched Morgan sorting her silks, creating patterns and imposing her own particular order upon them. "Morgan has more discipline and control than any other child I have known, but she is strong willed and, unlike her older sister, cannot easily be cajoled or persuaded into doing that which does not please her."

We had finally arrived at the castle gates and Yseult reined in her horse. "Igraine, we have no time today to discuss this further, but tomorrow, before I return to Treliggan, we must talk. These are difficult times, the old ways are being questioned, threatened by those who seek to follow the new pathways of the Risen God. Perhaps Morgan's destiny is to stem that tide, to strengthen Avalon, and to bring new hope and energy to the Goddess and those who serve her"

"And perhaps not," I thought uneasily, remembering the smile of triumph I had seen on Morgan's face as the old priestess bent the knee before her. I knew that my daughter had enjoyed the public display of power we had witnessed on the cliff top. It had given her pleasure to have all eyes upon her, and she had assumed the mantle of authority with relish. Over the past months, I had come to recognise that Morgan was remarkable, but this talk of power and destiny was troubling to me. With an unwilling heart I acknowledged a tiny flutter of fear. But now was not the time or the place to pursue this, so I nodded in assent, and as we rode beneath the archway I spotted Gorlois, deep in conversation with Jago.

I rode over toward him, and he smiled up at me and took me in his arms as I dismounted. Passing the reins to our steward, Gorlois asked him to see that my horse was stabled. "And then you may take my orders to the watch tower. All shall celebrate this day." Jago nodded and went to do his master's bidding. Gorlois kissed me, wrapping his arm around my waist as we began to walk across the courtyard. "You have been a long time, my love; I was beginning to worry that the sun would set before the rituals were complete."

"The causeway was busy, and my pace was slow. But I am here now, and there are, I think, still a few hours before sunset." I let my head rest on his shoulders as we neared the centre of the courtyard, where a second, smaller bonfire, was waiting to be lit. All was ready for the next part of the ceremony, but I was curious about his words to Jago. "What plans do you have for the watch tower?" I asked.

"I have told Jago to relax the watch and let the men join the celebrations; I want all to see us make our promises tonight."

"Are you sure that is wise?"

"The Goddess is watching over us, sweetheart. I am certain that all will be well."

I was not so confident, but I did not want to question either his faith or his judgement. His return and our reconciliation were still so new and so sweet to me that I was reluctant to threaten the harmony that now existed between us by appearing to take the responsibility for the protection of Tintagel more seriously than he did. Even as I pondered, Yseult, Jowanet, and Matilda walked together down the castle steps and took their places beside the pyre.

Gorlois had already gone to stand in his traditional position on the eastern side of the bonfire, with Jago standing a pace behind him. As I quickly took my place opposite him, Elaine appeared, looking a little anxious. "Is something the matter?" I asked in a whisper. "Where is Morgan?"

"I have taken her to her chamber. She was quiet enough, but told me she could not sleep. Too much excitement, I think."

"She has not been left alone?" Morgan's exploits earlier that day had unsettled me, and I felt some anxiety about leaving her to her own devices.

"No, the Lady Epona offered to sit with her." I nodded. Epona had been born a Saxon and I knew that the summer Solstice was not as important to her as the celebrations for Yule in mid-winter. Morgan knew Epona well, and although I would rather have had the comfort of knowing that my daughter was soundly asleep within the castle walls, I felt some reassurance that she was with the calm and dignified Lady of Tredarvah. However, I could not dwell on this. Whatever the situation, I had to put it from my mind. There were more pressing matters now calling for my attention.

The second stage of the ritual, where we would renew our vows to each other, had now begun. Matilda and Jowanet came forward, giving me the willow wands to light the bonfire. Once again, Yseult spoke the words that began the ceremony, and I held the wands up toward the departing sun saying: "Great Goddess, Mistress of the Sun and Moon, grant me the gift of fire."

The tips of the willow began to glow and soon they were blazing, casting flickering shadows in the purple dusk. I walked around the bonfire to hand one of the torches to Gorlois and, for a second, his features seemed to shimmer and shift, as if to dissolve into another face entirely. I blinked. The smoke from the green willow must have got in my eyes for when I looked again, I could see no trace of anything but the familiar countenance of my husband. I returned to my place and as Yseult raised her arms, we bent toward the pyre and thrust the burning wands deep into the bonfire.

Yseult now began the ritual that would reaffirm my bonds to my husband—and his to me. Last year at this time, Gorlois had agreed to take part only half-heartedly, and I now realised our vows had been nothing but a shameful travesty. This year, we would make our vows in earnest.

"Great Goddess, lady of the sun and moon," Yseult's strong, clear voice rang out in the stillness. "Before you stand the lord and lady of these lands, here to do you honour." At her words, I bowed my head, first to the Priestess, and then, across the bonfire, at Gorlois. He did the same.

"They stand before you, decked in gold and silver, symbols of Your favour and obedient to Your will. But they come to You, not in splendour, but in humility, to renew their vows of loyalty and love—to You and to each other."

At this, Jago began to help Gorlois divest himself of his sword and ceremonial robes, and Elaine came forward to assist me in unfastening the complicated lacing of the heavy, embroidered gown. This part of the ritual was very ancient. It recognised that all power and rights of sovereignty and governance were a direct gift from the Goddess. By removing our robes and surrendering the trappings of power, Gorlois and I stood before the priestess as man and woman, not Lord and Lady. This was a stark reminder that our status and position were not ours by right, but by the gift of Her favour. Unbidden, I remembered the words my mother would say, if ever she thought me too proud or haughty. "Remember, Igraine; what She has given, She can also take away."

Once our robes had been placed to one side Gorlois resumed his place at the east side of the bonfire and I at the west. We now wore nothing but our shifts. I handed the silver crescent moon to Matilda and Gorlois surrendered the chain of golden suns to Jowanet.

Yseult called us forward, and we knelt before her. Gorlois reached for my hand, and as my fingers returned his pressure, I felt his thumb softly caressing the inside of my palm.

"You kneel before me as man and woman, with humble hearts, and minds open to the truth of the Goddess, to ask for Her love and bounty for the year to come, and to renew your vows to each other in sight of all gathered here this Solstice night." Yseult's voice was low, but it was clear and strong and resonated through the silent courtyard. Matilda then handed her a coil of rope and Yseult gestured to us to raise our arms so she could bind our hands together, to symbolise the vows that would join us to each other, hand and heart.

Yseult now raised us to our feet and placed her long, slender fingers on top of our joined hands. "In the name of the Goddess I ask you to speak truth, have you chosen to love and cherish each other from this day forward?"

"I have," said Gorlois.

"I have," I repeated.

"And will you promise to nurture and protect each other, as the Goddess nurtures and protects the land?"

"I will," said Gorlois.

"I will," I repeated.

"Then, in the name of the Goddess, who resides within us all, and who has blessed us this day with her presence, I declare you to be handfast and bound to each other, as man and wife. May you love and have joy in each other."

She bent forward then and kissed us, and as she did so, resounding cheers rang out from the crowd. Gorlois pulled me to him with his left arm, holding me tight and kissing me long and hard. I loved the taste and the smell of him and, more than anything, I wanted these ceremonies to be over, so that he and I could honour the Goddess with our pleasure.

The courtyard was no longer silent. More barrels had been broached and flagons of wine were being carried out to our thirsty and appreciative guests. The sky was darkening now, and Jago had set the kitchen lads to light torches in the sconces around the walls.

As I began to untangle the ropes that bound us, Elaine appeared, with two beakers of spiced wine.

"Congratulations, my lord and my lady; that was well done." We thanked her and took the wine gratefully. As I drank, I realised that I had had nought to eat or drink since morning. The spiced wine was strong, and after one sip, I asked Elaine to fetch me water. The rituals had not ended, we still had one more vow to make before we leapt the bonfire, and I did not want the sweet, potent liquid to go to my head.

Gorlois finished his wine and threw the beaker into the fire. "It has been a long day, my lady, and I am tired of standing on ceremony." He spoke low, for my ears alone. "I would have you to myself, Igraine."

"And I would have you," I reached out and stroked his chest, and allowed my fingers to travel downward, tracing his body through the thin linen shift.

"Oh, Igraine," he groaned, pulling me to him so I could feel his hardness. "I want you."

"Then let us get this done. One last vow. One last ceremony. Yes?"

He nodded, and I went in search of Yseult, to let her know that we were ready to begin the last part of the Solstice ritual. I found her sitting at a long table with others from the Houses of Treliggan, Fowey, and Ynas Bray. She smiled warmly at me. "You have done well, Igraine. The Gathering is a success. I believe all now are certain that the Goddess is with us."

"And that is in great part to you, my lady. Your words have brought strength and courage to so many. Thank you for all you have done for us. If the Great Gathering has done its work, if we are now united, then it is in no small part due to you."

"And what you plan to do now, to offer fealty once more to Uther and to end this war… Are you sure, Igraine?" She looked at me, compassion mingling with concern upon her face. "Many people have suffered much. I know you want to bring that to an end, but people must not think their lives have just been wasted."

"Yes. I know."

She reached out and placed a hand upon my arm. "Do you, Igraine? Do you really know this? Have you sought guidance from the Goddess, have you listened to hear her words?"

"Yseult, you yourself said that all that has happened is part of a bigger plan, one which the Goddess has not yet made known. You don't know all that has taken place between Uther, Gorlois, and myself. So much of this is my fault, and I believe the people have suffered enough. We will have peace." I touched her fingers, placing my hand over hers. "But, tomorrow, when Solstice is over, will you join with me in sending messages in friendship to the Lady of the Lake? Together, we can ask for reparation, for mercy and compassion, to help rebuild the villages that have been destroyed and the lives that have been torn asunder."

She smiled. "Yes, my child. That is a good plan. And I will help you. But now, we have the final ritual to perform. Are you ready?"

I told her that I was, and we made our way back to the bonfire arm in arm. The flames had died down and the pyre was now just a circle of glowing embers, which sent the occasional spark glistening and tumbling into the night air.

As we walked across the courtyard, the atmosphere was merry. There were no clouds and the stars blazed with an incandescent brightness in the midsummer sky. It was warm and there was a gentle breeze from across the causeway, which caused the embers from the fire to dance and shimmer. Looking out to the headland, I could still see the remains of the litha fire. Our guests had eaten and drunk well. People were talking and laughing and from the orchard we could hear music, fragments of song, and the strumming of a harp; but, as we approached the bonfire, the crowd once again fell silent.

For the last time, Yseult took her place, but Matilda and Jowanet did not join her. Instead Gorlois and I stood with her, one on each side. As before, she raised her arms, to signify that the ritual was about to begin.

"Mighty Goddess, by whose bounty the land brings forth fruit, and to whom all things are known, we honour you.

"We bring to You the sorrows of Your children, that You may comfort us, and make us whole.

"We bring to You the foolish quarrels and divisions that have brought such suffering to this land.

"Tonight, as the sun sets on these, our Solstice rituals, so shall it set on the anger and divisions that have rent our land."

As she finished speaking, she stepped back and Gorlois began to speak.

"Mighty Goddess, we ask Your blessings and Your forgiveness. We seek Your mercy and Your compassion." And now, Gorlois knelt, raising his hands in supplication. "We humble ourselves before You.

"Tonight, under the eye of the Goddess and before you, my friends, vassals, and allies, we will renew our vows of fealty to the Pendragon, so that this realm of Cornwall and Lyonesse may once again be at peace."

At these words, there was some disturbance in the crowd. There were some shouts, whether of protest or surprise I could not be sure, and several people got up and walked away, out through the castle gates and across the darkening causeway. But the majority stayed where they were, wishing to hear what their liege lord had to say.

As we waited for the murmurings to cease, I took my place at Gorlois' side, kneeling before the High Priestess.

"Do you recognise Uther Pendragon as High King of all Britain and your liege lord by right, by conquest and by the will of the Goddess?"

"I do," said Gorlois.

"I do," said I.

A great sigh went up from the crowds at these words and, at first, Yseult had to shout to make herself heard.

"Great Goddess, give this man and this woman the strength and humility to defend their people and the wisdom to lead them. Help them to protect their land and subjects, and to seek Thy will in all things. Grant them the strength and fortitude to rebuild this realm that has been torn apart by war. Strengthen their resolve and give them courage but make their hearts gentle and full of Thy healing mercy."

Once more the crowd had become silent, as we prepared for the last part of the ritual. For this, we would be sky-clad. Jago and Elaine came forward to take away our shifts and we stood naked before the fire.

Yseult spoke the final words of the Solstice ceremony. "May the fire in your hearth burn brightly, the meat and mead on your table bring comfort, and your loins bring forth fruit to keep the land settled and peaceful, for this generation and the next."

As she finished speaking, Gorlois turned to me and taking my chin in his fingers, raised my face to his for a kiss. I took his hand and we retreated a few paces and then, together, we ran toward the fire. As we leapt over the bonfire, the flames surged, tawny red and deep crimson, and the embers flew, some settling on our cheeks and hair.

We landed safely in the courtyard and raised our linked hands toward the crowd saying together. "For this generation and the next."

And as with one throat, they shouted back to us. "For this generation and the next."

Before the cheering ceased, I was pleased to see Elaine making her way toward us with our cloaks. As we covered ourselves, we watched those who also wished to leap the bonfire, to bring them luck in the year ahead. I was not surprised to see the warrior woman from Ynas Bray approach the fire, hand in hand with the young smith. Pulling off their clothes, and oblivious to anyone but themselves, they ran naked together toward the dying flames. As they leapt high above the bonfire, the tiny golden sparks danced round them and they seemed to hang, frozen in the air, silhouetted against the pale midsummer night sky. And then, in a heartbeat, the moment passed, they landed in the shadows of the courtyard and I watched as she took him in her arms and kissed him. Without bothering to collect their clothes, they slowly walked away together to find a place where they could find their pleasure and honour the Goddess in the oldest and most powerful ritual of them all.

By now, the courtyard was nearly empty. The night was strangely still and the windows of the watch-tower, which would usually have been aglow with the torches of the night-watch, were dark and empty. Along the castle walls, the lights in the sconces were burning low but there was brightness enough from the pale moon for us to make our way. We climbed the stairs in silence; I walked just ahead of Gorlois, my hand held loosely in his, leading him forward. We closed the door and moved together, drawn by an urgent desire for each other that despite all our years of marriage, felt stronger than ever.

I pulled him toward me and kissed his neck. His old riding cloak smelt of smoke from the Solstice bonfire, and I undid the fastenings and threw it to the floor, so that I could breathe in the familiar scent of his body as he stood naked before me. I stepped back a few paces to look at him.

He was good to look upon, strong limbed and broad shouldered. The scars upon his chest and legs seemed only to add to the beauty of his body, making me realise once again how fortunate I was that he had been returned to me. He was not embarrassed by his nakedness but stood proud and smiling as he held out his hand to me, drawing me closer. He began to undo the fastening at the neck of my cloak, when the candle light glinted on the chain around his neck and the small amulet bag fell forward toward me. Once again, I was seized with a need to know what it contained and playfully, I reached up and took hold of it. It was so light and soft, it could contain nothing more than a feather, or perhaps a scrap of material. I looked questioningly at him. "What is this, my lord?"

He looked at me, an expression on his face I found hard to interpret. "Not now, Igraine, tomorrow…tomorrow I—"

But whatever he had been about to say was obliterated by the frantic pounding of hoofbeats on the courtyard cobblestones, and the sound of a voice screaming my name into the silent night. I ran to the window and stared down into the courtyard. A rider had entered through the unmanned postern; it was a woman, her hair flying around her face as her horse reared in pain and terror, an arrow in its flank, its legs beating the silent air.

"Igraine, where are you? Igraine…" It was Bennath, her face pale and harrowed in the silver moonlight. There was blood on her tunic, and I saw that one arm hung limply at her side.

"They are all dead: Gorlois, Lowen, Erec…" She screamed each name in increasing desperation, and then said no more as an arrow flew through the air and pierced her side.

As she fell to the ground, three more horses raced through our undefended gateway. One was the archer, who, after checking that Bennath needed no more of his attention, took up his position to one side of the courtyard. He held his bow high, trained on the small huddle of sleepy people who had been woken by the commotion and made their way out into the courtyard. The other riders quieted their horses and looked about them. One was a man, white-haired and dignified, his long beard braided into three plaits that fell below the belt of his dark green robes. The other, smaller and far more delicate of build, was dressed in robes of fine-woven white samite. Her dark hair was tied elegantly in a knot at the nape of her neck, and she held herself with regal dignity. I recognised them both. Merlin and Vivian.

Completely shocked by what I had witnessed, desperate to make my way down to the courtyard where Bennath lay bleeding, I heard a noise behind me. I turned and stared at the man who stood, still naked, in the shadows of my chamber. He had taken the amulet from his neck and held it out to me. Wordlessly, I took it, knowing with a terrible foreboding what it was that I would find inside. I pulled out a tiny fragment of cloth which glowed with a strange, milky iridescence in the moonlight and then looked up, into the face of Uther Pendragon.

"I'm sorry, Igraine," he said.

Chapter Fifteen

I have fractured memories of what happened next. I remember pulling on some clothes before running down to the courtyard, where, just as Morgan had foreseen, I knelt before Vivian with the flowers of Solstice still wreathed in my tangled hair. I begged to be allowed to tend to Bennath, who had lost consciousness and whose breath was now coming in slow and irregular gasps. Vivian looked down on me, a smile of triumph on her lips as she slowly nodded her assent, before dismounting and making her way toward the castle steps where Uther and Morgan stood, waiting to receive her.

I remember Elaine and I carrying Bennath to my chamber. She was still bleeding from the wound in her side and had hit her head hard upon the cobbles when she fell. I concentrated on cleaning her wounds, not wanting to think about what had happened, about the words that she had screamed into the night air before the arrow had silenced her.

Gorlois, Lowen, Erec… all dead. Gone, killed upon the battlefield at Demelihoc, pulled to the ground by a host of Uther's soldiers and slaughtered like dogs. And this man that I had thought was Gorlois, this man that I had shared my bed with, had kissed and caressed and opened my heart to, had promised before all Tintagel to love and care for…This man was Uther, the agent of their death.

It was too much for me. Elaine put me to my bed and there I stayed for days, weeping, and unwilling to eat or drink more than was absolutely necessary, refusing to wash or get dressed. I insisted the door remained locked. Only Elaine had a key and I would have none but my half-sister visit or tend me. Sometimes I heard noises outside, voices calling to me to let them in. Once, I was aware of Morgan's precise, measured tones, asking for admission. I turned my face from the door and covered my ears with my pillow and she never came again. Another day, Ened came to the door, sobbing and beating her fists upon it, calling me a bitch, a whore and worse until someone whose voice I didn't recognise told her she must stop and took her away, still screaming.

All this time Bennath lay, silent and unmoving, her breath still shallow, but regular now. Elaine had used a sleeping draught of borage and valerian to create an enchanted sleep, in whose calming depths her wounds would heal and her body regain its strength. I begged her to do the same for me, but she refused, saying that sleep would not heal me.

Perhaps she was right, for I slept little, and when I did, I found no comfort in my dreams. My rest was fitful and I was pursued by nightmares. I dreamt of Gorlois, sometimes terrible visions where once again my mind took me to the battlefield. I saw him dragged, screaming to his death, his corpse left exposed on the hillside, and a ghastly hole in his chest where his heart had been ripped, still beating, from his body. These dreams left me shaken and I would wake up and walk to the window, my limbs drenched in sweat and unable to get back to sleep. But they were not the worst.

In the other dreams, Gorlois and I were together, happy and content. We would laugh and he would kiss me. Sometimes I would rumple his hair or snuggle close beside him, spooning my knees into his back as we settled into sleep. And then he would turn toward me, coming closer and closer, and his face would be the face of the Pendragon. I would pull awake from these dreams rigid and screaming, wakening Elaine who now spent her nights on a truckle at my side. She would hold me gently, murmuring calming words until my sobs subsided. Then she would wash my face and bring me wine to drink and lie beside me in the dark, saying nothing, just holding my hand and being there.

And so the days passed with a painful, nightmarish monotony. I did not measure them and had no idea how long I had remained in my self-imposed isolation. But one day, there was a knock and I heard the quiet but commanding voice of Vivian. "Igraine, open the door. I depart tomorrow and we must talk." I said nothing and Elaine looked at me, questioningly.

There was another knock. "Igraine, if you will not unlock the door, I shall have it taken from its hinges. You are behaving like a foolish child." I did not doubt for a moment that she would do as she threatened and so I nodded to Elaine. She went to the door and turned the key, opening the door and standing aside to give the Lady of the Lake admittance. She was not alone, Morgan was with her, and they walked into the room together, taking their places side-by-side upon the settle.

I saw a look of disgust on Vivian's beautiful sculptured face and Morgan wrinkled her nose saying, "This room smells most unpleasant, Mother."

I looked around me, seeing my chamber through their eyes. The bed was unmade, and I had not allowed Elaine to change the sheets or provide me with fresh linen. The rushes by the fireside were dry and dusty, their sweetness long replaced with a stale, almost fetid odour. By the door stood the slop bowl, waiting for Elaine to empty it, and the stew that I had refused to eat for last night's supper stood cold and unwanted on the table, a hunk of bread hardening by its side.

"I have not been well and am ill-prepared for visitors," I said.

"So I see," said Vivian dryly. "Igraine, this room is a shambles and you look like an unkempt kitchen harridan. This is not what I would expect from a princess of the Welsh Marches and a daughter of Avalon."

"I don't care what you think. This is my room; I didn't ask you to come here. Just say what you have to say and get out."

"Indeed, that is a fine example of courtesy and hospitality to show your daughter." Vivian turned toward Morgan, who had opened my box of tapestry silks and was ordering them in neat rows upon the table. "Pay no heed to your mother, child, she is still somewhat overcome and has yet to accommodate herself to her new situation." Morgan said nothing, just nodded silently before returning her attention to her task.

Vivian ordered Elaine to remove the slop bowl and leftovers and to return with a broom and sweet rushes. She then turned and opened the shutters to let the fresh morning into the room. Despite myself, I realised that I had missed the smell of the ocean and the feeling of the breeze upon my skin.

"When was the last time you combed your hair? It is as matted and coarse as an old mare's mane. You look simply dreadful, Igraine. When I think of you at Caer-Lundein, crowned as the queen of beauty before Uther's Court, I can hardly believe I am looking at the same woman. If Uther were to see you now, I doubt he would even give you a second glance."

"I wish he had never seen me. I wish I had never gone to Caer-Lundein. Then none of this would have happened and Gorlois would still be alive."

"Possibly, possibly… But you know my dear, I don't think so." Vivian reached for my comb and began to stroke the tangles from my hair, her voice low and hypnotic. "If you had not gone to Caer-Lundein, it would not have been long before Uther came here on his royal progress. He would have seen you, and been entranced by you, and the story would still have unfolded…perhaps with a few changes to scene or setting, but believe me, Igraine, when the Goddess choses to work her will, we should have the humility to recognise that there is little we can do to thwart her."

"I don't understand."

"Don't you? I thought that Merlin had told you of the prophecy and the role that you were born to play. Your son is destined for greatness. He will be the Once and Future King, before whom all will bow down and acknowledge as their liege lord."

"I have no son. And now Gorlois is dead, I will have no more children."

"I would not be so hasty in making such pronouncements, Igraine. The Goddess has foretold that your son will be King both by right and by virtue, and it does not do to make so light of her intentions."

As she spoke, I remembered Merlin's last visit to Tintagel, just before the war began. He too had told me of this prediction and had tried to persuade Gorlois to make his peace with Uther by dangling the prophecy in front of us, implying that Gorlois himself could become the father of the next King.

"And so he could, Igraine." Vivian had always had an uncanny ability to know what I was thinking. "Had he remained true to the old ways. But I'd long heard rumours that your apostate husband had turned his back on the Mysteries in favour of the new religion. When I spoke with you in Caer-Lundein, you confirmed everything I had been told was true. I knew then that he could not be a fitting father for the new King, or even, if truth be told, a husband worthy of you, Igraine."

As she spoke, she continued to comb my hair. Her hands were gentle and deft, and she smelt of lavender and honeysuckle, reminding me of the gardens of Avalon. So many years ago, when I was but a green girl, it had been Vivian who had instructed me in herb craft and taught Elaine the healing magics; and, it was to Vivian that I had turned for comfort when my mother died. She had been part of my life for so many years, and until recently, I had loved and trusted her implicitly. Almost imperceptibly, I felt my shoulders relax and I leant back in my chair. By now, she had worked through all the tangles and the comb slid through my hair, smoothing it and making it sleek and lustrous once again.

Reaching over to the jug of water Elaine had left on the table, she dipped in a towel and began to clean my face, which was stained with tears and Bennath's blood. When she had finished, she took my hand and led me to the mirror. "See, child; you are still beautiful."

I looked at myself, hardly recognising the woman who stared back at me. My eyes were huge in my pale face, which seemed angular and almost sculptured. Days of not eating had removed the softness from my cheeks and brought into sharp relief the delicate shape of my jawline. "Sadness becomes you," said Vivian. "It has added a nobility to your features. This truly is the face of a Queen."

"I don't want to be a Queen."

"What do you want, Igraine?" And now her voice was soft and almost tender.

"I don't know…"

She said nothing, but came to stand beside me, so we were both looking deep within the mirror, holding each other's gaze in the burnished copper.

Finally I spoke. "What I want, I know I can't have. I want Gorlois back, I want my life like it was, with my daughters in their nursery and my husband in my bed. I want everything that has been taken from me. Without it, my life is nothing, I have…nothing."

"You are right about one thing, Igraine. We cannot undo what has been done. You cannot go back and your life will never be what it was. But you need to understand that what has happened has not been by chance. It has been of my making, at the will of the Goddess, and although you may not accept this now, I tell you true that it has been done for love of you.

"Can you possibly believe that I raised you, and taught you, and gave of myself to you, for this?" Vivian cast her eyes around the disordered chamber. "Do you really think that you are meant to end your days locked away in some far-flung castle, losing your looks and probably your mind, endlessly wallowing in self-pity? Oh no, Igraine; this is not where it ends. You can have a husband, and one who loves you more than that foolish hothead ever did. And you can be Queen." Vivian's voice was low and her un-blinking eyes continued to bore deeply into mine.

I was first to look away. "I am no puppet to be played with Lady. If you want me to listen to anything you have to say about my future, then you had better tell me what you have done—and exactly why you did it." And so she told me.

The story went back many years, to a vision granted to Vivian and my mother in the scrying bowl when they themselves were young girls sent to Avalon for schooling. They saw the birth of the warrior king, destined to wield the great sword Caliburn, that he would be born here in Tintagel, and that I was to be his mother. From that day forward, my future was planned and when Vivian brought about my marriage to Gorlois, she was certain that everything was now in place for the prophecy to be fulfilled. She had not anticipated Gorlois' growing disaffection with the Mysteries and had asked Merlin to visit us last summer to find out if the rumours she had heard were true.

Gorlois had treated Merlin shamefully on that occasion, and if he had but known it, it was on that day that his fate had been determined. The Goddess had made it clear that I was to be the mother of this long-awaited child, but the identity of his father had not been vouchsafed. If Cornwall's war duke had chosen to turn his back on the Mysteries, shifting his allegiance to the Risen God, then what could be more appropriate than to place the newly victorious Pendragon, loyal to the Goddess and acknowledged King of the Britons, at the very heart of the prophecy's fulfilment?

Merlin and Vivian began to lay their plans. Merlin was to speak to Uther of my beauty and accomplishments, Vivian to weave enchantments that would cause him to fall in love with me the moment he saw me. She ordered the creation of the dress of gossamer and swansdown that had so entranced him, and planned Uther's ceremony of allegiance to ensure that I would be crowned Queen of Beauty before the eyes of the whole court. In the aftermath of that evening, Gorlois had ordered the men of Cornwall and Lyonesse away from Caer-Lundein and declared war on his former friend and liege lord.

"And even then, even after Gorlois had traitorously declared war on Uther, Merlin was determined to give your husband one last chance. If you recall, he followed you to Tintagel and revealed certain details of the prophecy. At that point, Gorlois could still have made peace, could have kept Tintagel and, in time, fathered the child.

"But he would have none of it." Vivian's eyes flashed in anger. "No, instead of responding with humility and gratitude the man you called your husband threatened to whip Merlin from your court."

I remembered the scene quite vividly; Gorlois seizing Merlin and almost pushing him to the floor in anger, my horrified cry as I ran to support the ancient Druid and help him to his feet. Gorlois' abrupt departure from the room and then Merlin's gentle questioning. *"Igraine; tell me, can you honestly say that Uther does not please you?"* And when I side-stepped his question, again he had asked. *"Tell me Igraine, did Uther truly force you, or would you have given yourself to him if you could have done so without disgrace?"* Again, I had prevaricated, unwilling to lie to the venerable Druid, but not wanting to admit the truth even to myself.

"Merlin felt certain that you had feelings for Uther and you had told me yourself that your true loyalty was to the Goddess. What we did was in your best interests child, and it pains me that you still refuse to see that." Whilst she had been talking, Vivian had also been sorting through my closet and had chosen a pale underdress and a dark green kirtle.

"Now, don't you think it is about time you made yourself a little more presentable? That shift you are wearing is a disgrace and, without putting too fine a point on it, you smell most unsavoury."

Despite myself, I blushed, feeling once again as I had as a young girl in Avalon when my small faults and misdemeanours had been exposed to Vivian's implacable scrutiny.

"But I still don't understand, how did you do it?" As I spoke, I pulled off my shift and began to wash myself in the water Elaine had made ready earlier that morning. I felt incapable of resisting Vivian's commands.

"Do what, child?" Vivian handed me the shift, and I pulled it on haphazardly. She tutted and came to help me, straightening it at my shoulders and lacing the ribbons of my kirtle. "Carry out the enchantment that persuaded you that the man you welcomed into your chamber was not Uther, the man you were already half in love with, but Gorlois, the husband you had sent on his way to war with harsh words and anger in your heart?"

"That's not true," I said, "I loved Gorlois. He was my husband. If you and Merlin hadn't meddled in our lives, we would have been happy."

"Would you, child? How could you have been happy with a man who ridiculed your beliefs and mocked the things that you have long held sacred? And what about your daughters?" Vivian pointed toward Morgan, who had tucked her feet neatly underneath her and still seemed to be absolutely absorbed in her task. Sunlight shone in through the window, the pale, dappled rays playing on her glossy hair and creating a golden rectangle on the wooden table, in which she was laying out the tapestry threads.

"What do you mean? Gorlois loved his daughters."

"Did he love Morgause when he tried to remove her from the protection of the Goddess? Sending her to sea with just the benison of an old wooden cross?"

Remembering my own anger when I had discovered this, I coloured slightly, but said nothing.

"And what of Morgan?" At the sound of her name, my little girl looked up. Smiling to see me looking more presentable, she got down from the table and came over to us. Saying nothing, I reached out to touch her nose gently with the tip of my finger, the way I had always greeted her when I had been away. She looked up at me, curious and a little uncertain and then moved closer. I leant down toward her and she raised her head so the very tips of our noses touched. Finally, she smiled. "Hello, Mother," was all she said.

Vivian was smiling too. She reached out to gently touch my daughter's forehead. "Morgan is a very special child. The Goddess has blessed her with abilities that could, one day, exceed my own. You must know this, Igraine."

Slowly, I nodded.

"And how do you think Morgan would have fared coming to womanhood in Gorlois' household? A man who had declared himself the enemy of the Goddess…a man who had sworn to drive Her worship from the land. How would he treat a daughter whose every natural inclination is to seek the Mysteries and to learn how to wield the powers the Goddess has bestowed upon her?"

I had no answer to this, and I knew that she was right. I myself had seen the extraordinary nature of Morgan's abilities. This was a child who, at the age of four, had sufficient command of the rituals to use the sea itself as a scrying bowl, a feat of power so demanding that I doubted even Vivian herself would have attempted it.

Even if I had questioned the evidence of my own eyes, both Bennath and Yseult had told me that my youngest child's abilities were prodigious, needing careful schooling and instruction if she was to learn how to manage and control them without bringing danger to herself and others.

Morgan would never become the sort of woman who would be satisfied with home and husband and the management of a household. I had been raised in Avalon and schooled in the ancient crafts and although my powers were but one tenth of my daughter's, I recognised how much I needed my own freedom and independence of thought. How much more would this apply to my remarkable young daughter, who had been given great gifts and alongside them, almost certainly, a future that would contain great responsibilities?

The priests of Gorlois' new religion were critical of the Mysteries and of the power and authority accorded to Her seers and priestesses. I had heard him speak of a woman's place being at the hearthside, not in the schoolroom. I remembered how opposed he had been to my desire to send Morgan to Avalon, not just because of his antipathy to the Lady, but because he had come to believe that women should not have an education which would accord them knowledge and intellectual freedom.

I recognised that Vivian was right, but I was not going to join her in criticism of Gorlois. Yes, I had been angered and concerned by his rejection of the Mysteries, but he had been my husband and I had loved him. "Lady, Morgan has been promised to Avalon from the hour of her birth. I had hoped to keep her with me until a few more summers had passed, but it appears that is not the will of the Goddess." I looked at Morgan, who was still standing beside me, not speaking and looking intently at both of us.

"Morgan, sweetling, what do you want to do?" But even before she spoke, I knew what my daughter would say. "I want to go to Avalon," she spoke quickly, with an excitement in her voice that I had never heard before.

"Are you sure? Won't you miss your home, miss Tintagel?"

I wanted to ask, "Won't you miss me?" but I could not bring myself to say it.

Morgan reached across and took my hand, an uncharacteristic gesture of affection which I'm sure she made only because she knew it would give me comfort. "I care for you very much, Mother, but I am bored in Tintagel. I have learned everything you and Elaine can teach me. I need to go to Avalon."

I knew that she was right. Inside, I had been preparing for this moment for months. As a mother, I knew instinctively that this was what my daughter wanted and needed, but, at the same time, I dreaded sending her away.

Morgause had gone; Gorlois was dead. There was nothing for me now in Tintagel, but my daughter deserved more from me than grief and self-pity. I forced myself to smile and took my hand away, smoothing down the folds of my kirtle. "Well, child, you shall go. When shall I send her to you, Vivian?"

We agreed that Morgan would remain with me for the summer months and that we would travel together to Avalon for Samhain, the Autumn festival. As we made our plans, Elaine reappeared, bringing with her fresh rushes and a small jug containing the sleeping draught for Bennath. Vivian dismissed her, asking her to take Morgan to the Great Hall to break her fast.

"And now, Igraine, there are things I must tell you that are not to be shared with others." She went over to the bed where Bennath lay, deep in sleep, her breathing calm and regular. Satisfied that there was no one to overhear us, she motioned me to be seated and herself resumed her place on the settle.

"I will be frank with you, child. My words will not make you think kindly of me, but they are the truth. I hope that you will have both the intelligence to understand why I did what I did, and the sense to accept the gifts the Goddess is now offering you." I said nothing, but inclined my head, to indicate that I was ready for her to continue.

"Igraine, Uther loves you. Truly and, I believe, with absolute sincerity. This has surprised me. At the outset, Merlin and I intended no more than a passing entrancement, a rough magic to pique his desire and enflame his passion, but when he saw you, when he spoke with you at Caer-Lundein, he was lost.

"We had already decided that we would enchant Uther, making him assume the appearance of your husband, so that you would welcome him to your bed. The last time Merlin visited you, he took Gorlois' cloak with him, and we used this to conjure the enchantment. But Uther would have none of it. He refused to listen to me, saying that he wanted to woo you honestly and openly, that he would have no truck with what he called 'my deceitful trickeries.' Indeed, in his anger, he threw the potion on the fire and sent me from the camp."

At her words, I started. This was familiar. The story Vivian was telling me resonated in my mind. And then I recollected the vision I had seen with Morgan, the first time I had given her a lesson on the rituals of the scrying bowl. I remembered Uther, sitting in his shadowy war tent, his features illuminated by the glow of a small brazier. Vivian had been beside him, talking, cajoling, trying to persuade him to take something from her, but he had refused, and in a burst of anger had thrown the potion into the flames.

"So he wouldn't listen to you, but somehow, Merlin managed to persuade him," I said bitterly.

If Vivian was startled by my knowledge, she didn't show it. "Yes, child; you have it right. Merlin convinced Uther that you would come to care for him in time. He had seen how things were with you and Gorlois. How angry and bitter your husband had become, and how much it hurt you that he had turned toward the Risen God. I think you had even told him that you were attracted to the Pendragon."

I could not deny this. Merlin knew me well.

"Merlin is genuinely fond of you, Igraine. I do not think he would have agreed so willingly to the plan if he did not believe that the will of the Goddess was also the path to your future happiness. But the circumstances were such that we could not wait. There was no time for Uther to woo and win you."

"What do you mean, what circumstances?"

"Why, the Solstice. The vision I had all those years ago was crystal clear. The child would be conceived in Tintagel at Solstice. If the prophecy was to be fulfilled, Uther had no choice but to agree."

I stared at her in horror as my hands involuntarily flew to my belly.

VIVIAN LEFT TINTAGEL LATER THAT day. I watched her ride out through the postern gate and along the causeway and felt a sudden need to be outside. The morning sun had vanished, replaced by a leaden sky heavy with clouds, and I wrapped my cloak around me as I went down the stairs and out past the Great Hall.

There was no one to be seen as I made my way across the courtyard and into the kitchen garden. It had been weeks since I had left my room, and the castle now seemed very different. It was quiet, with no signs of the routine hustle and bustle that I would have expected. At this time of day, the kitchen maids and scullions would usually be running to and fro on errands for Jago or the castle cook. The soldiers from the garrison would be at practice—either at the archery butts or drilling with their wooden swords—watched by Ened and her friends, who enjoyed taking the castle children to see the display. But all was still and I was alone apart from a kitchen cat sitting silently on a gate post and staring at the seabirds.

As I walked in front of the castle I could still make out the remains of the litha fire, and there was a dark stain on the cobbles where Bennath had fallen. Averting my eyes, I walked on down the stone steps, past the stables, and under the archway that led to the garden and the orchard beyond. The seagulls were calling, screeching and diving in the grey sky and I heard the whinny of a horse followed by the gentle murmur of someone attempting to calm it.

I felt very strange. I had never known Tintagel to be like this, so quiet and ominously still. Since I had first come to the castle, as a young woman about to be wed, I had regarded it as my home. I had loved its noise, its wildness, and its tumultuous beauty, but now it felt alien and unwelcoming.

I walked quickly through the rows of vegetables—the beds of parsnips and carrots and the tall runner beans with their flame red flowers and on, past the bright yellow bells of the cucumber vines. I knew what I was looking for; tansy, pennyroyal, yarrow, and angelica. If Vivian was right and Uther had indeed planted his seed within me, then there was one thing I felt certain of. I did not want this child and, prophecy or no prophecy, I would do everything I could to remove it from my womb.

I had gathered handfuls of pennyroyal and tansy and was now making my way toward the rear wall of the garden where I could see the tall many-flowered heads of the angelica. Suddenly, I heard a noise behind me, a sharp crack that could have been a twig breaking or the sound of someone stepping on an empty snail shell. I was no longer alone.

"Igraine."

I knew that voice. I did not turn round.

"Igraine, I am pleased to see you out of doors once more."

Slowly, I turned to face him. Uther Pendragon.

He was dressed simply, his breeches tucked into plain leather boots and a homespun tunic belted at the waist. He carried no sword and his head was bare. It would seem that he too had not been eating. His face was pale and his tunic hung loosely on his broad shouldered but angular body.

"Get away from me. You disgust me."

He reached out his hand toward me, but I backed away, not wanting to touch him, not wanting to be touched by him.

"Igraine, I'm sorry." He remained where he was, his hand still outstretched. "Vivian has spoken to you, she's explained it. Don't you see, I had no choice. This was the only way." He spoke quietly, his voice little more than a whisper, trying to make me move closer. I stood my ground.

"I love you, Igraine; I'm so sorry that I've hurt you, but you must see that it had to be this way."

"Of course you had a choice. You are the King, Uther Pendragon, the most powerful man in Britain. Stop hiding the truth about your own desires behind a woman's skirts. You saw something you wanted and you took it. You killed my husband and you lied to me. How can I feel anything for you but hatred?"

"I never lied to you. Every word I said to you was true. You may have heard the voice of Gorlois, but the words were my words, not his. I told you that I love you, that no one means more to me than you do. Believe me. Please, Igraine; believe me."

"You lied to me with your body, with your eyes, with your tongue. Lies do not have to be spoken, Uther. Everything I said to you, I said because I thought you were Gorlois. I gave you everything. I opened myself to you. I shared my heart with you and it was nothing but a lie."

I remembered the way I had felt, the morning after he had returned to me. Closer to him at that moment than I had ever been to another person. And it had all been a deception. He had taken my trust and abused it. He had taken my body and used it for his pleasure.

"And I loved you for it. I have never known anyone like you. I know that I've hurt you, and I'm sorry for it. Had there been another way, believe me, I would have taken it." He moved closer, never taking his eyes from my face.

"You were born to be my wife. To sit beside me as Queen. To give me comfort and share my life. It is what the Goddess wants. And in your heart of hearts, I know it's what you want as well."

"I want nothing to do with you, Uther Pendragon." I held out my hands, showing him the herbs I had picked. "And that includes the bastard child I am carrying. I want rid of it as much as I want rid of you."

"You don't mean that, Igraine. The babe that grows within you is destined for greatness and I know he will bring you joy." His voice was low, caressing, seductive. "Marry me; our child will be no bastard. I know you care for me. I know you want me. I could tell the very first time I kissed you…," he reached out and touched my shoulder, putting his arm around my waist, pulling me toward him. His mouth sought mine, just as it had that other time, so long ago in the darkened corridors of Caer-Lundein.

I kicked and scratched his face, feeling the skin on his cheek tear beneath my nails. He gasped in pain and I broke away.

"No Uther, I will never marry you. My husband was Gorlois, Duke of Cornwall. He was your loyal friend and you murdered him. You plotted with Merlin and Vivian to make him jealous, knowing exactly what he would do. You lied and manipulated me and took my body through falsehoods and deceit. Yes, I admit that for a moment, there in Caer-Lundein, I was foolish, dazzled by you, taken in by sweet words. But I do not love you and I never will."

I don't know what I expected from Uther. Perhaps I thought he would hit me, or even take me by force. We were alone, no one would hear me if I screamed, but all he did was to take the bunches of herbs and throw them on the ground, crushing them beneath his boots. Then he took me by the arm and led me gently, but firmly, back to the castle.

◆ ◆ ◆

UTHER AND THE MAJORITY OF his soldiers were now planning to leave Tintagel. I learned that they meant first to journey to the Welsh Marches to my father's court, to see my brother and cement their alliance, and then farther North to treat with the Kings of Mercia.

Uther had instructed that I was still to be regarded as Duchess of Cornwall and to be treated with respect. He had not appointed anyone to act as regent and I was still nominally responsible for the affairs of Cornwall and Lyonesse, although in practice, I was prevented from any real decision making by the presence of Merlin who was to remain at Tintagel throughout the summer. Uther had also decided to reinforce the castle garrison with a troop of Irish galloglaigh, fierce and silent mercenaries who took up residence in the keep, to the discomfort and irritation of Jago and the castle guard.

It had been determined that my freedoms and privileges were to be severely curtailed. I was still allowed to go where I wished within the castle walls, but I was no longer permitted to travel across the causeway to the mainland. I could see Morgan and Elaine as often as I wanted to, and we were told that we could continue to care for Bennath, but there was not a moment of my day where I would be unsupervised. Uther was determined that no harm would come to the child I carried and he instructed Ened, Hild, and Epona to keep me under constant surveillance. If they did so to his satisfaction, he would permit their children to inherit their dead fathers' estates. If not, all of their lands, goods, and chattels would be confiscated.

Before he left, Uther came to see me in my chamber. Elaine and I were instructing Morgan in the preparation of a healing poultice, using charcoal and bread pellets mixed with comfrey and a little honey. Epona was sitting on a low stool by the fireside. Of the three women I had come to think of as my jailers, she was the least unwelcome. I felt that she tried to make her presence as unobtrusive as possible, and always said very little, unlike Ened, who would take any opportunity she could to insult or berate me.

Uther was dressed formally, in a finely woven tunic, soft leather breeches, and richly brocaded travelling cloak. His sword was slung across his back, and he had a dagger at his belt. I noticed with some gratification that his face still bore the signs of the scars my nails had made. "I have come to say goodbye, Igraine," he said, coming to stand beside me. He was too close. I could smell the dry, musky scent of his skin and the herbs that the laundress must have used to fragrance his clothing. It made me feel sick and I struggled hard not to retch, but I said nothing, simply continuing to pound the charcoal and honey to a sticky paste.

"I see that you are busy; I am sorry to disturb you." He spoke hesitantly, in a low voice as if he wished the others not to hear him. Then he reached out toward me, hoping, I think, to touch the fabric that hung loose across my still flat stomach, but I twisted myself sideways and his hand fell upon empty air.

"I had hoped to speak with you, Igraine, but I see that I am not welcome." Righting himself and clearly embarrassed, he looked toward Elaine and Epona and raising his voice said, "Take good care of my lady. I wish no harm to come to her, or the child she carries."

They both murmured something in assent, and, satisfied, he turned once more to me. "I will return to Tintagel at Yuletide. May the blessing of the Goddess be upon you." I said nothing. After a moment of silence, he began to walk toward the door but then he turned back, saying, "Do you have a message for me to take to your father and brother?"

I looked up at him, unspeaking and then got to my feet. As I walked across the room to him, he smiled, tentatively, hoping perhaps that I might send him on his way with some word of kindness. Instead, I spat at him, full in the face.

"Take that to my brother."

Without another word he turned on his heel and left my chamber, using the edge of his cloak to wipe the spittle from his cheek.

Chapter Sixteen

Tintagel is always beautiful, but that summer, I remember it to have been peculiarly, disturbingly enchanting. The flowers in the castle garden grew lush and lovely, scenting the air with a delicate sweetness that was particularly noticeable at dusk and sunrise. When I looked across the causeway toward the headland, I could see the crops beginning to ripen, golden fields of wheat and barley rippling in the warm summer air. In the orchards, the apples ripened and the berries on the brambles that grew around the castle walls began to turn from green to pink, to dusky red, and, finally, to deepest black.

The days were long and sunlit; if it rained, it did so gently, at eventide or during the hours of darkness. Perhaps to many it would have seemed as if the Goddess were smiling, blessing us with her bounty, but to me, and to Bennath, it felt as if she mocked us, taunting us in our misery and suffering. As the summer days shortened and harvest approached, Bennath regained her strength sufficiently to leave her bed. We walked together in the castle grounds, usually choosing to go out early before the household became busy, or after sunset, seeking cooling breaths of sea air to relieve the oppressive and stultifying heat.

We were never allowed to be alone. Ened, Hild, or Epona would always be there, walking behind us at a discreet distance, but close enough to hear every word spoken above a whisper. Sometimes we would find Merlin waiting for us in the courtyard, or we would come upon him unexpectedly in the herb garden. He would always appear surprised and delighted to have encountered us and would ask our permission for him to join us with disingenuous simplicity and charm. If he was with us, my jailers were permitted to withdraw, and for me, that was reason enough to accept his occasionally proffered companionship.

Hild and Epona rarely spoke. They did what Uther had required of them, anxious to assure their children's inheritance, but not, I think, with any specific feelings of ill-will toward me. Ened was another matter. Her grief at losing Erec was deep and violent, and I knew that she held me entirely to blame for the loss of her husband and the dramatic changes in her circumstances. She had always been a lazy, self-indulgent woman, who had enjoyed the pleasures of the table rather too well. Bereavement, and the bitterness and anger that accompanied it, had changed her. She was thin now, her eyes reddened with tears of rage and sadness that never seemed far from the surface. Her face was gaunt and she wore her straw-coloured hair tied back severely at the nape of her neck. Her youngest child, a boy named Edwyn who had inherited his father's long limbs and pale eyes, was now more than a year old and she ministered to his every need obsessively, only choosing to leave his side if it was her turn to watch over me.

It was a warm night and Bennath and I decided to take a walk in the orchard. Elaine declined our invitation to join us. She had spent the day with Morgan, teaching her the rituals and magics associated with summoning enchantments and was clearly exhausted. My daughter was becoming a demanding and challenging student, and I was not surprised that Elaine wanted a few hours to herself.

As we walked toward the door, Ened pulled herself up from her place on the settle, groaning with annoyance as she did so. "Yet another sign of your selfishness and lack of consideration, Igraine. Why can't you just go to bed like everyone else?" Ened reached for her cloak. Since losing so much weight, she felt the cold even in the middle of summer.

"This is the second time this week that you have had me traipsing about the castle in the middle of the night. I'd hoped to see Edwyn before he went to his cradle, but oh no, I have to wait until you see fit to lay your pretty head upon the pillows before I am allowed to go to my own chamber and see my poor darling." I could see that she was close to tears.

"My poor, fatherless boy. And it's your fault, you whore." She was hissing at me now, standing close beside me, a gleam of madness in her eyes. Elaine had risen from her seat in the window and Bennath had moved closer toward me, instinctively, laying a hand protectively on my shoulder. "If you hadn't flaunted yourself in front of Uther like a bitch in heat, this never would have happened. Erec would still be here and I—" But before she could complete her sentence, there was a tap at the door, and without waiting for an acknowledgement, it opened, and Merlin stepped into the room.

"Good evening, Ladies, please forgive this intrusion." His lips twitched into a brief smile as he took in the scene. His tone was light, but his grey eyes were cold and I could tell that what he had witnessed had displeased him.

"Lady Ened, you appear to have forgotten the respect you owe to the Lady Igraine, who may before long become your queen." Ened backed away from me, a look of absolute hatred in her eyes.

Merlin chose to ignore this. "On this occasion, I am prepared to make allowances… I know that you are still in mourning for the death of your husband. But you would do well to be mindful of your duty if you wish to see Madron's lands pass to the babe in your chamber rather than to one of King Uther's favoured Lords. Perhaps a good night's rest will provide you with the opportunity to regain your composure. May I suggest that you retire?" Merlin's tone was dispassionate, his face immobile. Ened received her dismissal without saying a word and once she was gone Merlin turned his attention to Elaine.

"You also look tired, child; I think the pupil demands much from the teacher?" This time, Merlin smiled and raised his hand to softly caress her hair. I knew that he often joined Elaine and Morgan in the nursery that had now become a well-equipped schoolroom, and I could see that he had become fond of my half-sister.

"She is making so much progress that soon she will outstrip me. If I am honest, I do not think I can have care of her much longer; there is little now that I can teach her."

"You have done what you can. And now, go, get some rest, I will stay with the Lady Igraine." Elaine sent a glance in my direction and I nodded. Although I knew that Bennath's experiences had made her mistrustful of the ancient Druid, Merlin had never been anything but courteous toward me and my daughters, and I felt that I had nothing to fear from him.

When Elaine had gone, I indicated to Merlin that he should take a seat, but instead he moved toward the doorway. "I was hoping to find you still awake, Igraine, and was wondering if you and the Lady of Syllan would welcome my company? The air is warm and the stars are beautiful. Shall we walk out across the causeway?"

Neither Bennath nor I had been beyond the castle gates since Solstice and we were feeling frustrated and diminished by the limits Uther had placed upon our freedom. We were both surprised by Merlin's suggestion, but pleased to accept his invitation and within minutes, the three of us had made our way quietly out of the castle and across the courtyard. At a word from Merlin the castle gates were opened and we walked out into the silent summer night.

The cloudless sky was the darkest blue, with faint traces of pink still visible at the horizon. The stars shone with an intense brilliance and seemed very close as we walked out onto the causeway where the gentle, rhythmic splashing of the waves was the only thing to disturb the silence. We walked without speaking for some time and were nearing the mainland when Merlin said. "My Lady of Syllan, I am pleased to see that you are recovering from your injuries. For many weeks we feared that we would lose you."

I was unsure how Bennath would respond to this. In the first few weeks after her injury, Elaine had administered sleeping draughts to keep Bennath sedated, just wakening her for a short time each day so she could eat and we could cleanse her. During her infrequent periods of wakefulness, Bennath had been confused and incoherent. I had learned nothing about what had happened when she had ridden away from Tintagel, furious with what she had seen as my naïve decision to sue for peace. But as her wounds healed and Elaine reduced the strength and frequency of her treatment, Bennath slowly began to come to terms with what she had witnessed.

It took a while, but, eventually, Elaine and I had been able to piece together what had happened. Bennath had chosen to ride along the coast path, not turning inland until she had passed the hamlet of Trewalder, and she had seen no signs of the outlaws who had attacked the men from the Tintagel garrison. She reached the edge of Goss Moor, less than an hour's ride from Demelihoc, just before noon and was lucky not to have ridden directly into the vanguard of Uther's troops. The host was not large; she estimated a force of no more than three hundred and she had hidden within a small coppice until they had ridden past. Once she was sure her road was clear, she made all speed to Demelihoc, only to find a battlefield strewn with the dying and the dead.

For many days, Bennath was unable to share with us the detail of what she had seen, and there were times when I urged Elaine to return her to her enchanted sleep as I could not bear to watch the agony of her remembrance. But my half-sister refused to do this, saying that the visions would simply follow Bennath into her nightmares. She was certain that the only way we could relieve her suffering would be to encourage her to give voice to the horrors she had seen, and that by doing so, help her find a path to understanding and healing.

Eventually, Bennath told us how she had found Erec, his throat cut, body disfigured by the blows from a battle-axe and rent by the vicious beaks of the carrion birds that circled the battlefield. She was silent for a while and then reached out a hand to grasp mine as she continued. Her fingers gripped tighter and tighter as she spoke of the next body she had found, a headless, disembowelled corpse, dressed in a tunic bearing the emblem of Syllan. Her eyes were dry as she told us that she had found her husband's head and cradled it in her arms. "His face was not marked," she said, in a voice as hard and cold as the steel that had taken Lowen from her, and she had kissed his lips and closed his sightless eyes.

The last body she went looking for was Gorlois, and I had no need of her description. I had seen his body in the scrying bowl, battered, despoiled, and degraded and, again, on the very morning of his death when my taibhse had been dragged to the fields of Demelihoc by his final, agonising scream.

Bennath told me that there was not a man left alive upon the battlefield, and her only thought now was to ride back to Tintagel and warn us of the army that was approaching. Demelihoc was but three hours, hard ride, and she knew that a single rider could cover ground more quickly than three hundred horses. What was more, she knew the country and was certain that she could reach the castle before Uther's troops arrived upon the headland. Her horse was not fresh, but she was a gallant beast, and Bennath was an experienced rider.

She covered the ground well, and at first was certain that she would arrive in time to warn us, allowing us to fortify the postern gate and do our best to ensure the garrison was ready to defend it. But as she approached the headland, she knew that she was too late. Uther's troops were now forming for attack, under the brow of the hill and out of sight of the castle.

It had seemed to Bennath that there was only one possible course of action: to move toward the leeward side behind enemy lines, cut out in front of them, and ride the last mile to the causeway across the exposed headland. She knew she would be pursued, but her one hope was that her unexpected appearance would take them off guard and give her enough time to force her exhausted horse onward. As things turned out, she was seen by Vivian as she broke cover, and an archer was instantly sent in pursuit. Merlin and Vivian followed, with Uther's army charging across the headland behind them. It was only because of the narrow causeway track that Bennath had managed to reach us at all. She was very familiar with the narrow pathway and drove her horse onward at a faster pace than her pursuers, screaming her warning as she galloped in through the undefended castle gate with an arrow in her horse's flank, her hunters at her heels.

I was very aware that she was still grieving for Lowen and had yet to forgive Vivian for the damage and destruction Uther's troops had wrought across the Cornish borderlands. I had taken her into my confidence regarding the deception they had played on me, and she blamed the Lady of the Lake for much of what had happened. When she was not with me, I knew she spent her time either alone, in quiet contemplation, or with Yseult. The priestess had remained at Tintagel and was trying to help my poor, wounded friend find some element of spiritual peace and consolation. I knew that Bennath was rarely in Merlin's company, seeing him only on those occasions when he had come across us in the courtyard or garden. When this happened, the Druid greeted her with courtesy, but then rarely spoke to her, choosing instead to converse with me on the topics of Morgan's education and my physical health.

I was not sure how she would respond to Merlin's words about her recovery, and sure enough, there was a bitterness in her voice when she replied. "Had your troops not chosen to attack Tintagel on the sacred night of the Solstice ritual, there would have been nothing for me to recover from."

"It was indeed an unfortunate necessity. The path the Goddess lays before us is not always an easy one, but it is not for us, child, to question her wisdom." He spoke quietly, without aggression, but with a calm forcefulness that spoke of absolute commitment and a certainty that he was right.

"And was it right to murder civilians and innocent children, to rape women and girls, and to burn the fields they had been working to ensure the bounty of the Goddess would come forth?"

"Sometimes atrocious things have to happen if the overall vision is to be achieved. I am not justifying the actions themselves, Bennath, but saying that there are times when a terrible price has to be paid for the greater good to prevail." He spoke slowly, calmly, as if trying to explain something to a much loved but recalcitrant child.

"I know you have talked with the Lady of Treliggan. She also is concerned for those who suffered during Gorlois' rebellion. She has made the case forcefully for reparation and compensation. Uther's council has agreed and we are already helping those who lost their homes and lands to rebuild and to start again."

"A new house will not bring back a dead child, or cure a family who have seen their mothers and grandmothers raped and murdered by Uther's soldiers." Bennath's voice was low, but steady. "Lord Merlin, I can't believe this was the will of the Goddess. I have always served Her. Lowen and I followed the old ways and honoured Her in all we did. And now he's dead, and I can make sense of none of it."

We had reached the end of the causeway and Merlin now began to walk down onto the beach, away from the headland toward the caves that interlaced the cliffs for miles along the shoreline.

"I suspected this was how you felt, Bennath, and I am sorry for it. That is one of the reasons why I wished to speak with you this night. I have spoken with Yseult, and we both feel that you should return to Syllan, to your people and Lowen's. To take your rightful place."

Bennath said nothing, and I stood stock still, trying to absorb what I had just heard. I had lost so much. Over the past months, I had come to love and depend on Bennath as much as I did Elaine. At Samhain, my daughter Morgan was to be taken from me; was I about to lose my friend as well?

"I know you find it hard to accept this, but Cornwall is a better place now. The people understand that Uther is their liege lord and that he will bring peace and prosperity if he is served with loyalty."

Merlin had taken a seat on a large flat rock at the mouth of one of the caves, and he gestured to us to join him.

"The suppression of the Rebellion has driven out the servants of the false religion; those itinerants who peddle the lies and nonsense of the Risen God know they are not welcome. Return to your people, Bennath; it will soon be time for first harvest and you would do well to observe Lughnasa by celebrating the Goddess' bounty in the fields and orchards of your childhood. It will ease you; I promise. It will help you find peace."

I looked at Bennath's face and I knew at once that Merlin's words had found a receptive audience. Her face had softened, and as she turned toward me, I could see the beginning of a tear glistening in her eye.

"But Igraine, Lady, how could I leave you?"

He was clever, Merlin. I now understood exactly how he had manipulated this situation. He guessed that I would never ask Bennath to stay with me if her well-being would be better served by sending her away. He was deliberately creating a situation in which I would become more isolated, where the only person I could turn to would be him. He knew me well. Just because I was in torment, that did not give me the moral authority to deny Bennath the chance to heal.

"Bennath, Merlin is right; your people need you. And I believe that you need them, too. Staying here in Tintagel is just making it worse for you. You need to return to the land."

"Are you sure, Igraine? Is this what you really want? Because I'll not go unless I am certain that you will manage without me." I turned to her and drew her close, wanting to feel the warmth of her, to breathe in the smell of her, to absorb her strength. She relaxed into me, her head upon my shoulders and we sat together, unspeaking. It was me that broke away first.

"I am sure, Bennath. It is the right thing for you. Your home is calling and you go with my blessing." She smiled at me through her tears. "And don't forget, Elaine and Morgan are still with me…and

I suppose Epona's not too bad. At the very least I can rely on her not to insult me."

This rather feeble attempt at humour found its mark and Bennath gave a half-hearted laugh. Merlin got to his feet and gestured to us to walk in front of him back toward the causeway saying, "I am glad that is settled. I will speak with Jago in the morning to make preparations for your departure. There is much to be done, and little time to do it in. If you are to return in time to celebrate Lughnasa, you needs must be on your way by the day after tomorrow at the latest."

I felt a deep dismay at these words. I had lost track of the days and had not realised how close we were to first harvest. Although I had given Bennath my blessing, her departure was a hard knock to take, and I had thought that I'd have several days to get used to the idea that my life was to become even more isolated and restricted.

"Merlin, I think you are right to counsel the Lady of Syllan to return to her homelands. But she is dear to me and I cannot spare her for long. May she return, to be with me when my time is upon me?"

Merlin looked a little startled at this request, which he clearly had not anticipated. "Your baby is due in the spring time I think, Igraine?" I nodded. He said nothing for a while and we walked on in silence, climbing over the rocks that led up from the beach onto the causeway. The wind was rising with the turning tide and the waves splashed us with salt spray as we began to walk back toward the castle.

"The roads should be clear by then." He sounded thoughtful, and I knew that he was weighing up the options, deciding where, for him, the advantage would lie. He soon made his mind up, saying, "If the Goddess wills it, Bennath, I see no reason why you may not return."

We thanked him and I felt Bennath reach for my hand. Together we walked back to Tintagel, with Merlin pacing silently behind us like a large and rather frightening guard-dog.

◆ ◆ ◆

ONCE BENNATH HAD LEFT ME, my world became very small indeed. We received occasional visitors, messengers from Uther or other members of the council for Merlin. I was not allowed to see anyone unaccompanied, although I was pleased that Merlin—since witnessing Ened's behaviour toward me—had relieved her of most of her responsibilities regarding my surveillance. If neither Hild nor Epona were with me, Merlin would take it upon himself to visit my chamber or join me on my monotonous and otherwise solitary walks around the castle grounds, rather than finding another lady of the castle to become my jailer.

As the days shortened and the leaves on the trees in the castle courtyard began to turn from pale green to golden yellow, I received word from Orkney that Morgause was well and, by all accounts, happy. She had sent me a small piece of tapestry, embroidered with a strange four-legged creature that I took to be a unicorn. I placed it next to my heart and would not be parted with it.

I also received gifts from Uther. Yards of fine cloth to be made into gowns to accommodate my rapidly increasing waistline, a beautifully crafted necklace of twisted copper showing two serpents entwined, two delicate crystal goblets that appeared to have been sculptured from a single piece of living rock. I accepted nothing from him and sent him no word of thanks. He had taken from me everything I valued: my honour, my liberty, my family. He had even taken my freedom to determine my choices about my own body. How dare he suggest that I could be bought by these inconsequential trifles? I threw the crystal from my window and heard it smash upon the cobblestones below with great satisfaction. I would have hurled the other presents into the fire had not Hild and Epona prevented me.

One day I was seated by the window of my solar, looking out across the courtyard when a rider passed under the postern gateway and dismounted. He was wearing the badge of the Lady of the Lake and was immediately greeted by a member of the castle guard and escorted toward the Great Hall. I guessed that this was a messenger from Vivian, come to escort Morgan and myself to Avalon in time to celebrate the Samhain rituals.

It would seem that I had guessed correctly, for a few minutes later I heard a knock on my door. I rose to my feet somewhat clumsily; this baby was very different from my daughters, lying heavily against my spine and causing my back to ache and pressing down on my bladder, resulting in a feeling of almost permanent discomfort. Although the early weeks of sickness had now passed, I suffered terribly from stomach cramps and was very frequently troubled with an unpleasantly ferrous taste in my mouth.

Elaine had helped me to dress that morning but was now with Morgan and I was alone, apart from Hild, who was sitting by the fireside working on her loom. She rose to her feet as the door opened and Merlin walked in; at his gesture of dismissal she left the room, taking her loom with her and not even giving me a second glance.

The Druid was smiling as he came toward me, bending slightly to kiss me on the forehead. He allowed his hands to rest for a second on my swollen belly. I resented the way he assumed these casual embraces were acceptable but knew that I would not help myself by making any objection.

"And how are you this morning, Igraine?" He reached out and helped himself to an apple, biting deep into its russet sweetness.

"I've been better. There is little to occupy me, and my allotted companions are not exactly witty conversationalists." I moved across to the window, looking out across the castle walls to the mainland. "I don't deny that my prison is a beautiful place, but I long to go beyond the walls of Tintagel."

"'Prison' is too strong a word, Igraine; you are free to go where you wish within the castle."

"Your view of freedom is not mine, Merlin." I made an effort to speak in measured tones, my voice low and calm. "I am watched all the time. I can do nothing that is not monitored, noted, observed. Even at night one of your lackeys stands guard at my bedside. I have no privacy, no opportunity to be on my own with my thoughts. You say that I am still the Duchess of Cornwall, but I have not been allowed to visit my lands or see my people. They will think I have deserted them."

The old Druid threw his apple core in the fireplace and came to stand beside me at the window, his features forming themselves into an expression of concern. "Child, I do not think you realise how foolish you are being. Do you not understand what the people of Cornwall really think of you? How much they hate you? They blame you for Gorlois' rebellion, for the death of their men-folk and the destruction of their villages. It's not safe for you out there. You must understand, Igraine; we do what we do because we have your well-being at heart. You must stay within the walls of Tintagel."

"It was not I who burned their homesteads. I did not order my soldiers to rape and murder innocent people. This was Uther's work, aye, and yours and Vivian's. But it was not of my doing." I was angry now, pacing the room. "I did all I could to prevent the war, and it was because of me that the fields did not lie fallow. From what you have told me, the barns and granaries across Cornwall and Lyonesse are full and we are well placed to face the winter months. I do not believe my people hate me."

"Igraine, your people saw you dance with Uther before all the court. They know he bedded you at Solstice when your husband was not yet cold. They know his child is growing in your womb."

I listened, appalled at the injustice of Merlin's words. "But you know I had no choice but to dance with him. Vivian made it absolutely clear that it was my duty to the Goddess, and as for Solstice, that was your doing, Merlin. You enchanted Uther, gave him Gorlois' face and form, made me believe my husband had returned to me."

"Igraine, it is not always what is true, but what is believed that counts in this world. Uther has shown the power of his anger, but he has also demonstrated his mercy to those who have returned to him in loyalty. Whom do you think your Cornish peasants will choose to blame for their misfortunes: the King who has rebuilt their villages and paid generous compensation for their losses, or the woman they believe betrayed their war duke to go whoring in Caer-Lundein?"

I thought of the look of hatred in Ened's eyes and knew that what the Druid was telling me was true. I felt so angry that the women I had worked so hard to support and protect should think of me this way. The unfairness was almost over-whelming. I sank into a chair, my head in my hands. I just wanted to be alone.

Merlin did not leave the room, but for a long time he said nothing. When I raised my head he was still standing by the window, gazing out across the causeway. He must have caught my movement from the corner of his eye, for he turned and smiled at me. "But you know, it doesn't have to be like this, Igraine. Uther loves you. You are carrying his child, the child the Goddess has destined for greatness. You could be Queen, your dignity and freedom returned to you. People have short memories and all of this year's trouble would be forgotten when they see you crowned, with a little princeling in your arms."

"Uther doesn't love me; he loves his idea of me. No one could do what he has done to someone that they love."

"Love is a very complex thing, Igraine. Did you truly love Gorlois? A man chosen for you, whom you met only on your wedding day? A man who had turned against the Goddess and everything that you hold dear?"

"He was my husband. He made me happy."

"You did not love Gorlois before he bedded you; he did not court you, woo you with fine words and presents. You married him because it had been arranged that you should do so, and in your obedience, you gave of yourself to your marriage and that is how you found happiness. I believe you could do so again. You are not a stupid woman and Vivian trained you well. I know that Uther pleased you.

Stop being so stubborn and you will see that everything will work out for the best."

So here it was at last. Merlin was ready to talk terms, to tell me what he wanted of me, what I would need to do to get some semblance of my life back. I thought it unlikely that I would find palatable any plan crafted by Merlin—and, I was certain, Vivian—but it would not hurt to find out more. "What would you have me do?" I asked.

"Send word of thanks to Uther for his gifts. Suggest that his addresses are not unwelcome, but that you must be seen to grieve for Gorlois before you can wed again. Intimate that, when he returns to Tintagel, he will not find you to be unfriendly."

"So you would have me lie, send sweet words to the man who killed my husband and took me through deceit and trickery? The man who ordered his troops to kill my people and burn my lands and who placed this unwanted bastard in my belly?"

"I would see your son born legitimate," said Merlin gravely.

I made a face, and said nothing, caring little for this unborn child.

"Uther is a better match for you than Gorlois," the Druid continued. "He is loyal to the Mysteries and his feelings for you run very deep. You would be his Queen and consort. Unlike Gorlois, who I know was loath to accord you your rightful place in the governance of Cornwall, Uther would consult you, involve you. Your years in Avalon will stand you in good stead, and you will have myself and Vivian to help and guide you."

"I am not sure I trust your 'help and guidance.' From what I can see, it is your interference, yours and Vivian's, that started all of this. If you had left well alone, Gorlois would be alive and I would not be prisoner within these castle walls."

"You remain very bitter, Igraine and that, I think clouds your sense of perspective." He reached out and placed his hand upon my arm, but I shrugged it off and turned away from him. For a second, I caught a flash of anger in his pale grey eyes. "I understand now that you have not had enough time to truly consider what would be best for you. You still spend many hours with Morgan. Perhaps once she has gone, you will have leisure enough to reflect on what I have said."

My anger at Merlin's suggestion had completely taken any thoughts of Morgan and her journey to Avalon from my mind. I had assumed that had been why the Druid had come to see me in the first place, and it had been my complaints about my situation and frustrations regarding the continued lack of liberty that had diverted our conversation from her forthcoming departure.

I turned back toward him and smiled, wishing to placate him. "I saw the messenger from Avalon arrive this morning. I assume he will be our escort on the journey to Avalon?"

"He brought messages from the Lady and will indeed be of the party who travel with Morgan on her journey."

"Party?" I looked at him in surprise. "How many of us are going to make the journey? I had assumed that Elaine and I would accompany my daughter to take her place on Avalon. Neither of us have visited the Lake Island for many years, and we were looking forward to celebrating Samhain on its shores."

"Certainly, Elaine will accompany Morgan; she has cared for her well and is an intelligent servant. They will leave tomorrow, accompanied by a small number of the castle garrison. The roads are still beset by shadow pads and outlaws, and Morgan is far too precious a child to travel unprotected. You, however, will remain here. Uther's orders were clear. You are not to leave Tintagel."

I stared at him, speechless and in shock. I had not prepared myself for this, not readied myself to part so suddenly from my youngest daughter. Of course I had known that she was leaving, understood it was unlikely that, once she began her studies at Avalon, she would ever live with me again, but I had thought that we would have days together on our journey, days before I need say goodbye. And then I remembered the vision in the scrying bowl. Morgan, travel-stained but happy making her way across the lake in Avalon's enchanted barge. She had been on her own, accompanied only by the Ferryman. It had not struck me then, but now I realised that this had always been the plan. Morgan was wanted on Avalon; Vivian desired her company with a jealous, single-minded intensity, and I knew that I would never be welcome on the Lake Island again.

"It is all as it must be child. You know that Vivian and I think of nothing but your best interests." Merlin smiled again, a cold smile that did not reach his eyes. "I will send Morgan and Elaine to you now. I am sure that you will wish to spend the remaining hours before their departure together."

He opened the door to re-admit Hild and left me to my thoughts.

I DID NOT WISH MORGAN to see my unhappiness, and by the time she and Elaine joined me, I had composed myself. Whilst waiting, I spent my time removing a few skeins of thread from my box of embroidery silks, putting aside just those I thought I might have need of, to patch or mend my clothing. The rest I began to sort into order of colour and thickness before replacing them in neat rows in the wooden box that had belonged to my mother. It was a simple, hypnotic task, and it gave me a new insight of my daughter, who so loved to sort and arrange the delicate bundles. As I worked, I felt myself entering a trancelike state, almost as if I was scrying and in my mind I saw my daughters, women, grown and beautiful.

Morgause held a baby in her arms, a tiny scrap with pale skin and auburn hair. She smiled as Morgan came toward her, belly distended and a look of tranquil pleasure on her face. Something I couldn't see must have startled them, for they both looked up and stared toward me, blue eyes and brown eyes, in familiar but now so different faces that creased with laughter as two small boys and a puppy came charging into the room.

My girls, my daughters, together and happy. I thanked the Goddess for sending me the vision, which calmed me and gave me strength, and when Morgan came to stand beside me I smiled down at her and handed her the box.

"This is for you, darling heart. Keep it safe and think of me sometimes."

Morgan thanked me saying, "Merlin had told us that you are not well enough to travel with us. That is a shame, but it is probably for the best." I met Elaine's eyes over my daughter's head. Her face was troubled and I sensed that, like me, she had only just learned of Merlin's proposals for the journey.

"I have been told that I must stay here and you will go to Avalon without me. But you are not to be frightened, Morgan. Elaine will be with you and there will be soldiers to guard you on the road."

Morgan put down the box and reached out her hand to touch my hand. "I'm not frightened, Mother. I am going to Avalon, where I belong. There is nothing to frighten me there." And then I felt her finger poke hard into my belly. "Merlin says the people are angry with you because of this baby and that is why you cannot travel with us." She jabbed again, and I tried not to flinch from the pain. "I hate this baby; he is not my brother. He is a bastard that never should have been created." She raised her head to look at me, her face set and her eyes flaming with a fierce anger. "One day I will make him pay for what he's done to you."

"Sweetling, whatever has happened, it is not the baby's fault. He will be your brother, and you must love him as you do Morgause." As I said these words, I suddenly realised that they were true. The child I was carrying was an innocent, who could not be blamed for the circumstances of his conception.

"I will never love him." She said these words with a calm finality as she bent to pick up the box of silks and as she did so, I felt a quivering inside me, and then another. My baby had quickened, and for the first time I thought of him with something other than anger and resentment.

Morgan and I spent the rest of the day together whilst Elaine oversaw the packing of her belongings. My daughter wished to take very little with her, saying that Vivian would provide her with what she needed whilst she was on Avalon. I was pleased to see that she tucked the box of silks into the corner of her trunk, covering it carefully with her Solstice robes and saying, "I will treasure this, Mother, and when I look upon my silks, I will always think of you." I reached toward her, trying to draw her to me in a hug, but she wriggled to one side and would not allow me to hold her. I think she must have seen the tears that welled involuntarily in my eyes, for she came to stand in front of me and reached out her finger to touch my nose, remaining close enough for me to touch hers, as I smiled at her through misty eyes.

MERLIN CAME TO MY CHAMBER an hour before sunrise and told Morgan and Elaine they were to go with him to break their fast. He asked me if I wished to join them in the Great Hall, but the thought of hundreds of eyes upon me, judging me, possibly relishing my misery as I prepared to say goodbye to my daughter, was more than I could bear.

I hugged Elaine to me. "Take care of her; please be careful. And come back soon."

My half-sister was weeping, unable to speak. She nodded her head and I placed a kiss upon her brow, sending her on her journey with my blessing.

Merlin nodded toward the doorway and Elaine was gone. Morgan hung back, for once uncertain. "Will you be alright, Mother? Will you be lonely? I wish that you could come with us."

"Morgan, child of my heart, that cannot be. I send you to Vivian with my blessing." I smiled and raised my hand in a gesture of benison. "I am certain that you have been favoured by the Goddess. You will learn much in Avalon, but darling girl, please always remember to be true to your heart. Don't wield the power you have been given unthinkingly."

Morgan looked at me, a slightly quizzical look on her face which resolved into a cold, hard smile. "Oh, don't worry, Mother; I will always be true to my heart." And with that she was gone.

I took my seat by the window. The stars had disappeared and the full autumn moon hung low over the waves. The sky at the horizon was turning from deepest blue to a tawny orange as the pale sun cast its first rays across the dark sea. It was still too dark to see clearly and the torches in their sconces had been lit. As I watched, the gates of the castle were flung open and Elaine and Morgan rode out across the causeway, followed by an ox-cart piled high with barrels and boxes, gifts that were none of my doing, but sent, I was certain, in my name from Tintagel to the Lady of the Lake. A small squad of mounted soldiers brought up the rear.

As Elaine passed under the postern she turned in her saddle, looking up at my chamber and raising her arm in salute. I raised mine and forced myself to smile. Beside her, my daughter rode through the gateway without once turning back, leaving both me and Tintagel behind her.

Chapter Seventeen

In the weeks that followed, I was indeed lonely. I could, I suppose, have tried to find some solace in the day-to-day life of the castle, but after Merlin had told me what my people felt about me, I was loathe to do this. Instead, I had taken to calling the great seabird to me, taking possession of her mind and flying way beyond the boundaries of Tintagel, relishing the freedom to skim the waves and soar high above the clifftops, but I could only do this when Hild or Epona were my companions. They very rarely spoke to me, but simply sat with their sewing or worked at their looms, uninterested in what I was doing. As long as I remained quiet and still, they would just have assumed I was napping, or that I was lost, deep in thought as I sat at my accustomed seat by the window, gazing out toward the headland.

But when Merlin chose to be my companion, it was very different. He was at all times gentle and solicitous, bringing me salves to ease the almost constant pain in my lower back, or delicately flavoured herbal drinks that calmed my stomach and helped to mask the unpleasant metallic taste in my mouth that had been a feature of this pregnancy from the beginning.

He would sit beside me, in front of the fire, watching the flames and encouraging me to talk about my early years in Tintagel. He wanted to know all about the births of Morgause and Morgan, asking questions with a keen and unembarrassed interest as we discussed details that I had never thought to share with anyone but my half-sister and the wise women who had helped me at the births.

Merlin felt that my preference for remaining in my room was bad for my health and the health of the child. He insisted that I take a walk within the castle grounds every day, always accompanying me when he could. He understood my reluctance to expose myself to the eyes of the castle servants, who I now believed to be consumed with hatred and anger toward me, and so when he was my companion, we would walk together in the hours just before dawn. I preferred this to the days when Hild or Epona would make me walk around the orchard in the early morning, after we had broken our fast. No one spoke to me, but I was certain the eyes of Ened and the other castle ladies followed me with looks of loathing as I manoeuvred my increasingly clumsy body through the narrow lychgate and along the uneven pathways, taking care not to miss my footing or trip on one of the windfalls that lay rotting in the grass beneath the trees.

It was as we were coming to the end of one of these walks that the messenger wearing my father's emblem rode into the courtyard. Hild had just closed the orchard gate behind us and we were making our way across the courtyard. I watched him dismount at the stable block, looking around for someone to take his horse, but there was no one else to be seen. He approached us, and as he came closer, I recognised him. It was Huw, the son of my father's steward. I had known him since I was a little girl but had not seen him for many years.

By now, Hild and I were at the foot of the steps that led up to the castle. Huw stopped a few feet away from us and his eyes went straight to my belly, which I carried high and distended as I entered the sixth month of my pregnancy. His expression was grim as he bent forward and bowed to me. "My Lady Igraine, I have news from the Welsh Border."

"You are welcome, Huw. Hild, please send for one of Jago's boys to see to this man's horse." The visitor from my father's court intrigued me, making me eager for news of the outside world and, as result, I spoke with my old authority which appeared to surprise

Hild so much that she did not question me and instead made her way toward the buttery.

"What news do you bring from Amlawdd's court? How is my father?"

"My lady, I have sad news for you, your father died at Samhain. These are messages from the new King, Gareth, your brother."

From the corner of my eye, I saw Jago approaching, followed by Hild and one of the stable boys. I was feeling tired and did not want to engage anyone in conversation and I knew Jago would look after the needs of the messenger. However, I was keen to hear what he had to say as soon as possible.

"I see Jago, my steward, approaching. You may leave your horse here, Huw; Jago will see that it is well stabled and will bring you refreshments. Please ask Hild to show you to my solar when you are rested." I turned and began to climb the steps to the great front door.

"I'm sorry, my lady; the messages are not for you. They are for Merlin."

I stopped in my tracks, little able to believe what I had been told. "But I am still Duchess of Cornwall. Tintagel is my castle, not Merlin's. Are you certain that my brother sent no message to tell me of the death of our father?" I glared down at him and he fumbled uncomfortably with the hem of his tunic.

"No…I'm sorry, my lady. There is no message for you. The King made it extremely clear to me, the messages I bring are for the ears of Merlin alone." He looked shamefaced, unhappy, I believed, to have unwittingly become part of yet another of my humiliations. I forced myself to smile. "It is of no matter. You have ridden far and must needs be in want of refreshment. Jago will see to you." I continued to mount the steps, and then turned back toward him saying, "I am tired and will return to my room. I doubt I will see you again before you depart. Please send my regards to your father and mother."

His face was ablaze with embarrassment as he nodded, allowing himself to be led away toward the buttery by Jago. Hild climbed the stairs after me, exclaiming about the news and even offering me her condolences on the death of my father, but I said nothing. The incident had upset me, and I felt utterly exhausted. I wanted nothing but to lose myself in sleep.

It was not until the evening of the next day that I gained any knowledge of the news from the Welsh borders. It was cold and, although the sky had darkened early, I had asked Epona to leave the candles unlit as a darkened room was more in keeping with my mood. The fire burned in the grate and I was sitting on a low chair, a cushion at my back and my feet raised up on a footstool, staring at the shapes that danced before me in the flames. I was lost in thought and did not hear Merlin's knock, so was a little startled when he entered my chamber, followed by two pages. The smaller one was carrying a vast candlestick, which he proceeded to place upon the table. As he began to light the candles, the second page put a tray containing a jug of mulled wine and a bowl of sweetmeats on the low chest before the fireplace.

"What is this, Igraine? Sitting in the darkness? Summoning up visions of discontent? Unhealthy thoughts cannot be good for the babe you are carrying." Once again, Merlin reached across and stroked my belly; this time I found it impossible to conceal my shudder at his touch. He ignored this, however, waving instead to the page boy to bring me some wine. I took a sip, and, despite myself, was warmed by the rich spiced liquid that seemed to caress my throat and settle gently in my stomach. "It's good, isn't it?" Merlin drank deep and held out his beaker for a refill. "The wine was a present from King Gareth. I thought it fitting to bring you some, in memory of your father."

I said nothing.

"I'm sorry for your loss, Igraine. Amlawdd was a good man. You were close, I believe?"

Still, I said nothing, but nodded, remembering the father of my childhood, a bluff, hearty, laughing man who would throw me high in the air as I screamed, half in joy and half in terror. He had been a father as much as he had been a King, and I had loved him, but I also knew that he had lived too long and that for him death was not a tragedy, but a release from pain.

I took another sip. "You have news from the Welsh court, I believe?"

"Yes," said Merlin, putting down his drink and stroking the tips of his beard in a thoughtful and contemplative way. "Interesting news, and not just from Gareth. The new king has high favour with the Pendragon…indeed, Uther is with him presently."

"Gareth always knew which side his bread was buttered. I am sure that he and Uther are getting along famously."

"King Gareth would indeed be foolish to court the displeasure of the High King, particularly when the High King could soon become more intimately related to him," Merlin smiled at me and offered me a sweetmeat.

"Here, child; try one of these honey cakes. Uther sent them to me, asking most especially that I share them with you." I grabbed a handful of the honey cakes and rather childishly threw them in the fire, where they bubbled and hissed and finally gave off an unpleasantly acrid smell.

"That was rather wasteful child, and the honey would have provided good nourishment for the child. You look tired, Igraine, and I am worried that you are not eating enough. The cares of Tintagel are clearly too much for you."

"What cares? As you well know, I have done nothing, have been forced to do nothing, for months. Jago has not spoken to me about the harvest, all matters of law and arbitration are dealt with by you, or Lord Madoc. I have not spoken with Yseult or any of the High Priestesses. I have been little but a prisoner in this chamber."

"Child, you exaggerate. You are under strain and we have done what we can to take the burden from you, to ensure that you are not troubled and that all of your energies and strength are concentrated on the child." Once again, he reached out, but before he could touch me, I had pulled myself up from the chair, moving away from the fire and the bright lights of the candles to my old settle in the corner of the room.

"You see, you are restless. You need calm, tranquillity, and today's decree from Uther will, I'm sure do much to reassure you."

He said nothing further, but settled himself more comfortably in his chair, sipping his wine and taking appreciative bites from the remaining honey cakes.

Finally I spoke. "What news?"

Merlin shook himself as if he had fallen into a light slumber, stretched and spoke through a half yawn. "Oh…yes…Well it would seem that Uther Pendragon is most pleased with your brother and in addition to confirming his right to rule the Welsh Marches, he has awarded him the regency of Cornwall and Lyonesse, to be held by him until your son comes of age."

"But I am Duchess of Cornwall. By right, by marriage, with the blessing of the Goddess. I made my vows at Solstice and it is not for Uther to undo them." I was shaking with fury and disbelief. Cornwall and Lyonesse were mine to rule. I had sworn to honour the Goddess and protect the land. I knew that I could do little to win back my people until after the child was born, but I had been certain that, once I had regained my strength I could ride amongst them, show them that I was still one of them, and win back their loyalty and trust.

"Igraine, he is the High King and he most certainly can dispose of his fiefdoms as he so desires." Merlin brushed a crumb of honey cake from the cuff of his robes and got to his feet. "But it is late and you must sleep. I should tell you that both Vivian and myself fully support Uther's decision. As you know, we have nothing but your best interest at heart. From now on, your title will be 'Lady of Cornwall', unless—or until—you choose to take a new one, and one which is much more exalted than that of a mere Duchess."

He gestured to the pages to blow out the candles and collect up what was left of the wine and sweetmeats. "Good night, my dear." Merlin smiled and made as though to leave, but as he stood on the doorstep, he smiled and wagged his finger at himself in mock serious admonition. "Silly me, there is one more thing that I had to tell you. As he promised, Uther will celebrate Yule at Tintagel. He plans to be with us by the time the moon is new, and to stay until the Year has turned."

TWO DAYS AFTER MERLIN'S ANNOUNCEMENT, Elaine returned from her journey. She had been escorted by the Irish mercenaries, the galloglaigh, who Uther had installed in the garrison at Tintagel; although they had not been the most sociable of companions, they had ridden fast and hard and nothing had threatened the safety of the little band of travellers. Elaine told me that she had been allowed to go as far as the Lakeside, and it had been she who had summoned the enchanted barge to carry Morgan across the Lake, to where Vivian had stood to receive her.

I was overjoyed to have my half-sister and friend with me once again; to be able to talk freely, to laugh and to work together at our sewing, albeit under the dour and disapproving eyes of Hild or Epona, was nothing but a delight. By now my pregnancy was very obvious: my breasts were swollen and my belly was large, and although I was carrying high, none of my kirtles, and few of my under-gowns, would fit me.

I almost wished that I had not spurned Uther's gift of dress material, until Elaine had the ingenious idea of undoing the seams of my current shifts and enlarging them by adding in lengths cut from older garments that I had put aside. It was less easy to make any presentable adjustments to my kirtles, and I was forced to wear odd, rag-tag garments, cobbled together from sources as varied as old blankets and several of my mother's shawls. Still, I was not concerned about looking beautiful. I simply wished to keep warm and comfortable as the winter storms began to pound the walls of Tintagel in earnest.

The baby was no longer pushing against my spine and bladder, and although he kicked lustily at all hours of the day and night, the final few months of my pregnancy promised to be rather less uncomfortable than the first. With Elaine at my side, I began to feel more comfortable in the company of others, and on several occasions, we chose to dine in the Great Hall.

The second time we did so, I was slightly bemused to find Jago, the pages, scullery maids, stable hands and cooks lined up before me, each carrying a bunch of herbs, a small bottle or barrel of wine or cider, or a delicacy they had prepared in the castle kitchens. Ignoring the glint of anger in Merlin's eyes, Jago came forward with his arms outstretched and bowed before me. "M'lady, it do warm our hearts to see you 'ere, where you belong. We're loyal people, y'er at Tintagel, and you'll alus be our Duchess, no matter what anyone else says." With this, each and every one of them came forward, bobbing a curtsey, or bending in a bow, before putting their gifts in a great pile in front of me. If anything could have raised my spirits, this could. My people did not hate me. They understood, and cared for me, and knowing this, I grew strong.

As Yule approached, I saw less of Merlin. The castle grew merry, as guests arrived from the Great Houses across all of Cornwall and Lyonesse. Lesser lords and nobles who had been accustomed to spending the winter festival at Tintagel also made their appearance and Jago took both pride and pleasure in finding space for them all. He also supervised the decoration of the Great Hall with vast boughs of greenery, ripe with berries, and wreaths of ivy hung in lush green swags at the windows, as was Tintagel's custom. Outside in the courtyard the Yule tree had been cut and left to dry under a temporary structure of willow twigs and tanned horsehide. Jago would bring it into the Hall on the first day of Yuletide when we would light it from kindling left over from the previous year's celebrations. It would burn, uninterrupted, throughout the festival, symbolising the light and warmth of the Goddess and her promise of a bright future.

There were but two days to go before the new moon, which would also see the first day of the festival. Elaine and I were standing together at the top of the postern gate, looking out across the causeway. Epona was behind us, silent as always, but even her dour countenance was lifted by the beauty of the morning. It was a glorious day. The seabirds whirled above us, calling out to each other as the winds lifted them, sending them soaring high into the chill, crisp winter sky and then wheeling downward, to skim the wavetops, diving below the water when a glint betrayed a fish swimming close to the surface.

Elaine's cheeks were pink and her eyes glistened in the cold wind. I felt a tingle on my own nose and cheek bones, which probably indicated that we had been out long enough in the icy wind. We had just agreed to make our way to the Great Hall in search of warmth and comfort when we noticed a horse riding hard along the headland. Its rider was small and dressed in green but was too far away for us to tell if it was a man or a woman.

"It looks like we have another visitor. Is anyone else expected?" I asked Elaine.

"No. No one until new moon."

As the rider came closer I could tell it was a woman, with black hair and pale skin. Her horse had raced across the hazardous turf of the causeway as if each inch of ground was familiar. As they approached the postern, the rider reined in her palfrey and gazed up to where we were standing. The gates were now always locked and manned with a full complement of the Irish galloglaigh. Merlin, it seemed, was taking no chances.

Putting up a hand to shield her eyes, the rider raised her other arm in a gesture of salute. "Greetings, Igraine; I had forgotten how pregnancy suits you. You look beautiful. But what on earth are you wearing? I shall have to take your wardrobe in hand before the festival." Her blue eyes flashed brilliant in the chill winter sunlight. It was Vivian. "Now, hurry down and get the gates opened, I can see that there is much for me to do."

By the time we reached the ground the gates were already standing open and Merlin had appeared in the courtyard, holding out his arms in welcome. Vivian dismounted, throwing the reigns to a stable boy and instructing him to make ready for her carriage which she said was following on behind her and should arrive in Tintagel well before nightfall. She permitted Merlin a rather cursory embrace before making her way toward me.

"Child, you look frozen." She reached out and touched my cheek with her finger. "You feel like ice. I would have thought that Elaine would have had greater care of you."

"I asked Elaine to accompany me to the top of the tower. I have little enough freedom, and at least when I stand there, I can imagine that one day this castle will cease to be my prison. Please do not blame her for my decision. If anyone is at fault, it is me." My voice was hard and unwelcoming, and for an instant, I thought I saw an expression of uncertainty in Vivian's eyes.

"Igraine, you are very touchy. It is only my great concern for your well-being—and for that of the child—that makes me a little overprotective. I'm sorry if I have offended you. Do you not have any words of welcome for me?"

Her words caused an instant flame of anger inside me. How did she have the gall to describe herself as "overprotective"? This was the woman whose scheming had led to Gorlois' death and who had shown no scruples about using me as a puppet in her intrigues. I would have liked nothing more than to tell her to get back on her horse and return to Avalon. But I could not forget that she now had sole guardianship of my child, and so, grudgingly, I smiled and bent to embrace her. She offered her cheek for a kiss.

"Welcome Vivian, Lady of the Lake, we are honoured to receive you here in Tintagel. I offer you the freedom of my home and hearth this Yuletide." Vivian smiled as I made the formal words of welcome.

She tucked her hand under my arm and began to lead me across the courtyard. "Now first, we must get you warm and then we will discuss your appearance. You have lost too much weight and your kirtle is little more than a mockery. Elaine, please instruct Jago to make ready my usual chamber and then I would like you to join

Igraine and myself in her chamber. I believe your skills as a seamstress are not too shabby, and we will have need of you." Elaine did as she was told, disappearing in search of Jago, whilst Vivian and I joined Merlin and made our way to the Great Hall.

The room was warm and welcoming; the fire had been lit and the smell of burning apple logs mingled pleasingly with the fresh tang of pine resin and the sweet, spicy fragrance of mulled wine. Vivian looked about her approvingly, and when she took the wine Jago offered her, she complimented him on the beauty of the room.

"You have done well. It looks as lovely as I remembered from my last Yuletide visit. When was that, Igraine? Six years ago…seven?"

"It was eight years ago, Lady. The year that I married Gorlois."

"Yes, yes child, now I think about it, you are right," Vivian raised her wine and took a small sip. "Delicious. Try some, Igraine; it will warm you and bring some colour to your cheeks." She gestured to Jago, who immediately ladled some wine into a beaker and handed it to me. "Eight years ago," she continued. "How well I remember it…and now, we are perhaps about to celebrate another wedding here at Tintagel." She took another sip of her wine before placing it on the table. "There is much to do, Jago. We must talk about preparations for the feast and I must satisfy myself that you have followed all my instructions regarding the comfort of the King."

I looked up, astonished. Jago had not once mentioned any messages from Vivian, or any special preparations regarding Uther Pendragon. We had discussed the Yule feast yesterday, and I had been satisfied that, as always, Tintagel would make its guests welcome and the bounty of our hall and hearth would compare favourably to any in the land. "Vivian, I am still mistress of this household. You can be assured that all is ready, and as it should be. Is that not so, Jago?" But Jago would not meet my eyes and a guilty blush spread across his face.

"Igraine, child, it pains me to have to make this point in front of your household." Vivian placed her hand on my sleeve as if to placate me. Her face wore an expression that many would have taken for genuine concern and she spoke low so that none but myself and Jago could hear her. "I know this cannot be easy, but you must accept that you no longer hold any authority here. It is the King and his Regent who determine what happens at Tintagel, and I speak with their blessing and authority. I am surprised that you still do not appear to have grasped this." She looked angrily at Jago, who shrugged his shoulders and shuffled his feet a little shamefacedly but said nothing. "Your erstwhile servants may well have been humouring you, but you know, it is not for you to determine how we will celebrate Yuletide." She patted my arm again as if to console me. "Think of it this way: you will be treated as a guest, an honoured guest, with nothing to do but look beautiful and enjoy the company of your King. What could be more wonderful than that?" She reached out and stroked the curve of my belly. "You have been through so much, Igraine. Now is the time to let others do the work and take the responsibility."

I found I could not reply, for I was certain that I would be unable to control the rage and frustration that were surging through me. I feared my voice would betray me, and I raised my hands to wipe away the bitter tears that were forming, unbidden in my eyes. Putting down my wine, I turned away from the fire and instantly Vivian joined me, putting her arm through mine to lead me gently, but firmly, from the room.

As we made our way to my chamber, Vivian murmured pleasantries that echoed the words I was by now so used to hearing from Merlin. That she had my best interest at heart, that all I had to do to regain my place, my status, and my authority was to marry Uther, that I should realise how lucky I was that a man so blessed by the Goddess wanted no one but me to be his queen.

I listened but made no response until we were inside, with the door closed firmly behind us. The room was not empty; Elaine was standing by my bed, carefully unpacking bales of cloth and other finery. This did not bother me. I had no secrets from my half-sister. "Vivian, whatever you may say, I am still the Duchess of Cornwall."

I spoke slowly and clearly, trying to control my anger. "I made my vows to the Goddess at Solstice and as long as I live and breathe, this is my country, and no one can take it from me."

Vivian sighed and raised her eyebrows as if dealing with a loved but rather troublesome child. "I thought that Merlin had made this clear to you, but obviously he has not. This disappoints me. As I realised very quickly when you were with me in Avalon, you were never a particularly talented scholar, and many are far more gifted in the workings of the Mysteries, but one thing I have always admired in you is your ability to understand and do your duty. You say you made your oath of obedience to the Goddess at Solstice?" She looked at me, and I nodded slowly, suddenly dreading the direction she was taking.

"Yes…I see you remember. I believe that you swore, in front of everyone, that you would 'honour and follow the paths of the Mysteries.' Am I right?" Once again, I nodded.

"And is it also true that you made an oath, again in a hallowed place and in the presence of the High Priestess, that you recognised Uther Pendragon as High King of all Britain and your liege lord by right, by conquest, and by the will of the Goddess?"

I said nothing.

"Igraine, did you, or did you not, swear allegiance to the Pendragon?"

The room was silent. Vivian did not move and Elaine had stopped work, holding one of the bales of cloth tight against her as she looked at me, compassion in her eyes.

Finally, I spoke. "Yes. I swore allegiance. But I was tricked, deceived by you and Merlin and most of all by Uther. The Goddess cannot hold me to it."

"Igraine, I have spoken with Yseult, Lady of Treliggan. She told me that before the Rituals here within the castle that she questioned you, asking if you had taken counsel before making your vows, seeking assurance before you made them that they were your will and your desire. You assured her that it was."

And I remembered the words I had exchanged with Yseult just before we began the final part of the Solstice ritual, the look of concern upon her face when I told her what I planned to do. She had sensed that all was not right, and perhaps she had tried to warn me. But I had not listened to the underlying doubt couched within her words. I had believed that Gorlois had been returned to me. I had been certain, confident and oh so foolish, utterly convinced that I was doing the right thing, absolutely unprepared for the web of deceit that at that very moment had been tightening around me.

There was nothing I could say to contradict Vivian. Yes, I had been tricked, but I had also connived at my own destruction. I had so wanted to believe that I was doing the right thing that I had not listened to Yseult, not listened to Bennath when she had warned me so passionately against my unconditional surrender. I had made my vows, and I could not escape them.

My back was hurting and suddenly I felt exhausted. Lowering myself into a chair, I closed my eyes and let my head fall back. "What is it you want of me?"

"That's better child. I knew that I could make you come to your senses. Women such as you and I are not as the common stock. We have a destiny to fulfil and cannot always follow the paths of our own desiring." I looked up and was surprised to see the lineaments of compassion and understanding on Vivian's face. "But you know, Igraine, the Goddess can be kind. If you will submit yourself to her instruction, you can have love, or power, beauty and riches. She will reward those who serve her well."

"As she has rewarded you?"

"Exactly. But we are not here to discuss my life, but to prepare for the next stage of yours. And the first thing we must do is to make you presentable. We cannot have you looking like a scarecrow at the feast tonight." Vivian beckoned toward Elaine, gesturing to her to bring with her some of the bales of cloth that were now piled high upon my mattress.

"Now, let me see…we need something that makes you look better than skin and bone with a swollen belly. You have got far too pale and thin, and even my arts can do nothing to rectify that in but one afternoon." Sighing at the challenge she had set herself, and with the tip of her tongue caught between her lips, her face took on a look of deep concentration. Vivian began to unfold the material. She held swag after swag against my cheek and I looked in the mirror as she discarded the pale yellow, rich purple, delicate white, and deepest blue. The green and the ruby red she set to one side as possibilities, but it was only when she got to the last of the bales that a smile appeared on her face.

"Ah. Now, here we have a possibility." She held out her hand and raised me to my feet so that I stood before the mirror. The cloth that rippled before me was samite, woven in shades of russet and tawny and shot through with gold and copper thread. Despite its richness, it was not as heavy as I had expected and it fell into beautiful elegant folds as Vivian held it against me, talking all the time about how she wished it to be cut and sewn together.

"Of course, you will need an underdress of cream linen. I had several made in Avalon, all in differing sizes. One of them is certain to fit you." She dispatched Elaine to look through her trunk and sure enough, she soon lifted out an exquisitely made shift of the finest linen I had ever seen, delicately embroidered at the neck and hem.

"Ah yes, this one is perfect… See, here." She pointed to a beautiful tracery of pale green ivy leaves. "Do you recognise the stitchcraft? This was worked by Morgan. She will be pleased when I tell her that you wore her work on the day that you married the Pendragon."

"Vivian. I have not agreed to wed the Pendragon."

"Child, you must do your duty." She gave a heavy sigh. "At the very least, will you promise me to listen to him and to consider what he has to say? Think about it. When you are married, and after the child is born, you can travel together to Orkney, to see Morgause.

You and Uther would always be welcome guests in Avalon, you can spend time with Morgan, see how she progresses in her studies. And you will be reinstated as Duchess of Cornwall. If you so wished it, you could live peacefully here, in Tintagel, watching over your son as he grows to manhood." She took my chin in her hand and stared straight into my eyes.

"Is that so bad a future, Igraine?" I looked, unblinking, into those cold, blue eyes. "Is it not worth forgetting the past in order to have a life like that?"

I felt the baby kick and once again, a wave of exhaustion overwhelmed me. "Lady, I am tired. I would sleep now."

She did not let go of my chin. "But you will consider what I have said?"

"Yes, Vivian. I will consider it." With that she let go of my chin and ran her fingernail softly down my cheek.

"That is sensible, child. Now, Elaine will help you to your bed and we will leave you. I have much to do to finish preparations for the Yule feast and Elaine must needs work hard to get your kirtle ready for tomorrow."

I SLEPT FOR HOURS, AND I woke to find Elaine asleep upon the truckle bed and the dress laid out upon the settle. It was beautiful, soft, and supple, and I could not help but feel delighted at the idea of wearing something other than the makeshift smocks Elaine and I had cobbled together out of oddments and discarded clothing.

After we had broken our fast, Elaine helped me to wash my hair, combing it dry before the fire and twisting it into soft braids. I took off my nightgown and raised my arms to allow Elaine to lower the undershift carefully over my head. It felt soft and cool against my skin and I smiled as I touched the delicate embroidery at the neckline, thinking with pleasure of Morgan and delighting in the deftness of her work. Then Elaine helped me into the kirtle, lacing it below my breasts, emphasising their fullness above the swelling of my rounded belly. The skirts fell in soft folds, and the sleeves fitted tight to the elbow, then falling away in an elegant cascade of russet, copper, and gold.

Elaine was helping me into a pair of soft, tawny-gold slippers that she had found in the trunk that Vivian had brought with her from Avalon, when the Lady herself walked into the room. Nodding appreciatively, she came over to me, tweaking the folds of the kirtle so it hung more to her liking, and smoothing an errant lock of hair back into its braid.

"You look charming, Igraine. Tintagel will have no need to be ashamed of its Lady this Yuletide…at least not on the grounds of her appearance." She looked at Elaine and gestured toward the doorway. "You have done well and if I have guessed correctly, you have been at work half the night and have had little sleep. Am I right?"

"It was nothing. I was happy to do it," but as she spoke, I saw my half-sister stifle a yawn, and I could see that her eyes were dark-rimmed with tiredness. Vivian waved toward the door once more. "Go, get some rest. I will stay with Igraine. You may join us this evening at the feast. I will instruct Jago to lay a place for you."

As Elaine left the room, Vivian came and stood behind me. She was holding something that glistened and shone in the flickering torchlight, and as she drew nearer I recognised it as the necklace of twisted copper that Uther had sent me and which I had tried, unsuccessfully, to throw in the fire.

"I would rather not wear that," I protested as she reached to fasten the chain around my neck.

"Oh, but look how it becomes you…" She directed my gaze toward the mirror and I could not help but agree. I knew that I had not looked so beautiful or well cared for since Solstice. The necklace nestled against my skin, two delicately wrought serpents twined together, their scales catching the flickering firelight, creating tiny glimmers of light that warmed my skin, making it seem soft and lustrous.

"But I do not want to wear his gift. I want nothing from him."

"Igraine, remember what we talked about last night? You promised me that you would think more about your future, that you would do nothing hasty. This necklace sends a message, it tells Uther that you are willing to consider his proposals." I reached my hand to my neck, involuntarily. Strangely, the necklace seemed warm to my touch, not like a metal at all. I stroked it, not sure if I liked the feel of it against my skin, but I recognised that it suited me and added much to the restored beauty of my appearance.

Vivian smiled. "It does become you—and wearing it will help you to remember the vows you made at Solstice to the Goddess. With this around your neck, you will listen carefully, and I hope you will be persuaded to do your duty."

We made our way together down to the Great Hall, where the Yule Log was being put in its usual place in a central firepit that ran down the whole length of the room. It was used only for the midwinter festival and was usually boarded over for the rest of the year, preventing anyone who had perhaps indulged themselves a little too enthusiastically from falling into it.

Jago was directing a small gang of pages and kitchen lads who were staggering under the weight of the enormous log and everyone seemed relieved when it finally settled into place. Conjuring the Yule flame from a branch left over from the previous year had been my task since I had been Lady of Tintagel. Last year, I had allowed Morgause to help me, as she had finally mastered the spells needed to create fire. If things had been different this year, I would have had both my daughters with me, and together, we would have set the log ablaze. Now, I was not even sure if I would be asked to take any part in the Yuletide rituals. Perhaps it would be Vivian who would play the role of Lady of the Household, summoning the living flame that would blaze throughout the festival, representing life, warmth, and a promise of good luck for the year ahead.

Jago must have heard us approaching for he turned round with a smile on his face, which appeared to freeze when he realised that the Lady of the Lake was right behind me. It was clear from his words that he also did not know who was to undertake the ritual that signified the beginning of the festival. "M'Ladies, all is ready. Are you here to light the Yule Log?"

"What can you be thinking Jago? We cannot light the Yule Log until all our guests are with us. The High King has not yet arrived. When we have received him and he has taken refreshment, Uther and the Lady Igraine will undertake the ritual together." Having made that clear, Vivian took the Steward to one side, probably to discuss the finer points of the evening's entertainment, and I looked around me to see if there was anyone I would feel comfortable talking to.

I noticed Ened and Hild sitting at a table sharing a jug of spiced wine with two other women that I didn't recognise. Beyond them, I saw Lord Madoc, deep in conversation with a woman with her back to me. She was wearing the robes of a Priestess and when she turned her head to look at something Madoc had pointed to, I was delighted to recognise Matilda, the Priestess of the House of Fowey, whom I had known from my days in Avalon. She had arrived earlier that day to celebrate Yuletide with us, as had been our custom for many years. She embraced me, and we spent a few pleasant hours, reminiscing about our girlhood. She asked me for news of my daughters and was able to tell me that she had heard from Bennath, who had asked her to travel to Syllan in the New Year. I was delighted to hear this and asked her to come to my chamber before she left Tintagel to take messages and a gift from me to my friend. We both avoided talking about my pregnancy, the events at Solstice, or the fact that I had been little more than a prisoner for the best part of half a year. I was grateful for her tact, but I began to find the mutually self-imposed limitations on our conversation rather tiring and as the shadows began to lengthen and there was still no sign of Uther, I told my old friend that I was tired and excused myself.

I made my way to my chamber, where I found Epona asleep in a chair by the fireside, an empty wine jug at her feet. Not wanting to risk waking her and having to endure her tedious and terse conversation, I chose not to light any of the candles and made my way carefully across the darkened room to the window seat, where I could look out across the headland. Placing a cushion behind my back, I tucked my shawl tightly around me and gazed out into the darkness.

Dark clouds hung at the horizon, where the sky was grey and still streaked with the last traces of the departing sun. A mist had rolled out across the water, covering much of the headland and it was hard to see where the water ended and land began. I turned my head to look out across the ocean, where the crescent moon was still low in the sky. I could see only three stars, but they shone with a strange brilliance, casting their light on the waves to make shining pathways all the way to the horizon.

I felt strangely at peace, sitting there, in the darkness, watching the waters. I did not want this moment to end, for I knew that once Uther had arrived I would need to make an irrevocable choice. I knew myself to be confused and uncertain. If I was honest with myself, I was tempted by the future that Vivian had painted for me. To be able to see my daughters as they grew to womanhood, to carry on living here, in the place I loved, with my position and reputation restored to me. To be a queen, and mother of a future king, able to guide and shape him, to teach him kindness and wisdom. All these things were attractive.

But to have them meant accepting as my husband the man who had killed Gorlois. The man who had betrayed and deceived me and who had taken my body without my consent. The man who had kept me prisoner for months, starved of companionship, humiliated and belittled.

Suddenly, I wished that I could set my feet on those shining pathways and walk away from Tintagel, to a place where no one could find me, where I could find peace. I raised my eyes to the moon, symbol of the Goddess, and cried out to her: "Help me. I do not understand what you want of me. Please, show me the way." As

I looked out across the waters, the mists began to clear and I saw, not the headland or the causeway, but a strange castle, grey-walled and turreted. Ivy grew down from the battlements and its heavy iron gate looked as if it had not been opened for many years. Yet the place did not look threatening. There were lights at the window and as I looked closer, I saw into one of the rooms high in the southernmost turret. Inside, there were two women, sitting together before the fireside. One of them was laughing. There was something familiar about her, about the colour of her hair and the way she held her head. And then she turned and looked at me, and smiled.

I was looking at myself.

Startled, I rubbed my eyes, unable to understand what I had just seen, but when I looked again, there was nothing but the clouds rolling across the headland and, rapidly approaching, the dancing flickers of lights that I knew could only be Uther and his party riding toward Tintagel.

What had I seen? Had the Goddess sent me a vision, another future, one where I could find the solitude and peace I now recognised I craved? Or had I just been dreaming? Whatever the truth of the matter, I was unable to consider it further as there was a knock at my door and Vivian walked into the room

"I thought I would find you here. But what are you doing, skulking in the darkness?" She looked down at Epona, who was now snoring gently, and gave her a sharp smack, which woke her in an instant. "How dare you forget your duties. It is freezing in here; the fire has almost gone out and you have failed to light the candles."

"Vivian, Epona is not a servant." There was little love lost between us, but I felt Vivian was being far too high-handed, and to be fair, I had not wanted the other woman to tend the fire or light the candles. But Vivian would not listen. "She owes service to the Goddess, as we all do, and her duty is to watch over you and keep you safe. I find you half frozen, wrapped in an old shawl, in a room so dark you easily could have fallen." She noticed the empty wine jug, which had now rolled into the hearth and, picking it up, threw it at Epona. "Get out. I will tell Merlin of this."

Epona left without a word and Vivian conjured lights to blaze in the wall sconces. "Let me look at you." She pulled me to my feet none too gently, straightening my hair and adjusting the folds of my kirtle. "You look well enough. Now, we must make our way downstairs. It is for you to greet the High King and welcome him to Tintagel."

Strengthened by the vision I was now certain the Goddess had sent me; I was disinclined to fall in with Vivian's instructions. "I do not wish to make him welcome. Last time he arrived like a thief in the night. He needed no welcoming committee. I do not see why he needs one now."

"Don't be so stupid, child; he is the High King. You are the Lady of Tintagel. You must make him welcome."

"He has stripped me of my titles and my honours as he stripped me of my virtue. It is not my job to make him welcome."

Vivian looked at me uncertainly. "I don't understand you, Igraine. When we spoke this morning you said that you would listen to him. You agreed that you must do your duty to the Goddess. Why are you behaving this way now? What has happened to you?"

"Perhaps my duty to the Goddess is not exactly what you would have me believe, Vivian." She looked at me, anger causing a flush to race across her high cheek bones and for a second there was a flash of what looked like pure hatred in her eyes.

"You are speaking nonsense, but I have no time to argue with you now. The High King and his followers will be with us at any moment. Listen, can you not hear the horses riding across the causeway?" We both turned and looked out of the window. The postern gate was being swung open and I could see the soldiers of the garrison had already lined up to welcome Uther the Pendragon.

By now, Vivian had regained her composure. She reached out and took my hand. "There is no time to talk now, child. Your guests await you and you must take your place amongst them."

So saying, she led my down to the hallway, where the great door to Tintagel stood open. Riders were already dismounting and as it turned out, our argument over who would greet the High King was made irrelevant by Merlin, who was already standing on the castle steps, his arms outstretched in greeting.

Vivian moved forward to stand beside him, but I hung back, taking cover in the shadows behind the doorway. I heard a great cheer and saw first Merlin and then Vivian embrace the man who had haunted my nightmares.

Uther stood in the hallway, looking about him. His head was bare and he was dressed in simple travelling clothes, a sword strapped across his shoulders and his cloak and boots worn and mud-stained. He was clean-shaven, his skin tanned by the sun and wind. He did not look like a man who spent his time with courtiers or counsellors, but a warrior, who was most at ease on horseback or the battlefield.

His hair looked as if it had not been cut since I'd seen him last and it fell in a single plait below his shoulders. I had forgotten how tall he was. He towered over Vivian, and stood at least a head higher than Merlin, who though by now an old man, was still of good stature. He made his way across the hallway, smiling and nodding at those who offered him greeting, but not stopping until, finally, he found me. In my mind, I had turned him into a monster, but now, as he stood before me, I could see that he was just a man.

When he saw me, a smile lit up his face and he bent on one knee before me. "Igraine, I knew I would find you here, ready to welcome me." He took my hand, bringing it to his lips and kissing it. As he did so, I felt once again the delicate touch of his tongue, inserting itself between my fingers and I gasped and pulled away from him.

He smiled. "No words of welcome, Igraine?" I looked up and beyond him, to where Merlin and Vivian were standing. Both of them looked implacable, grim-faced in their determination that I should do their bidding. I could see no one who could help me. No one to give me the strength to refuse to bid him welcome. And besides, as Vivian had reminded me so eloquently the day before, I had sworn allegiance to this man but six months ago in this very castle.

He continued to kneel and so I gestured for him to rise, saying as I did so the ritual words, "Welcome Uther Pendragon, High King of Britain. We are honoured to receive you here in Tintagel. I offer you the freedom of my home and hearth this Yuletide." Uther bent to kiss me on both cheeks and together we walked into the Great Hall.

Chapter Eighteen

After the flame for the Yule Log had been conjured, Uther went to his room to change out of his travelling clothes. By the time he returned the feast had begun in earnest. I was pleased to see that Vivian had kept her promise and a place for Elaine had been laid toward the bottom of the Hall. I would have been happier if she could have been seated closer to me, but it was still a comfort to see her sweet, familiar face. I had been given a place of honour on the dais, Uther sat beside me, with Vivian to his right, whilst Merlin had taken the empty seat to my left.

The pot-boys circulated, ensuring that no one would go short of ale or cider, whilst Jago and two of his trusted pages poured wine for those with a more sophisticated palate. With a fanfare of trumpets from the heralds, four pages carried in an enormous roast boar, stuffed with apples and mushrooms. To great applause, Uther cut the first slice with his sword. He presented it to me, but as I looked at the meat, swimming in grease and still slightly bloody, I felt faint and knew that I would be unable to eat it.

In addition to the boar, great haunches of beef and venison were carved, platters of steaming vegetables were brought in from the kitchens, and everyone began eating, drinking, and talking with a hearty enthusiasm. Uther had not spoken to me since our conversation in the hallway, and Vivian was busily monopolising his attention. Merlin had tried to talk to me, but I was feeling too hot and uncomfortable to say anything remotely interesting or entertaining. The hall seemed to be getting hotter and hotter and

I longed for nothing so much as a pitcher of pure spring water and the cooling freshness of the night air.

As Jago began to supervise the arrival of yet another dish—this time a monstrous pigeon pie as big as a cart wheel—Uther finally turned to me saying, "You keep a good table at Tintagel. I have not feasted so well for many a month."

"I am surprised that you were not well fed at my brother's court," I said tartly. "My father always prided himself on his hospitality to his guests." Uther seemed surprised that I had mentioned his time in the Welsh Marches. Perhaps he had assumed that I would not want to talk about anything that might lead to a discussion of his humiliating decision to strip me of my titles and make my brother regent of Cornwall and Lyonesse.

"I must give you my condolences for your father's death. King Amlawdd was a good man and an honest ruler."

"He was a good father, and a better king than my brother will ever be." I was about to say more, when Merlin, who had been listening to our conversation, chose this moment to intervene. "Igraine, you look tired. I think the feast is too much for you. Shall I summon Elaine to take you to your chamber?"

Much as I disliked Merlin for preventing me from telling Uther exactly what I thought of my brother, and how angered I had been by the decision to give him sovereignty over me, I could not deny that I was feeling very uncomfortable. I nodded. "It is hot, and the child is pressing hard against my spine. It would please me if I could walk in the night air for a while, before retiring to my chamber."

I was surprised to see that Uther instantly got to his feet and moved to help me from my chair saying, "Please, let me accompany you. I long to talk to you in private, away from all these people."

"But you cannot leave the feast so early, what will your guests think?"

"They have wine and ale aplenty. They have food to fill their bellies. They will hardly notice if we slip away."

Merlin had been quick to assess the situation and very clearly approved of Uther's suggestion. Speaking quietly so only we could hear he said, "There is another door from the Great Hall, at the far end, behind the hangings. If you leave now, whilst Jago is releasing the singing birds from the pie, I believe that no one will even see you leaving." Merlin smiled at Uther and gave me an encouraging pat on the arm. I scowled at him, furious at his suggestion, but once again unable to think of anything I could do to oppose it. Trying to think positively, I reasoned that at least this would get me away from the noise and clamour of the feast and allow me to stretch my legs, hopefully relieving the pain in my spine that was becoming less bearable with every second.

We walked toward the far wall and made our way out through the small doorway that led out into the courtyard. The air was chilly and Uther took off his cloak, offering to place it round my shoulders, but I waved it away, enjoying the crisp purity of the night air. There was a slight breeze and I could taste the salt tang of the sea.

"It is too cold for you to be out long, Igraine. Let's walk around the courtyard and then, I think I should take you back to your chamber," Uther spoke gently and took my arm to walk with me across the cobbles. He was right, it was cold. Frost glinted on the trees and our breath hung upon the air. Although I did not like the feel of his arm upon mine, the cobbles were icy and my uneven gait would have caused me to fall had he not been there to steady me. We walked slowly, each step helping to stretch my spine and ease the pain. By the time we had walked twice around the courtyard and were standing in front of the castle steps, I had begun to feel cold and knew that it would be sensible to make my way back to my room.

Uther had said little as we walked, limiting himself to comments about the night sky and remarking on the weather conditions each time I almost slipped. My replies were both stilted and formal, determinedly quashing any possible opportunity to use a casual pleasantry as the way into a more intimate conversation. I was eager to return to the peace and solitude of my room, but much to my annoyance, Uther did not leave me at the foot of the stairs. Instead he followed me as I made my slow, inelegant way up the curving stone steps to the door of my chamber, which he then opened and held gallantly aside, leaving me little choice but to enter.

The room was empty but the fire had been re-kindled and the candles in the sconces had been freshly lit. Wine sat warming in the hearth and on the table there was a jug of fresh water, delicately flavoured with mint and borage. Uther poured water into a beaker and set it down on the table saying, "You should drink, Igraine. You took little earlier of either meat or mead." It was true, and I was thirsty, so I took the water from him and drank, but although I was tired I did not sit down. I was not comfortable in his presence and despite my promise to Vivian to listen to what he had to say, I did not want him to be here.

Uther seemed oblivious to my discomfort. He was gazing round the room, looking first at the brass mirror above the settle, then running his fingers across the tapestries that hung on the walls, keeping out the worst of the chilly Cornish air. Finally, he walked over to the bed, where he reached out and gently touched the pillow that still bore the faint imprint of my last night's slumbers.

"Do you know, Igraine, I have known more true happiness in this room than anywhere else I have ever been." He smiled at me and held out his hand, gesturing to me to come closer. I simply looked at him in bewilderment. The last time he had been in this room, I had spat in his face. Since then, he had kept me here as a virtual prisoner. I found it hard to believe what I was hearing.

"I know I wronged you, but what I did, I did out of love for you. There was no other way. I think you understand that now." He was looking at me, a tender expression on his face. "Vivian has told me that you are ready to listen to me. When I tried to speak to you before…after Solstice…I know now it was too soon. I acted like a callous fool, and, believe me, I am sorry for it."

Still, I said nothing. I could not bear this; putting down my water, I moved toward the doorway, but he was too quick. "Where are you going, Igraine?" He caught my hand and pulled me toward him. I wanted to scream, but when I tried to open my mouth I felt a sharp pain at my throat, as if tiny, burning needles were being driven into my flesh. Involuntarily, my free hand clutched at my neck and I felt the necklace of serpents that Vivian had placed there getting tighter and tighter. The copper fangs bit into my skin, and the pressure on my throat increased; I was finding it difficult to breathe.

Uther was still talking, but I hadn't taken in a word. I moved back toward the table and sank into a chair and as I did so, the necklace loosened and there were no more needle-sharp stabs of pain from the tiny fangs.

"So will you agree, my darling? Will you be my wife in truth?" Uther still held my hand but he was now kneeling before me, looking up at me with devotion.

"I'm sorry, my lord, a faintness came upon me. I did not hear what you said."

"Merlin was right. This has all been too much for you. I will take you away from here, take you somewhere where you can be properly cared for, where the child can be born in comfort."

"But I love Tintagel. It is my home."

"It is all very well in the Summer I suppose, and yes, I do concede it has a certain bleak grandeur…but it is not a fitting place for my Queen."

"I am not your Queen." I just managed to get the words out before the necklace once again tightened and the tiny fangs began their vicious stabbing.

"Igraine, you were born to be my Queen. Merlin knows it, Vivian knows it. It was prophesied that you would bear the child who will be the Once and Future King. It is my child you are carrying and I would have his birth legitimised." I tried to speak, but once again, the necklace burned into my throat.

"I have loved you from the moment I saw you. When I was with you here at Solstice I made my vows in truth to you. In my heart, and in the eyes of the Goddess, I can have no other wife."

He got to his feet and began to walk about the room. "Whilst we have been apart, you have never been far from my mind. Vivian counselled me to wait before I spoke again to you, and hard though that was, I have taken her counsel. But I have not been idle. I have made such plans. Let me tell you." As he spoke, Uther had become more and more excited. "After we are married, we will go to Caer-Lundein and there await the birth of the child. It is warmer there and you will be safe and cared for in a way befitting to a Queen. In the Spring, when you are well enough, we shall travel. I will take you North, to Orkney, where we shall be the guests of King Lot and you can see your daughter. We shall progress throughout the land and all will bow down before you. They will see you are my Queen and they will love you."

There was a flush upon his cheeks and his eyes were sparkling as he returned to where I was sitting. "Tomorrow our new future will begin. In front of all the Court you will repeat the vows you made at Solstice, but this time, you will make them knowingly, to me, Uther Pendragon, and I shall in truth become your husband."

I got up and moved toward the window, hoping that the cool air would help ease the burning pain at my throat.

"Uther, I have listened, but…" The necklace tightened. Uther moved toward me and tried to take me in his arms. "I…don't…"

"My darling, don't say that you don't deserve this. I knew one day you would come to love me." He held me to him, his lips trying to find mine as the copper wire burned and tightened round my throat.

"I… I…," His arms closed in around me and I tried to push him away, but I had no strength left, no breath to speak a word of protest and as his lips met mine, everything went dark.

◆ ◆ ◆

WHEN I REGAINED CONSCIOUSNESS, I was lying on my bed. Elaine was kneeling beside me, holding my hand and gently pressing a cool compress of thyme and lavender against my brow. She smiled when she saw my eyes open and got to her feet. "My lord, she is awake." Uther was sitting, head in hands, at the table. At her words, he raised his head. "How is she?"

Elaine fetched some water and I took a welcome sip before sinking back upon the pillows. "She is in no danger, my lord, but tired. I think she needs no more excitement this night."

Uther came to stand beside me, a gentle smile upon his face. He reached out and touched my belly before sitting down on the bed beside me, taking my hand in his. "My love, you must sleep now. I know that you have been ill-used and unhappy, but all of that is going to change. The ceremony will take place tomorrow and we shall truly be man and wife. I will take care of you and you will want for nothing." So saying, he bent to kiss me and I found myself unable to move. The necklace tightened, the needle-sharp fangs sending a chilly paralysis that spread throughout my entire body. I was unable even to flinch away from him; it was impossible to resist. After he had kissed me, he stroked my cheek. "Have you no smile for me beloved? You must be tired indeed. Now rest, and I shall see you on the morrow."

As the door closed behind him, Elaine flew to my side. "Igraine, what was he talking about, have you agreed to marry him?" I shook my head, uncertain if I would be able to speak, but the necklace did not tighten and the fangs remained sheathed. Despite this, my throat still burned and my voice was hoarse. Hesitantly, worried that any moment the pain would begin again, I explained what had happened. Elaine tried to undo the clasp to remove the collar from my neck but as she did so, the serpent's fangs struck out at her, piercing her fingers until they bled, and despite her best efforts, the fastening would not give way.

◆ ◆ ◆

I SLEPT FITFULLY. THE BABY was restless and I found it hard to get comfortable. Before the sky began to lighten I got out of bed and went to sit by the fire. I wrapped myself in my shawl and sat, watching the flames and thinking about my future. All my life I had done my duty, honoured the wishes of my father and mother, acted in obedience to the will of the Goddess. And I had not been unhappy. My marriage to Gorlois had been arranged when I was but a young girl, but we had found love, my husband and I, and from that love, my two daughters had been born, bringing me more joy and delight than I could ever have believed possible.

I was being offered a future that many women would envy. The chance to marry Uther Pendragon, the High King. A man who was not just powerful, but good to look upon and, so it would seem, deeply in love with me. The chance to spend the rest of my days in comfort, raising my third-born and visiting my daughters, being part of their life as they grew to womanhood. Was that so bad a fate, I asked myself.

And what was the alternative? If I refused Uther, would I be forced to spend the rest of my days here, little more than a prisoner, my rights and titles stripped from me and subject to the whims of my brother, who was now regent of Cornwall and Lyonesse until my unborn son reached his majority. I could expect little kindness from that quarter, and I was certain that, if I refused to obey them, neither Merlin nor Vivian would concern themselves with my future comfort or happiness.

Then, in the flames, deep within the heart of the fading embers, I saw once again the battlements and towers of a distant castle. This was a place that I was certain I had never visited, but I recognised it instantly from that other vision, seen through the mists across the headland. I had seen myself here, happy and at peace. Was this another future? Another chance?

I must have fallen asleep pondering the possibilities for I was still sitting there, wrapped in my shawl when Elaine, who had spent the night on the truckle bed in the corner of my room, came to wake me. She helped me to wash and dress, and before I had chance to break my fast, there was a knock at the door and Merlin and Vivian walked in.

They were both smiling and first Vivian and then Merlin placed a kiss upon my brow. Vivian beckoned to the doorway and two serving women entered. One carried what I took to be a new robe, a beautiful green and gold confection which she laid out on the bed. The other placed a large inlaid wooden box upon the table. At a gesture from Vivian, they both curtsied and left the room. Vivian waved a hand and the lid of the box sprang open. Inside, I could see many shiny things: coronets, necklaces, rings of gold and silver set with emeralds and rubies, great ornate brooches and heavy chains of state. Vivian picked out a slender chaplet of burnished gold and held it out to me saying, "Here child, this will become you. A coronet fit for a queen."

I hesitated, my hand resting on the necklace that still sat at my throat, my fingers holding it away from my skin in an attempt to prevent it from tightening as it had before. Beneath the necklace my skin was still bruised and raw. Not knowing if I would be able to speak, I looked to Elaine for courage and she placed her hand upon my shoulder. Its warmth gave me strength and the determination to at least try to speak the words I knew I needed to say.

"Vivian, Lady, you know that I have always done my duty. I have been a good daughter to the Goddess," She smiled again and came toward me, as if to place the chaplet on my head. I moved away, close to the window, with Elaine now standing between me and the others.

"I do not believe the Goddess wants me to make this marriage." I waited. Would the serpents sting? Would I feel that terrible burning once more around my throat? But nothing happened and I felt emboldened to continue. "Yesterday, you made me wear this necklace, telling me that, with this around my neck I would be sure to listen carefully to whatever Uther had to say to me. Your enchantments made it certain that I could do nothing but listen. You knew that I would not be able to speak, would be unable to tell Uther that I will never willingly be his wife." At these words, Merlin looked at Vivian, raising one eyebrow in an unspoken question. She nodded and gestured dismissively. "It was necessary. Despite your educational advantages, you have always been a fool, Igraine. You do not know what is best for you. Sometimes you are in need of protection from yourself."

"And so this is to be my life now? Shackled like a slave, never able to express my true feelings. Living in fear if I ever chose to contradict my lord and master?"

Vivian looked at me contemptuously; "Oh I do not think it will be long before you become reconciled to your lot. A slave who dresses in silks and sleeps on fine linen—and in the bed of a king to boot—is a slave that many would envy."

"You do not know me as well as you think you do. Yes, I was a biddable child. I honoured the wishes of my mother and, oh, how I stood in awe of you, Lady. I married Gorlois because there was no reason not to. It was what was expected of me. And not for one moment did I wish to do otherwise. But this is different. Now you want me to marry the man who killed my husband. Who took me by deceit and against my will and who has kept me prisoner here for months."

"Igraine, my dear, I think perhaps you are too harsh on Uther." Merlin had stepped forward, holding out his hands to me as if in supplication. "Much of the fault is mine. I counselled Uther to behave as he did, telling him that you would be more receptive if you had been deprived of company, forced to remain solitary, isolated from your friends, and stripped of your titles and authorities. I see now that perhaps I read you wrong. But do not blame Uther for my poor counsel."

"That's as maybe, Merlin. I thank you for your honesty, but your words do nothing to change my mind. If Uther had any true feelings for me, he could never have agreed to follow your counsel. Perhaps your methods would have worked if he had been trying to tame a wild dog or force an unbroken stallion to obey him, but with me, they never would. He was only thinking of his own desires and pleasures, and not of me. That isn't love." I reached out and took Elaine's hand.

"I call upon the Goddess to witness these words. I do not consent to marry Uther Pendragon. I will not become his wife freely and I call down Her curse upon the match if you force me to go through with it."

With a screech of anger, Vivian ran toward me. "You little fool. You understand nothing." She slapped me round the face with a force that threw me backward against the wall. Elaine helped me to steady myself as Merlin placed his hands on Vivian's shoulders and drew her away before she could hit me again.

"Igraine, I understand now that we have treated you shabbily, but is there nothing that could change your mind?" Merlin spoke quietly, fixing me with his sharp grey eyes. "I beg you, don't make a hasty decision. At least let us talk further about the matter. Promise me that you will give Uther more time, to help you reconsider." He put out his hand and gestured toward my swollen stomach. "If not for me, then for the sake of your unborn child. Do you want him to be born a bastard, with no one knowing for sure who his true father is?"

Before either of them could stop me, I leant on Elaine's shoulder, pulling myself up on to the settle and from there to the ledge of the window. "I will not marry Uther, and I do not want this child. If you won't accept my decision, then believe me when I say that I would rather hurl myself to the cobbles below than spend the rest of my days in a forced and loveless marriage."

No one said anything. Elaine came to stand in front of me, stopping either of the others from reaching up to grab me and prevent me from carrying out my threat.

Finally, Merlin spoke. "Are you certain that this is what you want? You will not marry the Pendragon?"

"Never."

"You are foolish, child. We sought only to help you. But no matter." He moved slowly toward the window. "I know Vivian wished to see you upon the throne, to make certain that Avalon would remain at the heart of Uther's power. Without you there, her influence may wane, but that is not my concern." At these words, Vivian hissed and moved away from the Druid, a look of pure hatred on her face. The thought that Merlin had just made himself her implacable enemy flicked through my mind, but I continued to listen.

"I am concerned only with the child. The one destined to wield the great sword, the Once and Future King. I cannot allow any harm to come to him, and if you will promise to do nothing foolish and to give me the boy when he is born, then I swear that I will help you."

I looked at his stern, cold face. His eyes were not smiling now. Could I trust him?

"And how will you help me, Merlin? What will you do for me if I do as you say?"

"I will take you to Carbonek, the hidden castle ruled by the Fisher King, and sanctuary for those who wish to remain veiled from the world."

As he said this, I saw once again the mysterious castle with its ivy-covered battlements and tall, graceful turrets. Was this Carbonek? Of course I knew the stories of the strange enchanted castle that moved from place to place, hidden from the world. It was supposed to hold many treasures, including the horn of plenty, the cornucopia of Bran the Blessed, and was ruled over by the maimed Fisher King, dreadfully injured in battle and yet unable to die. It was a mystic place that many believed to be nothing more than a legend, but I remembered one of the old, wise women in Avalon who claimed to have been born there. She had been sent to Lake Island to learn the Mysteries only to discover that, despite all her magics, she could never find the way back. If I went to Carbonek, not even Vivian would be able to find me. I would be safe.

"Do I have your word on this, Lord Merlin?"

"You have my word. I swear on the life of your unborn child, on the blessed blade of the sword Caliburn. I will not play you false."

"Then I agree to your terms." I held out my hand and allowed him to help me down. Taking a seat at the table I turned to Vivian. "Please, send for Uther, but before he arrives, remove this collar from my neck. There can be no more misunderstandings." She did as I asked and Elaine gasped when she saw the livid marks around my throat. She went to get a salve to sooth my wounded skin, but I waved her away saying, "No, I would have Uther see this."

I did not have long to wait. Uther arrived clean shaven and dressed in his wedding finery. He looked somewhat askance at my uncombed hair, the shawl wrapped tight around my nightshift, the green and gold dress still lying limp and abandoned on the bed.

"What is this, my love? You had best make haste, we are expected presently by our guests in the Great Hall."

I picked up the necklace and handed it to him. "Do you recognise this?"

"Why yes, it is one of the small trifles that I had sent to you, to show you that you were always on my mind and in my heart. You were wearing it yesterday I think?"

"And do you know that it has most interesting properties?" He looked at me blankly.

"I don't love you, Uther." As I spoke, the serpents began to writhe and one of their needle-sharp fangs sank itself into Uther's hand. He gave a cry of pain and dropped it instantly.

"I don't love you. I don't love you." Each time I spoke, the serpents writhed, twisting and tightening upon the floor, their fangs shooting out impotently into the air.

"What is this thing?" Uther stamped hard upon the necklace, grinding it beneath the heel of his boot.

"This trifle was enchanted by the Lady of the Lake, who made me wear it yesterday. When I tried to tell you how I truly felt, it burned my flesh and pierced my skin. See." I showed him the livid scar that circled my throat and he gasped in horror.

"Believe me, I had no knowledge of this."

"I do believe you. And now you must believe me. I do not consent to marry you." I bent down and picked up the necklace. It was no longer moving but appeared to have suffered very little damage under the heel of Uther's boot. I placed it on the table between us. "I cannot prevent you from instructing the Lady to place this once again around my neck." The serpents began to writhe. "I cannot prevent you from using this rough magic to force me to go through a ceremony with you today. But know this, every night of our marriage you will have to rape me anew, as I will never consent or go to your arms willingly."

The necklace was now spinning wildly and we could hear the serpents hissing. With a look of disgust, Uther unsheathed his sword, using the tip to pick up the vile thing and hurl it into the fire. There was a shrill crackle and green and copper flames surged upward. I was worried that they would set light to the chimney, but in a moment they were gone, leaving nothing of the necklace but a few strands of burned and twisted wire.

Uther was looking not at me but at Vivian. "How dare you use your magics in this way? You swore to me that Igraine was destined to be my wife, that the Goddess herself had chosen her to be my queen.

"I see now that you have lied to me. You are no longer welcome at my Court. Get you gone to Avalon, and if I hear that you have left the Lake shores, be certain that you will feel my anger."

"As you will, my lord." Vivian stood and moved toward the door. Despite Uther's anger she still appeared calm, and her voice was steady. "I will be waiting for the day the Goddess brings clarity to your mind and you send for me to counsel you once again."

"Then you will wait until the sea itself freezes over. Now go. I would see you no more." Vivian left the room and Uther turned his attention to me.

"I will not force you. This night has brought me much to think on, and whatever you may think of me, Igraine, it would bring me little pleasure to have a wife that I needs must drag, unwilling, to my bed."

"And what of the child?" Merlin spoke quietly.

"I care nothing for the child. I do not want to see it or to hear what becomes of it."

"Do I have your permission to become his guardian, to raise him and educate him as I see fit?"

"I want no one to know of his existence, but apart from that, you may deal with him as you wish."

Merlin nodded. "It will be as you say, Sire. And what of today? We have many guests assembled. What are your wishes?"

Uther stepped toward me, reaching his hand out to touch my hair. Without the necklace to restrain me I flinched involuntarily. "Do you hate me so much, Igraine?"

I looked at him, knowing that if Merlin kept his promise, I would never see him again, and wanting to answer honestly. "I do not hate you, Uther." A flicker of hope appeared on his face. My feelings for this man had always been complex. Merlin and Vivian had both witnessed an attraction between us that I still was unable to deny. Perhaps, if things had been different I could have learned to care for him. If Gorlois had died at someone else's hand, if Uther had not deceived me so subtly and cruelly at Solstice. If he had had the wit to recognise that I could never love anyone who tried to master me by imprisonment and neglect.

I knew now that much of what had happened had been engineered by others. Merlin and Vivian had conspired against me for their own ends, but I also had to recognise that Uther had been complicit. In some ways, his was the worst fault of all, for he had allowed his own desires and selfish passion to blind him to the suffering he was inflicting on a woman he claimed to care about and love. Looking him in the eye, I took his hand in mine. "I could never love you, Uther. But despite all you have done to me, I wish you no evil. All I ask is that you leave me now, and I pray you never return to Tintagel whilst it is still my home."

And so he left.

I'm not sure exactly what Merlin said to the guests assembled in the Great Hall, but they too began to depart, riding their horses out across the causeway until, by early afternoon, Elaine came to tell me that only one of our guests still remained. It was Matilda, the Priestess from the House of Fowey. I remembered that I had asked her to come to see me before she left and told Elaine that I would be willing to see her.

Matilda did not stay long. I think she felt uncomfortable in my presence, embarrassed by the cancelled wedding and uncertain what to say to me. I asked her to send my love to Bennath and to remind her of her promise to come to me in early spring. "I expect the child to come with daffodils. Please, ask Bennath to come to me before they are in bloom." I took a ring from my finger and handed it to the Priestess. "Give this to her, with my love." She nodded and went on her way, leaving me alone in my darkening chamber.

THE NEXT FEW MONTHS PASSED quickly. As Merlin felt assured that I would not take any steps to hurt the child within my womb, he no longer required Hild or Epona to keep a watch on me. Realising that I had seen neither woman for some days, I asked for news of them from Elaine. She told me that Uther's promise to allow their children to inherit their father's lands had been honoured and that they had returned home. Ened had also been granted her promised inheritance rights and was gone, taking her children back to Madron. I was interested to hear that she had not travelled alone.

Lord Madoc had chosen to accompany her and according to Elaine, it would not be surprising if we were to hear the news of a match between them. Madoc was much older than Erec had been, and he had lost his lands and position in the Welsh Marches as a result of my brother's treachery. But he was a good man and although I had never been fond of Ened, I knew she had suffered much and did not begrudge her a second chance for happiness.

The castle was quiet. We received few visitors; no one came to see me, but the occasional messenger arrived with news for Merlin, who continued his habit of spending an hour or so each evening in my chamber. He told me that Uther was planning to travel to Brittany to see his friend and ally King Budic. Rumour had it that he intended to make King Lot of Orkney regent in his absence. This made me smile to think that one day, my little daughter Morgause, as wife of the King's regent, might well sit upon the throne that had been so recently offered to me.

Of Vivian there was no news, but twice Elaine and I had seen visions of Morgan in the scrying bowl. In one, she was still a child, perhaps eight or nine years old, gathering herbs in the gardens of Avalon. She seemed happy, content with her task, choosing each plant with care and placing them with the precision I knew so well into her willow basket. She was not alone; at her side was a beautiful young girl who looked to be two or three years older than my daughter. She had long, dark-gold hair and strange, hazel-coloured eyes. As we watched, we saw Merlin walk across the grass toward them. The three of them stood together and talked awhile, before Merlin took each girl by the hand and they returned together to the lake house.

In the second vision, Morgan was older, a woman grown. She was still small and slender and had now come into the full promise of her beauty. Richly dressed in a beautifully embroidered blue kirtle, her hair was long and lustrous, falling almost to her waist. It was kept in place with a delicate coronet of silver, which she touched now and then, almost involuntarily as if she did not feel comfortable wearing it. She was sitting in a room that I recognised; the ladies solar at Caer-Lundein. It had changed little since I was last there; the rose bowl still sat upon the table and the sun shone in on the ornate tapestries that graced the walls.

Morgan appeared to be waiting for someone, and as I watched, the door opened and a young man, long-limbed and rangy, entered the room. His face lit up when he saw her, and he hurried toward her. He too seemed taken by the coronet, smiling as he reached out to touch it, appearing to straighten it slightly before leaning forward to place a gentle kiss upon her nose. He opened his arms to her, and she appeared to go to him willingly, but as the perspective changed, I was able to see her face, resting on his shoulders and could only shudder at the look of spite and hatred that I saw there. I did not understand what was happening Whoever this young man was, he was clearly falling in love with my daughter, and she appeared to be encouraging him, despite the loathing and repugnance I had seen upon her face. I wanted to know more, but the vision faded, and despite our entreaties, the Goddess sent us no others.

IN THE LAST FEW WEEKS of my pregnancy, whilst the daffodils were still in bud, Bennath joined us. I was very happy to see her and delighted to hear her talk of the work she had been doing on Syllan. Matilda of Fowey was still with her, helping her to build a new House, which would provide care and shelter to those children who had been left homeless and helpless after the war. All her old passion had returned. She was full of energy, fired up with her plans, and I loved to listen as she spoke about the people who had come to her and whose lives she was enriching. There was only one thing we did not speak of.

No one but Merlin and Elaine knew of my plans regarding Carbonek. When I had first told my half-sister about Merlin's suggestion, I had assumed that I would be going alone. I felt that I could never ask another person to go into what was, to all intents and purposes, self-imposed exile. To live in a place so hidden from the world, a place that no one could find unless they knew the right enchantments, was to me a promise of peace and tranquillity; I was not so certain that other people would see it in that light.

But when I told Elaine, she asked immediately if I truly wanted to be alone, or if it would make me happier to have her as a companion. I had been delighted, for she had been the one person

I had always been able to trust and rely on. She had come to my father's court when I was but seven years old and had been my friend and helpmate ever since. The thought of leaving her behind had been almost unbearable and now that I knew that this would not have to happen, I was looking forward with eager excitement to my new life.

For many weeks now, we had been making plans, about what we would take and what we would leave behind, what we would need and what would already be there for us. We did not know how we would travel to the hidden castle, but despite this, the small storeroom behind my solar was gradually filling up with trunks and boxes. Merlin had raised an eyebrow when we had taken him there, asking once again to be given some idea about our journey. But Merlin would not even tell us if we would travel across land or sea. He had simply sworn us both to secrecy, saying that he could not reveal the enchantments and that we would have to trust him to take us there safely when the time came.

I let Bennath believe that I intended to remain at Tintagel once the baby was born. She could see that I had more liberty and knowing now that there were no more plans for marrying me to Uther, she suggested that I pay a visit to Syllan in the summer, when the child was old enough to travel. I nodded and told her that we would see.

The last few weeks before the child was born were easier. Perhaps the babe could sense my new contentment, or maybe he had found a position that suited him and did not play merry havoc with my spine. For whatever reason, he was calmer and I found myself able to sleep well at night and, as a result, had more energy during the day.

Maybe because of this, I became restless and wanted to be outside. Often, I would walk with Elaine or Bennath through the orchards, looking for the first sign of this year's blossoms, or we would take long walks across the causeway to the caves beneath the headland, looking out to sea and listening to the crying of the seabirds. For the first time, I had the opportunity to think clearly about the baby I was carrying. I had not asked for him to be planted in my womb, and for many weeks I had done nothing but resent his existence.

This was so different from my other pregnancies. With my daughters, I had dreamed about the child that I was carrying, falling in love first with Morgause and then with Morgan before I had even seen their faces or held them in my arms. And both those girls were gone. I knew that once I travelled to Carbonek, it was most unlikely that I would ever see them anywhere but in the waters of the scrying bowl. But I knew that I had already lost them. They had been taken from me and whether I blamed fate, or circumstance, or the machinations of Vivian and Merlin, there was nothing I could do to get them back.

And I was planning to surrender this child also, to give up my babe within a few hours of his birth. We had discussed it together, Merlin and I, and had both agreed that it would be better if I let him go immediately. Merlin was worried that if I held him in my arms, I would not be able to keep my promise, and I had a suspicion that he was right. He had already arranged a wet nurse from the village, installing her in the small room next to mine that had previously been used to store my trunks and travelling clothes.

She had a small daughter, almost weaned, and I would sometimes waken in the night to the sound of her crying, only to hear her mother's soft voice soothing her and nestling her to the breast. It was during one of these incidents that my pains began. I woke Elaine, who went to fetch Bennath and within hours, my baby had been born.

He was a beautiful child, long and slender with delicate, fine-boned hands and feet. His hair was a dark blond and his eyes a deep grey-blue like the sea in winter. Bennath cut the cord and, after he was cleaned, Elaine wrapped him in linen swaddling and handed him to me.

I couldn't help it. I placed him to my breast and felt his tiny mouth latch on. He fed for what seemed like hours, until the sky was light, and both of us fell asleep.

When I woke he wasn't there. The chamber was empty, all traces of the birth had been cleaned away and my travelling clothes were laid out on the settle. I got out of bed, feeling weak and hungry and poured myself some wine. There was bread on the table and although it looked dry and stale, I tore off a piece and began to chew on it as I went to look out of the window.

The courtyard was empty apart from Merlin and one of the kitchen maids who were helping the wet nurse into a small cart. Once she was settled, Merlin handled her a bundle that I knew must be my baby, and the maid got in behind her, carrying another, older child. For a second I was paralysed, uncertain about what I was feeling, but then I knew with absolute clarity that I wanted my child and I would do anything to have him. Without even reaching for my shawl, I ran toward the door, nearly colliding with Elaine who was carrying a tray of fresh bread and savoury smelling broth.

"Oh please, help me…Elaine, I have made such a mistake…what have I done…I want my baby…please help me." Putting the tray down on the floor, Elaine held out her arms to me, a look of the deepest sadness and pity on her face. "Igraine, sweetling, it is too late. I'm so sorry, but the deed is done." She held me in her arms and rocked me, as if I were myself a babe, and we cried together as the cart drove away across the causeway.

Eventually, she calmed me and I recognised that I had to reconcile myself to what had happened. Although I felt that Merlin had acted high-handedly in removing the child whilst I slept, he had, in truth, done nothing that I had not previously agreed to. It was not unusual for a child to be sent to live with its wet nurse, and although Bennath was a little surprised that I had not told her that this had been my intention, she saw nothing strange in the fact that the babe was gone.

Once the baby had been born, Bennath asked me for leave to return to Syllan as there was much that demanded her attention. I smiled at this, telling her that she longer had any need to ask my leave, and sent her on her way with my blessing. She departed the following day, once again urging me to visit her in the summer. Before she mounted her horse, I embraced her with tears in my eyes. I knew not what would befall her, but it was unlikely that we would ever meet again, and I was certain that I would miss this brave and spirited woman, who had been my champion and my friend.

And so, I prepared to leave Tintagel, the place that had been my home for most of my adult life. The Marcher flag of my brother's forces now flew next to that of the Pendragon on the battlements, and I had heard from Merlin that my brother was already on his way here, planning to reinforce the garrison and to spend the summer months becoming familiar with his new territories.

I had no wish to encounter him. There was now nothing here for me and all I wanted was to leave. Within three days of Bennath's departure, Merlin, Elaine, and I took ship from the harbour. Never one to ask questions, Jago had ensured the carts loaded with our belongings were safely stowed on board and we set sail at sunset, with a fair wind.

Merlin was still being secretive. He refused to tell us anything about the voyage, not how long it would be, or even in which direction we would be travelling. Finally, when it became clear that we would get no answers, Elaine and I made our way to the small cabin we were sharing and although it was still early, we felt tired from our exertions and sought our bunks.

The next morning we were woken by the dazzle of sunbeams playing on the walls and a sweet smell of flowers in the air. We dressed hurriedly and went on deck to find that the sky was no longer the dull grey we had left behind us in Tintagel, but clear blue like the most glorious of midsummer days. I knew not how, or where we had travelled, but we had arrived at a place the like of which I had never known. The castle was not grey, as I had seen it through the mists, but white. Its walls shone in the early morning sunlight, red and yellow flowers cascaded over the battlements, and as we waited for the gangplank to be put into position we saw the gates of the castle swing open and a young woman step outside.

She walked toward us, her gaze compassionate, her arms outstretched in greeting: "Welcome to Carbonek," she said.

All at once, I felt myself overcome with emotion; to be greeted with courtesy, when I had come to expect only disdain, to be welcomed, when for so many months I been merely tolerated, was so overwhelming that I felt a sob rise in my throat. Looking toward Elaine I saw that my half-sister was smiling, but that her eyes too were bright with tears. Reaching out, I took her hand and together we walked across the sand toward the beautiful white walls, and the promise of peace.

◆ ◆ ◆

THE END

Author's Note

As with all the tales of Arthur and his court, the lives of my characters are interwoven with genuine historical figures and real events.

Early fragments of the Arthurian story can be found in Welsh poetry dating from the seventh century, but it was not until 1138 that Geoffrey of Monmouth's *History of the Kings of Britain* told the story of Arthur in any detail. Monmouth presented Arthur as an historical figure, positioning what may be called the Arthurian period between the end of the Roman occupation in 406 AD and the beginning of the Anglo-Saxon era.

According to Monmouth, after the death of the last Roman Emperor, Constantine III, the throne passed to his eldest son. He trusted his father's counsellor, Vortigern, to advise him, but instead the traitorous Vortigern murdered the young prince and set himself upon the throne. Emperor Constantine's two surviving sons, Aurelius and Uther, escaped to Brittany where they gathered their forces, eventually returning to England to wage war on Vortigern and the Saxons.

Aurelius defeated his enemies and assumed his rightful crown. However, before the realm of Britain could be returned to peace, the treacherous sons of Vortigern, allied again with the invading Saxons, rose up against the rightful king. Things went badly for Aurelius; he, just like his elder brother, died at an assassin's hand. And thus the crown and throne of Britain passed to Uther, who seized it gladly.

Although Monmouth's *History* has been proved to be inaccurate, the legend of Arthur has caught the imagination of many writers, who have told and retold the stories of the fabled knights and the tragedy that lay at the heart of Camelot.

Like many of my predecessors, I took some historical and architectural liberties within these pages, reasoning that if authors such as T. H. White and Thomas Malory can allow their characters to inhabit what are, to all intents and purposes, medieval castles, then who am I to quarrel with literary tradition?

Acknowledgements

I would like to thank my father, who first introduced me to the Arthurian stories, and my mother, who taught me that all women should have a voice.

I am indebted to my marvellous agent—Lindsay Guzzardo—who had absolute faith in me and in Igraine, and to the wisdom and deftness of my amazing editor—Toni Kirkpatrick. You are a joy to work with.

Finally, no acknowledgement would be complete without my heartfelt thanks to my husband, Colin, who has trudged the length and breadth of the British Isles with me in search of this story—from Tintagel to the Isles of Orkney, keeping me supplied with endless cups of tea.